FROM THE BEGINNING

Uncommon Bonds – 3

A Novel by

WILLIAM E. NOLAND

FROM THE BEGINNING
Uncommon Bonds - Book 3

FIRST EDITION SOFTCOVER
ISBN: 162253719X
ISBN-13: 978-1-62253-719-8

Editor: Lane Diamond
Cover Artist: Kris Norris
Interior Designer: Lane Diamond

EVOLVED PUBLISHING™

www.EvolvedPub.com
Evolved Publishing LLC
Butler, Wisconsin, USA

Printed in Book Antiqua font.

BOOKS BY WILLIAM E. NOLAND

UNCOMMON BONDS
Book 1: *Playing with Fire*
Book 2: *Hammer to Fall*
Book 3: *From the Beginning*
Book 4: *Day of Judgment* [Fall 2023]

DEDICATION

To Nick, Sharon, Chris, Valerie, and Tess, and to bonds reborn.

PROLOGUE

I am fleet as feather, fierce as flesh, staunch as stone.

Forged by a god, then gifted to his son, who became my master, I served both with savage loyalty. By their decree, thousands died.

Countless more knelt before our unyielding might. But fortunes change more rapidly than the surging eddies of the Southern Winds. When my master became imprisoned for his perceived avarice, all for me went still and silent... until now.

Once again, I am fleet as feather, fierce as flesh, staunch as stone.

This night, I am *reborn.*

CHAPTER 1

Radicofani, Italy (roughly eight miles west of Sarteano), August 2015

"Try to hold it steady! You're wiggling it around too much!" Lotte's words resounded like the sound of dumpsters being loudly emptied by spiteful trash collectors at 4:00 a.m.

Eric took an extremely deep breath. This was not going as planned, but then very little had gone as planned so far on this, his and Lotte's first big vacation together. He froze in place and glared at her where she crouched by the laptop and the rack of data collection equipment.

He struggled mightily to maintain his composure. "Can you remind me what this contraption is called?"

"It's the WHG, Eric. You know this." With her German pronunciation, "WHG" sounded like "vey-ha-gay."

"Yeah, I do, but humor me. What does WHG stand for again?"

She heaved a great sigh of frustration. She was already covered with sweat, and it wasn't even noon.

Under the Tuscan sun, indeed!

After three days of this, she looked like a boiled lobster. Even copious sunblock and an oversized Aussie safari hat couldn't save her pale skin from the fierce solar bombardment, and it definitely wasn't improving her mood.

"*Alter!* It's the *Werner Hand Gehalten!* I've told you this before. Can you please just hold it steady? And remember, take exactly equal steps... one second each... and keep the sensor about six inches from the ground. *Scheiße!* We have to start this pass again!"

Not wishing to make the situation worse, he restrained a bitter laugh and backtracked to the starting point. "Well, reviewing our joyous German lessons, I seem to recall that *Hand Gehalten* means 'hand-held,' right? Last time I checked, hands tend to move around, particularly when you're walking over rough terrain. In other words, I'm holding the damn thing as steady as I can while I help *you* get all these readings... sweetheart."

Her tone changed to one of dismay as she fiddled with the settings on the computer. "Oh, I know! I'm sorry. This is all such a disaster. We were supposed to have plenty of time, but that ridiculous train strike threw everything off schedule. Stupid Italians!"

On this, she's right. Well, about the train strike, anyway.

Eric had found the Italians to be lovely people, and he knew she was just venting. The WHG, however, was supposed to have arrived in Florence from Berlin five days ago. The plan had been to drive up from Murlo, near Poggio Civitate, where they were staying, get the device in Florence, and then go on to Sarteano.

The Werner Institut was sponsoring Lotte to give a talk at the upcoming WIA Conference in October, which would feature their new portable data collection technology. She got to pick the spot to survey, which was really too good to be true. Overtly, she chose Sarteano because of the ongoing digs around the Tomb of the Infernal Chariot, plus the fact that she and Eric had already planned a nice vacation in Italy. No matter that none of their intended program had included archaeological data collection, but that was a different issue.

Covertly, of course, this presented a perfect opportunity to survey the area around where Mason and Emilia had found Charun's portal. Despite eating a good chunk of their vacation time, Lotte couldn't pass up the chance. Even Eric had eventually agreed, if a bit begrudgingly, though he kept that to himself. Unfortunately, with the train strike, their schedule had been totally messed up. Things had gotten pushed back, and what was supposed to be done over four days had to be squashed into barely three, with only one day to get all the data around the once-buried temple.

The Sarteano samples for Werner had been collected over the past two days. Jose, who had taken over for Mason two years ago as Dig Supervisor, and some of his dig team helped out. All of them stood to benefit greatly if Lotte found anything.

Eric mostly just sat around and watched, sweltering in the intense heat.

Hey, if there were tents to set up, I'd have set them up.

Now, however, his services were required. They both worked secretly and frantically near the overlook that had washed into the river two years ago, hoping to find some indication where another nearby temple, presumably Vanth's, might be buried, before the Werner equipment had to be packed up and shipped back.

"I know you're frustrated," he said, trying to calm both of them, "but this thing isn't so easy to use, and we've been at this for hours. I'm getting tired. I really am doing the best I can."

The WHG looked like a large metal detector, a square sensor about two feet on each side attached to a long pole with handles. The device was deceptively light, and an arm attached to a shoulder harness helped the operator with additional support, but it was still a tricky piece of equipment to wield manually. It could be mounted to a small chassis with four large wheels, but that only worked on pavement or extremely smooth terrain.

The WHG was essentially a feature-packed ground penetrating radar, or "GPR," unit. It used triple-frequency stepped ultra-wideband electromagnetic pulses in the microwave band of the radio spectrum to map subsurface objects and structures up to almost fifty feet deep, depending on soil and other conditions.

Its sensors combined the advantages of pulse and stepped frequency radar, along with a magnetometer to measure concentrations of magnetic materials that might disrupt the radar readings, such as fine-grained clays and silts whose high electrical conductivity caused loss of signal strength, or dense, rocky, and heterogeneous sediments that scattered and weakened the GPR signal while increasing extraneous noise.

The device transmitted the data it collected to a nearby receiver, which was stored in a rack-case along with an amplifier, a specialized band-pass and spatial filtering module, and a spot for the removable laptop, with proprietary software that recorded the processed signals. The final scans would later be uploaded via an encrypted link to Werner's mainframe in Berlin, for deep analysis by sophisticated artificial intelligence programs, and from which 3D stratigraphic models of the subsurface could be interpolated.

At least, that's what Lotte had said. Eric didn't pay too much attention to all the techno-geek talk.

Train strikes notwithstanding, the WHG was far cheaper and easier to employ than having to arrange aerial scans. The drawbacks were the relatively small effective range, due to the amount of data the device collected, and the fact that particularly rough areas might need many passes to get a steady and complete reading of the area. This made using the device somewhat tedious, but for taking detailed scans in the field, the WHG really was a revolutionary, reasonably portable, and imminently affordable apparatus. Werner had more powerful systems that operated on helicopters or drones, but they were vastly more expensive to set up and operate—not to mention less... well... secret.

"I know," she replied. "I'm tired too. This is all I've done for the past two days. Thankfully, Jose and the others helped out so I could take breaks. You're doing fine, and I really do appreciate it. I'm just so wound up."

No shit.

She continued as she typed on the laptop. "You're supposed to be able to make multiple passes to get a larger sample size, which Werner's AI modeling can use to create the most accurate image. With all the delays, though, we just don't have time. We've already cancelled Siena, and we have to be in Florence tomorrow. All you've done for days is sit in Sarteano and wait. I'm ruining everything for you!"

Eric halted once again. "Say what? What do you mean you're ruining everything for *me*?"

She flashed him a look as though he was an idiot. "I mean this isn't what we planned. It was already bad enough that Werner cut into our time, but this delay has been awful. If Alberto and I hadn't driven to Milan to get the stupid WHG, we'd probably still be waiting. That was a whole day lost, and you had nothing to do, on top of the past two while you were just sitting around."

"Well, I basically knew it was gonna be like this. I'd have helped you and Jose if anyone had asked, but apparently you all had it under control. If you recall, I also offered to go to Milan. I'd have even driven. We have the car."

"I know," she moaned, "but Alberto knew the way and how to avoid all those ridiculous speed traps so we could move fast. Plus, he knew who to talk to at the station, and how. It just seemed silly to have you stuck in the car for eight hours, plus all that insane running around trying to find what train the WHG was trapped in. I thought you'd be happier here. Really, it was quite hopeless either way."

Perhaps. Alternatively, maybe you were just enjoying a little alone time with Alberto.

Even Eric had to admit this guy was pretty easy on the eyes, and he doted on Lotte as if she were the Queen of Tuscany.

Which, of course, she is, but Lotte's ego doesn't need that kind of stroking. Or does it? She seemed to be having a fine time when Alberto was around, laughing and smiling – no sign of the stress case she turns into when we're alone together.

Eric wasn't quite certain where all this was going. Leaving aside what was probably just petty jealousy, lately, it seemed things often followed this pattern – Lotte finding herself overcommitted, under stress, and feeling bad for neglecting him, and him feeling bad for asserting his minimal desires on a continuously overextended Lotte. It wasn't always awful. In fact, it wasn't really "awful" at all. It just felt like things had settled into something of a rut.

Those first months after Lotte relocated from Berlin, when they moved in together, had been amazing.

They don't call it the honeymoon *period for nothing. Yeah, it was crazy, buying stuff for the apartment, her getting set up at school, me finishing Margot's training and then transitioning to a new Schneider project. But it felt like an adventure, and that we were in it together... like we were a team, and the strengths of our differing perspectives and temperaments always seemed to produce a mutually satisfying solution.*

With so much emotional baggage seemingly behind them, they had finally been able to express the genuine joy they had in each other's companionship, which they did—frequently— and to their great and mutual satisfaction. For Eric, it had been validation of what he'd come to realize: that this was who he was, and who he wanted to be, and that he'd been right not to equivocate or compromise, despite the potential for problems.

Unfortunately, all honeymoons eventually end, and all too soon, some of those "potential" problems started to manifest, especially as Lotte became increasingly involved with her program. It could have been worse. Her Master's of Research degree was largely independent, and her focus on computational archaeology involving data analysis, geophysics, and geoinformation meant she didn't need to spend as much time in the field.

On breaks and during the summer, Lotte did travel to Europe, where quantitative archaeological techniques seemed to be more prevalent, though Harvard was trying to change that by taking her on as a star student. She'd spent most of this past June in Berlin at Werner, which was hard on both of them. With the vacation to Italy coming up, they'd both managed through it, but pressures on her time were increasing, and Lotte did plan to participate in more fieldwork, focusing on data collection, during the upcoming PhD portion of her program.

In some sense, it felt to Eric like this was the natural push and pull of a developing relationship, coupled with the stress of super-busy schedules.

Well, one super-busy schedule, anyway. Mine is more manageable.

Given that they had plenty of time to figure things out, he wasn't in a panic about it. Just as his father had warned him, however, it was no picnic either, despite the fact that today they'd brought a lovely picnic lunch.

You really couldn't miss with the food in Italy, and Eric had enjoyed his share. In truth, the day Lotte and Alberto went to Milan, Signora

Nocenzi, who ran the B&B where they were staying, took pity on him and produced a wonderful lunch, which she drafted Eric into helping her prepare. Her English was spotty, but she got her points across with a few prods from a rolling pin, exhortations to various saints for patience and serenity, and no small amount of red wine. It was Eric's best day in Italy so far, and he'd barely seen Lotte at all.

I think I'll just keep that to myself, though. Especially since I had a little bit of Signora Nocenzi's wine. Well, maybe more than a little *bit.*

He wished Lotte would just calm down, but that seemed to be against her nature, though not totally. Eventually, she would always crash, and they'd have a quiet day or two where she largely couldn't get off the couch, or out of bed.

No problems with that!

In such moments, Eric became everything to her again. Those interludes sustained him, but he felt they were both struggling to solve the riddle of much of their other time together. Problems weren't unanticipated pairing a tortoise with a hare, but the devil is always in the details, and how the specific patterns of their relationship would unfold were just now, after two years of living together, becoming apparent.

Eric lowered the sensor of the WHG to the ground. "Lotte, if you think you're ruining everything for me because we missed Siena and I spent a couple of days sitting in Sarteano, you're wrong. I think you care about all that stuff more than I do. You planned the whole itinerary anyway. Not that I had a problem with any of it, but you were more upset than I was when we had to move things around after Werner contacted you. Do you not get that all I want is to be with you? All I want is for us to have fun together. I don't care if that means seeing the Uffizi or sitting all day in the sweltering sun watching you walk in corn-rows with your archaeology buddies. So, if you want to stay here longer to collect your data, the hell with Florence. I just want to be with you, but I want you to be happy while we're together, not stressed-out *'Fraulein Kommandantin* Bossy Pants!' Does that make any sense?"

She froze and squinted intimidatingly. Without taking her eyes from Eric, she removed her Aussie safari hat and wiped her brow. "Eric," she said in a menacing tone, "put down the WHG."

"Umm, why?"

"Because I'm going to *kill* you!" she squealed as she tossed her hat aside and launched to her feet.

"Uh, oh!" he yelped, as he quickly unhooked the handle from the harness and gently laid it in the grass before he skedaddled. Even with the delay, he had a bit of a head start, and he was taller and faster... but that was all theory. In practice, he could never outrun Lotte. By sheer force of will, she always caught up, and sure enough, he soon heard the pounding of her Euro-style Adidas close behind, then felt a tug at the back of his shirt. She pulled, and he surrendered into her arms, feeling the tight squeeze as she locked her hands around his stomach.

"Eric, do you mean it?" She pressed her head into his left shoulder, awakening memories of the pain from his battle with Charun, which only now was beginning to give way to near normalcy. "Can we really stay another day, or two?"

"Of course, I mean it," he emphatically replied, even though the thought of potentially two more days of this made him grimace inwardly. "If it makes you happy, it makes me happy. Florence will be there. We can come back. We have all the time in the world. Does this make you happy?"

"Yes, this makes me happy, and much calmer. Thank you so much. You know how much this means to me." She squeezed even more forcefully, and he had to tighten his abs to avoid having all the air crushed from his lungs. "But now—" She giggled. "—what did you call me, you little shit?"

"Umm, I can't remember. Running makes me forget stuff. Who are you again?"

"Apparently, I'm *Fraulein Kommandantin* Bossy Pants! Are you going to take that back, or will I need to kill you after all?"

"Hey, I just work here. You'll need to take that up with the union."

"The union?" She seemed genuinely intrigued. "You're in a union?"

"Yeah, the IBLM. That's my union."

"Oh, this will be good, I'm sure. What does IBLM stand for?"

"The International Brotherhood of Lotte's Minions. Proudly serving Lotte since 2005."

She gave a little whoop of a laugh and then whirled him around to face her. "*Alter!* 2005! That's ten years this year. Can you believe we've known each other for that long?"

Only ten years? Feels like way more. "Wow, you're right. Pretty unbelievable. What will we do to celebrate?"

"Well," she said with a sly look, "we have our picnic, and it's getting close to lunch. How about we run down to the river to cool off before we eat?"

Kuuuul off. "Umm, I don't think I brought my bathing suit," he sheepishly replied.

"Neither did I," she said with a seductive grin, then turned and ran for the water.

As always, Eric followed.

CHAPTER 2

Somerville, Massachusetts, Saturday, October 10, 2015

Eric opened his eyes and glanced at the clock: 8:30 a.m.

Under normal circumstances, this would be cause for alarm, exactly why they *had* an alarm, typically set for 6:30. Today being Saturday, there was none of the usual rush to get anywhere. He planned to have lunch with Margot and Jessica, who were spending the day in Boston, and he had to pick up Lotte at the airport around 6:00 p.m. Otherwise, it was an unusually quiet day, and he spent a few more minutes lounging in bed before jumping in the shower.

When he emerged, the familiar strains of opera drifted up from the first floor. Obviously, Mrs. Binson was up and about, which reminded him he had some books of hers to return. He'd do that in a bit. Now, he needed coffee, though it never tasted as good when Lotte didn't make it, even with the fancy new French press they'd bought recently in Boston's North End. While the coffee steeped, he fed Langsam some berries. He'd take her out later if the weather cleared. Right now, it was lightly raining.

"Don't give me that look," he said to his turtle. "I know you'd love going out in the rain, but I just got out of the shower. I don't want to have to clean up again." Langsam just stared at him, non-plussed as ever.

He gazed out the window into the little backyard while he drank his coffee and ate his yogurt and Alpen with honey. The rain made things still, which he liked. Only the opera below broke the silence, a small price to pay for an unbelievably great living situation.

Gloria Binson's husband, George, died in early 2013. An English professor at Tufts University, he'd only been in his early sixties when he suffered a fatal stroke. As it happened, the Binsons had already converted part of their second floor into an in-law apartment with a small kitchen when Gloria's mother had lived with them. So, not wanting to move, Gloria decided to rent the upper floor, as much for company as income.

Mrs. Binson also volunteered at the Museum of Fine Arts, and knew Carolyn Booth, Mr. Schwarz's girlfriend. When Lotte told her father she needed a place to stay near Harvard—and oh, by the way, that Eric would be living with her as well, which thankfully was A-Okay—Mr. Schwarz talked to Carolyn, Carolyn talked to Gloria, and that was pretty much that. The house on Rodgers Avenue was only a ten-minute bike ride to Harvard, and only a fifteen-minute walk to the Davis Square T stop, though Eric usually drove Lotte in when the weather was awful.

Much as it rankled her, Lotte owed one to Carolyn for hooking them up with such a nice place. For her part, Mr. Schwarz's girlfriend was absolutely lovely, just as Lotte had said. Even ten years on, though, she still frequently brought up Dr. Esfahani, whom she'd known quite well. That always cast a bit of a shadow over otherwise enjoyable gatherings.

Eric had figured Carolyn would bring up the subject when he first met her, which she did. He was, after all, with Lotte at the MFA the last time Dr. Esfahani was seen.

Well, the last time that anyone knows about.

Somehow, the matter seemed to creep into many conversations, as if Carolyn felt a bond with Lotte and Eric over the loss of a mutual friend. He began to see why Lotte had been so annoyed by it two years ago, but they both simply had to endure, obviously more so now that they were in Boston and saw her father more frequently.

Big aria coming up.

When that was over, he planned to bring down Gloria's books. He'd enjoyed Amy Chua's *Day of Empire* about the correlation between tolerance along racial, ethnic, or religious dimensions during the rise of a hyperpower, and increasing intolerance as the hyperpower declined. Of course, no mention of Afrits or other supposedly mythical monsters in the rise and fall of the empires in the first place, but that wasn't exactly a surprise. History definitely took a different slant for Eric, knowing what he knew.

He also found it interesting to re-read Freud's *Civilization and its Discontents* ten years after Mr. Schwarz had loaned it to him. The key point that civilization exacted suffering on the individual by repressing aggressive instincts still came through, but Eric caught more this time, particularly the pervasive anti-religious sentiment, which hadn't made such an impression when he read the book as a teenager. He found it ironic, because civilization had its birth in a society centered around religion, where the temples wielded both political and economic authority.

Perhaps more troubling, though, was Freud's idea that humans are torn between Eros and Thanatos, the desire to live and the wish to die. Eric couldn't really understand this, and frankly sort of found it to be bunk. Put more politely, perhaps, he felt this concept was simply too much a reflection of the pessimism of a man who had lived through a horrible war, saw the signs of another one likely rising, and who suffered with excruciating pain from the mouth cancer that would eventually push him to take his own life.

In any case, Eric still found some resonance with the idea that the benefits of civilization often came at a price.

Is Lotte really better off for her super-specialized intellectual pursuits? Is she happier for all this? Is she really even happy at all?

Eric could easily imagine himself living in a primordial paradise, lying around until hunt time, chasing down some game, then lying around again before the great feast. Not a lot of decisions to be made there. That would suit him perfectly, and as he'd learned, hunter gatherers had far more leisure time than people in the modern, industrialized world.

Why do we bend ourselves into pretzels like this, causing at minimum neuroses, and at worst psychoses? What the hell are we doing all this for? Flush toilets and smart phones? I'd happily kiss that shit goodbye, but at this point, it seems like it's just too late to go back.

As good as it sounded, Eric knew he'd simply starve. He didn't have the knowledge to live off the land in some small, nomadic band. Nor did the vast majority of others. That ship had sailed.

How the hell did we get started down this path in the first place?

Of course, greater minds than his probably didn't know the answer either. So, he did what everybody else did and went with the seemingly inevitable flow. He did, however, find it interesting to ponder.

The aria ended, so Eric gathered the books and proceeded downstairs. The bathroom, kitchen, living room, and one bedroom of their apartment were at the back of the house behind a single door in the upstairs hallway. Gloria had happily let Lotte have the other upstairs bedroom, which faced the street for her study. It used to be the Binson's daughter Melinda's room, and its perfect location afforded quiet in the evenings when Eric was also home.

Well, perfect for Lotte anyway.

She spent countless hours in her little lair, sequestered behind the two doors that she now habitually closed for quiet. Eric often wished her study were better integrated with the rest of the apartment. He didn't really have a place there, not even anywhere to sit down, and he felt it created a certain distance between them. Of course, this was all temporary while she was so busy in school, but school for her was like a lifetime—possibly up to ten years depending on how things went.

Two down, eight more to go? Yikes!

He walked by the open door across the hall and saw her desk piled high with books and papers, surrounded by similarly stuffed shelves. Even the floor had accumulated substantial piles of folders and notebooks. He wondered how the heck she found anything in this mess, but didn't dare try to clean up.

That would really freak her out.

The door to Gloria's apartment lay on the left at the bottom of the stairs, next to the main exit that led to the front porch. She rarely locked it, and often just left it standing open, encouraging Lotte and Eric to visit whenever they liked. Right now, it was closed, more likely to dampen the sound of the music than for any concern for privacy. Eric lightly knocked.

"Come on in, it's open!"

He entered and found Gloria where he figured she'd be, sitting on the living room couch near the big front window, reading a magazine.

He smiled. "Good morning. I wanted to return these books. Thanks for letting me borrow them. The Amy Chua was really good, like you said."

She smiled in return. "Oh, it's my pleasure. Have a seat. Do you want anything to drink? I hope the music wasn't bothering you."

"No, I'm good. I just had coffee. And the music was fine. I was in the shower when you started, so you didn't wake me up."

"Oh, good. You two are so quiet, I can't believe it. Sometimes I forget you're up there. Don't you ever listen to music?"

He laughed. "Well, Lotte does. She has a lot of old vinyl records of bands that I think are weird. She listens to them wearing headphones in the rare instances she has time. I'm not much of a music fan, and the little I like is pretty mellow. So, the loudest sounds you're likely to get from us is Lotte, furiously typing."

"She really is a go-getter. Where is she? I thought I saw you two leave in the car yesterday and she had a bag with her."

"Yeah, I took her to the airport. She had to go down to the University of North Carolina for a couple of days."

"Didn't they have that big storm down there? Hurricane Joaquin that we got some rain from on Wednesday?"

"Yeah, I don't think it hit the Raleigh area that bad. It was more South Carolina and the coast that got nailed. Anyway, they didn't cancel the conference, and I got a text from her last night saying she got in fine."

"Well, that's good. So, she's attending a conference down there?"

"Actually, she's the featured speaker today, giving a big presentation this morning, probably starting right around now. She's presenting the results of the Werner data we collected when we were in Italy a couple of months ago."

"Incredible! That's so exciting. Did you find anything?"

"No, not really," he glumly replied.

They'd sent the results back to Berlin for AI scrutiny, and the Sarteano samples had come up negative. Even more disappointing was that the data from the river Lotte had quietly slipped to her friend Jürgen for some surreptitious after-hours analysis had also produced nothing. The site had clearly been occupied. There was evidence of a narrow road or path leading up the hill on the north side, and the WHG had detected some small items buried in the soil. But if Vanth had an underground portal chamber like Charun's, its location would remain a mystery for now.

"It's okay, though. She still had plenty to talk about in terms of the process of data collection and technical analytics. That's what the lecture was really about."

Gloria seemed impressed. "I'll bet she did. I'll bet they're all buzzing about the big robbery too."

"What are you talking about? I haven't had the TV on this morning."

"Oh, my, there was a big robbery at the Louvre in Paris. Actually, it seems like they did more damage than steal things. Somebody broke a display case, and it looks like they only took one thing, some kind of old stone mace."

Eric shuddered slightly, thinking of Charun's hammer. *But Charun is gone... right?*

"The incredible thing, though," Gloria continued, "was that they somehow got out through a glass ceiling in some covered courtyard. Nobody knows how they got up there, or why they chose that way to get out, but there was broken glass everywhere. Apparently, they used some kind of electrical pulse that disabled all the power and security cameras in that wing of the building, so there's no video. I guess a guard heard the noise and triggered something manually in another part of the building. The whole complex was going off like a thousand car alarms for two hours."

"When did this happen?" he asked, utterly amazed and secretly somewhat concerned about what it might mean.

"It would have been about three a.m. their time, so about nine last night ours."

"Wow. I was in bed finishing that Amy Chua book, then I went to sleep. I'll bet the WIA is going nuts over this."

"Sorry, WIA?"

"Oh, my bad." He chuckled. "Everybody has an acronym these days, don't they? WIA stands for 'Women in Archaeology.' That's the conference Lotte's attending."

She gave a somewhat skeptical look. "Aren't there already a lot of women in archaeology? Do they really need a conference?"

"Yeah, there are, but they started this up a few years ago to try to address gaps in publication rates and tenure positions between women and men. Also, with more and more reliance on technology, you're seeing the same thing that happens with a lot of STEM programs. Women get discouraged and don't stick with it for the same reasons they leave science and tech. So, among other things, WIA are doing a lot of mentoring. In fact, the whole afternoon today is geared toward that, which is why Lotte is leaving early and I have to get her tonight."

"Doesn't she want to be a mentor? She'd be fantastic."

Eric smiled knowingly. "Fantastic doesn't even cover it, believe me. She's a great teacher and would be a perfect mentor for undergrads. She's just really busy and overextended, so she's trying not to get sucked into any more commitments just now. She just finished her Master's. Maybe once she has some traction with the PhD, she'll feel differently."

In truth, Lotte had some reservations about the whole concept of the WIA. Mentoring was one thing, but having a conference with programming and a small awards ceremony geared only at women sort of rubbed her the wrong way. She felt men and women should be seen as equals, and that having a conference for women might have the unintended consequence of creating an even greater divide between genders than currently existed. Eric didn't really see a big problem, but if the Werner Institut hadn't sponsored her to present on their technology, she'd have never gone. Ironically, Werner chose her because she was the *only* female involved in the institute who had enough knowledge of the technology to represent them. To Eric, this was exactly the point of WIA.

Gloria nodded. "Yeah, that makes sense. George tended to go overboard too. He just loved what he did, and he had that kind of voracious curiosity about... well, everything! He was involved in so many things—committees, curriculum development, writing articles—and so much work with his students, trying to help them see that an English degree wasn't an economic death sentence. He tried to get students to understand that people who could think and write could do so many things, and that the money would come in the end. He was always running off to something, doing all kinds of projects with all sorts of people, but he didn't look after his health. At least it was fast, no suffering, unlike my poor mother."

"I'm so sorry," Eric said, sensing all of this still hovered awfully near the surface for Gloria, even after several years of losing both the people she had lived with and loved. "You've never mentioned what happened with your mother."

"It was cancer. We took care of her as long as we could here, but in the end, she had to go into a nursing home for continuous monitoring. She hated it, and I think that broke what little spirit she had left to fight. Then it was just a slow process of watching her waste away in hospice. She died about six months before George did. Such a good person. I wish she could have just gone quietly and peacefully, avoided all that suffering, but I guess we don't get to make that choice for people, do we?"

He didn't know what to say to that, so he kept his mouth shut. It was true. Even people suffering didn't appear to have the choice to end their lives when they felt they were done. That seemed silly to him, and he thought of Freud's antipathy toward religion. Maybe there was more to his feelings than just the pessimism of a weary and sick old man. Interesting also that his final act was a finger in the eye of those who opposed doctor-assisted suicide on so called "moral" grounds. Freud was far from a perfect person, but Eric perceived that for the time in which he lived, and died, he did so by the ideals that guided his life's work, which was ultimately geared at reducing human suffering.

Gloria sighed deeply. "In any case, that's why George had books on so many subjects, not just his dusty old lit crit. He read about everything so he could talk to people about anything. He'd be happy somebody was getting some use out of them. Most of them are just packed up in boxes in the basement. Do you want some more?"

"Absolutely!" Eric responded with enthusiasm, trying to lift Gloria's spirits. "You pick. I like everything, but you know I prefer non-fiction."

"Gotcha!" she winked. "Stop back this afternoon and I'll have some for you, or I'll just leave them on the stairs if you're busy. You say Lotte is coming home tonight?"

"Yeah, she leaves around three, and I'll get her at Logan around six. She's been super busy with school starting back, but maybe we could plan to do dinner sometime in the next couple of weeks. I'll pry her away from the computer. She'll hate it, but she'll thank me in the end."

Gloria laughed. "That's sounds lovely. You two are so sweet. Are you ever going to get married?"

Yikes, where did that come from? "Wow, uh... gee... I honestly don't know. We haven't put much thought into that. Maybe, some day. I'm not sure. I'd have to ask the boss."

"Well, that's usually how it works, isn't it?"

"Yeah, I guess it is at that. I suppose I meant that at some point, she and I would need to talk about it... try to figure out what advantage marriage would bring us. I'm not sure it would change our basic commitment to one another. We have an especially strong and kind of... well... *uncommon* bond."

"I can tell. You're the poster children for 'opposites attract.' I think that's so cute. I'd love to hear how you two got together."

Yeah, that's never gonna happen.

"All I can say is, for George and me, marriage just greased the skids. It made certain practical things easier. For better or worse, it's what people expect. Not people, people, like your friends, but people at banks, and with the IRS, and mortgage companies... and people who aren't your friends, who judge you only by what they see on the outside. It's also usually the step folks take before they have children. Guess that was a factor for us, too."

Children, yowzah! Now there's a frightening concept. "Well, I appreciate your input. It's definitely food for thought."

"Yeah, something to consider," she said, appearing to sense she'd struck a nerve. "You'll be fine either way. Don't worry about it."

Yeah, right. That's kind of like asking me not to breathe.

They bid *adieu*, and he scurried back upstairs. He'd need to leave to meet Margot and Jessica soon. They wanted to have lunch in the South End, and Eric was damned if he was going to drive. He'd take the T... plenty of time to sit on the train and contemplate what it might be like being married to Lotte. Or, more to the point, what it would be like for Lotte being married to him... with children.

The mind boggles.

Rather than ponder the imponderable, Eric spent most of his time on the train looking at videos from Paris on his phone. Most of it showed aerial footage of the glass canopy of the *Cour Marly*, the enclosed courtyard of the Louvre that now housed a magnificent collection of sculptures.

The damage was impressive. Glass and debris littered the roof. Whatever had been inside had clearly burst out, likely at great speed, almost as if they'd ridden a tiny missile from the floor below. The gaping hole was about six to eight feet wide. The authorities had no idea how the thieves got in, but this was without a doubt the method of egress.

They also seemed clueless as to why, of all the incredible treasures in the vast museum, only the one display case in room 236, Ancient Mesopotamia, had been broken into, or, according to reports, utterly destroyed. No images from inside the building had been released, and the mysterious electrical malfunction, likely initiated by the thieves themselves, had disabled all the security cameras, so they'd captured no video of the culprits or their astonishing escape. Equally puzzling was why only one item, identified simply as a "votive mace head," had been taken. Nevertheless, French police spokespeople assured the public that the miscreants would be rapidly found and severely punished.

Eric had his doubts. It had been twenty-five years since the theft at the Isabella Stewart Gardner Museum in Boston, and they didn't seem any closer to catching those miscreants or finding the stolen artwork than when he was a nine-month-old baby. The whole Louvre thing, however, totally creeped him out. It just didn't seem natural. Given his experiences, that might just be paranoia creeping in—seeing monsters where none existed.

At least, I hope that's the case.

Margot and Jessica wanted to go to a tapas place on Washington Street, so he made the change to the Orange Line at Downtown Crossing and got off at Back Bay. It wasn't the nearest stop, but he liked walking through the South End, and since the rain had let up, he took advantage of getting a little exercise. Tapas was good because he could eat fairly light and maybe go for a bike ride in the afternoon before picking up Lotte. It felt nice not having to run around for a change.

"Hey stranger!" Margot called as Eric stepped inside the restaurant. "Long time no see. You behaving?"

He gave his friend and co-worker a big hug. "If behaving badly is behaving, then sure." He turned to hug Margot's partner. "Hi Jessica! How have you two been?"

"Fine, good to see you Eric," Jessica replied. "Busy as ever. School is back in full swing, and your dad is running Margot ragged, as usual."

"What? My dad never ran anybody ragged but me. You're either making it up, or you're more incompetent than I thought."

Margot smiled and countered the joke insult. "No, things are far more efficient in the office than ever, now that *you've* been exiled to Eastern Mass!"

Eric made a play at being wounded, but he knew she was probably telling the truth. "I think they want to seat us. We'll hash this out when we get to the table."

After sitting down and ordering drinks and some starter tapas, Eric turned to Jessica. "So, school... how is old Southby High? Lotte and I should drop by sometime and see the place. That would bring back memories."

"Oh, it's fine." Jessica sighed. "This is my third year, and I guess I've got the drill down. I think they'll want me to start teaching geometry next year, which will be something new."

He groaned. "Ugh, geometry. Kill me now."

She laughed. "Yeah, that seems like a 'love it or hate it' kind of subject. I take it you were the latter. I've always been a math geek, so I'm excited. That's about all I'm excited about right now, though. It just feels like the school is moving backwards."

"How so?"

"Well, it's not the kids. I mean, kids are kids, right? They're an echo chamber for what their parents do and say. I guess I've gotten used to a certain amount of self-centered entitlement in Southby, though that's probably true in a lot of places these days. I just can't believe all the incidences we've had of bullying and hateful speech. I didn't hear this stuff three years ago when I started, but last year, and now with the new year, it's just seeping out of the woodwork. There seems to be so much... *anger* out there, and it all just seems to be bubbling to the surface. I don't know if it's people reacting to Obama, or fucking Facebook, or what, but it feels like people are coming unhinged. I'm really dreading next year's election."

Eric had voted twice, both times for Obama. He didn't especially follow politics all that closely, but his sense was that Republicans had very much dug in their heels over his policies and things had gotten more divisive. The debate over immigration reminded him of Amy Chua's book, and how intolerance toward minorities in your midst correlated with a hyperpower's decline.

Is this all symptomatic of the end of the "American era?"

Hard to tell, but it was interesting how these issues seemed to be playing out in his old high school. Southby had always been a conservative and insular place. For a while there, it seemed like things were changing, but progress is rarely linear, and it didn't surprise him that his hometown had given back some of what he, at least, saw as the gains that had been made. He'd never felt truly at home in Southby. Cambridge and Somerville were much more to his liking, though a far more urban environment, which meant there were tradeoffs in space, noise, cost, and other factors.

"Wow," he said, shaking his head. "I remember the day I met Lotte. There was an incident with a kid who made a Nazi salute. Lotte slapped him. I'm not joking. He was on the freaking football team, but she was fearless. It's something I'll never forget. It was so shocking. It's the only time I remember anything like that happening, but I'm not gonna say there wasn't some pretty disturbing stuff going on under the surface."

"Yeah, well," Jessica said with distaste, "things are changing, and not for the better. It's gonna be a wild ride over the next few years. Whatever, I don't mean to be a downer. Hey, speaking of Lotte, how is she? I miss seeing you two at Peaches."

"Yeah, we've got to get back down there the next time Margot is playing. Lotte's fine... super busy, but she's killing it in her program. Surprise, surprise. I'm not sure if Margot mentioned, but she's down in North Carolina at a conference giving a talk for the Werner Institut. In fact, it's probably done now. Maybe she'll call and tell us how it went."

"And how are you?" Margot asked. The look she gave him, and the context of Lotte, gave him a clue what she was really asking.

"I'm fine. We're fine. It's not perfect, but what is? She's usually really busy, and she gets kind of wound up about all the stuff she feels like she has to do, but that's Lotte. I expected that. I'm exactly where I need to be, and deep down, I think she feels like she is too. There are things to hash through and figure out, but we have time. No panic. It's a work in progress. *Lavori in Corso*, as the Italians say. There, how'd I do?"

Margot laughed. "Not bad! I almost believe you. Actually, I'm proud of you, Eric. You sort of surprised me doing what you did two years ago. It took guts. I thought it could go either way, but I kind of bet on you staying with Erica—money I happily lost."

Eric shook his head. "Oh, God. Erica. Poor Erica. How is she?"

"She's fine. I see her at the bank when I go. We've never discussed it, but I'm sure she knows I have most of the details of what happened. It's probably hard for her, having that constant reminder, but as far as I can tell, she's moved on. Sometimes that's just the way it has to be."

"Jeez!" Jessica interjected. "Is this what you two spent all your time talking about when you worked together?"

Both Eric and Margot gave a somewhat uncomfortable laugh. "Margot helped me out of a jam two years ago. We talked about stuff like this then, and if we hadn't, I'm not really sure where I'd be today. Definitely not in as good a place. I say that with certainty. Otherwise, we were all business. Right?"

He winked, and Margot winked back. "Right, boss. Ex-boss, actually. Speaking of work, though, I've been wanting to talk with you about something, but I wanted to do it in person, and I knew you'd been busy with the new team, so I didn't ask if you could come down."

She was referring to the new flooring team for which Eric was partly responsible as Assistant Project Manager. When he'd told his dad he wanted to move to the Boston area, Mr. Schneider acted on a plan he'd had in mind for several years but never executed. From among his Central Mass flooring personnel, he formed a new group that was willing to work in the Boston area, and he drafted Eric to help with project management.

Schneider Industrial Flooring had a great reputation in Central Mass, Rhode Island, and parts of Connecticut and Western Mass, but the Boston area was a different ballgame. So far, the city itself hadn't proven especially fruitful, but the northern part of Route 128 around Woburn and Burlington had turned out to be a goldmine. Eric could easily drive up there after rush hour to meet with the team when jobs were in progress, or help his dad with the occasional sales call.

It wasn't full-time, which was fine because it had given him the opportunity to finish grooming Margot for the Business Manager role. For the hours worked, though, the money he made was better than anything he could get elsewhere, and over two years, business had increased steadily, to the point where his dad had briefly considered creating a second Eastern Mass unit, though Eric hadn't heard much about that since the spring.

After the waitress came and they ordered more tapas, Eric picked the conversation back up. "So, what's going on? What have I screwed up this time?"

Margot laughed. "Nothing, for once. Actually, I need to talk with you about your dad."

"He's not sick, is he?"

"No, no, nothing like that. Actually, he's great. He *is* working me to death, but I'm loving it. I hate being bored. He's finally starting to let go of things, let others do stuff, probably because he's spending so much time in your area. Which is why what happened was so strange and made me wonder what it was about. And you know me: if something's going on, I want to know what it is."

He smiled as he remembered Margot's interest when Lotte showed up at the office two years ago. In others, that trait might have been considered "nosy" and annoying, but he'd always trusted her, and somehow knew her interest was grounded at some level in concern for him, in addition to her love of a juicy piece of gossip. No harm in that, given she'd never used it against him.

"So," she continued. "September 30th, the Wednesday before last, three guys in suits came to the office. Keisha and I got them coffee and whatnot. It seemed strange to me. They weren't clients or prospects, otherwise she or I would have known about this and prepped materials, had all our ducks in a row. So, while they were meeting, I took a little spin outside. Sure enough, in the parking lot, there's a minivan with the EastCoast Flooring logo on it."

EastCoast was a large industrial flooring company based in Hartford. They didn't really compete with Schneider, usually focusing on bigger jobs and larger clients in Western New York and along the Connecticut coast down toward Stamford and White Plains.

"What the hell would they be doing in Southby?" he asked.

Margot's tone turned serious. "Eric, I think your dad is considering selling the business."

He ceased chewing his tuna tostada. If true, this was an interesting development. It wasn't totally clear what his dad selling the business might mean—maybe nothing, or maybe they'd want to keep the crews and replace all the management and administrative employees. Not that there were many of these, just himself, Skip and Ernie helping his father oversee the Central Mass teams, Tony, who served as shift supervisor on the Boston crew, and, of course, Margot and Keisha.

"What do you make of it?" he asked, wanting her opinion, as she'd had more time to consider the ramifications.

She was quick to answer. "If he sells, I'm gone for sure. To EastCoast, I'd be dead wood, Keisha too. They'd centralize what we do down in Hartford. You're probably safe. Your dad would make a stipulation for you. The teams would be fine. Not sure about Skip, Ernie, or Tony. It would depend on what EastCoast thought of their skills. I'm not sure they'd stay in supervisory positions, especially Tony, because he's so new at it, but I don't really know."

A fair assessment. It's strange to even contemplate this happening. "Do you think I should talk to him about it?"

She winced a bit as she answered. "Well, yes and no. I don't think you should confront him about seeing EastCoast people in the office, but if there was some way you could... I don't know... get him talking... you might get a better sense of what's on his mind. My guess is, if he knew you eventually wanted to take over, he'd pass the business to you. I don't get the sense he thinks that's what you want right now, so he's looking at options. But if it *is* what you want, then you should probably consider it seriously and maybe plant the seed now, before it's too late."

Eric consternated. *This is not part of the plan. I like my role at Schneider. It gives me enough money, plenty of flexibility, and when Lotte's done with her program two hundred years from now, I'll know if staying is an option, or if I'll need to follow her wherever the artifacts take her. Dad's moving too fast. What's his problem? He's only, what... in his mid-50s? Is he really ready to go out to pasture so young? Why is my nice little situation getting short-circuited? Or is it? Hmmmmm....*

"Yeah, I think talking with my dad is a good idea," he finally said. "The problem is, I'm just not sure what to say to him right now. Let me think it over, and then I'll try to set up some time with him. Thanks for letting me know, Margot. It took me by surprise, but I guess that's the way things happen. I'm glad you have my back. Jessica, you're a lucky girl."

Jessica smiled. "I sure am. Now if you two are through sorting out Eric's life, can we get more tapas? I'm still hungry."

CHAPTER 3

The rest of lunch passed pleasantly.

Margot and Eric had been unable to resist a bit more work talk, but it had centered on how she was doing as Business Manager. He couldn't help but be impressed, both with the types of work his dad was handing off to her and how Margot had risen to the challenge. The basic bookkeeping, accounts payable, and purchasing had always been part of the Business Manager's role, but contracts and project budgets had always been the sole purview of Eric's father.

Naturally, Eric had been exposed to those areas as Assistant Project Manager, but it really was a big change for his dad to open up those processes in the home office. Both Margot and the new receptionist Keisha Henderson had stepped up. Eric was pleased by how Margot let Keisha take on aspects of her role as she took on the new duties. There might come a time they would need another person in the office, assuming, of course, an office remained to staff.

Eric ruminated on that after they'd said their goodbyes as he ambled through the South End toward Back Bay station. It had started to rain again, but he'd brought an umbrella, and the light mist wasn't enough to force him into an Uber. The thing that troubled him most about a potential sale was the prospect of losing Margot. She'd been right: his dad would likely secure his position, at least in the short run. In a sense, that was all he needed because of the uncertainties around Lotte's future whereabouts. He recognized, however, that it would be hard to justify roles like Margot's or Keisha's.

I wonder if maybe I could somehow take over the business, assuming that's what Dad wants. Has a sale always been part of his plan? Does Dad need that money for the retirement he envisioned? Could I actually run the business? Of course, what happens when Lotte finishes her studies and most likely gets a job outside of Boston? What then?

A lot of questions to consider, seemingly as always.

He laughed to himself. *A* Lotte *questions.*

Right on cue, the opening guitar riff to Soundgarden's *Black Hole Sun* came from the phone in his jacket pocket. He wasn't much of a Soundgarden fan, but this song understandably resonated with him and made a great ring tone for when Lotte called. He wasn't exactly sure how she'd feel about that, so he'd kept it his little secret.

He fished the phone out of his pocket, a process made more difficult by holding his umbrella. "Hey, how'd it go?"

"Hi!" She seemed a little breathless, and from the background noise appeared to be walking outside, as he was. "The talk was fine. They loved it, but... Eric, you won't believe what happened at lunch!" She seemed super excited.

"Tell me. Sounds interesting."

"I think I found one!"

"Found one... what?"

"A portal! I think I've found another portal!"

Despite the rain, he stopped dead in his tracks. "What? How? Where?" *What the hell, do they serve portals on the lunch menu at UNC? I'll have one with a side of fava beans and a nice Chianti.*

"It's just so unbelievable! There was a student sitting at my table... she'd gotten an inquiry about something in a picture she'd taken and posted on Facebook. She was passing her phone around, wondering if anyone knew what the item might be, and if it might be valuable. I wasn't really paying attention, but the person next to me gave me her phone and... there it was! It took me a moment to see it, because it wasn't the right way up, and it's a little different, but I really think it's a portal!"

"What do you mean it 'wasn't the right way up'?"

"Well, it's hard to tell exactly. The whole thing is in the back of a flooded room. All I could see were what looked like pieces of wood formed into a semicircular arch that was sticking up out of the water. At the apex, there was a sort of stepped, conical shape with little curved protrusions coming out of it... kind of like a witch's hat with tiny, upturned hooks. I know I've seen something like this before, but I can't place where. In any case, it was the semicircular form that got my attention. It's exactly like the stone slabs and the black marble board the *Sadat Alnaar* used to summon the Afrit."

"Well, that could be a coincidence. I mean, there have to be things in semicircular shapes like that, other than portals. Plus, this one is upright. The slabs and the marble board go on the ground. Where's the doorway?"

"It's on the floor! When I saw this shape, I asked the student if there were more parts to this item, and she said yes! There are more of these interlocked pieces of wood, or whatever it is, forming a circular area on the ground in front of the arch. Apparently, it's rather small, only about five feet in diameter, but think about it.... If that's the doorway, whatever comes through would come from beneath, so the opening itself wouldn't need to be as tall. It's like the whole thing is tipped on its end."

Geometry. Not my strong suit.

With some concentration, he began to envision what she was describing, and he couldn't disagree. It sounded like a portal. "Holy shit. What are you gonna do?"

"Not me, silly... we! You think I'm going to see this thing without you? Not a chance!"

She'd never know it, but it was little moments like these that he lived for... to do things with her, together, as a team, and to know she wanted him by her side and that he had a place in her life. He knew it was probably stupid, but he felt overcome with joy.

"Can you get on a plane and come down tomorrow morning? The student said she could drive us to where it is when you get here. I'm actually staying with her tonight since I only booked my hotel room at the Carolina Inn for Friday. She was super nice and let me stay with her. She's at the Hampton Inn nearby. That's where I'm headed now."

"Do you want me to come sooner? I could probably get down there this evening."

"Oh, don't bother," she wearily replied. "I have a place for tonight. It's not worth getting another room, and since I'm here, I'm going to attend their big dinner celebration after all. The organizers were ecstatic that I was staying on. They've been fawning all over me since yesterday. So tedious! I'm like their wet dream... a *girl* who's into the techie part of archaeology. They want me to join... do mentoring. They'll probably have me on the bloody *board* in two years. I just don't have time for all this."

He laughed. "Sounds like a great opportunity to me. Think of all the connections you'd make. I mean, how else will you find more portals if you don't go to WIA luncheons?"

"Ha, ha, ha. Actually, it would be a fantastic way to meet people, and they really are lovely. It's just... well... you know how I feel about all this. I don't want to be seen as a *woman* archaeologist. I want to be seen simply as an *archaeologist,* and I think that's what *all* women should want. I know females have these barriers and often face institutional prejudices, but that hasn't been *my* experience, and I don't expect it to be in the future, or I'll raise holy hell about it!"

Of this, I have no doubt.

"I don't know. I'm conflicted, so I'm hesitant to get too connected. In the end, I think I'm just too busy to get involved in something else, so I'm going to try to fend them off for now. We'll see down the road. Anyway, can you come?"

"Of course, I can come. I'd come to see you even if there wasn't a portal."

"You sweetie. I miss you. I don't sleep right without you anymore. It's quite troublesome. Maybe you'll just need to go everywhere I go."

If I must.

"How are you, by the way? How was lunch with Margot and Jessica?"

"Great! They both say hi. I have some interesting news to tell you, but not now. I'm gonna head home and set up my flight. I'll text you when I have the details."

"Sounds good. I just reached the Hampton. Olive gave me her key. I'm going to rest up this afternoon. They're doing the mentoring sessions now, trying to pair people up, and I want to be as far away from *that* as possible. Oh, I almost forgot... did you hear about the robbery at the Louvre? Everyone at the conference has been going crazy!"

"Yeah, Mrs. Binson told me about it this morning and I looked at some footage on my phone. Absolutely unbelievable. What do you think happened?"

"Honestly, I think it was a stunt... somebody showing off, trying to make some kind of point. I wouldn't be surprised if the item that was taken turns up with a crazy political message attached to it, probably tied to one of the messes in the Middle East—take your pick which one... some supporter of ISIS, or ISIL, or whatever they call themselves. Or who knows, maybe it was the Paris sewer workers trying to say they hadn't had a raise since the time of fucking Hammurabi! Good reason to hit the Mesopotamian room. All I know is that if it were a true theft, they'd have taken much more, or something far more valuable."

Eric laughed about Lotte's Hammurabi quip, and imagined a votive mace head found languishing in some surprised Parisian's *bidet.* Otherwise, though, what she'd said made sense, and he was relieved to hear she didn't think it was a portal-related catastrophe. "You're probably right. They definitely got people's attention, though, especially with the way they got out."

"Yes, quite spectacular, but this is exactly why I think it's just for publicity. Real thieves wouldn't go to trouble like that. If they had the ability to get in, they must have been able to find an easier way out.

Anyway, I'll see you tomorrow. Can you try to arrive in the morning? I think it's a bit of a drive to where this thing is... some kind of turtle-leech place. I can't understand a word Olive says, she has such an accent."

"Hey, you should talk. What, is Olive not from the States?"

"No, she's from the States. I think she said she was born in South Carolina, but grew up mostly in Georgia. It's this Southern accent... worse than the damned Swiss or the East Londoners. Well, maybe not *that* bad. Anyway, where we're going must be like a swamp."

He shuddered. "Yeesh, that sounds awful. Do you need some more clothes? I don't think you brought very much for such a short trip."

She squealed with delight. "Oh, Eric, that's so thoughtful! I wasn't even thinking about it. You're so practical. I knew I kept you around for some reason. Yes, please. It's quite warm down here, but not as hot as right before I arrived. I think that hurricane pushed up a lot of warm air, but it's still near eighty."

He hoped she meant Fahrenheit, otherwise the only thing that would be living down there would be the Afrit.

"Anyway, just bring me some shorts, jeans, some knit tops, and maybe a t-shirt or two... and my sneakers and some socks, if you have room."

"Jeez, anything else?" *Where am I gonna fit my clothes?*

"Yes, some undies, if you don't mind... tops and bottoms."

"Well, okay. I like going in that drawer."

"I'll bet you do, you deviant!"

"Guilty as charged. Hey, with all this stuff, how long are you thinking we're going be down there?"

"Probably just Sunday and part of Monday. I've already called the airline and they gave me a credit for another flight when we book. I'd like to be back by Tuesday. I have a million things to do. Thankfully, I have my laptop and I can do a little work this afternoon."

"So, you need all this stuff for a day-and-a-half? *This* is why your suitcases were so overstuffed in Italy."

"I know! I never know what I'll need, and I never have time to plan, so I just bring everything. You're so much more organized about stuff like this. Why can't you just quit your job and be my valet?"

He chuckled, secretly thinking that might truly be his calling in life. "It's an alluring offer, but I hear you can be a really tough boss. I don't want to have to file a *Lotte* union grievances against you with the IBLM! Get it... a *Lotte* grievances?"

"Oh, I got it," she dully replied, "and you're going to *get it* when I see you! I'll show you what a tough boss I can be. Little shit. I do love you so."

"I love you too. I'll text you when I have my flight details, and I'll see you tomorrow."

"Great, see you then! *Tschüss!*"

Note to self, he thought as he put away his phone and shook off his umbrella under the awning to the Back Bay station entrance. *Lotte likely to be in good mood when she finds portal. Must find many portals. I wonder if I should join the WIA so I can attend all their luncheons, a surprising but apparently lucrative portal identifying activity. It doesn't matter that I'm a guy. I don't need mentoring or any of their services. I'm just there for the food and to look at people's camera rolls. I'll pay my membership fee. That should fly. Hey, with all that experience, maybe the next time I see the Afrit, I could pass for a woman.*

He came to a dead halt as the turnstile door to the train platform swung open.

What the hell am I saying? Hopefully, there is no damn next time with that thing!

"You gonna move, buddy?" someone said from behind.

He fumbled before he finally remembered where he was. "Oh, sorry. My bad."

I just had Afrits on my mind. I'm sure it happens to you all the time.

Eric felt the plane level out. It was a beautiful, clear day, and had he been next to a window, the ground would have been in full view. The flight would take under two hours, and he'd arrive just before 11:00 a.m. He recalled texting Lotte the night before.

Arrive hotel around 11:30. Will text you when I get in...

She responded shortly thereafter:

He laughed. She'd never really been much of a texter. He figured she was at her event, so he decided to have some fun:

How's the WIA dinner?

Her comeback said it all:

Too funny! That had been enough. He didn't want to bug her. Plus, he'd been tired. When he'd gotten home from lunch, Gloria Binson had caught him.

"Hi, Eric," Gloria said as he came through the front door. "I didn't forget about your books, but some of the ones I think you'd like best are stuck in some lower boxes. Would you be able to help me move some stuff around?"

"Yeah, absolutely. Listen, Lotte called me and wants me to go down to Raleigh to see something with a person she met at the conference. I have to book a flight, but after that, I'm free. Do you have dinner plans? I could come down and we could fix up the basement before supper. Not that I'm inviting myself over, or anything."

She laughed. "That would be fantastic. You know you're welcome any time. I'll make my Manicotti. That's very simple and you'll love it. When are you flying out?"

"Hopefully tomorrow morning. I'll have to see what's available."

What turned out to be available was a direct flight at 9:00 a.m. – not cheap, but if this really was a portal, it would be money well spent.

Dinner was not quite Signora Nocenzi quality, but still fabulous. As advertised, Mrs. Binson's basement was literally full of boxes of books. They had that "musty book" smell that reminded Eric of the Southby High library stacks, the first place he'd physically touched Lotte, and had felt gravity and mass giving way. He could still feel her sleeping under his arm, which he'd dared not move even though a stampede probably wouldn't have woken her at that particular moment.

In addition to the books, the furnace, and the washer and dryer, the space at the back of the basement, near the bulkhead, was dominated by some unused furniture.

"That's all Melinda's stuff," Mrs. Binson explained. "She went to school at the University of Oregon, and now she lives outside of Portland. I kept all this for her in case she wanted it, but she wound up being more interested in my mother's furniture, so we shipped that to her after Mom died. Would you and Lotte be able to help me sell this stuff on the internet? I don't need to make much money. It's just not doing any good sitting around, and it sure would free up some space down here."

"Absolutely, no problem. Let me look into that when I'm back. I'm sure we can find a good home for it." He'd wondered if maybe they could wrangle a little space for their bikes in the winter, too. They'd stowed them under the back stairs, which wasn't optimal when it rained or snowed.

With all the moving of boxes, dinner, and splitting a bottle of wine, along with a gin and tonic, Eric found himself exhausted, not to mention a little tipsy, when he finally got back upstairs. Thankfully, he remembered to text Lotte. Being with her had been decidedly good for him in terms of learning how to moderate his drinking. She enjoyed wine when they went out to eat, and even beer on occasion, but rarely drank a lot. So, when she stopped, he stopped, and that had worked well. When she wasn't around, he occasionally slipped a bit, but after that awful night in New Hampshire, he'd never tasted rum again, and had completely avoided getting really drunk.

He went straight to bed, and felt fine when he got up early to pack. Even with all the stuff Lotte wanted, he still fit everything into his two carry-on items.

Despite getting plenty of sleep, he dozed off during the flight, and only woke up when the captain announced their imminent arrival at the Raleigh-Durham airport.

With no bags to claim, he quickly booked an Uber bound for the Hampton Inn. Despite the inevitable delay getting out of Logan, he still arrived by 11:30.

The car pulled up at the hotel, and after he completed his transaction, he texted Lotte. She didn't immediately reply, so he went into the lobby and scanned around. 10:00 a.m. was usually checkout time, so unless they'd asked for a little extra leeway, Lotte and her new friend, Olive, should be around somewhere. He had no clue what Olive looked like, so he searched for the droid he knew.

She was nowhere in sight. He moved to a spot where he wouldn't block the doors and checked his phone. His text to her seemed to have gone through.

Maybe she's in the bathroom, or they're somewhere getting coffee... or tea, in Lotte's case.

He stood and waited. Fifteen minutes passed, and still nothing. He texted again, just in case the first hadn't gotten through. Unwilling to stand around looking like an idiot, he finally moved to one of the lobby's couches. Ten more minutes passed. As noon approached, he felt hungry. The second text also appeared to have been received.

Am I in the right hotel? You know what, enough of this! I'm just gonna call her.

He punched her number from his call log and almost immediately heard a phone ring from the couch abutting the back of the one where he sat.

"Hello?"

The female voice that answered came through in stereo, coming from the speaker of his phone, but also from the person right behind him.

Eric turned around.

"Hello," he said, both into his phone, and into the ear of the woman who he now realized was holding Lotte's LG G3 to her ear. She turned around, and a moment of confusion ensued, as she wasn't Lotte. She was incredibly Lotte-like, however, with black hair that, though not as straight, was about the same length. Her eyes and eyebrows were also dark like Lotte's, though she didn't have that sort of sharp, "devilish" look. Overall, their features were strikingly similar, and they seemed to have a similar build, though this young woman was perhaps a bit taller and lankier.

"Oh, my gawd!" she proclaimed in a deep Southern drawl. "Are you Eric?"

"Yes, I am indeed Eric. And you're Olive, I presume."

She smiled and extended her hand, which he shook in greeting. "Yeah, I'm Olivia Carter, but everybody calls me 'Olive.' Gawd, you're as cute as Lotte said you were."

He blinked and gave a quick shake of his head. *Did I just hear that? Well, at least Lotte doesn't speak badly of me when I'm not around. Unless she calls me a cute idiot.*

"I'm sorry. Sometimes I just blurt things out when I'm nervous. My momma's always sayin', 'Olive, just shut your damned mouth, that way you can't stick your foot in it!' Too late for that, I guess."

He tried to make her feel at ease. "It's okay, really. I've been called much worse things than 'cute,' believe me. But listen, why do you have Lotte's phone? And where is she?"

She began to get flustered. "You mean you don't know? I figured she was with you! I haven't seen her for more than two hours. She left all her bags in the room. I had to bring them down 'cause the maids were wantin' to get in to clean!"

"What do you mean you haven't seen her for over two hours?"

"So, when we got up, Lotte wanted tea, but she'd gone and drank all the darned teabags that were in the room while she was hangin' around yesterday afternoon. That girl really likes tea."

"Yes, she does," he said, as soothingly as possible despite his growing impatience. "Please go on."

"Right, so anyway, we were basically all packed and ready to go by nine-thirty. I was posting pictures of the conference to Facebook, and Lotte said she really wanted to find some tea and that she'd be right back.

She went out, and the next time I looked up, it was past ten! I waited in there as long as I could, but round a little past eleven, I heard the cleaners comin'. I had to make two trips getting our bags down here. I thought maybe she found you and was sittin' in the lobby, but nothin'. I asked at the front desk, but they hadn't seen her neither. She wasn't really supposed to be staying with me anyway, it was all a last-minute thing."

Eric scratched his chin and considered. "Can I see her phone?" She handed it to him, and he swiped the password. He saw his recent text messages, but no other texts, and no new voice mails. He opened her email. She hadn't sent any messages since yesterday afternoon, and the only things in her inbox were replies to those emails or routine archaeology-related subscriptions—nothing that would give any clue where she might be right now.

"What room were you two in?" he asked.

"Room 237."

"What? You can't be serious!"

"I swear on my grandmother's grave, that was our room! Why is that so strange?"

"I take it you've never seen *The Shining?* Never mind. Listen, I'm gonna take her phone and go check it out. Maybe she's waiting up there for some ridiculous reason. Stay here, and I'll be back soon."

She just nodded, seeming to sense his agitation.

He didn't waste time with the elevator. He found the stairs and bounded up two at a time. He exited the stairwell into the second-floor hallway and tracked to room 237, which sat quite nearby. Lotte was nowhere to be seen. He took a chance and knocked. No answer. New guests must not have arrived yet. He poked his head into the room with the ice and vending machine as he scampered toward the elevators. Still nothing. Then he had an idea.

He backtracked to the stairs and went down. Just as he'd surmised, at the bottom of the stairwell was a door. He exited into a parking garage. There weren't a lot of cars, it being Sunday, so he walked up and down and looked into each vehicle parked near the door to the stairs. Nothing. His heart began to race. Something clearly wasn't right. He went out where the cars exited and walked along the pavement, scanning for anything that Lotte might have dropped on the pavement outside.

He couldn't see anything, so he briskly walked to the front entrance of the hotel, took a moment to compose himself, and went inside.

Olive still sat on the couch, but now had her arm over the back as she surveyed the room. She saw him as he approached. "Did you find her?"

He sat beside her. "No. Listen, Olive, I need you to tell me what happened. Can you start by going over how you met Lotte at lunch yesterday?"

She visibly tried to suppress her nervousness and concentrate. "Okay. I went to Lotte's talk at ten-thirty. Well, everybody did... it was a real big deal. She was amazing! She knows so much. I was mighty impressed. Afterward, people were just there talking with her, asking questions about that German institute she works for... what was up with their technology... all kinds of stuff. I just wanted to tell her I thought she was incredible, but the minute I got to her, the WIA folks whisked her away to lunch. So, I tagged along, and darned if they didn't seat me at her table!"

"Lucky break. What happened next?"

"So, we're eating lunch when I hear my Facebook Instant Message go off. Nobody was paying any attention to me, and they were talking about stratospheric data analysis that's way above my pay grade. I'm more into conservation and archives. I just love to be around old things, always have since I was a little girl. My momma used to say—"

"Olive, can we just try to focus on what happened? There may not be much time. Also, it was probably *stratigraphic* analysis. The stratosphere is in the air. Not many artifacts up there."

She pondered for a moment. "Gawd, you're right. See, I was out of my league. Anyway, I check my phone and there's this message from a guy along with a friend request. He says he saw a picture I'd posted yesterday, meaning Friday, because it was Saturday at the time. He wanted to know if I was lookin' to sell the item in the picture. He called it the "hoop-shaped" object in the back of the room, but it's really semicircular. Lotte knew that!"

"Can I see that picture?"

She produced her phone, opened Facebook, and after scrolling past her posts from this morning, came to some she had submitted on Friday. Most were of the conference, but one appeared to show a small house, or perhaps a two-story cabin. The entire area, both inside and out, was completely flooded. A sliding glass door on the back porch stood open, and the first floor of the interior was covered with perhaps a foot-and-a-half of standing water. At the back of the room, near the wall and next to a stairway, a "hoop-shaped" object protruded from the water, seemingly made of interlocking pieces of wood. As Lotte had described, what looked like a little stepped witch's hat, with eight upturned hook-like shapes sticking out of it, sat at the very top. The photo's caption read, "Daddy's house, after the flood."

"Do you know what this object is?" he probed. "Is it your father's?"

"I think it's my daddy's, unless he gave it to my uncle as a present. They share the fishing lodge. It's not really Daddy's house. He lives here in Raleigh, and my uncle lives down in Longs, near North Myrtle Beach."

Myrtle Beach... turtle-leech. The mystery is solved. It does sort of sound like turtle-leech when Olive says it.

"As far as what it is," she continued, "I think my daddy brought it back from Iraq when all the Americans had to leave in 2011. I've always thought it was some kind of weird sculpture."

"Is your father a soldier?"

"No, he works for a private military company called Black Arrow. They're like Blackwater, except smaller and supposedly even more specialized and highly trained in combat and armed security-type stuff. 'Better than the best,' my daddy says. I think that's their motto or something. He's back over there now, helping train the Kurdish fighters against ISIS. He's usually overseas on missions. That's why my momma left and took me to Georgia. She finally had enough."

"I'm sorry to hear that," he said, trying to be nice, but also wishing she'd stay focused. *Time might be of the essence.*

"That's okay. It was a long time ago. I was a little girl. It all worked out. So where were we?"

"Well, I'm trying to understand what happened with this photo. I think Lotte has disappeared, and I have reason to believe it has to do with what's in this picture, but I can't figure out the connection. Do you have the message from the person who wanted to buy the object?"

"No," she said sadly. "When I got the message, I figured, 'Well, here you are surrounded by people who know about artifacts. Maybe someone knows what this is worth?' So, I showed the picture to the folks next to me, and asked them to pass the phone around, hoping someone knew something. Honestly, I don't think half of them even looked at it. Not very nice. Lotte did, though, and she almost jumped clean out of her chair when she saw it! She grabbed me aside and started asking me all kinds of questions, like about what was under the water. How could she have known there was more to it? But she did. She described it almost perfectly, and I told her what she was sayin' was exactly how I remember the thing looked, from the times I saw it before the flood."

"So, what did you do with the person's message?"

"I deleted it. Lotte was so interested and wanted to see it so bad, I just told him I had another buyer, thank you very much, and deleted the IM and the friend request."

"I'm not so good with Facebook. Can you recover that kind of stuff?"

"I don't think so. Let me try." She fiddled with her phone for a bit, but eventually shook her head. "I don't see how to do it. I'm so sorry. I always do the wrong thing."

He began to sense that Olive was a bit fragile "I can't believe that's true, and you did nothing wrong. You had no idea who this was or what they might have wanted. You said it was a guy. Do you happen to remember his name? Maybe we could look up his profile."

"Oh, gawd. It was John something. Began with an 'R.' Sounded like he was on a ship."

"Like rigging?"

"That's it! Riggins! John Riggins."

Eric did a facepalm. "You've got to be kidding. Do me a favor... type in that name into your Facebook search and see what comes up."

She did. "Well, there's several people. None of them are the guy whose picture I saw. His profile seems to be gone. There wasn't much information on there, anyhow. It looked a little fishy. Hey, one of these guys is a famous football player."

"No shit. I suspected that was a fake profile the minute you said that name. Well, we know whoever it was likes the Washington Redskins. What I want to know is, of all the billions of photos on Facebook, how the hell did he find this one picture? Where did you take this, anyway... and why?"

"I told you. I took it at my daddy's fishing lodge that he shares with my uncle. It's near North Myrtle Beach in South Carolina. That area got hit by the floods last weekend. Since my daddy is in Iraq, and my stupid uncle can barely operate his cell phone, let alone send pictures, I decided to stop by there on my way to the WIA Conference. I was there on Thursday and the waters were still pretty high, as you can see. All them rivers down there are still cresting, or they were a few days ago. In all the time they've had this place, I don't think it's ever flooded like that. I emailed my daddy the picture and told him that despite the mess, everything was under control."

"Wait a minute," he said, holding up his hand to stop her. "So, in addition to posting it on Facebook, you also emailed this picture to your father?"

"That's what I just told you. I don't have his phone number over there in Iraq. It's real restricted. He checks email when he can."

"Did you say anything about where it was, or being with your uncle?"

"No. We were out on the boat. I didn't want to type up my life's story while we were flopping around on the water. He probably figured I was out with Uncle Clint. How else would I get there, with the flood, and all? I just wanted him to see what happened and know the lodge had survived basically okay."

"But you signed your name," he slowly said, while thinking through all the ramifications. "What email address did you use?"

"My Savannah State University address. That's where I go to school. It seems more 'professional' than Gmail—to me, anyways."

He wiped his brow. *This isn't good.* "John Riggins, or whoever this is, didn't see your photo on Facebook. That's utterly impossible. He was watching your father's email. He got onto you from that, and found your profile on Facebook because you're the Olive Carter that goes to Savannah State University. He tracked you here because of the photos you posted from the WIA Conference. He tried to lure you out with the offer to buy the object, but you turned him down, so he took a different approach."

"Whuut?"

"He kidnapped you. He probably followed you after the conference yesterday to see what room you were in, and he grabbed you as you came out this morning. Except it wasn't you. It was Lotte. He got the wrong archaeologist."

CHAPTER 4

Things seemed bad, but then they got worse.

Olive began to cry. "I can't believe this is happening! What are they gonna do when they find out Lotte isn't me? Kill her? Then what? Come after me again? This is awful!"

Eric had many of the same thoughts, but the hotel lobby wasn't the place to hash all this through. "Olive, I know you're upset, but try to be calm and keep your voice down. We don't want to attract attention. We need to stay cool."

She pulled herself together as best she could, then whispered over sniffled tears. "Shouldn't we call the police? Maybe somebody saw something, or there might be video of this guy taking her... maybe a shot of his car leaving the parking lot."

She has a point. If I'm right, the person who took Lotte staked out the second-floor hallway. Guests, cleaners, and other staff could easily have seen something suspicious. There also may well be video, inside or outside of the hotel, but... there's a problem.

"That's really good thinking," he said encouragingly. "You're totally right, but we can't involve the police."

"Why not? Are you and Lotte criminals?"

He almost laughed. In a sense, he and Lotte *were* criminals. They had the blood of at least one person on their hands, and if the evidence could be traced, they'd likely be convicted in the death of a police deputy and probably several others. Add to this hiding an artifact—as well as knowledge—of incredible historic and scientific significance. Eric felt he could justify all these actions, or at least Lotte could, but looking at it from the outside, he wasn't so sure everyone would see things the way they did. In truth, maybe to some extent, they were right, just as Dr. Esfahani may have been. Things weren't so clear-cut.

"No, we're not criminals, but we know... secrets... and the secrets we know involve artifacts like the one in your father's fishing lodge. We can't involve the police because we can't risk knowledge of this thing getting out."

"But it's just a stupid plastic sculpture! It looks like some big ol' Iraqi Lego project. I'll bet they sell them over there for nothing. What's all the fuss about?"

He had to chuckle a bit. "Tell you what... go on eBay and see if you can find something like this for sale used. If so, I'll buy one, and we can give that to this guy in exchange for Lotte. I guarantee, you won't find anything. You won't even find something like it in a museum, except one place: the Museum of Fine Arts in Boston. The fact that you say this is made of 'plastic' only convinces me more that we've got the real deal on our hands. This is an incredibly rare, incredibly valuable, and incredibly dangerous artifact. I have no idea who's after it, but we can't give it to him, and we can't involve the police in a way that knowledge of this thing's existence comes to light."

She stared at him wide-eyed and, for once, silently. "So, what do we do?"

"I have an idea, but I don't want to pull the trigger on that just yet. Is Lotte's wallet in the bags of hers you have?"

"I didn't check. Here's her pocketbook, though."

Eric opened the sleek little purse and looked inside. This wasn't her day-to-day purse, rather one she took to more formal occasions, or when she didn't need everything—and *everything* wasn't much of an understatement—handy all at once. It contained almost nothing, and not her wallet.

"Nothing. I figured she'd take that with her if she needed money to buy tea. So, she has it on her. Eventually, our buddy John is gonna figure out he nabbed the wrong person, and the wallet with her ID will prove it. When that happens, he'll do one of three things. He might decide the whole mess just isn't worth it and simply let her go. I'm not holding my breath on that scenario, but it would be awfully nice. Most likely, he'll try to call someone, probably you or me. Does Lotte have your number?"

"I don't think so. I don't remember giving it to her."

"Okay, so she'll give him my number, or he'll call us on Lotte's phone. I guess he might call your father, assuming he has that information, which he may or may not. If he's not holding you, though, his leverage over your dad is pretty minimal. So, I'm thinking he'll call me in some fashion."

"That makes sense, but you said three things. What else might he do?"

He hesitated. "Lotte doesn't know exactly where this thing is, right?"

"I told her what I told you, that it was in my daddy's fishing lodge down near Myrtle Beach, but she doesn't know *exactly* where it is. Like... she couldn't give him the address or nothing, or directions."

"Right. Well, it's highly unlikely, and I don't want to upset you, but you called it before... he may kill her."

She put her hands over her mouth in shock.

"Just... stay calm. He'd be an idiot to do that. He'd lose any possibility of negotiating with us and finding what he really wants. I truly don't think that's what he's gonna do. So, this is a long-winded way of saying that we'll just have to wait until he contacts us."

"What'll you do if he does?" she asked through her tightly laced fingers.

"I'm gonna try to stall for some time. Like I say, I have an idea, but it will take some work to pull it off." He paused and thought for a moment. "Listen, let's try to drive it home to this guy that he's got the wrong person. Can you just send your dad a real simple email and attach a picture or two from the conference? Just tell him you had a great time, and here are a couple of photos... no other details."

Olive grabbed her phone. "Sure. How about this one?" She held the phone out for him, and there was Lotte at the podium giving her presentation.

She looked amazing, and in complete control. For whatever reason, seeing this photo rattled him, and he actually felt the urge to cry.

Will this be the last image I'll ever see of Lotte alive?

"That's perfect," he whispered, coughing a bit to cover for the fact that he was choking up. "Send that one, plus one other that's more general. We'll see if we can get a rise out of him."

She did as he asked. "Y'all okay? You want some water or something? You poor thing. Here I am crying, and it's *your* girlfriend that's missing. I'm so sorry. I'll do anything I can to help you find her."

She put her hand on his knee, and he couldn't help but remember how he'd tried to comfort Lotte in the same way while sitting in the MFA food court, as she told him about discovering her mother's dead body hanging from a chandelier. That was almost ten years ago to the day. Time flies, but some things seem to stay with you forever, and Eric had a bevy of intense memories from those first weeks of knowing Lotte that still frequently overwhelmed him.

"I'm fine, thanks. Actually, I'm not fine. I'm starving. I don't feel like eating, but I know I need to. What about you?"

"Oh, gawd, I'm Starvin' Marvin! There are all kinds of places on the street toward the university, or my car is here. We can go anywhere you want."

"Where exactly is your car?"

"It's in the parking garage."

"I think we should get out of here. I just realized that when this guy does discover he's got the wrong person, he may come back looking for you instead of calling."

"Isn't that what you want, him coming here where we can catch him? If we could identify who he is without him seeing us, maybe we could follow him and find out where he's hiding Lotte."

At least she's trying, and it's not the worst idea.

"I hear what you're saying. The problem is, he has a total advantage on us. We'll have no idea who he is, and he knows what you look like, at least basically. Plus, even if we identified this guy, I think there's too much risk of him noticing us, and that'll most likely lead to a confrontation, in which case, we're screwed. I want to maintain some distance from him. We have a window of time now to drop out of sight. I think we should take it."

She seemed to get it. "We could go to my daddy's real house. He lives in a townhouse condo over in Knightdale. I have a key and the alarm code. He just put that in after he got robbed last December when he was in Syria. I think the thieves knew nobody was home. They didn't get nothing, though. All his real valuable stuff is down with Uncle Clint."

"No, that's too obvious. If our buddy, John Riggins, has your dad's email, he probably knows where he lives too. We need to pick somewhere we'd have no reason for being. Durham isn't far from here, is it?"

"No. Only like thirty minutes."

"Perfect. He'll have zero clue where we are, but we're still nearby. Are you ready? Do you have everything here?"

She nodded, and they both hustled to the parking garage. Eric stayed alert, trying to see if anyone was following or watching them. If they were, they were successfully discrete about it, as he didn't see anything. Olive's car was a black Volkswagen Jetta with Georgia plates.

Perfect car for Lotte. German and black!

They piled the bags into the back seat, exited the garage, and after snaking out of Chapel Hill were soon on Durham-Chapel Hill Boulevard headed toward Durham. Eric wrapped his arm around the seat and looked past the headrest out the back window. He tried to see if any cars pulled out that might be following them. Again, if they were, he couldn't tell. It appeared they were in the clear.

As they neared Durham, he noticed what appeared to be a German café and biergarten on the left side of the road.

"Hey, can you pull in there?"

He'd never lost his taste for German cuisine, partly from his grandmother's cooking, but mainly from the wonderful meals Lotte's father prepared on Sundays when he and Lotte were in high school. They'd been inseparable in those days, and he'd almost felt he was a part of Lotte's family, and assumed she felt similarly about his. His grandma, in particular, had taken a liking to her, and many weekends Lotte would visit with Eric and his parents. As a result, some weekends, he had two German meals, and that never bothered him one bit.

With the beautiful weather, Eric and Olive sat outdoors. He positioned himself where he could see a portion of the parking lot, and as best he could monitored who came in. Everything seemed normal, a sharp contrast with the intense feeling of abnormality that, in truth, shook him to his core. Still, he tried to remain calm and keep his wits. He couldn't help Lotte if he was a quivering mess. Plus, he had to project a feeling of confidence to Olive, who was clearly a bit emotional. He needed her, so he had to try to make her feel safe.

"Are y'all gonna tell me what's so important about that dang ol' thing?" she asked after their waiter had brought drinks and taken their order. Olive had changed her iced tea to a glass of Riesling when she saw Eric get a beer. "What's so super-secret? Does it have magical powers or something?"

He snarfed his beer and almost spit it on the table.

What am I gonna say? Tell her that most likely this object sitting in her father's fishing lodge summons a creature from another plane of existence? If she freaks out, it'll cause a scene. People will hear strange things. Someone might call the police and report that there are a couple of crazy people in this nice little biergarten. Hell, maybe we are crazy! Too risky.

"I'll explain at some point," he said, wiping his mouth and sniffing to get some dregs out of his nostrils. "This just isn't the place, or the time. Trust me, you'll know what you need to know when you need to know it."

God, I sound just like Lotte! He suddenly had better insight on the push and pull she must have experienced about when, and how much, to tell him regarding the portal Mason had found. He always felt like she was holding things back from him, but maybe it was truly as she had said—just a matter of timing.

Olive didn't seem pleased, but she took it in stride and changed the subject. "How did you meet Lotte? Are you into archaeology too?"

"Well, I am a bit through her." He chuckled. "But no, I'm not an archaeologist, and that's not how we met. We've actually known each other since high school."

"You two are high school sweethearts? Now *that* I'd have never predicted! Doesn't seem like Lotte's style. You, I'm not so sure about, not meanin' any offense. You just seem more like the quiet, stay at home type."

He found himself surprised by her insight and quick and accurate assessments. "No offense taken. Lotte and I became really close in high school almost by accident. We're extremely different types of people, and if a lot of... well... *unusual* things hadn't happened, we'd have probably never even spoken, let alone been friends. And you're right: I went to college not too far from home, but she went away to school, to freaking England! We didn't see each other for years. I assumed she'd go her way, and I'd go mine, but a couple of years ago, again due to some weird circumstances, we got back together, and we've been together ever since."

She smiled. "True love! That's so sweet. I know what you're talkin' about. I really wanted to go to college and study history, but my boyfriend back in Marietta didn't feel like leaving. He expected me to stay too, but I just couldn't. I have things I want to do. We tried to make it work, but in the end, he met someone else. It sort of broke my heart, but in other ways I felt really free. That's weird, isn't it?"

"Not at all. I've come to realize that ambivalence is virtually inevitable, almost natural. Even when things work out, there will be aspects of a situation that might still tug at you. It's rare that something is clear-cut and perfect, especially with relationships."

"How old are you? You're so *together*. I mean, here you are, your girlfriend has disappeared, but you seem so calm. You also totally get how I feel, and you don't hardly know me. I thought you were a lucky guy to be with Lotte, but now I see she's pretty dang lucky too."

"That's very nice, Olive. Believe me, I'm nothing special, and I'm not nearly as calm as I might look. I've just been through some experiences that maybe give me some... well... perspective on things. I've been through stuff with Lotte too. It's not all as perfect as it looks from the outside. Nothing is. I guess you learn as you work on building a relationship, and it is work—work that in some sense never stops. As I said, Lotte and I are pretty dissimilar, so we have certain challenges, but you do the best you can, and over time, you get better at finding that middle ground. At least I hope so."

"I hope so too. I've never met anyone I could really connect with, who really seemed to value what I wanted to do. I don't care what you say, I think you're a special person. I know this is an awful way to have met, but I'm really happy to know you."

Nice to hear, but we'll see how you really feel about me in a few days... after some of those secrets I mentioned have been revealed.

The food tasted good, but Eric didn't really enjoy it. Maybe German wasn't such a good choice after all, as it only exacerbated Lotte's absence in his mind. The more time that went by, the more unsettled he became.

Why doesn't he fucking call? He has to know she's the wrong person by now.

After lunch, they drove the rest of the way to Durham, parked, and walked around a bit. There wasn't a huge amount to see, but he felt restless and wanted to walk, so they started off in the direction of Duke University. About halfway there, Olive needed to rest, so they took a diversion into Maplewood Cemetery. Oddly, this gave him a strong sense of closeness with Lotte.

Olive found a bench under a shady tree, but he couldn't sit still. He wandered around the cemetery and perused the historic grave markers. Under normal circumstances, this might have been interesting, but his concentration failed him. Instead, the gravestones reminded him of death and its often-unpredictable inevitability. He was supposed to have met Lotte this morning, and they were meant to have embarked on an adventure together. Instead, she had disappeared... just like that. It reminded him of Mr. Binson, who'd probably said goodbye to his wife, like he did every morning, before he headed out to his enjoyably hectic schedule, never to return.

What if she's dead?

Contemplating that possibility made him realize that, if true, he would want to be dead too. Maybe Freud was right about Thanatos after all... that wish to die. Maybe people simply couldn't understand it, or didn't have such an urge, until they'd experienced existential loss—despair so great that they preferred the end to carrying on.

Obviously, most of the time, people carried on, as evidenced by his grandma and Mrs. Binson, not to mention Lotte and her father, whose lives continued after the deaths of the ones they loved the most. He wondered, though, if maybe Thanatos now had a foothold in them, and it was a battle for them to keep going where it may not have been before.

If I lost Lotte, I'm not sure that's a battle I'd want to win.

Almost 3:30 now, the waiting was wearing him down.

Why doesn't he call?

He returned to Olive, who still sat on the bench as she flipped through her phone. "You feel like going on?"

"You sure do like to walk," she commented. "Maybe that's why you're in such good shape."

Eric was in good shape because he still hit the gym three times a week and rode his bike whenever possible. He and Lotte took shared pleasure in biking the Minuteman Rail Trail on weekends whenever she had time, and he wished they could do it more often. He wished they could do a lot of things together, but time always seemed too short, and Lotte too busy. It frustrated him, and now there might be no more time. He wondered what exactly she'd accomplished by doing all those other things besides being with him, and whether she felt it was worth it.

This isn't helping. I have to stay focused and stop thinking so negatively.

"I walk when I get nervous," he said. "I find it helps distract me... burns off some of that bad energy. Listen, why don't we go on to Duke, walk around a little, and then we can take an Uber back to your car. That sound okay?"

She smiled. "That's just fine. I can do it. I just wish I had my better walking shoes. These are the flats I brought for the conference."

"Do your feet hurt?"

"Nah. They just slow me down, but I'll be fine. I also needed to kinda' recover a little after those glasses of wine. I'm not used to drinking in the middle of the day."

"We'll get some water on the way. You need to stay hydrated."

The Duke University campus was absolutely stunning, particularly around the Chapel. It seemed to be a fairly quiet Sunday, with students enjoying the nice weather. The relaxed atmosphere and the lovely stone architecture soothed Eric's mind a bit. He remembered days like this at UMass with Jennifer, hanging out near the pond with her friends, playing frisbee, watching the ducks swim around. Good times.

Please, just call. I can't take much more of this.

He suddenly felt tired. It was getting close to 5:00. Even he had finally surrendered and sat with Olive on a bench in some shade, restlessly checking his phone every five minutes, as if all the noises and vibrations the stupid thing made wouldn't have alerted him had a message actually come in. He kicked himself for not acting on his plan. He'd miscalculated, but the risk of missing the call had been too great. Painful as it was, he knew it had been better to wait.

"We've got to figure out our next move," he finally said as he yawned. "I think we're gonna have to find a place to stay for tonight. I thought he'd call sooner than this, but I was clearly wrong. I'm not sure what's going on, but we need to be patient. I know you probably need to get back to school. Is this gonna to be a big problem for you?"

"I ain't leavin' you alone like this. Plus, this guy knows where I go to school! If I go back there before all this is settled, he may come after *me.* I'm scared, and I feel like I'm better off hiding out with you."

"I think that's a wise choice. It could be dangerous if you went back. I appreciate your standing by me, too. Truth is, Olive, I may need you for something incredibly important, so I'm really glad we're sticking together. Can you get out your phone and look for something nearby that has two rooms?"

"I can, but, Eric, I don't have a lot of money. Most of what I had I spent on coming to this conference. I really need to start making some connections if I want to break into archaeology, and this seemed so perfect. I spent almost everything I'd saved from my student job. I did meet some people, and a couple of them could be possible mentors, but the most interesting person I met was Lotte. She and I had a such nice time at the dinner and got to know each other after. Now I know you, too. It's just been great. Sorry, I got off track.... What was I sayin'? Oh, yeah, the hotel rooms. I'll pay you back some time... promise I will."

He laughed. *She's starting to grow on me. She has a good heart, and she's a fair bit shrewder than her scattered demeanor might lead you to believe.*

"Don't even worry about it. I work for my dad, who owns an industrial flooring company. I make plenty of money, and this is nothing. You just keep focused. We're in this together. You're part of the team now."

She leaned over on the bench and gave him a hug. "You're so sweet! I won't let you down."

CHAPTER 5

Light filtered in past the edges of the room-darkening curtains, just shy of 7:00 a.m. Eric sat near the window in the big red chair with a white crisscrossed pattern, legs outstretched on the matching footstool. His and Lotte's phones sat on the desk nearby, batteries charging.

He'd been in this spot for nearly three hours. Occasionally, he dozed off, then awoke with a frightful and fitful start. This inability to sleep had ultimately driven him from the bed, and he hadn't wanted to wake Olive, who still slumbered on the opposite side, nearer the door of the hotel room.

He briefly pondered how she'd managed to come into sole possession of his bed.

The Marriott had been close to where she'd parked her car, and it was reasonably priced.

After they grabbed an Uber back from Duke to Durham, they booked two rooms at around 6:00 p.m. Eric intended to collapse into bed and blissful unconsciousness, but tired as he was, sleep proved elusive. He wound up watching the end of the Patriots-Cowboys game, though he found it difficult to focus. The Pats were destroying them, which was fine with him. He'd never cared for "America's Team."

Close to 8:00 p.m., someone knocked. He threw on his jeans and found Olive standing at the door with a pizza and a sixer of beer, wearing shorts and a t-shirt, with no shoes or socks.

She smiled. "I went and got some food. You must be Starvin' Marvin! I just couldn't wear them flats no more. They was driving me crazy. You don't mind, do you?"

He didn't know if she meant that he minded her bringing food or going barefoot, but before he could answer, she brushed past him into the room. In truth, he didn't mind either. Being alone hadn't really been working for him, and the company might distract him from his constant worry.

"I asked them for German beer at the liquor store, 'cause I seen you liked that at the restaurant today." She slapped the six pack and the pizza on the desk. "This was all they had. Hope it's okay."

Beck's... from Bremen... where Lotte was born and grew up. "Actually, that's a great choice. Thanks, this is really nice."

"It's my pleasure. You been so nice to me. This is the least I could do. Plus, truth be told, I was gettin' a little lonely and figured you might be too. I know we're probably safe here, but all this kidnapping stuff is still freaking me right out."

"Well, you figured right. I can't really sleep. I'm too stressed out. I'm glad to have some company. You like football? The eight-thirty game is Giants-49ers."

"Are you teasing me? Of course, I like football. I grew up in Georgia! I watch more college than pro football. Just my luck that I had to be a Georgia Tech Yellowjackets fan. My momma works in the financial aid office there, so that was my team, like it or not. 'Course then they go win the Orange Bowl last year when all my attention was on school. Why couldn't Tech have done that when I was watching them all the time as a little girl?"

He laughed. "Yeah, college football is king down here, isn't it? It's not such a big thing where I grew up. The University of Massachusetts upgraded their program to FBS the year after I graduated. It's been pretty ugly. We've got a long way to go to compete with big name Southern schools."

"I want to go up there so bad. I love all that Revolutionary War history. I want to see Lexington and Concord, and Gettysburg. I know that last one's a different war, but I like that too. I guess that's my daddy in me... got me into all that war history, and that led to my love of the whole period of American history through World War Two. After that, I start to lose interest. It just seems like the world changed so much when technology started goin' crazy and everybody got the atomic bomb. I like reading stuff about early America, and when I'm around the things from that period, I just feel like I'm part of a simpler, better time."

Eric had his doubts. His reading of history was that despite a veneer of civility among the wealthiest parts of society, life for most people had been pretty merciless, and in many parts of the world still was.

The good old days... boy, were they terrible.

It wasn't worth arguing with her about it, though. He was glad she found pleasure and a sense of solace in her interests. There were far worse ways to spend your time.

They talked and enjoyed the game, which was surprisingly competitive, though he was bummed the Giants won. He'd never forgive them for beating the Pats in the 2007 Super Bowl. Still, he had fun watching football with somebody else. He usually watched the Pats games alone while Lotte worked. Even when she wasn't busy, she didn't care much for American Football. Olive had also been right about him being hungry. The pizza had easily disappeared, and the beer too. He was surprised when it was all gone.

How many did I drink... four? Yikes.

That definitely took the edge off, but he remained tense.

Seeming to sense this, Olive offered him a backrub. He hadn't realized how tight his shoulders actually were until he felt her hands working out the knots.

The contact felt good, and somehow, he drifted off.

He woke around 2:00 a.m., lying on top of the sheets, still wearing his jeans. He clicked on the light, intending to get undressed and go pee, and found Olive sleeping in the bed next to him.

"Do you mind if I just stay here?" she asked in a groggy voice. "I know you paid for my own room, but I just feel safer."

He understood. Honestly, it felt good having her here. It made him at least try to be still, and he got a couple more hours sleep before an anxious dream finally woke him for good.

Not wanting to wake her with his tossing around, he moved to the chair.

Here he still sat. The clock on the nightstand now read 7:15 a.m. He closed his eyes and hoped to catch a few more precious minutes of sleep before he had to face what he feared would be another brutal and useless day of waiting.

Then it happened: his phone rang.

He popped on the desk light and saw Olive looking up from the bed. He put his finger to his mouth, instructing her to remain quiet, then grabbed the phone and looked at the display: "Unknown Number - (111) 111-1111." He'd never seen anything like that.

This has to be it!

On the fourth ring, he swiped the phone and answered in as confident a voice as he could summon. He then placed the phone on speaker so Olive could hear as well.

"Hello?"

"Is this Eric Schneider?" a man said in a fairly deep voice with a mild Southern accent. He sounded a bit older – *fifties maybe, or early sixties?* His tone was menacing and accusatory, and his words seemed slightly muffled, as if he might be wearing a mask.

"No," Eric sarcastically replied. "This is Tom Brady. It sure is a pleasure to make your acquaintance, Mr. Riggins. I look forward to joining you in the Hall of Fame. Maybe we could meet in person at my induction ceremony."

A pause came at the other end of the line, just as Eric had hoped.

"You're quite the little wise-ass, aren't you? Listen to me, you don't know who you're dealing with. If you want to see your little girlfriend again, you better do what I tell you."

"Actually," he replied, projecting greater confidence and cockiness than he felt, "I have a pretty good sense of who I'm dealing with. You're the guy who can't kidnap the right person... and I'm not doing anything you say until I talk with Lotte."

Again, a pause. Eric felt he had the guy off balance, which is what he wanted.

"Hold on!" the man barked.

Eric again put his finger to his lips, urging silence from his companion. After what felt like an eternity, he heard some noise in the phone's speaker, and then someone spoke.

"Eric?"

His heart raced at the sound of Lotte's voice, but he tried to remain calm. "Lotte, are you okay? Did he hurt you?"

"No, they didn't really hurt me, but... Eric, you need to give him what he's asking for. Do the right thing."

"Okay!" The man's voice returned as he seemed to rip the phone away from Lotte. "That's enough of that! All right, wise-ass, you've got your proof of life, so now you're gonna listen very carefully. You know what I want, and you're damned well gonna tell me where it is. When I get it, you get her back. It's that simple. Understood?"

"I've got it, and you're in luck there, John. I don't give a crap about the thing you want. I'm happy to let you have it... but there's a little problem. I don't know where it is."

"Bullshit! The girl you're with knows exactly where it is. She took that damned picture. Put her on the phone and make her tell me where it is."

"That's just not possible, John. She's not here. She went back to school last night. We had no idea when, or if, you'd call, so she left. She's not with me."

"So call her!" he said, barely containing his rising anger. "Call her on the damned phone and get her to tell you where it is!"

"No can do. You've got her so freaked out, she shut her phone off thinking you might be tracking her like you did her father's email. She's gonna get a new one with a new number and call me tomorrow. When she calls, I'll tell her you *finally* contacted us, and I'll tell you what... rather than asking her where it is, I'll have her go and get it for you and bring it here. You call me back tomorrow, say around five p.m., and we'll figure out how to make the switch. That's the best I can do. Deal?"

More silence as the man weighed his options. Eric felt he had him.

"Okay," he finally replied, somewhat exasperated. "Tomorrow at 5:00... sharp! If you don't answer, and you don't give me what I want, I'm gonna kill her... and if you contact the police, I'll *definitely* kill her... and believe me, I'll know if you contact the police."

"Well, then you probably know I *haven't* contacted the police, and I have no intention of doing that. Again, neither Olive nor I give a *shit* about the thing you want. We'll give it to you. Lotte is way more important. Even Lotte agrees—you heard her—so it sounds like we have a deal, right? I'll talk with you tomorrow... John."

The phone went dead, and Eric collapsed, shaking, into the big red chair with the white crisscrosses. He'd been rehearsing what he wanted to say since yesterday, but it still took all his courage to follow through. After a moment, he noticed movement from the bed where Olive waved, trying to get his attention. She looked at him questioningly.

"Yeah, you can talk now. He hung up."

"Oh, my gawd, Eric! You were so... I don't even know the word... so... *tough*! I can't believe you talked to him that way. I just don't understand why both you and Lotte think we should give him that sculpture thing. That's not what you told me. Also, why did you say I was back at school?"

He grimly laughed. "Because I lied. So did Lotte... well... in a sense. She didn't say give him the object. She said, 'Give him what he's asking for.' He's asking for trouble. She also said, 'Do the right thing.' Believe me, I know all too well that implies the exact *opposite* of giving this artifact to him. I know it's hard to believe, but she'd sooner die herself than turn it over. So, as I guessed, we're on the same page. We also know there's more than one of them."

"How?"

"Because she said *they* didn't hurt her. Not *he*."

She nodded. "It's like you two are telegraphic. You know what each other is thinkin'!"

"That's telepathic," he said, and chuckled. "And yeah, we sort of are... at least when it comes to this stuff."

"So, what about me going back to school? What's that all about?"

"That is *exactly* what this was all about. I just bought us the time I need, with as close to a guarantee as possible that he won't hurt Lotte. Now, we just need to take full advantage of it. We've got to get to the airport immediately. You always wanted to go to Boston. You're about to get your wish."

"Boston? Why are we going all the way up there?"

"Because there's something we need to get... to rescue Lotte."

Eric had already purchased a return ticket to Boston for Monday night, figuring he could change it, if necessary, but he wanted to get back before then. They quickly checked out of the Marriott, found a parking garage for Olive's Jetta, and took an Uber back to the Raleigh-Durham airport. Many flights were booked up, so the two were lucky to get seats on a plane departing at 2:30 that afternoon. He bought Olive a one-way ticket. They wouldn't be flying back.

"It's later than I'd hoped," he said with disappointment once they'd completed the complex and myriad transactions. "We'll stay the night at our apartment, then drive down to Southby in the morning. I need to call Ricky Vitis to get a van. He'll be thrilled to hear from me... not."

"We're driving all the way back? Why would we do that?"

"As I said, we need something. It's a rather *large* something... actually several rather large somethings. I'll explain everything, trust me. It'll take about twelve hours to get back to the Raleigh area, assuming minimal and quick stops. That'll get us in about nine or ten tomorrow night, which is perfect. We just have to pull over in a spot with good cell reception before five o'clock, so we don't miss the call."

She was still confused, but he knew she'd survive for now. He dreaded what he'd need to tell her, but as Lotte often said, "There's nothing for it." Securing the van was the next priority. Eric still had Ricky's cell number in his phone, so he called directly rather than go through the Vitis Brothers office.

"Eric Schneider!" Ricky said when he answered, obviously seeing Eric's name on the caller ID. "What the fuck is up? Haven't seen you since you totaled our van two years ago!" He laughed.

Eric felt that was a good thing. In truth, other than losing the vehicle, it hadn't cost Vitis Brothers anything. The van was old, Eric had taken extra insurance, and he paid the deductible without complaint. Hopefully, it was just a distant and somewhat odd memory for them.

"Well," Eric said as cheerfully as possible, "funny you mention that old van, because I need another one for a few days... maybe through the weekend. I'd like to pick it up tomorrow. Can you hook me up?"

Ricky was silent for a moment. "Are you actually serious? Man, do you even fuckin' remember what you did to that damned thing? The top was ripped open like a giant can-opener had been at it! Why the hell do you think we'd give you another van?"

D'oh! "Yeah, I remember, Ricky, but you probably remember how sorry I was, and how I didn't give you kind folks any shit. I paid my portion for the damage, and insurance took care of the rest. I'm not going out in the woods this time. I'm taking all main roads. There should be no problem. Please, Ricky, I'm asking for a second chance."

"Man, Eric, you're putting me in a tough spot. My dad didn't give a shit about what happened—actually, he thought it was funny as hell. 'Nice to know that Schneider kid has some fuckin' balls after all' is what he said!" Ricky laughed his ass off into the phone.

Nice. Good to know my balls impressed his father. If I'd known that's what it took, I'd have shown them to him before. Well, probably not, actually.

When he'd recovered from laughing and the smoker's coughing fit it had produced, Ricky went on. "But my uncle really runs the show here, and he wasn't so happy. Tell you what, I'll type up the paperwork and keep it tucked away, then I'll drive the van to where you are... I assume in Southby? You drive me back to the shop so my uncle doesn't see your car parked in the lot and start asking questions, and then you return the goddamned thing in good shape! Got it?"

"I got it! Ricky, I can't thank you enough. I'll call you around eight tomorrow morning and tell you where I am. Is that okay?"

"Yeah, fine, but Eric... one more thing."

"Anything, man, you name it."

"Take the extra fuckin' insurance again, okay?"

He happily agreed. He could have probably gone to one of the big guys, but if a problem did arise, the possibility of which he didn't completely dismiss in the back of his mind, then he knew he'd be better off working with Vitis Brothers to resolve it.

Now, it was time to call Margot. He was already late for something. The rest of his life had essentially flown out of the window when Lotte disappeared. He couldn't bring himself to open his calendar or work email yesterday. It was just too much, like lifting a weight that was a bit too heavy after pre-exhausting your muscles. It just wasn't going to happen... and it didn't.

Eric dialed her cell phone instead of the office number. Though Schneider business, he needed something more personal from Margot, even if he wasn't quite sure what.

"Hey!" she cheerfully answered. "Wasn't expecting you to call. Weren't you supposed to be out with Tony's team this morning at that new job in Billerica?"

Fuck! That new job in Billerica. Now that you mention it, yes... that's exactly where I was supposed to be. "It's entirely possible, but something came up. I can't make it. I should have called before but I... but I... well... I didn't. I'm sorry, Margot. I'm... I'm... so, so sorry." Suddenly, it just all felt like too much to bear.

"Eric, what the hell is wrong? What happened?"

He didn't have a story. All the thought and consternation he'd put into talking with John Riggins—the planning, the details, the lies and the posturing that made the kidnapper give up that little bit of control, and bought him the time he needed—but he hadn't planned one word of what he'd say to Margot. That was a mistake, because with her, he slipped. The depth of his fear and uncertainty came pouring out.

"I... umm... well... umm... it's Lotte! She needs my help. I have to help her." He tried to regroup, tried to focus his thoughts. "She needed some things. I had to bring them to her. I'm down in North Carolina. She needs help lugging some gear around." *God, that was feeble!* "It'll be a few days... maybe the rest of the week. I'm sorry for the late notice, but can you help me cover what I have on my calendar this week?"

Silence came in response, but he heard the clicking of keys in the background.

"Is your calendar up to date?" she asked.

"I think so. Honestly, I haven't been checking my email, so I'm not sure if anyone has added or changed anything. Margot, I'm so sorry."

"Shut up. You've got a follow-up meeting in Burlington at that new Mexican restaurant on Thursday at ten a.m. Can you make that?"

He was silent.

"Okay, that's the only really important thing. I'll talk to your dad, see if he can cover it, or if he thinks it can wait until you're back. Otherwise, it's just routine stuff. There's nothing I can do about today, but I'll call Tony and tell him you're sick and to let them know you'll reschedule something when you're feeling better. I think I've got it under control, but if you have a chance, can you look at your email and just send me anything that looks important? I'll take care of it."

He struggled to find the words. Near tears, both as a result of the situation with Lotte and of hearing Margot's familiar and comforting voice, he marveled at her efficiency and effectiveness under fire. "I don't know what to say, Margot. Thank you so much. I owe you a big one."

"No, you don't. This is my job, and you don't pull last-minute shit very often. In fact, the only other time I remember you falling off a cliff like this was when Lotte showed up two years ago. Funny, this feels kind of similar. Coincidence?"

Despite himself, he laughed. "You know me too well. Maybe we should get married."

"I'd marry you, as long as you don't mind me seeing other girls. Ha! But, Eric, I really hope this isn't like last time, when you came back looking like you got beat up by a gorilla!"

Well, more like a giant bird of prey with a fucking magnetic hammer of death, but close enough.

"I hope it isn't, either, Margot. That was pretty rough—in more ways than one."

"You gonna tell me what this is all about, or will it be another great mystery like two years ago?"

He really did want to tell her. He trusted Margot, and realized that the secret he carried could often be a tremendous burden, one that he bore alone without Lotte at his side. He began to grasp that this was what he really wanted and needed. He missed Lotte's cocksure confidence, her take charge attitude, and her keen intelligence. Margot had many of those same qualities. This explained much of why Eric liked and respected her so much. If he told her the truth, he'd no doubt benefit from her support, but he simply couldn't make the decision to talk with her without Lotte's approval, and in the end, had Lotte been here, he wouldn't even feel the need.

"Yeah, it's complicated. Probably a story for some time, but not now."

She quickly navigated away from the subject, seemingly void of disappointment. "I understand. I'm here if you need me, you know that. Try to give me a little more notice next time, and get your sorry ass home in one piece. That's all I want from you. Oh, and this time, make sure you bring Lotte too."

I will try. With every fiber of my being, I will try.

CHAPTER 6

Olive called out from behind the open refrigerator door. "Can I open one of these bottles of wine in your Frigidaire?"

"We have wine in our fridge?"

"Yeah, a bottle of Riesling and something that starts with a 'G.' Don't even ask me to try pronouncing that. I'll bet most German people can't even say that word!"

He laughed. "It's Gewürztraminer—not as hard as it looks. God, those bottles are still in there? I think a friend of Lotte's gave them to us when we moved in here. Sure, open the Riesling. That'll probably go better with Thai food."

"Awesome. I like Riesling. I drink Relax Riesling when I can. That's really good."

Relax Riesling sounded more like a command than a wine. *Relax, Riesling, Chardonnay and Gewürztraminer will be here any minute, then we'll go show those damn reds what's what! Just chill, and stop giving me that blanc stare!*

Eric giggled to himself as he recalled their trip back from North Carolina.

The flight out of Raleigh-Durham was delayed—*surprise, surprise.*

They didn't arrive in Boston until close to 6:00. Poor Olive nearly suffered a heart attack on the descent into Logan.

"Eric, I don't see land!" she said, tension in her voice. "Only water! Is there something wrong?"

"Nothing's wrong. The airport's on... like... an island. It'll be fine."

She grabbed his hand and held tightly as the plane landed.

"There, see?"

Her look was a mixture of relief and disbelief. "Who in the H-E Double L puts an airport on a tiny little pissant island like this?"

He laughed. It was a fair question.

She recovered quickly upon arrival, and looked at everything with the thrill of newness, particularly enjoying a brief glimpse of the Bunker Hill Monument as they exited the tunnel on the cab ride from the airport.

Once home, he showed her around the apartment and helped her get settled in the bedroom. He planned to sleep on the couch.

"Would Lotte mind if I borrowed a sweatshirt or something and some heavy socks? It's freezing up here, and I didn't bring many clothes for that conference."

"Absolutely. Look in the dresser there. You'll find something."

She opened a middle drawer. "Gawd! She sure has a lot of black band t-shirts. Who are 'The Sisters of Mercy'?" She held up a specimen he wasn't sure he'd seen Lotte wear before. Under the band's name appeared a round logo with a drawn image of a man's head, superimposed over a five-pointed star.

"I have no idea," he confessed. "She likes a lot of weird bands from the eighties that I've never heard of." The Sisters of Mercy didn't even sound like a band Lotte would particularly enjoy.

Now, if it was The Brothers of If You Don't Like It... Tough!*, that might be more up her alley.*

He brought the takeout Thai food they had gotten from Davis Square into the living room while Olive opened the wine. They were both starving, this being the first food either of them had eaten since a crappy sandwich in the Raleigh-Durham airport. They ate largely in silence, nestled on the couch watching Monday Night Football pre-game. The Riesling actually went quite well with the Pad Thai and Ginger Chicken. He took note for when Lotte was back.

Lotte! Will I ever even see her again?

His confidence wavered, and he suddenly lost his appetite, but forced himself to finish his food. He'd need the energy.

They made short work of the Riesling, and Olive really wanted to try "that weirdo wine that I can't pronounce," so she cracked the Gewürztraminer as well. As always, Eric found it hard to resist drinking more as his inhibitions decreased, but this time he consciously fought the urge. It would be an extremely long day tomorrow, for Olive as well—little did she know.

Perhaps it's time to change that. Maybe it's time to let her in on what's going on, see if she's really up for this, and find out if I can rely on her in a pinch.

He waited for Olive to finish eating, then took the dishes and empty food containers to the kitchen. When he returned, she'd wrapped herself in the blanket he'd taken out for later and had poured the last of the Gewürztraminer into her glass. She'd already had the lion's share of the bottle and seemed to be getting a little tipsy.

He sat beside her and muted the TV with the remote. "So, listen, we need to talk."

"Did I do something wrong?"

"No, no, not at all. You're fine. We just need to discuss what's gonna happen tomorrow. You don't know it, but things are about to get really weird... even weirder than they already are. You're gonna see things that will change your perspective on life forever, and Olive, I won't lie to you: people are gonna die, and you'll be party to their death."

A serious look came over her face. "Y'all gonna kill those people who took Lotte?"

"That's the plan," he affirmed with equal gravity. "We can't let them have what they want, and if we don't give it to them, they'll kill Lotte. That can't happen either. So, I don't have much of a choice, but you do. You can stay here, and I'll deal with this on my own. I was in your position once, not knowing which choice to make, but I didn't know what it really meant when I agreed to go on... what the real consequences might be. I mostly did it for Lotte. I don't regret my decision. I just want you to really understand and be ready for what you'll be in for."

She sat silently ruminating on that and sipped her wine. When she spoke, she sounded dispirited. "I thought you said you needed me. If I'm here and you need me, how can I help you?"

"I did say I needed you, and it may be really helpful if you're with me... potentially critical. It's just that the reasons I need you are almost as terrible as killing. If you come with me, you'll never be like you were. You'll never see the world the same way again. I know that sounds crazy, but I promise you, it's true. It happened to me, and to Lotte. As much as possible, I want you to go into this with your eyes open. If you're not up for this, I'll figure out a way. You have a choice, Olive, and I'll support whatever you choose."

He could only imagine what thoughts coursed through her mind as she processed all this. He remembered himself ten years ago as he mulled the same question. Would he have chosen differently if he'd known it would mean Dr. Esfahani's death... or Mason's... or Vern's? It's possible those people would have died anyway, or Lotte would have. Other than losing Lotte, he would never have known... never been involved. Would that have been better? Would he have preferred to shield himself from the terrifying fact that monsters are real?

Olive stirred and shook her head with a sort of resigned determination. "I don't care. Those people who took Lotte deserve to be punished, and if things are like you say, then we don't got much of a choice. That don't bother me none. I just... I... I don't know."

"What? Tell me."

She began to cry. "You say it like it's a big deal... me choosin' what to do! It ain't! It ain't no big deal at all! In case you haven't noticed, I'm not exactly settin' the world on fire like you and Lotte."

Interesting choice of metaphors, but please continue.

"It's not like I have a lot to offer, exactly. Even my daddy calls me *Airhead*. So, what difference does it make if I see and do terrible things? What else am I here for? And if it means helping Lotte, then I guess you can say I'm in the same boat as you were. I'll do it for her. Plus, I want to help you. I told you I wouldn't let you down, and I'm not fixin' to. If I don't help you, then what good am I really, as a person, or as a friend?"

She burst into tears, the depth of her insecurity and feelings of inferiority revealed.

Eric feared maybe he'd pushed too hard. He slid over on the couch to give her a comforting hug, and she wailed into his chest.

"Olive, that's not true. You have plenty to offer. You're a wonderful, thoughtful person, and I've really enjoyed getting to know you the past couple of days. Whatever you choose, we'll still be friends. I like you for who you are. You don't need to do this to prove your worth—to me, or to anyone."

That only made her cry harder, so he went to Plan B: he shut his mouth, which had always seemed to work for him in the past. He held her and stroked her black hair as she sobbed. She grasped him tightly and moved her head to his shoulder. Gradually, she calmed, and he lifted her chin and cradled her face as he wiped tears away with his thumbs.

"You okay? I didn't mean to—"

His final words were muffled as she pressed her lips to his. Again, she clung tightly as she pushed her body against him, and her hands danced fervidly across his shoulder blades. For a brief moment, he felt a rush of passion. His excruciating longing for Lotte's touch, to feel her warmth, to hold her again, was suddenly and joyously fulfilled.

Except this isn't Lotte!

As her movements became more urgent and intense, he regained his senses and pulled back.

"Woah, woah, woah. Stop, stop, stop. Olive, I'm sorry if I gave you the wrong impression. I just can't... well... we can't do this."

She gave a couple of quick shakes of her head, and then opened her eyes wide with shock. "Oh, my gawd. What did I just do? I was just so upset, and I think I had too much of that wine that I can't pronounce. Man, I always do stuff like this! I always find a way to mess things up. I just lose my damned head. I'm sorry, Eric. I'm so sorry. I hope you can forgive me."

She leapt off the couch, bounded through the kitchen, and a moment later the door to the bedroom slammed shut.

Shit. Where did that come from?

He briefly considered going to talk with her, but then decided maybe they both needed a little space. It had been an intense couple of days, and they'd been together a lot. In truth, he found it extremely easy to be with Olive. She liked a lot of the things he did, and she was totally... *present.* In fact, she practically hung on every word he said. It suddenly occurred to him that he'd been enjoying that attention—being the focus. Usually, conversations with Lotte were about what Lotte was up to, and her mind was almost always on all the things she had to do.

Did I lead Olive on? Did I inadvertently blur the boundaries because of, because of... what? Because I was so naturally comfortable with her in a way I'm not with Lotte?

The game had started—Steelers at Chargers. Eric watched the images on the muted television.

I'll get Lotte back, or I'll die trying. Assuming I succeed, though... what then? Is love enough? Love doesn't help that much when you wish you didn't have to watch Monday Night Football alone.

Of course, it was more than just that. It was all the little Monday Night Footballs that Lotte eschewed in favor of her seemingly all-consuming intellectual pursuits. It wasn't the *Über Liebe,* the great love, at issue. It was the *Kleine Dinge,* the little things. Eric had always figured there would be time to work all that out, or that things would eventually work themselves out as Lotte's life became less hectic.

However, as he watched the Chargers silently celebrate the game's first touchdown, he began to doubt that assumption. That led to the big question: what would he do about it?

Eric knew it was Ricky the minute the van came into sight, white and gleaming, in front of his grandma's apartment building. It felt like seeing a ghost, or perhaps a being resurrected and healed of its scars and the ravages of time, like Gandalf the White emerging from the ashes of Gandalf the Grey.

Gandalf the White Van.

Ricky pulled the sparkling machine up to where he and Olive waited in the parking lot next to his little red Mazda 3, which had absorbed its share of bumps and bruises over the past two years navigating the treacherous Somerville streets.

Despite being close to 60 degrees, Olive shivered in the misty rain. She wore Lotte's black anorak, which fit loosely enough that Olive could wear it comfortably. The darkness of the draping garment seemed to match her mood. She'd barely spoken all morning.

"Hey, man!" Ricky said as he jumped out of the van and handed Eric the keys. "Hey, Lotte! Long time, no see. You look different. Did you change your hair or something?"

Olive drove her hands deeper into the pockets of the long coat and sunk her head to her chest.

"That isn't Lotte," Eric intervened. "This is our friend Olive. She's helping me get some stuff Lotte needs, and we're traveling down to meet her. That's why we need the van."

Ricky looked her up and down. "Damn! Sorry, Olive. You do look a lot like Lotte, but then I haven't seen her much – only that time when you two returned the other rental. I wasn't sure which of you were more fucked-up. Did you both get into a massive fistfight or something?"

"Yeah, something like that. You should have seen the other guys. Listen, Olive, would you mind running Ricky back to the shop? It's not far from here." He gave her the keys to his Mazda, and she hopped into the driver's seat, happy to get out of the drizzle.

Or is she just happy to get away from me?

Ricky gave Eric a light shove. "Damn, Schneider! You sure do have an exact type that you're attracted to, don't you?"

Eric groaned. "It's not like that, Ricky. She's a friend of Lotte's. They met at a conference. We're just moving this gear because Lotte's... well... kind of tied up right now."

Ricky grinned. "Kinky! You don't have to explain anything to me. I don't give a fuck. You were always such a freakin' little nobody in high school. I'm just over-fuckin-joyed you're finally gettin' some damn action!"

Eric just rolled his eyes. It was hopeless.

"Just sign here for the van, and here for the insurance rider. This thing is pretty new, so you better get it back in good shape."

"Thanks, Ricky, I will." He brusquely signed the papers, not wishing to belabor the conversation, then headed to where Olive sat in the car and knocked on the window, which she rolled down. "I'm going up to get the keys from my grandmother and start bringing out the stuff. You can help me get it in the van when you're back. If you want, you can stop for coffee or something to eat. I have plenty of money. What do you say?"

"I'm fine," she unenthusiastically replied. "Y'all want something?"

He shook his head. "I'm good. We'll stop later. We need to buy some stuff anyway, and I want to get you some better shoes... maybe some pants too. You'll need them."

Ricky jumped in the Mazda, and they drove off. At some point, he and Olive would need to talk about what had happened, and about what soon was *going* to happen, but right now, he needed to start bringing the cases out so they could get the van loaded and hit the road. They had time, but if anything went wrong, that time could vanish pretty quickly.

He got out his phone and dialed his grandma's number. It was 8:15 a.m. He hoped she'd be up. In theory, this was her best time of day, but at 88, Grandma was clearly slowing down, so it was always a throw of the dice. This time, he got lucky.

"Eric, you never call me this early. Something must be wrong."

What do you have, trouble radar or something?

"No, no," he cheerfully replied to cover the truth. "Nothing's wrong. I just need to get at the gear Lotte stored in your basement space. She's out of town and needs me to bring it to her. Can you buzz me up so I can get the key?"

She did, and he grabbed the elevator up to her apartment. How long had it been since the two of them had last visited? It had definitely been before they went to Italy.

Damn, she wanted to see our pictures!

Things had just been so hectic, so hard to find time. If they made it out of this, he'd make sure he and Lotte came down. Grandma always loved it when Lotte visited, but then, Grandma had always loved Lotte.

The door already stood open when he arrived, and he gave his aging grandmother a big hug.

"Eric, it's so good to see you. You never visit your old *Oma* anymore. I miss seeing you and Lotte so, but, your busy lives bring you to me now, *ja*?"

He genuinely felt riddled with guilt. It really was a massive oversight on their part, one he committed to correcting. "I'm so sorry, Grandma. We miss you too. We'll come visit the minute we're back, promise." *Assuming we make it back, that is.*

"Oh, Eric," she said, seemingly untroubled. "I'm not mad. Visit when you can. I too was young once and know how life can sweep you away. Speaking of being swept away, did you hear about Mrs. Thompson?"

Mrs. Thompson, an elderly woman who lived in the building, was one of Eric's grandmother's closest friends. "No. Is she okay?"

"Well, yes and no. She had a fall last week and broke her hip. She was able to call her daughter, who arranged an ambulance and got her to the hospital. She's stable now, but she won't come back here. They're putting her in... what is this they call it... assisted living. She was my only remaining friend in the building. They say I can visit, but what good is this? We saw each other most every day. Now, it will be once every few months. So life goes, I suppose."

His grandmother's voice seeped a kind of tiredness. He wasn't sure what to say, so he remained silent.

"So, what is it you need, and where is Lotte?"

"Umm, long story," he said, surprised he had to repeat what he'd just told her. "Lotte's down in North Carolina. She just needs some of her gear that's in your basement, and asked me to bring it to her."

"Ah, *richtig!*" she said, and then shuffled toward the kitchen. "Now, where did I put those keys? Just a minute while I look for them, *ja?* Do you want something to eat?"

"No thanks, Grandma." He wandered into the TV room. The coffee table was covered with black and white photographs, seemingly from a box that sat on the floor nearby, which still contained many more. "What are all these?" he asked over the sounds of his grandmother rifling through kitchen drawers.

Slowly, she shuffled back into the room. "What is what?"

"All these photographs. I don't think I've ever seen these." He sat on the couch to get a better look at the pictures.

"No," she quietly said as she sat heavily next to him. "These I had put up long ago. You would never have seen them. I don't know why I got them out. Perhaps just to see if I could still remember."

A picture of a young man in a *Wehrmacht* uniform caught Eric's eye. He held up the image and felt like he was looking into a mirror. "Grandma, who is this? He looks just like me."

"That is my brother, Stefan." She took the picture from his hand. "I have always seen him in you. He was maybe nineteen when this picture was taken at the beginning of the war."

"I... I didn't know you had a brother. I only know of Great Aunt Gisela, but she died when I was little."

"*Ja,*" she sadly replied as she reached for another photo. "Here is Gisela as a little girl. Wasn't she cute? She was a year younger than Stefan, and I was two years younger than her. Stefan died in the war, near Nijmegen in *die Niederlande.* When I came here, it was not so good to speak of having a relative who fought on the German side. One can almost forget, putting things in a box, pretending they never existed... but exist they did, and now, there's nothing for me to lose in remembering. It's all gone anyway, or going quickly. So quickly it all goes, Eric."

He watched silently as his grandmother stared at the pictures of her lost siblings.

So quickly it all goes... or, so quickly it all can go.

Three days ago, he was headed to meet an excited, happy Lotte, and then... *whoosh*! Now, of perhaps equal concern, he witnessed something he'd never seen before in his grandmother—a sense of resignation, a weariness that blunted her normally indomitable spirit.

"Grandma, are you okay? Is there something I can do?" *Besides visit more often, you moron!*

His voice seemed to bring her back to earth a bit. "No, dear boy, I'm just old and facing the inevitable. Every year, another friend gone, and less and less that I can do. I get so tired, and it's hard to remember things now. It's easier to remember my brother and sister, and my parents, than it is to recall what I did yesterday. I fear this, Eric, more than anything. I hope fate spares me having to waste away in some 'assisted living' facility, barely knowing those who I love, or even who I am."

He thought about Mrs. Binson's mother, how she had lost her will when she was taken from home and removed from her familiar surroundings. He hoped it wouldn't come to that with Grandma.

"Or like your grandfather at the end," she went on, "barely conscious and just trying to manage the pain while he waited to die. I've lived a good life. I only pray now that the end comes quickly for me, but it seems we don't get to choose our fate in matters such as this."

Eric sat speechless. He never saw Grandpa in that condition--his parents must have shielded him from it at a certain point. He wasn't exactly sure how he felt about that, but he'd have to mull over that revelation later. Right now, he wanted to support his grandmother, but he didn't really know what to say.

"I'm sure Mom and Dad will help you do what's best," he suggested, though he was sure of no such thing, "and Lotte and I, too. I'm really sorry, Grandma. We all love you."

She rallied and produced a kindly smile. "I know you do. Oh, and Lotte! How thrilled I am that you and she found your way back to each other. I hoped at least you could be friends again, but seeing the two of you together this way is more than I could have ever imagined. I want nothing more than for both of you to have a long and happy life together!"

Long and happy, huh? Yeah, and I want a pony and a lifetime supply of Afrit repellent. Right now, it doesn't look like either of us are going to get our fondest desires.

His shoulders slumped as the weight of his troubles again permeated his mind.

"What is it, Eric? Something is obviously wrong. I knew this the minute you called. Tell me!"

You have to hand it to her, memory fading or not, her powers of perception are as sharp as ever.

Obviously, he couldn't get into the kidnapping, as that would send her over the edge and create all manner of problems, but there were other things bothering him, exacerbated by what happened last night with Olive.

"I don't know, Grandma. Lotte's just so busy, so caught up in everything she's doing. Sometimes, I feel like I'm just along for the ride. That wouldn't be so bad, actually. I love that she's so driven and interested in things, but sometimes it's hard to figure out where I fit in. It's not like I didn't know this going in. Dad pretty much called it. He said it would always be a struggle for me with her, and I believed him, but... I guess the reality of what that truly means is just starting to become apparent. It's not a crisis, but you say you want me to have a 'happy life.' Right now, I think I'm more 'content.' Maybe that's not so bad, but it feels to me like there ought to be more, and that if it goes on this way... well... I don't know. Maybe, at some point, I won't be so content anymore."

"Eric," she said, her tone tender. "Always there are things to work on in a relationship, always challenges to face, compromises to make, but no matter how much you love them, you cannot look to one person to bring you happiness. You must first be happy with yourself, with what *you* are doing. Your grandfather had his work, the business he built that you and your father now run. What was I to do? I left my country to come with him. I had few skills, and in those days, married women were not expected to work. For me, it was easy. I had a baby, your father, to look after, and that became my joy. Later, I volunteered at the Lutheran church, and I had all my friends. For me, this was enough. For you, there will be different things, but you cannot define your happiness strictly through Lotte, especially since she has such a clear sense of what she wants."

He felt transparent, like his grandmother could see right through him. As much as he'd grown in the past ten years, in many ways, he was still the sixteen-year-old kid who sat on the floor of this very room, dazzled by a girl who had purpose and direction in her life. Yeah, she was a hot mess back then too, but that wasn't exactly her fault. Being tormented by monsters in your dreams will kind of do that to you. Still, the contrast between himself and her could not have been starker in his adolescent mind.

In some twist of fate as unlikely as being hit by a meteor, he'd wound up with that dazzling girl, and it had been through her that he found his way, and through losing her that he had lost it. Now, she was back again, hopefully for good, but Eric could see that Grandma was right. He'd never confronted the fundamental question that made Lotte so beguiling in the first place.

What do I want out of my life?

Lotte was obviously a part of the answer, but being hitched to her star had, in a sense, insulated him from having to make some difficult decisions. Many he'd simply kicked down the road, such as what he'd do with his job at Schneider. That made some sense because of the uncertainty around where they might be in the longer term, but it also had day-to-day ramifications. His lack of real *commitment* to anything meant that he looked to Lotte to find fulfillment and meaning in his everyday existence—and so it had ever been, at least since they became friends, and eventually lovers, in high school.

He had to laugh. "A clear sense of what she wants. That's pretty much it. You certainly know Lotte. Sometimes I wonder what she sees in me, because other than her, I'm not sure I have a clue about what I really want."

"I know two Lottes, Eric," she stiffly replied. "Lotte as she is today, and the Lotte you brought to my door all those years ago—a lovely girl with all the promise in the world, but despite her best efforts, I could see the depths of her troubles. I'll never know what happened, but at no time has there been a doubt in my mind that you were a part of her transformation. Do not question why she loves you. Lotte has made her decision, and she is not one to choose lightly, but if you want her to see more in you, give her more to see. In the end, this would be better for both of you, I think. *Ja*?"

He couldn't fundamentally disagree with that, and despite the challenge this posed, what she said brought a sense of clarity. "Yeah, Grandma, that's really good advice. Very helpful. You're pretty smart, huh?"

"Not smart, just old. When you're my age, you'll have it all figured out as well. Then you can make *your* grandchildren think you're so smart."

"Whew, grandchildren... that's a stretch. I'm not sure Lotte even wants kids. I'm not even sure I do."

"Well, it is none of my business, but you would be excellent parents. Of this, I'm sure. There is so much of your father in you—his patience, his kindness. I see this in you, dear boy."

He beamed, though inwardly his stomach still clenched given the precarious situation. "Wow. That's incredibly nice to hear. I'm flattered, really."

"Don't be. Something is either true, or it isn't. I say this to you just as I say in other ways that you need to do better. Both are true. I say these things not to flatter or scold, but to help you make the best choice you can. So, if it is your choice to have children, I think it would suit you well, and make you and Lotte tremendously happy." She winked as she added, "And your old *Oma*, too."

Well, that was a sneaky but endearing way of applying a little pressure. Come to think of it, I wonder why Lotte and I have never once discussed having children? Shit! Lotte! I've gotta get going!

"I hear you, Grandma, but listen, if I don't get this equipment to Lotte, she will not be happy. Of this, *I* am sure! I've got a long drive ahead of me. Did you find those keys?"

"What keys?"

"Umm... the basement keys, to the storage area...."

"Of course! Why was I looking in the kitchen? They're hanging on the coat rack by the door. Lotte put them on a string for me because I was forever losing them in drawers."

"Great! I'm gonna grab the stuff and start getting it outside. I have a friend helping me. Lotte and I will be back to visit soon, I promise! We'll show you our Italy pictures."

She gave him a quizzical look. "When were you in Italy?"

He just smiled and headed for the keys.

CHAPTER 7

Olive just stared at him, but Eric figured that was better than forlornly gazing out the window, which she'd been doing most of the morning. He'd spilled the beans, let her in on the whole shebang.

"So, I was right all along," she finally said. "The damn thing *does* have magical powers—at least, yours does. Now I know why you was acting so confident, like, with that kidnapper. You don't think he expects nothin' like this... us coming after him. He wants the one my daddy has, though, that... portal... if that's what it really is. Don't you think he has some idea what it can do, and that he'll be prepared?"

"I don't know. I have no idea what John Riggins, or whatever his real name is, truly understands about the portal in your father's house. I have to say, he wasn't what I thought he'd be like on the phone. Given where this object came from, I guess I was expecting someone from the Middle East... maybe with some kind of ISIS connection. That may still be correct, but at this point, I have my doubts. In any case, no matter what he may or may not know about your father's portal, I can't imagine he'll be expecting the Afrit, or that he'll even anticipate us finding Lotte. I'm counting on that element of surprise."

She chewed on that, and everything else he'd told her, as the gleaming white van charged down I-95 toward New Rochelle and The Bronx.

After loading and securing the flight cases carrying the un-mirror and the various other items that made the portal function into the van, they'd driven in silence for a couple of hours before stopping at the Dick's Sporting Goods in Norwalk, Connecticut, a little before noon.

He had to coax her out of the vehicle. "Come on, Olive. We're gonna get you some clothes and shoes here. You pick out what you need. It's on me. I have to get some stuff too. Then we'll get some food. Aren't you hungry?"

She finally, and silently, acquiesced.

The shopping seemed to cheer her a bit, but she was surprised when she saw he planned to purchase a hunting knife, some stiff cord, and two baseball bats. "What are y'all fixin' to do with that stuff?"

He just stared at her.

"Oh," she said, finally getting the picture.

For lunch, they grabbed some subs to go, and hit the road.

Olive had changed into her new cargo pants and sneakers in the bathroom of the sub shop, and seemed much more comfortable. They ate as Eric drove, not wanting to lose precious time. At one point, their hands met over the shared bag of chips tucked into the dashboard cubby.

"Sorry about that—" "'Scuse me—" they both said in unison.

"You first, please—" "Y'all go ahead—"

They both laughed, a bit uncomfortably.

"Tell you what," he said, sensing an opportunity in the awkward moment that had served to break the ice. "You eat some chips, while I finish telling you what's gonna happen tonight. I guarantee, you won't have an appetite when I'm done, and then they'll be all mine."

She nodded, and with that simple gesture, Olivia Carter, who everybody called Olive— except her daddy, who apparently called her Airhead—*That really isn't very nice!*—came finally and formally into the fold.

He finished warning her of what would come, and awaited her response.

She now knew about dreams, and portals, and Afrits, and bargains, and broken bargains, and broken spines, and Etruscan demi-gods, and menacing magnetic hammers, and severed arms in white vans almost identical to the one they were in now—except older and smellier—and lost companions, and great battles high on a hill to the north, and a great love that was forged, and then lost, and then re-forged in the crucible of all this... impossibility.

Now, she knew it all, because you never could tell which detail might matter, or be the difference between life and death, or who would, in the end, survive to carry this knowledge forward. Lotte understood this long before Eric had grasped it, and on this point, she'd been completely persuasive.

Perhaps of greatest importance, however, was that Olive now knew that Afrits really preferred girls to guys, and that this is why she'd likely be needed tonight. She also realized that she'd have to be courageous, and strong, and confident.

Eric finished off the chips.

The parking lot sat utterly silent. They'd been watching for almost an hour, and it was now close to 11:30 p.m. Traffic on the main road had slowed to a sporadic car here or there, none of which made the turn into the condo complex where Eric and Olive sat in the white van.

They'd made pretty good time. Olive had slept for a bit, after they ate lunch while they drove and had their difficult conversation. Then she spelled him at the wheel somewhere around Princeton, New Jersey so he could catch a nap. Their only major stop had come just outside of Washington, when they pulled over to take the all-important call, which was punctual practically to the second.

John's voice was as pleasant as ever, a mixture of aggression and impatience that Eric thought made the Afrit sound downright suave.

Well, almost.

"You got it?"

"You're in luck there, John," he replied, trying to keep up his confident façade. "Olive called me a couple of hours ago. She's leaving early tomorrow to go get the... well... whatever the hell it is. She'll be in Chapel Hill with it tomorrow morning around ten. Does that work for you, or would another time be more convenient?"

"You little shit!" he spat. Eric briefly wondered if he'd gotten that expression from Lotte, but then dismissed the thought. "Don't you fuck with me. Why can't she get it here tonight?"

"Well, it's quite a ways up here from Savannah, Georgia, and she doesn't have access to where the thing is kept until morning. Then she has to drive it here. It simply takes time. Where do you want to do the switch?" He hoped his story would hold water and buy them the last bit of time he needed.

"If it isn't getting here until tomorrow, I'll call you then. Ten o'clock, sharp... and you'll go where I tell you, and do what I say. Understood?"

Blah, blah, blah. He understood. Of course, he had no intention of meeting John Riggins at "ten o'clock, sharp," tomorrow. By then, he'd be long gone with Lotte, Olive, and the Afrit. Or else he'd be dead.

They ate dinner, then made the rest of the drive back to Raleigh and their final destination... Olive's father's condo in Knightdale.

They'd been surveilling that condo for the past hour.

"Eric!" Olive said with urgency. "My eyeballs are floatin'! Can't we just go inside? Y'all done looked in every car already. There was nobody in them and no new cars have parked. There ain't nobody watchin'!"

She's probably right.

If someone were casing the complex, there were only so many places they could possibly be—inside one of the other condos, which seemed highly doubtful, or in the trees off to the left, across the way from the building. The chances of someone being outside like that literally all day and all night on the slim chance that Olive showed up seemed close to zero. Still, he felt nervous. If there were any other place to go that might suit their purposes, he'd have tried it, but there really wasn't.

He finally capitulated. "Okay. Do your keys work on the doors in the back?"

"Umm, I don't think so. Actually, I don't know. The alarm panel is by the front door, though. That's the only way in that I use, and we sure don't want to be settin' off no alarms."

"Shit. All right, jump out and go in the front way. I'll watch from here for a while and see what happens. When I think it's secure, I'm gonna park the van in that last spot down there and circle around back. I want to see what the ground is like for moving these things. I'll knock three times on the back door, then pause, then three more. Don't open them if you don't get that pattern. Got it?"

"Yep." She eagerly exited the van and purposefully strolled along Tallula Lane, behind the cars parked neatly in front of their owners' town home condos. Near the end of the road, she walked up the cement sidewalk to number 216, second to last in the tidy little row. The last three units seemed a bit smaller than the others on the street, and of more recent construction. Olive's dad apparently lived alone, and was rarely home, so a smaller place likely suited him well. It would also suit them quite well, and the Afrit, who would need an easy and discrete way to exit the building. The double doors to the small cement patio in back that Olive had described to him sounded perfect.

She successfully opened the door, and since no alarm went off, he figured she'd disarmed that as well. He carefully watched for any signs of activity in the parking lot, fearing John Riggins, or one of his co-conspirators, may yet be watching the place. Nothing stirred, so he started up the van and drove to the final parking spot on the tiny road, which was fortuitously open.

He locked the vehicle and circled around back. There was no sidewalk here, just a somewhat scraggly grass lawn, likely shaded during the day by some trees a short distance behind the building. He saw all this by the back porch light, which Olive had turned on. He walked up to the glass double doors and saw light coming through the large Venetian-style blinds that otherwise blocked his view into the room. He knocked in the agreed upon pattern.

"Everything clear?" she asked as she opened the door.

"As far as I could tell. Can you point me toward the bathroom? I'll just be a minute, then we'll start unloading the gear."

They tried to be quiet, but you can only be so quiet when moving large cases on wheels across rough terrain.

At least it's flat!

The double doors were a blessing, far easier than having to squeeze through narrower openings, like the one in Mason's cabin or the tight entrance to Grandma's storage space. They didn't need everything. They left the case with the documents in the van. Eric wasn't even sure they'd need that at all, but if they did and he'd left it in Southby, Lotte would have never let him hear the end of it.

He kept a sharp lookout, but apparently no one heard, or didn't care about the gear being moved. He hoped their luck would hold when they had to load it all back into the van later. Once everything was inside, he surveyed the parking lot from a front window.

"Okay," he said, "everything seems clear. Do you need a little rest, or do you want to start setting it up now?"

Her eyes widened. "I want to see it now! I've been waitin' all day since you told me what it is."

That settled it. He went to the case with the un-mirror, used the hydraulics to ratchet it into an upright position, then unlatched and opened the front of the large case.

She gave a little cry of wonder behind him.

It was a wonder. The frame gleamed in the light of the room, cleaned and polished of the grit and dust from the mountain in New Hampshire. That had been one of the first things Lotte and Eric had done together when she'd arrived from Berlin. For a full day, they'd washed and organized all the gear that had been so hastily and haphazardly stowed. Just having Lotte near him had made him revel in the work. Now, he bit back memories of that seemingly meaningless moment, lost in time, as he secured the stand for the frame and removed the back of the case, lamenting all the while that his love wasn't with him.

They had plenty of room to set up in the sparsely furnished condo. With Olive's assistance, the ancient frame of the fire portal soon loomed above them, near the stairs to the bedrooms on the second floor. Eric placed the black marble board near the base of the un-mirror while she carefully removed the bowls from their boxes. Once they'd put everything in place, he retrieved the familiar knife from its spot in the flight case, along with two boxes of high-quality candles he'd ordered from Amazon.

No more shitty candles, ever!

He opened the package and handed it to her. "Grab the hunting knife I bought. You can help me. We're gonna cut the candles into thirds, expose the wicks, and then crush down the bottom a bit so they stand up in the bowls. I'll show you."

Together they made enough candles so there could be five per bowl, the seemingly magic number to summon the Afrit quickly. He didn't plan to fool around, as they had no time to waste. When they'd cut the candles and placed them in the bowls, he produced the gold ring and gold filigreed bracelet that had been bent to fit one of the Afrit's talons. He placed these, and the two aluminum baseball bats he'd bought at Dick's, near the apex of the black marble board.

"What do you need those for? This thing ain't gonna attack us, is it?"

"I hope not, but better safe than sorry. As I told you, the Afrit can be unpredictable. It looks exactly like how you'd picture the devil... horns, fangs, bat wings, barbed tail, the whole deal. When it's in a bad mood, you'll have your hands full. I still have the scars to prove it. For all that, though, I've come to understand that regardless of what it looks like, it isn't evil. It has its own logic, its own rationale. It's willing to bargain, and it honors its word, as long as you honor yours. So, the bats are a last resort if the negotiations go south... umm... I mean, don't go as planned."

She scowled a bit but recovered quickly. "That's what you want me to do, right? Talk to it? Try to get it to help us find Lotte?"

"That's basically right. I'm gonna start. This thing knows me, and it knows Lotte. I'll lay out the deal. I don't think it will just attack me outright, but if it does, or if it won't complete the bargain with me, that's when I'll need you to step in. Don't be afraid. Lotte uses a really commanding tone with the Afrit. She doesn't take any crap. I've never seen it threaten a female without being seriously provoked. So, just project confidence and I think you'll be okay. Are you ready?"

"I guess so," she replied, not exactly projecting the commanding confidence he'd hoped for. "It's just so unbelievable. You make summoning this thing sound almost normal-like."

He chuckled. "Well, I guess it shows that you can get used to practically anything. You're right, it does seem almost normal to me now.

There's probably something not normal about that, but that's how it is. If the Afrit can help us get Lotte back, I'll trade that for a bit of abnormality in my life." With that, he moved to the frame to begin lighting the candles.

"Wait!"

"What is it?"

She folded her arms in front of her and lowered her head. "I just wanted to say that I'm sorry... for what happened last night, and all. I, well... I don't know... I just never met no one like you. You're so easy to talk to. You make me feel... how can I say it... good about myself. I think I let that go to my head, what little there is up there. I just wanted you to know I was sorry, in case somethin' happens."

He took a deep breath as he absorbed what she'd said. So many responses came to him, but now just wasn't a time for a deep discussion, especially when he wasn't sure he'd even sorted out his own thoughts and feelings about it.

He resumed lighting the candles. "I don't think that's something you have to apologize for, but for what it's worth, I accept your apology. I still consider you my friend. For me, nothing has changed."

Not strictly true, as something *had* changed, but he wasn't sure he could pinpoint exactly what, or how it would affect things with Olive going forward. So, this was the best he could do at the moment. Thankfully, he sensed his words brought her comfort.

A good thing, because the candles were lit and the *Alkuartiz Alnaar* was heating up. Soon, they would need to sit side-by-side at the apex of the black marble board and reach out with their minds to the Afrit, something Lotte had always done, and something Eric never imagined he would have had the desire or the courage to do himself.

They'd both had to take breaks to stretch, drink some water, and to pee.

It took *way* longer than Eric had anticipated to attract the infernal creature's attention, and it was nearly 1:30 in the morning when a wisp of shining black ash finally appeared in the glass of the frame. Olive gasped, but he calmed her and told her to keep her concentration on calling the creature, lest they lose its attention.

The dark, shining ash billowed out from the un-mirror and swirled toward the large bowl at the center of the black marble board. The candles had burned down considerably, but Eric guessed there was enough life in them to complete the summoning and the Afrit's assembly.

At least, I hope there is.

The tendril of ash wasn't as thick as he remembered. Unsurprising, as the beast had lost much of its substance when Charun's magnetic touch had disrupted whatever force held the monster together. It had almost died, but then, so had he and Lotte. No being had departed that hill unscathed.

As anticipated, the shining ash shot upward when it reached the central bowl and began to twirl in a clockwise direction. Soon, the familiar form of the Afrit's head began to coalesce.

Again, Olive gasped as the goat-like horns took shape above the menacing eyes and fanged mouth of the monster. Eric put his hand on her shoulder and urged calm and silence.

After what seemed an eternity, the torso, arms, and eventually the bat-like wings of the beast began to form. The rotation stopped as the trailing tendril of ash filled in the creature's powerful legs and cloven hooves. The otherworldly being now stood on the beige wall-to-wall carpeting of the condo's living room. Its barbed tail lashed as the Afrit surveyed its surroundings and sniffed the air with its snout-like nose while its wings flexed as if preparing for flight. Surely, it must have been a mighty sight for wide-eyed Olive to behold, but to her credit she remained calm.

Eric, however, was aghast. Once fully formed, the Afrit stood barely four feet tall, hardly bigger than the stub of the monster he and Lotte had fought after part of the shining black beast had become separated during an interrupted summoning. He knew the creature could still help them locate Lotte, but his confidence in its ability to intimidate or fight the kidnappers eroded dramatically.

I should have considered this possibility, but in the end, it wouldn't have changed my plan that much.

'Why do you summon us?' the Afrit demanded. Despite its diminutive size, the beast's harsh and unintelligible words still resonated in the room, and in their heads.

Olive reeled at her first encounter with the creature's mind-to-mind contact, which allowed them to understand its ancient and alien tongue.

Sounds like we didn't catch it in an especially good mood.

He cautiously stood, and tugged on Olive's arm to indicate she do the same. Facing the beast head on, he channeled his inner Lotte. "We wish to bargain, great Afrit! We need your help in locating one who has been taken. She's familiar to you. You've had dealings with her before." He concentrated on Lotte's image and tried to project his thoughts at the being before him.

The Afrit cocked its head in seeming confusion. *'You wish the* Sadat Alnaar *dead?'*

The Sadat Alnaar*? What the hell do they have to do with it? They've been gone for thirteen hundred years.*

Suddenly, it dawned on him. "Oh, you mean Lotte!" It had never occurred to him that Lotte might be considered *Sadat Alnaar*, a Master of Fire, but in a sense, she was. In truth, she represented the last of the *Sadat Alnaar*, or the first of the new *Sadat Alnaar*.

Now there's a scary thought. He tried to file that image away permanently. "No, no! Not at all, nothing like that. She's been taken... kidnapped. We need your help to find her and free her."

The beast started to sway from side to side. Its barbed tail flicked in quick motions and its wings pulsated.

Eric knew he had its attention.

'She lives,' the creature announced. *'I can sense her, not far from this place. What do you offer us to help you save her?'*

Gotta hand it to ol' Chuckles: no beating around the bush – unless it's a burning bush, that is.

Relieved that she was still alive, he said, "She's being held against her will. I don't know how many are with her right now, but I have reason to believe that more than one person is involved. So, there could be two, three...? I don't know. Those who are with her, who hold her prisoner, are yours... spoils... as long as Lotte... umm... the *Sadat Alnaar,* is unharmed."

Again, the ashen creature listed from side to side before it jerked its bat-like wings to full extension. Olive jumped, but Eric held her elbow to steady her, and she quickly regained her composure.

'Of what manner are they?' the Afrit cautiously asked.

Eric was confused. "I don't understand. Of what manner are who, and what do you mean by, 'manner?'"

The beast loudly chuffed, and he jumped with alarm.

Maybe I should have added, 'oh, great Afrit,' *or something at the end there.* He tried to quiet his rapidly beating heart.

'Those that hold the Sadat Alnaar!' the creature roared, *'Of what manner are they? Mortal beings of this dreary world, like you, or like the other – the one you called Charun? The one who... damaged us?'*

My God, Eric thought with a mixture of dismay and ironic humor. *It's afraid. The damned Afrit has discovered fear!*

"As far as I know, they're all humans, like me. We think we've discovered another portal, but I don't believe any beings have come out of it, and it's a long way from here. In fact, it was that portal that led to Lotte's kidnapping, but that's a story for later. Right now, we don't have much time. I need to know if you're willing to help. If you're in, we're gonna help you." He gestured at Olive, who stiffened as the Afrit brought her into its stony gaze. "We'll work together, like we did against Charun, except we'll be fighting humans... mortal creatures... and the spoils will be yours. What do you say, in or out?"

He held his breath as the beast approached Olive. Even having lost practically half of its height and mass, sight of the monster still terrified. It brought its face close to her body and sniffed with its snout, seeming to taste the air around her with its oversized mouth. The creature's razor-sharp teeth gleamed in the light from the candles as its barbed tail traced with graceful menace along her jawline, barely touching her skin, while its talons outlined her arms and torso, as if measuring her for a demonic dress.

To Eric's surprise and wonder, Olive spoke. "You touch me, and I'm gonna whack the livin' shit out of you with one of them baseball bats, you damn ol' thing!"

The creature froze.

"Do we have a bargain, or not?" she continued. "If not, I got better things to do with my evening than being drooled over, thank you very much."

The Afrit backed away slightly, and Eric swore he saw the barest hint of a smile on the monster's fanged visage.

'Let the rings bind our pact,' it said with quiet satisfaction.

Eric reached to the ground to pick up the rings, but the Afrit barked its displeasure. He froze in place, half bent over, and gestured with one hand to Olive. "My dear, would you do the honors?"

She reached down and picked up the ring and the bracelet. The ring she put on her finger. It was a bit tight, but she managed. She then took the bracelet and fit it over the reduced Afrit's talon. It was far too big, and there wasn't enough play left to bend it further.

"What do we do?" she asked.

Eric thought fast. *Maybe we could tie it to a string, put it around the Afrit's neck. Where the hell can we get string?* Suddenly, it came to him. "Try one of the horns. Slip it on as far as it can go, it should stay."

Olive took a deep breath as she walked up to the creature and reached out with the bent filigreed bracelet. Past the tip, the dramatically diminished horn was now roughly the diameter of the full-size monster's claw. Remarkably, the beast didn't seem to mind, nor did it make any move to touch Olive while she secured the ersatz ring in place.

It was quite a sight, not one Eric ever thought he'd see. He laughed to himself. *You look pretty good there, Chuckles.*

When Olive was done, Eric said, "We have to load all this stuff into our van. Then we'll go. Can you direct us to where she is?"

'We will fly above, and make signals so you can follow.'

Eric didn't figure it would want to ride in the van. This would have to do. The time was upon them. He just hoped they had enough firepower to get the job done.

CHAPTER 8

At some point, Peebles became Jonesville Road.

It didn't seem to matter. After they'd re-packed and loaded all the gear into the van, the Afrit had shepherded them out of Knightdale. They traveled north, following the trusted little beastie who knew the way and could guide them. To impart directions, the creature would periodically swerve down to the passenger side window where Olive sat, glued to the back of her seat in seeming terror. Eric worried that someone might see the monster, but the roads at this hour were largely empty, and the ashen-black Afrit melded seamlessly into the darkness of the night sky.

"It says to go right when you can't go no farther," she relayed, as the impish demon spread its wings and launched back into the air, briefly visible in the van's headlights as it rocketed upward. "Gawd, Eric, that thing is still creepin' me out. I know you warned me, but seeing it yourself, and having it touch your mind like it does, is a whole 'nuther thing."

He couldn't disagree. Lotte had told him what she'd experienced on her first summoning, but not until Eric actually saw the beast for himself did the magnitude and reality of the situation fully register.

"I know," he said. "It's almost impossible to comprehend, but you're doing great... seriously! I wish your father could have seen you stand up to the Afrit that way. He'd have been proud. You definitely surprised me."

"Well, I guess almost peeing my pants in fear brings out the best in me. Not really sure how that helps getting a better grade in American Culture, 1600 to 1876, though. Just my luck."

He chuckled at her pragmatism while he took a right turn onto Route 401, just as the Afrit had instructed. He'd had his doubts about her, but so far, she'd come through. The true test, however, was yet to come.

"My daddy's office building is straight up there," she said, pointing through the windshield at the road ahead. "They bought some farmland off of Zebulon Road a few years back. They have a big ol' shooting range there, and places for people to train on combat skills and such. He took me there once, let me shoot his M4 rifle and everything. That was before he got sent back overseas."

"Really? That seems like an awful coincidence, that we'd be heading this direction. Are you sure there's no way to get in touch with your father besides email? It would really help to be able to talk with him."

"I don't got his number. He don't give it out... says it's for business only. I'll bet you ten dollars Uncle Clint has it, though. Like he'd ever be callin'. Freakin' once in five hundred years flooding hits their fishing lodge, and I ask him if he's contacted his brother. 'Do you think I should?' he asks me. 'Hell *yeah*, I think you should,' I told him, but it's *me* gotta do everything. I think my daddy just don't want me bothering him. Oh, shit, here it comes again."

The Afrit swooped in and grasped the passenger side mirror for stability. *'Where the lanterns flash ahead, reorient yourselves toward the northern skies.'*

She moaned once the little monster had again gone airborne. "I have no idea what it's tellin' us to do!"

"I think it wants us to bang a left at the lights."

"Why don't it just say so? Damn ol' thing."

Soon they turned onto East Young Street, again headed in a northerly direction, but away from where Olive had indicated Black Arrow's headquarters were located.

Maybe that was *just a coincidence.*

The road passed directly through the little township of Rolesville, and then became West Young Street on the opposite side. Having momentarily lost their guide, he slowed down on the dark road as the settlement receded from view. Eventually, they passed a cemetery on the right.

Seriously? What next? He surveyed the graveyard for any sign of zombies.

At the last moment, he slammed on his brakes. The Afrit stood in the middle of street, which thankfully was dark and quiet. It pointed down a road to the left, and Eric maneuvered the van in that direction as the beast strode toward Olive's door and scrambled onto the roof.

It pointed to the right as it loomed over her open window. *'The first structure, behind these trees. She is there, your* Sadat Alnaar.'

Eric drove slowly along the street for about a hundred and fifty yards until he saw a sign dangling on a white frame in front of a driveway.

For Sale
2406 Chalk Road, Rolesville
Contact Christine Harris – (919) 555-0193
KW Realty

The sign bore the image an older blonde woman whose perfect white teeth smiled preternaturally in the van's headlights, as if she promised the path to all happiness. If Lotte were in this house, then Eric figured Christine might well be able to deliver.

He shut off the engine, flicked off the headlights, and eased out of the van. The Afrit, seemingly all the more dexterous for its diminished size, landed smoothly beside him.

"This house?" he asked, and the creature bowed slightly in confirmation. "Okay, we need to spec it out. Olive, you stay here. I'm just gonna do a once around with Chuckles, try to see what's what. We'll be back, and then we can make a plan for how to approach this."

She voiced no disagreement, so he began to cautiously creep down the driveway.

The Afrit took to the air, where it would be able to scan in places Eric couldn't see from the ground.

Once he passed the trees near the main road, a house came into view on the large property. A light shone from a second-story window, but otherwise the place seemed dark.

The long driveway meandered around the front of the building to a two-car garage near the rear. He circled around the side and peered in a window. By the light of the moon, he could see a pickup truck parked inside. Quietly, he navigated to the back of the garage where there was a door. It was locked, but it had glass panes they might be able to break if he couldn't find another way in.

To his right, a large wooden deck at the back of the house looked out over some gardens. He slinked up the steps and tiptoed to the big glass doors leading to the interior. These were also locked, but as he tested them, he noticed a faint, flickering, whiteish light coming from another room somewhere to the right—probably a TV.

Shit!

He slipped as quietly as possible off the deck and continued his circuit of the house. When he reached the opposite side of the building from the garage, he again saw the flickering light. It had been obscured from the driveway by some bushes, which is why he hadn't noticed it before. Shades in the windows prevented him from seeing whether anyone was actually watching the TV set. To the front of the house on this side was a large, enclosed porch. It had a door with glass panes, but it was too close to the room with the TV to risk breaking. If the Afrit didn't find a way in, the garage seemed the likeliest entrance.

He stealthily inched back to the driveway and then jogged toward the van. The barest sound of fluttering wings alerted him that the Afrit had landed behind him. "What did you see?" he whispered. "Is there some way in on the second floor?"

'Many ways in, all through glass. We can enter, but we will make noise, and you cannot follow.'

Much as he'd anticipated, it looked like the garage would be the best bet. "Okay, I have an idea. Let's go back to the van. We need some stuff, and we need to get Olive."

"What are we gonna do?" she asked as they arrived. "How many of them are there?"

"I have no idea," he confessed as he opened the side door of the van and started pulling out gear. "Make sure you still have your knife on you. You'll need it. Also, take this bat."

He took the other baseball bat and tucked Dr. Esfahani's knife into his belt. Additionally, he grabbed the rope he'd bought at Dick's and one of the padded packing blankets from the back of the van.

He turned to the Afrit. "Okay, we're gonna break in through the garage, the big room at the far end of the building. There's a door in the back. Meet us there." He gestured, and the Afrit took to the air.

He and Olive marched back toward the house.

This time, he circled wide to avoid any chance of being noticed. The Afrit already waited for them when they arrived at the rear of the house. Eric unfolded the packing blanket and held it to the window. As quietly as possible, he tried to punch into the lowest pane of glass, closest to the doorknob, with his aluminum bat. He hoped to crack it enough that they could remove the shards, but found it awkward and difficult to get the right angle, so his first couple of attempts failed.

He stepped back. "Olive, can you hold the blanket so I can get a better—"

The Afrit casually thrust its muscled talon directly through the pane of glass, which shattered and fell with a loud jingle into the garage. Olive and Eric froze and held their breath, praying no one had heard. After a few moments, all still seemed quiet.

He whispered angrily at the Afrit. "We were trying to be quiet."

'We grew weary of watching you navigate that small obstacle. We meant only to assist.'

He bit back his frustration with the impatient creature and pulled away the blanket. As silently as possible, he removed the remaining shards of glass. Now, he worried whether the door had an alarm, and whether it was armed. He reached inside, twisted the locking mechanism on the door and, baseball bat in hand, pushed it open.

All remained silent. There appeared to be no alarm, at least not on this door. The entrance to the interior stood just to the right, up three wooden steps. If this door were locked, it would be a major problem.

He twisted the handle, and mercifully, it turned. Ever so slowly, he cracked it open and peeked into a hallway that led into the heart of the house. A large open area sat at the end of the hallway, probably a living room, and the dim light from the TV came from a doorway at the back of this space. It didn't appear as if the television's sound was on, or else the volume was quite low. To his immediate left, a door stood open, and to the right, one stood closed.

He crept in, crouched low, and peered into the opening on the left—an empty bathroom. The other door was probably just a closet, not worth risking the noise of opening. He continued down the hallway until the kitchen appeared on the left. He could see the side of the refrigerator and the tiles of the floor which abutted the hardwood flooring of the hallway. He stood up enough to see that a long counter separated this area from the large room just beyond.

He motioned for the Afrit to go into the kitchen and approach from the other side, while he went on ahead. When he reached the open area, he saw a dining table to his right, in front of the big glass double doors that led to the back deck. To his left sat some cushioned chairs, a coffee table, and a couch. The furniture appeared staged, not really looking like it fit well in the large space, and two of the chairs were missing from around the chintzy dining room table. He heard no noise and saw no movement, so he gestured to Olive and indicated she should stay where she crouched near the bathroom. Then he slipped out into the open area.

By the time he registered the motion, it was too late. A large object crashed into his back and the base of his skull. It knocked the breath from his lungs, and caused a loud ringing in his ears as pain engulfed him. He collapsed to the ground, and for a moment, he could do nothing more than gasp for breath. A forceful hand gripped his shoulder as someone tried to flip him over, and he heard angry words from above him, but they were a complete blur.

Then, another noise came—shriller than the deafening ringing in his head. From behind, Olive screamed, and the forceful hand let go of his shoulder.

"No!" he breathlessly wheezed, but he couldn't move. He couldn't go to help her. He desperately tried to regain control of his body, but for now it was all he could do to get breath in his lungs, though his hearing finally began to return.

A man's voice yelled, "Siddique! We got company. Git your ass down here!" He had a deep Southern drawl, and seemed to have the voice of a younger man.

Eric didn't think this was John Riggins.

"What you gonna do with that, little lady?" the man taunted. "You think you can—*aaahhh*!"

Something landed hard on Eric's legs and thrashed around as if in a panic. With all his concentration, he turned to look behind him. The man had collapsed onto the floor and now desperately fought off the Afrit, who clawed viscously at his head and shoulders.

"What the gawddamned fuck!" he screamed. "Siddique! Help me you sumbitch! There's a fuckin' animal clawin' at me down here!"

Eric fought to free himself from under the weight of the man, who was a bit heavyset, to put it mildly. He'd regained his breath, but still felt dazed, and sharp and agonizing pains radiated from his back and neck. In the dim light, he saw one of the missing dining room chairs, discarded where it lay on the floor. Two legs had broken off from the concussion with his body.

Good thing this is cheapo furniture. Solid wood might have broken my back.

He'd almost freed himself when a light went on dead ahead. A foyer appeared, with a stairway leading up, just to the right of the room that housed the muted television. A black man, probably in his twenties like Eric, stood at the bottom of the stairs, eyes wide with shock.

So much for surprise.

He had no idea where the baseball bat had flown when the chair hit him, so he reached for the knife tucked in his belt and prepared to face a new combatant. At that moment, however, the Afrit careened haphazardly over his head. The heavyset man had apparently thrown the creature off of him, and Eric could hear him as he scrambled to his feet. Fortuitously, when the man at the staircase saw the Afrit, he screamed in terror and ran back up to the second floor.

It's now or never. I have to move, or the dude behind will be on his feet, and he'll be in an extremely threatening position.

Almost instinctively, he rolled to his left, toward the couch. His back screamed in protest, but this was the quickest way. When he felt the couch, he got achingly to his knees, and scrambled around to the other side near the coffee table. Feeling more secure, he looked back toward the kitchen.

In the light now flooding in from the stairwell, he could see the dude who'd attacked him. The guy was probably in his late twenties or early thirties. He wore work boots and jeans, and sported a jean vest over a t-shirt for the band:

LYNYRD SKYNYRD

The garment displayed the odd juxtaposition of an American eagle alongside two Confederate flags. Blood dripped from multiple cuts and scrapes on his face and neck, and the man's left forearm had a nasty slice in it from the Afrit's barbed tail. He steadied himself on the kitchen counter, dabbing with his other hand at the various wounds.

"Siddique!" he bellowed. "You 'lil motherfucker! Git your sorry ass down here and help me! I'm bleedin'!"

Eric ducked back behind the couch to avoid being seen, and drew the knife from his belt. Like his opponent, he tried to recover from the recent onslaught as he gasped for breath and massaged his bruised neck. He looked around for the Afrit, but couldn't see it. Suddenly, he remembered that Olive was still near the door to the garage.

Maybe she went out.

He doubted that. More likely, she was still back there, maybe in the bathroom. He'd need to act. As cautiously as possible, he crawled toward the kitchen countertop, then veered right, away from the dining area where he'd been taken by surprise. Another entrance to the kitchen stood at the end of the counter, and he peered around the corner, back toward the refrigerator and the hallway where they'd come in. He didn't see the guy in the vest and Skynyrd t-shirt but knew instantly where he'd gone.

"Get out of there, you bitch!" The man screamed as he pounded on the bathroom door. "I'll bust this fucker down. I don't give a shit! Ain't my gawddamned house!"

Eric had no idea how strong that door was, but this was a big dude. If he slammed his body into it, the latch, or the wood around it, would almost certainly break.

Eric got to his feet, ran through the kitchen, and switched the knife to his left hand as he hung onto the refrigerator to whip himself around the corner.

It wasn't the most perfectly considered maneuver. The corner was tight, and the stainless-steel fridge was slippery. He lost his balance and crashed into the far wall of the hallway with a thud. He lost all his momentum, and almost dropped the knife.

The heavyset guy saw him and pounced. "Little fucker! I got you now!"

Eric swiped with the knife, but had drastically reduced thrust with his left hand, and the large man knocked the weapon out of his hand with minimal effort. It dawned on Eric that this guy knew what he was doing in a fistfight. Remembering his experience hitting the biker in the abandoned quarry building in New Hampshire, Eric threw his right elbow at his adversary's head. To his surprise, the blow found its mark and the guy stumbled back, seemingly stunned. Eric bent over and frantically searched for the knife.

Big mistake.

The heavyset man kicked out and caught him square on the jaw with his thick boots. The taste of blood filled his mouth as he collapsed backwards onto the floor. For a long moment, he entirely lost motor control. He couldn't move his arms to fend off the inevitable blows to come, and he didn't bother to attempt to skulk away on legs that had no hope of carrying him.

Through his dizzy haze, he heard the big man right himself against the door to the garage. "Oh, that had to hurt. You're dead now, asshole." Heavy footsteps came closer.

Eric vainly lashed out with his weakened leg.

His assailant howled in pain as foot met shin. "Gawdammit!" the guy screamed.

Before Eric could strike again, he felt the full weight of the heavy man on top of him. Eric feebly raised his arms, but they were easily knocked aside and secured to the wooden floor of the hallway by meaty legs. Then, stubby but strong fingers wrapped around his neck, and again he found himself gasping for breath.

I'm sorry, Lotte. I tried. I did the best I could. I love you.

The burly guy's foul breath assaulted his face as he fought to take in air, and his head began to swirl as he awaited the end.

Eric had played Little League Baseball. Like most things, he didn't take it particularly seriously. He usually covered an inning or two in right field, took one at-bat, and then spent a lot of time on the bench saying, "Swing, batta, batta, batta, swing, batta, batta, batta...." Whether this caused the opposing batter to swing at bad pitches or not, he had no statistical evidence to confirm or refute, but it was what you did, and he did it.

Perhaps the one thing, the only thing, which stuck with him from his Little League experience, was the sound of the bat contacting the ball. That ring of hollow aluminum as it connected, causing the solid little baseball to streak inevitably, directly toward his manhood, seemingly as if guided by radar—or the hand of God Himself—intent on Eric never reproducing.

Klank!

The familiar sound comforted him, as did the feeling of soft hands on his sore jaw, wiping away the blood that dripped from his mouth.

Did the ball hit me in the face? How embarrassing. That'll teach them for putting me on second base. They know I suck at ground balls.

'Eric.'

The word came from outside, and from inside—from memories of a field with eager and enthusiastic boys doing what eager and enthusiastic boys do, and from some dark place in a dark room in a dark house in a dark situation that Eric, whoever that was, didn't want to deal with.

'Eric.'

What more do they want? I'm dead, aren't I? Let me rest in peace.

"Eric," Olive implored. "Honey, you gotta come out of it. Please, you gotta help me."

Honey? My mother calls me honey. Is my mother here? That would be nice.

He opened his eyes.

"Oh, my gawd!" She gushed with relief. "You're alive! Eric, I got him, but you have to help me. He ain't dead. We gotta tie him up. Come on, sugar, come back to me."

Sugar. I like sugar in my coffee, especially when Lotte makes it. She must use a lot of sugar, or a lot of coffee, or both. Anyway, it always tastes better when Lotte makes it.

"Lotte!" He gasped as his senses returned. "Olive, what happened? Ow, shit! I bit my tongue really bad." He spat blood on the floor, next to the hulking frame of his opponent who lay face-down beside him.

"I heard him say he was gonna kill you. I knew he weren't at the bathroom door no more, so I looked out and saw him there strangling you. I grabbed my bat and clocked him good, right in the head. I was afraid I'd killed him, but I can see him breathin'. We gotta tie him up."

Eric felt stunned, in more ways than one. He grabbed her arm, both to steady himself as he tried to rise, and to get her full attention. "Olive, I think you saved my life. I don't know how to thank you."

"You don't have to thank me. I heard you comin' when that asshole was poundin' on the door. He'd have killed me, or worse, if he'd gotten in that bathroom. So, you saved my life, too. Plus, I told you I wouldn't let you down. Nobody ever believes me when I tell 'em stuff. Why is that?"

He gave her arm another squeeze before letting go. "I'll watch him. Can you go get the rope while I try to get my shit together? It's just outside the garage. Where the hell did the damn Afrit go?"

"I think he went up the stairs after that other feller. I ain't seen him since then."

"Damn. Okay, we have to hurry."

She dashed away to fetch the rope.

Dizziness still assailed him. The pains in his jaw and mouth distracted his attention from the excruciating welt on his upper back, until he tried to get up and the searing agony reasserted itself. He dragged himself over to the prone man and checked to see if he was still unconscious. Blood had dripped onto the floor and pooled at the back of his head.

He's not going anywhere.

Olive returned with the stiff cord.

"I don't think this guy will be waking up any time soon," Eric said. "Can you tie him up? Use your knife to cut the pieces to size and tie his legs together, then tie his hands behind his back. I have to get upstairs to see what's happening."

She nodded, so he staggered through the large living room area and located his bat, which he'd rolled right past earlier where it lay near the couch. He then painfully dragged himself up the stairs. The staircase looped at the bottom and top, and he found himself in a hallway that bisected the middle of the second story.

He peered around the corner and, to his amazement, spotted the Afrit crouched in the center of the hallway. Its wings flapped and its tail twitched with agitation. The creature had planted itself in front of an open door, from which light streamed out into the corridor.

Eric calculated this was probably the room he'd seen lit up earlier. Slowly, he lurched forward, still reeling from his recent fight.

The Afrit hissed in fury as it saw him approach. *'He threatens the Sadat Alnaar! We cannot dispatch him. It would mean her end.'*

Eric painfully craned his neck around the doorframe and took in the scene. He saw a bed, along with a nightstand and dresser—likely more staged furniture. A black ski mask sat on the nightstand, surely meant to hide the kidnapper's identity from Lotte.

That's a good sign. They probably had intended to let her go. Not that it matters now.

In the corner to the right sat the other missing dining room chair, akimbo in front of an open closet door, beside the man he'd seen earlier on the stairs. That man now stood with his back to the wall, where he held a knife to Lotte's throat.

"Eric!" she cried out when she saw him, but the man tightened his grip around her neck.

Eric bristled, brushed past the perturbed Afrit, and entered the room. "Let her go!" he demanded as he raised his bat as threateningly as possible.

"Are you crazy?" the man screamed. "If I let her go, that, that... thing... that black devil, whatever it is, will kill me for sure!" He had an unusual accent, not Southern, that was clear—at least not U.S. Southern.

He's not from this country, and he's obviously terrified. He can slit Lotte's throat with no effort at all.

"All right, hold on."

Eric backed away. He didn't wish to escalate the situation. He walked into the hall and pulled the door shut.

"Listen," he whispered to the Afrit. "Go outside. Fly up to the outside window of that room and wait. I'm gonna try and reason with him, get him to give up. I doubt it'll work, because you have him totally freaked out. If I can't get him to surrender, I'll try and lure him out. If I do and you have a shot at him, on my signal, take it. We can't let this drag on forever. I'm afraid more people may come."

The Afrit assented and whisked down the hallway toward the stairs.

Eric pushed the door open and reentered the room.

The man hadn't moved, but it appeared he'd relaxed his grip on Lotte just a bit.

Eric tried to calm his voice. "Okay, the creature's gone. I sent it away. It did its job. It led us to her. If you let her go, I won't hurt you. All I want is Lotte."

"No fucking way, man," he retorted as he brandished the knife. "I'm bringing her downstairs. Me and Mr. White are taking her with us in his truck. We're getting the hell away from you and that crazy monster. You're a sorcerer! I don't trust a word you say."

"He's telling you the truth," Lotte yelled. "If you want to live, let me go now."

For her trouble, the man again jerked at her neck and brought the knife close to her face. "Quiet, lady! I been good to you, right? I don't want to hurt you, but I will if I don't get what I want."

"All right, all right," Eric intervened. "Mr. White, huh? I don't think Mr. White will be going anywhere for a while. My partner downstairs hit him pretty hard. He's unconscious, and we've tied him up. You're all by yourself, Mr. Black... if I can presume to call you that. Or, would you prefer I call you Siddique?"

"Oh, shit! Why the fuck he go be callin' my name? Stupid fool! Now I'm in even deeper crap! This is *not* how it was supposed to be!"

"How was it supposed to be, Siddique? Tell me what this is all about."

"Oh, man, I don't know. My boss, he ask me if I want a job. Good money, he say. Five-thousand dollar! All we gotta do is grab this girl, take her to this house... keys and the alarm code will be in the mailbox. Then, we give her a little scare, find out where this thing in a picture is at, and let her go. Nobody gets hurt... a few hours maximum. Sure didn't go down like that."

"Who's your boss? Who put you up to this?"

"Fuck you! Why I tell you anything like that? Just let me get the hell out of here!"

"The reason you want to talk with me, is that I know your name and what you look like, and so does my partner downstairs. Even if you get out of here, you'll have to kill us both to hide your involvement in this, and that's not happening. I can call my little devilish friend back anytime I want. So, I'm asking you again... who's your boss?"

Siddique stiffened and then sadly shook his head. "My boss runs the Alley Cat strip club in Raleigh. Me and Wayne, umm... oh, shit... I mean me and Mr. White, we bouncers there. Saturday night, boss come to us, say some VIP member called him with a job. Don't give us his name, but I think he showed up here later... like Monday... after he find out we got the wrong girl at that hotel."

That made sense. Eric had received the call from John Riggins on Monday morning. "What did this guy say to you when he got here?"

"Oh, man, he was fuckin' pissed. Said, 'How can you grab the wrong stupid girl?' All they told us was to take the black-haired girl in room 237.

Look at her!" He gave Lotte a little push forward, and she grunted defiantly. "Look like she got black hair to you?"

"Okay, okay... easy. Did you get a look at his face? Did you see his car?"

"No, man. We all wear masks, like that one." He gestured toward the nightstand where the black ski mask still sat. "He must have parked by the street, because I don't hear nobody drive up... then suddenly he's at the door. He was hopping mad at us, but he say not to hurt her. He tells us to get her food, take care of her. He say when he gets what he wants, we let her go. We take care of you... right, lady?"

"Oh, I've been so well looked after," Lotte bitterly replied. "I particularly enjoyed spending the last three days locked in that fucking *closet*! Yes, it's been such a lovely stay. I'm already thinking about booking for next bloody *season*!"

Despite the situation, Eric smiled. *That's my Lotte!* If she could have given Siddique a patented right hook, he felt certain the standoff would be resolved, but she was in a tight spot, so he'd have to think of another way.

"All right, Siddique, I get it. You're just muscle for this job, and you don't know anything other than what you've told me. I believe you. Now, I'm asking you to believe me. We'll let you go. Your buddy downstairs, not so much, but you can leave in that truck. You just can't take Lotte with you. Get me? That's not negotiable. Let's just end this peacefully, and we'll all pretend it never happened."

Siddique mumbled something he couldn't make out.

"What was that? I didn't catch what you said."

"I can't drive! It's Wayne's truck. Plus, I got nowhere to go, man. If I lose this girl, I'm fucked. I'll lose my job, and that guy who come here, he be after me for sure. I guess I have to walk out, but I'm doing it with her. I got no choice."

He'd done his best, but he realized he wasn't going to convince him to let Lotte go. He had to do the next best thing, if he could. He dropped his bat on the floor and stepped aside from the door. "All right, I understand. You can go. Just relax. Don't hurt her, and please... stop choking her."

"Eric," Lotte gasped. "What are you doing?"

"Don't resist him. This is the only way. We have to give him what he's asking for."

Realization spread on her face as she relaxed into her captor's arms. "I'm ready. I won't fight you."

Siddique started pushing her away from the wall, but never took his eyes from Eric, who stood near the bed on the far side of the room. He gestured with the knife for Eric to stay back as he cautiously guided Lotte toward the doorway... and directly in front of the window.

Eric waved his arm.

An explosion of glass shot into the room with a thunderous crash. Siddique impulsively turned his head and screamed. The Afrit shot toward him, wings tucked tightly to its sides. Their bony protuberances extended menacingly in front of the ashen monster's head. The kidnapper madly turned and violently pushed Lotte in an attempt to escape the room. At that moment, Eric made for the knife in the terrified man's hand, but the Afrit got there first. The sharp points of its wings raked across Siddique's back and ripped a gash in his flesh. He dragged Lotte down with him as he cried out in agony and collapsed hard to the floor.

The beast's momentum carried it through the open door and out into the hallway. It collided with a resounding thud against the far wall.

Eric saw that Siddique had dropped the knife, so he dove onto him. They were nearly the same size, and now they both had injuries to cope with. He tried to pin the struggling man down, but Siddique was strong despite his wiry build, and his almost hysterical panic made him fight with reckless abandon. He quickly slipped out from Eric's grasp and reached for the fallen knife.

I can't let him get to that weapon.

With all his might, he lunged onto his opponent's back, wrapped his left arm around Siddique's neck, and began to pummel him repeatedly with his right hand.

Siddique howled in pain and fear, but still fought back. He grabbed Eric's right arm and gave it a mighty twist. The man's grasp was strong.

Eric couldn't free himself, and feared his arm might break. The pain reached a crescendo as he felt tendons begin to give way in his elbow when, suddenly, another shriek of agony rang out and the pressure finally relented.

He looked up and saw that the Afrit stood above them. Blood dripped from its barbed tail, and Siddique grasped at a wound in his left shoulder. He began to cry, seeming to sense the futility of continued struggle.

"I'm sorry, lady," he wailed. "I'm so sorry. It wasn't supposed to be like this. We'd never have hurt you. I wouldn't have let them hurt you. I take care of you, right, lady? I take care of you!"

The Afrit raised its deadly tail in the air and prepared a final killing strike.

"Wait!" Eric commanded. "Why are you killing him? I thought you liked to take your victims when they still had a little life left in them?"

'This one is extra. Too much for us now. We favor the one below.'

"Okay, then don't kill this guy. We'll deal with him. You can have the other."

He'd never intended to let Siddique go, with or without Lotte. He'd assumed this man was part of the bargain with the Afrit... doomed. Suddenly, however, he hesitated to simply let him die.

"Eric!" Lotte cried from where she'd crawled to get away from the melee. "Think of what he's seen. We can't just let him go. This way is... cleanest."

The Afrit loomed hesitantly above while Eric recovered Siddique's knife and positioned himself over the inconsolable and incapacitated man.

He extended his arm to Lotte. "Come here."

With effort, she crawled shakily toward him and met his embrace. The room began to spin with the euphoria of her touch.

"My God," he said. "I missed you so much. I was so scared."

"You didn't look frightened to me," she said tearfully into his shoulder, "but was this really your rescue plan?"

He laughed. "Totally. I had him right where I wanted him: knife at your throat... completely under control."

She laughed over her tears. "Little shit. I knew you'd figure it out somehow. Saving my life seems to be your forte. But what the hell is going on, and what do you plan to do with him?" She gestured at Siddique, who still lay on the floor, crying and clutching at his bleeding shoulder.

"I don't know, but, jeez... Lotte.... What are we gonna do, kill everyone who sees the Afrit or knows anything about a portal? This guy did a really stupid fucking thing, and he deserves to be punished, but does he deserve to *die*? I've already got more blood on my hands. I had to make a bargain with the Afrit to save you. That's done now. There's no going back from that, but if the damned thing doesn't want two victims right now... maybe there's another way."

She wiped streaks of tears from her face. It appeared she'd already cried away all her black mascara, so there wasn't the mess that usually resulted from these episodes.

"What are you thinking?"

"Let me handle it." In truth, he wasn't exactly sure what to do, but felt he could figure something out. "For now, go downstairs and send Olive up here with some rope."

"*Olive* is your accomplice? I suppose it makes sense, especially for bargaining with the Afrit."

"Exactly, but she's been really helpful the whole time. She even saved my life just now. Anyway, speaking of saving lives, get me that rope. We'll tie him up, and I'll see if I can do something for that cut. It's bleeding pretty bad."

She looked at him skeptically. "Very well. I hope you know what you're doing, but you did rescue me, even if I nearly died in the process. *Alter!* It looks like you nearly died too! Are you all right? You poor thing. I don't mean to sound ungrateful, it's just that there are so many things to think through. This whole thing is just so... *aaaarrgh...* crazy! But, Eric, thank you. You're my hero. You always have been, and you always will be. When we have time, you'll have to tell me everything. I can't wait to hear how clever you were."

He smiled as he once again hugged the love of his life. "Hey, we've got nothing but time, once we get the hell out of here, that is. So, let's get going, eh... so we can get going."

She hugged him once again, and then staggered past the Afrit through the door.

Eric turned his attention to the little beast. "When we get him tied up, you can go too... back to the garage, the big room where we came in. We'll set the portal up in there, and you'll have your spoils. Then our bargain will be complete."

The ashen creature gazed at him with empty, black eyes. Its tail twitched and its wings softly pulsed in obviously eager anticipation. The beast was a wolf among sheep, and Eric felt the weight of being the bearer of the lambs to slaughter.

CHAPTER 9

Unsurprisingly, Lotte had been right. There *was* a lot to think about, and as Eric went about completing the necessary and gruesome tasks before him, he contemplated the troubling larger questions.

This makes no sense. Who the hell gave these guys the keys and alarm code for this house? Is John Riggins the seller? Is the phony smiling real estate agent on the for sale sign involved somehow? Did the kidnappers steal the keys from the realty agency? Why bring Lotte here?

He also wondered as to the whereabouts of the man who'd been making the phone calls, and what Eric would say to him when he called tomorrow morning—assuming he did. Maybe John would just give up when he saw that his men, and his captive, were gone. Yet deep down, Eric feared that tonight wouldn't be the end of the situation.

He tied up Siddique with the rope Lotte brought him, and used the man's already tattered shirt to tend as best as possible to his wounded shoulder. Then he went outside and backed the van up to the garage. The exhausted trio unloaded the cases and set up the portal while the Afrit watched with unexpected and somewhat ominous patience.

Dragging Wayne into the garage weighed on Eric's soul as much as his painful back and arm. Olive had hit the large man quite forcefully. He barely stirred as they pulled him through the hall, down the little flight of stairs, and across the oil-stained cement floor. Had the circumstances been different, he'd have surely needed medical attention. As it was, only the last rites would be called for.

Well, that and a chair.

The Afrit was still too small and weak to *consume* its victim by holding him over the flame. So, they pressed one of the chintzy dining room chairs into service. They placed it on the floor of the garage near the black marble board, then laboriously hoisted Wayne into the seat and tied him to the back. In this spot, the flames could easily reach him from beneath. The Afrit seemed pleased.

How was I supposed to know they didn't really mean to kill Lotte? Even if I'd known, who's to say they wouldn't have changed their minds when I refused to hand over what they wanted? What choice did I have? It just felt like it was them or Lotte, and for me, that's really no choice at all.

At the moment, that knowledge provided little consolation. He knew when he'd made the bargain with the Afrit that it would eventually come to this. As he closed the door to the garage, he saw the bowls lit with flame. The portal already radiated its unearthly glow, and the ashen monster had taken position behind Wayne's limp body, which drooped in the cheap chair. This would add another image to the carousel of horror in Eric's troubled mind.

God help me, he briefly entreated, though he rapidly had a change of heart, fearing that God might actually show up, and Eric had no idea what the going rate for *His* services might be!

Leaving the Afrit to its own devices, Lotte and Olive collapsed wearily on the staged couch while Eric dragged himself back upstairs. He needed to talk with Siddique, an additional consideration among the myriad issues swirling in his head. He entered the second floor room where the prisoner lay, tied up and bleeding, on the bed.

"Where are you from?" He adjusted the makeshift bandage, which was already soaked with blood. "You don't sound like a Raleigh native."

Siddique was wary for a moment, but then answered. "I'm from Sierra Leone. Come here, maybe three years ago. I have family in the United States... fled the Civil War in my country back, maybe, fifteen years ago. My cousin said I can work with him, doing landscaping. He had his own business... doing good... but he got hurt, can't work no more. So, I get this job at the Alley Cat. Crappy job, crappy pay, no-good business... but it's all I can get. That's why I do this, with the lady. Need the money. Don't work out so good, me coming here. I'm desperate, man."

Eric leaned forward and stared straight at Siddique. "You're not desperate. You're dead."

His eyes went wide with fear. "You gonna kill me, man?"

"No, I don't need to. In a sense, you're already dead. The old you, anyway. That's what you're gonna have to accept. From this moment forward, Siddique... umm... what's your last name?"

"Alieu."

"From this moment forward, the old Siddique Alieu is dead. It'll be up to you to build a new one from his ashes. I'm willing to help you, but there's gonna be a price, and if you don't pay it, then that monster you saw *will* kill you. No second chances on that. It's too important, and the lives of people I love would be put at risk."

His look of terror subsided somewhat. "What do I have to do?"

"You have to keep your mouth shut. You can never, and I mean *never*, say anything to anyone about what you saw. You'll also have to go far away from here, leave your friends and family, and really limit contact for a while."

"Where will I go, man? What'll I do? I've got nothing, just half the money I was promised... was gonna get the other half when the job was done."

"I have an answer for you. Your shoulder is bleeding. Good thing you only met the pint-sized version of my little devil friend. The real monster might have sliced your head off."

He gulped.

"Anyway, it's too dangerous to take you to the emergency room. We'll go to a pharmacy, get some bandages to seal up that wound, and get you some fresh shirts. When we've fixed you up, we'll take you to the bus station. Is there anything critically important that you need from home, like your ID? Where do you live, anyway?"

"I have a room in an apartment, with some guys. My Green Card is in my wallet. It's just my clothes at home, and my bike. Oh, and my phone. We weren't supposed to have them on us when we did the job. The guy didn't want anyone being able to trace where we were. Wayne had to drive all the way home on Sunday to call our boss and tell him there was a problem."

Interesting. "Okay, forget your phone. Just find somewhere to get a pre-paid phone and use that for a while. At the bus station, you need to get your ass to Worcester, Massachusetts. When you're there, you're gonna call a woman named Margot. I'll write all this down for you, along with her number. She'll come get you... help you get set up... and she's gonna give you a job. It'll be a shit job, but it's how I started, and there's opportunity to learn and move up. This is the best I can do for you, Siddique. What do you say?"

He seemed confused but also obviously intrigued as he pondered his options. "Why you doing this, man?"

Good question. On the one hand, where else can I stick you where I can keep my eye on you? How better can I sweeten the pot to entice you to stay quiet than offer you a path forward? What I'm offering you serves my purposes, but really... it's more than that. Maybe I'm trying to make some kind of atonement. If so, it's probably completely insufficient, but at the moment, it's the best I can do. I feel a little bit better for at least making the attempt.

"Let me worry about that. We have to get out of here. I'll assume we have a deal. If you can help me find Wayne's first installment of the money, you can have that too. You've got to start completely fresh, no contact with any friends, and just a quick call to your cousin to let him know you're okay. Tell him you got a job out of state, and that the deal was too good to pass up. That's basically the truth. You just have to lay really low for a while, understand?"

"I understand. I did wrong. I pay the price... except not like Wayne. You kill him, right?"

"The creature you saw did. That's the bargain. We get what we want, it gets what it wants. You're lucky it didn't want you too. I wouldn't have been able to save you."

He slowly nodded as he took that in.

"Okay, we have to get moving, and I don't want you to bleed to death here. I'm gonna untie you. You won't fight me, right?"

He didn't.

Lotte bolted out of the van when they pulled up near the bus station. She'd held her tongue outside the Walgreens while Eric and Olive had tended to Siddique's wounds and helped him into a new t-shirt, but she'd become distraught when she found out where they were taking him, and why.

Olive still closely monitored Siddique, aluminum bat at the ready, so Eric hopped out and caught up with Lotte.

She turned on him when he touched her shoulder, tears in her eyes and a look of rage on her face. "He held a knife at my throat, and now you're going to give him a bloody *job*?"

He tried to explain his reasoning, that with Siddique nearby, they could keep an eye on him, as well as his own intense discomfort at the prospect of taking yet another life.

Clearly exhausted, she didn't have the strength to put up much of an argument. She angrily marched back to the van and threw open the side door. "Get out! You're lucky my boyfriend is so merciful. I'm not sure I'd have been so fucking magnanimous. I never want to see your face again. You should be ashamed of what you did!"

Siddique absorbed her venom without complaint. In truth, he looked completely chastened as he slipped out of the van and shuffled, head down, toward the bus station.

Lotte collapsed in the passenger's seat as they sped off. Eric drove for about a half-hour with a bag full of ice from a nearby 7-Eleven clutched to his swollen chin. Finally, the urgent need for sleep had overtaken him. Olive had likewise been exhausted, and of course, Lotte couldn't, or wouldn't, drive despite the ordeal she'd just been through.

Eric eventually pulled off of I-40 headed south toward Myrtle Beach, navigated onto Route 70, and finally brought the van to rest behind a giant Walmart Supercenter at about 4:30 a.m. The trio slept in the cargo area on the dirty packing blankets, squeezed into what space remained around the cases containing the portal and its various accessories.

"I think you could have left the case with all the documents in Southby," Lotte dryly observed as they fell asleep, seeming to have abandoned some of her fury.

Well, there's a perfect example of the 50-50-90 rule. Anytime you have a 50-50 chance of getting something right, there's a 90 percent probability you'll get it wrong. With Lotte, it's like more like 50-50-99.

He stopped grousing when she pressed her body close to him and told him how much she loved him. Soon after, he blissfully lost consciousness.

The light of the sun and the distant sound of passing cars woke him. Lotte was nowhere to be seen.

They'd cracked the back and side doors to get some ventilation in the stuffy van, which had no windows at all in the cargo area. In truth, the three of them smelled awful after the exertion of their ordeal, and Lotte doubly so for her three-day confinement. The fresh air had been welcome, but the open doors had allowed her to slip out unheard.

Olive still slept soundly, so he crept silently out of the van and scanned the area. At a little past 7:00 a.m., the sun just began to make its presence felt in the morning sky. They'd parked near a forested area to the side of the building. After a few moments, he spotted Lotte farther toward the rear of the parking lot, sitting with her back to a scraggly tree as she gazed into the dense underbrush beyond.

He quietly approached and knelt beside her. "You okay? How long have you been here?"

She stared into the trees with a distant and troubled look. "I slept for a bit, but... well... I don't know. I got this feeling of panic, like I was falling. It woke me up. I just felt like I needed to get up... think about some things."

"Are you still angry with me?"

"Angry at you? No, why should I be? Siddique? I'll admit, I'm still angry with him—furious, really. Probably always will be. But no, I'm not mad at you. I think what you did was brilliant, once I got used to the idea. In retrospect, it was probably the best thing possible. I don't want or need to be a part of that, but I totally trust you to handle it."

He felt relieved. "So, what's on your mind? Just kind of recovering from what happened? They didn't hurt you, did they?"

"No. Well, yes... a bit, I suppose... when they first grabbed me. That big one put his hand around my mouth. I thought I was going to suffocate. He told me he'd break my neck if I struggled, and I believed him. I knew he could. They threw me in the truck, and someone put a bag or something over my head. When we got to the house, they tossed me in the closet. After that, they came in with those ski masks on and showed me the picture... demanded to know where the object was. Like I'd know! They never touched me, but they threatened me. I tried not to cry, or beg, or bargain, or go through all that bullshit that captives go through. I tried not to show it, but... Eric, I was scared. There were times I worried I might actually die."

"I'm so sorry. I came as quickly as I could. I didn't want to leave you there so long. I just didn't know what else to do."

She flashed him a weak smile. "Don't be foolish. I'm not upset with you. I knew you were out there. That was the only thing that kept me going. I *knew* you'd know what to do. I knew you'd come. I just *hated* being in that position. I felt so... *powerless*, so out of control. It made me... how can I say it... it made me question. What if it had all ended there? What would I have had to show for my life? Is there anything of value that I've really contributed? What was the purpose of it?"

He'd heard a lot of things out of Lotte's mouth over the years, but this truly surprised him. "You've got to be kidding me. You're like an archaeology rock star. People look up to you, Lotte. They're blown away by you. *I'm* blown away by you! Okay, maybe you haven't contributed a lot to the field yet, but you're still a freaking student. All that's gonna come, but given where you are, you should be proud of your accomplishments."

She smiled and put her hand on his knee, possibly the one part of his body that didn't ache from the violent encounters of the previous night. Still, she shook her head. "You're so sweet. I do love you so, but that's not what I'm talking about... *accomplishments*. In fact, that's exactly what I started worrying about in that damned closet. I've allowed my life to be defined by my *accomplishments...* all the things I've done... or am doing... or want to do. All I could think about while I sat there, though... sat there, in the dark...."

She started to cry. "All I could think about was... was... well... what a damned mess I made of Italy."

What? "You mean our trip to Italy? What does that have to do with anything?"

"Yes, our trip, if you can call it that once I'd ruined it, and it's not just Italy. Italy is just what I kept coming back to, such a perfect example of how everything I want to *do* keeps me from *doing* what I probably *ought* to be doing, but don't... if that makes any sense."

It took him a minute, but he eventually untangled her words. It began to dawn on him what she was saying.

"Umm, I guess I understand. My only hesitation is that I think you *ought* to be doing exactly what you *want* to be doing. If that's taking field measurements with Werner equipment, then that's fine. I knew it would be like that with you, and I accepted it, and I still do. If I have issues, it's more that I'd like you to be happy while you're taking those field measurements, and that I wish I could find a bit more of a place in your day-to-day world, but I don't think you *ought* to be doing different things... unless you want to be."

She wiped tears from her thankfully mascara free eyes. "Well, I suppose that's the question, isn't it? I guess, in that closet, with the prospect of dying, I actually thought about what I'd have preferred—to have spent a day with you, or to have gone to Milan with Alberto. It seemed so important at the time, but now... I wonder if I made the right choice."

He smiled. "Wow. That's really nice to hear. Honestly, I'd have thought you would have enjoyed a day with Alberto regardless. He certainly seemed smitten with you."

She laughed as she wiped her nose with the back of her hand. "Smitten? Well, there's no question he was being especially nice. I suspect he wanted a good look at the Werner equipment—he's been dying to work for them for years—but smitten? I doubt it. You do know Alberto is gay, right?"

His eyes widened with surprise. *Umm, no, I did not know that.*

"Demetrios, the Greek guy who was around a bit, is his boyfriend, or at least, he was at the time. Who knows who Alberto's off with now. You weren't jealous of him, were you?"

"No, not at all." *Yes, completely!*

"All right, but Alberto or no, that day comes back to me, and I just wonder if I should have made a different choice, or a bunch of other different choices so that day would seem more trivial."

"Or you could have just let me drive, or brought me along. It doesn't have to be either-or."

"I *know* you'd have come. I know you'll do anything, and I appreciate that and try not to take advantage of it, even though I almost certainly do... but that's not the question. That's not what I'm thinking about. The question is, what did *I* really want to do that day, or lots of days like that? I guess it takes sitting in a dark closet thinking I'm going to die to make me even consider that in the end, when I really think about the true value of my life, maybe I'd have made a different choice. I don't know, but there it is. There's nothing for it now."

He anxiously bit his lower lip. What he heard should have sounded like music to his ears, but instead, he found it deeply troubling. Surely, he wished at times that Lotte would take her foot off the gas a little, be a bit less of a hare and not always have to charge forward, but he didn't want her to be intimidated into that by a traumatic situation. Her confidence and drive were as much a part of her makeup as her keen intelligence and her casual, what-you-see-is-what-you-get charisma. He could accept if she made different choices at times, but this seemed to be a deeper questioning, and behind her words, he perceived something he'd only rarely seen in the girl who, for him, bent space and time—fear.

"I hear you. It's probably something you'll need to think about, which is exactly what you were doing before I so rudely interrupted you."

She giggled. "You silly. It helps to talk to you. I don't know, maybe this is all nothing. Possibly, I'm just rattled and not thinking clearly. I'll say this, though: the only thing I had to fall back on in that closet was knowing you loved me, and that I love you. Maybe that means something, *Ja*?"

"You sound like my grandma. It means a lot to me, that's for sure. I just think you need to take some time to figure out what it really means to you. If it means you spend more days with me and fewer with Alberto, though, then I'm all for it."

She laughed. "*Tüddelkram!* I can't believe you were jealous of him. That's as ridiculous as me being envious of Olive."

Yikes!

After a quick breakfast at the Waffle House across the street from the Walmart Superstore, they hit the road. Exhausted as they still were, getting to Olive's uncle's house seemed the priority, so they pressed on.

The food had finally lulled Lotte into much-needed sleep. She lay on one of the blankets in the back, and barely stirred when Eric's phone rang a little after 10:00 a.m.

Late, he observed with some amusement. This time, he didn't bother to pull over.

Olive rode shotgun. She swiped to answer the call and put the phone on speaker before she passed it to him.

"John!" he called in cheerful greeting. "So nice to hear from you. Having a good morning?"

"How the hell did you find her?" he barked, barely able to contain the rage in his voice.

"Well, it's kind of a secret. I could tell you, but then I'd have to kill you. Like we did your two men. Not exactly top-notch talent, but I guess it's hard to find good help at five-thousand dollars a head. I suppose they did put up a bit of a fight."

"Those weren't my men! Those were just some damned hired goons. My men are the best. They're better than the best!"

Olive and Eric's gazes locked in wide-eyed shock and wonder.

This guy is Black Arrow, or he was!

Eric brought his finger to his lips and urged Olive to remain silent. This didn't present a problem as her hands were tightly clenched over her mouth.

The man on the phone went on. "I will admit it, though: I underestimated you. I have no idea how you pulled it off, but impressive as it may be, it ain't gonna change a damned thing. You're still gonna give me what I want."

"Why would I do that? You have no leverage on us now."

He chuckled. "I don't? Well, Mr. Eric Schneider, who works at Schneider Industrial Flooring and cohabitates with Ms. Liselotte Schwarz at 67 Rogers Avenue, Somerville Massachusetts... it seems I know quite a bit about you and that feisty little filly. I could grab one or both of you any time I wanted, when you least expect it. Or, maybe I'll just pop one of you... get you back for all the trouble you've put me to, and that's to say nothing of what I might do to Olivia Carter, student of history at the Savannah State University, currently residing at—"

"Okay! You made your point. What do you want?"

"I want what I always wanted, you damned fool. I want that statue thing, the one from the picture, and I'm through fucking around. You're gonna get it to me today. No more delays! Got it?"

Eric gave a deep sigh. Just as he'd feared, John had no intention of giving up, and he clearly posed a threat to all of them. Much as Eric hated the idea, he realized this guy would have to be eliminated. The problem was, no one had seen him, so they couldn't just send the Afrit out on its own. They'd have to lure John to them.

"All right, if you insist on pushing this, I guess there's no choice. We're headed to get the thing now. It's gonna take us a few hours, plus we all have to get some rest. I have no idea how portable it is. We haven't really seen it yet. So, you're gonna have to call back later, say like four o'clock this afternoon? I'm not trying to jerk you around. You'll have it tonight."

"Just a reminder, you little twerp: you call the police, you're *all* dead. I think you finally get my point, so I'll give you one last chance, but this is it. You hear me?"

"I hear you. No police. You'll get what you're asking for. I promise."

The phone went dead. Eric and Olive stared at each other in horror until he broke the silence. "He's Black Arrow. He works for your father's company—or did. He said *his* men. Maybe he's like a manager or something. Do you know any of your dad's co-workers? Ever meet any of them?"

"A couple of times. That day I went to their facility, I met a bunch of people, mostly out at the shooting range. I don't remember any of their names or what they did. My daddy just introduced us real quick-like. I met two others right after Christmas last year, at my daddy's condo. They came over one day when I was visiting, had some beers. They was nice. One feller was named Clarence. He was always laughing. The other one was more the quiet type, but he said he'd been robbed recently, just like my daddy had. I don't remember his name. I think both of them did similar stuff like my daddy, and the quiet guy was even in Iraq with him. They weren't like managers or nuthin', though."

"Hmmm.... Who owns Black Arrow? Is it a private company?"

"I have no idea. Let me look it up on my phone." She spent a moment searching. "Here it is. Black Arrow, a private military company. Founder and CEO Mr. Blake Harris."

"*What*? Harris! That was the last name of the realty agent on the sign at Chalk Road. My God, what if that's, like, his wife or something? No wonder he could get the keys and the alarm code, and that explains why this guy has access to your father's email. Olive, I think your dad's boss is John Riggins."

"But why would my daddy's boss be after this thing, and if he is, why don't he just ask my daddy for it? Why would he come after me?"

"I'm not certain. The only logical explanation is that he didn't want your father to know he planned to take it. He must have been aware your dad had it, or thought he *might* have had it. Otherwise, why watch his email? I don't know. It's still confusing, but the pieces are starting to come into place, and we'll have a chance to get more answers."

"Why, what are we gonna do?"

"We're gonna do what we did before. We're gonna give him what he's asking for."

"You mean feed him to that Afrit thing, like we did with Wayne."

Eric nodded.

"I wanted to watch, but Lotte said I shouldn't, that it was pretty awful. I reckon she was right. I just never killed nobody before, or took part in anything like that. I just thought maybe somebody ought to have stayed with him there... you know... at the end."

He remembered the horror of hearing Dr. Esfahani being consumed. "Lotte was right, but it's not really the end for Wayne. In some sense, he'll live on in the Afrit, be a part of its makeup, maybe even its intelligence at some level. We don't really know, but that may be as close to immortality as a human can achieve, odd as that may sound."

"Do you believe in God, Eric? Do you believe in an afterlife in Heaven?"

"There was a time I'd have answered 'no' to that question, but with what I've seen, I have to say, I'm just not sure anymore. It's possible, but from what I've learned, the reality isn't really like the myths. It's similar—you can see where the stories came from—but there's a lot of misunderstanding and twisted facts. It seems like human religions interpret these beings in their own way, and the beings themselves start to conform to those expectations. It's weird. Lotte described it as *symbiotic*. So, I really don't know what to think, but I'm more open to the possibility than I used to be. What about you?"

"I was brought up believing Jesus Christ is my Lord and Savior, but now I'm almost like the opposite of you. Seeing all this makes me wonder. I mean, that damn ol' thing looks exactly like Satan, but it helped us save Lotte from those bad men, and it don't really act evil. It didn't kill that feller you let go when you asked it not to. Heck, we were as responsible for Wayne gettin' killed as the Afrit was, and I don't think I'm evil either. Maybe things aren't as simple as everybody says they are."

I can't disagree with that. I've never found life to be simple. Dealing with these otherworldly beings only added to the complexity. She's now discovering the pitfalls of her newfound knowledge, just like I did. I tried to warn her, but it wasn't enough. It could never have been enough.

CHAPTER 10

It wasn't long after he talked with John Riggins, or as they now assumed, Blake Harris, that Eric pulled the van into the driveway of an old farmhouse on Happy Drive in Longs, South Carolina. He parked next to a motorboat strapped onto a trailer hitch.

Lotte yawned as she stretched. She hadn't stirred the entire trip. "Where are we? Are we there?"

"Well, we're somewhere," Eric replied, happy to be on Happy Drive, but still troubled by the continued threat from the orchestrator of her kidnapping. "This is Olive's uncle's house. She said we could stop here, clean up a little, and then it's just a short way to the fishing lodge where the portal is."

"*Alter!* I've never needed a shower more in my life, and I've done fieldwork all day in 38 Grad."

Olive and Eric exchanged a confused look, not knowing exactly how hot that might really be.

"It don't look like my uncle is here," Olive observed. "His truck is gone, and Rebel would be barking his head off if he heard us coming. They might have gone down to the lodge to start the clean-up after the big flood."

"Is that a problem?" Lotte asked with concern. "Can we not get inside? I mean, I was really hoping for that shower."

"Oh, no. Uncle Clint don't care. He'll be happy to have the company. He lives alone in this big ol' place. This was the house he and my daddy grew up in, and he took care of my grandparents until they both died. Now he's here all alone. My uncle is sort of a quiet type anyway, but he don't mind visitors from time to time, and he likes me... probably more than my daddy does." She scowled briefly before she hefted her bag out of the van and strolled toward the house.

Lotte and Eric followed, though slowly, as the bruises on Eric's back were now quite painful, having stiffened up overnight and during the drive.

"Just leave those," Lotte scolded. "I'll come back to get them."

"No, no, it's fine. It's not that far to the door. I just need a shower too, and some ibuprofen. Should have taken some before. I'll be good."

"You poor thing. This always seems to happen. Good thing you go to the gym."

"Seriously, what I really need to do is start taking self-defense lessons. I never figured fighting skills would be that useful to me. Boy, did *that* turn out to be wrong."

Olive just walked in. Apparently, the door wasn't locked. The old house seemed to be well-tended. Pieces of potentially antique furniture that likely belonged to Olive's grandparents created a genteel ambiance.

"Y'all come on upstairs," Olive said. "I'll put you in the actual guest room. I'll sleep down here in my daddy's room."

Bathroom. Shower. The words took on almost Homeric proportions. They dropped their bags on the bed, and after a short, "you first, no you first, no you first" argument, Lotte made a hasty exit to wash off the grime of her captivity.

Eric painfully peeled off his shirt and examined himself in the old-timey mirror, on the old-timey dresser, in the old-timey bedroom. Angry, greenish-purple bruises had formed on his chin from Wayne's kick, and on his back and shoulders where he'd been lashed by the chair. His elbow still felt shaky from Siddique's savage twisting.

I'm lucky no bones were broken. Screw the self-defense lessons, what I really need is armor!

In truth, he needed sleep, and despite his best efforts, it overtook him while Lotte was cleaning up.

When she emerged from the bathroom, she woke him with a kiss to the cheek as she slid into bed beside him. She wore only a towel, and her damp hair smelled of some unidentifiable variety of synthetic citrus.

"It's all yours, unless you want to take a nap. You must be exhausted."

"I could sleep for a week. Sadly, we don't have the luxury. The guy who's behind your kidnapping called while we were on the road. You're not gonna believe this, but Olive and I think it's her father's boss at Black Arrow who's behind what's going on, a guy named Blake Harris."

"Why would he do this? What possible motivation could he have to kidnap me? Of course, I suppose Olive was the target, but still, why didn't he just ask Olive's father where the portal was?"

"Your guess is as good as mine. He's not giving up, though, and he knows who we are, and where we live. He probably has all kinds of connections for information, including with law enforcement, which is why he keeps saying he'll know if we contact the police. He's threatening to grab us, or hurt us, if we don't give him the portal. It's something we're gonna have to... *deal* with."

Her shoulders sagged, and the look of happiness faded from her freshly washed face. "This is not how I anticipated things going. Not at all. Maybe you were right. Maybe we should have just destroyed the fire portal. I never wanted this power... never wanted to be judge, jury, and executioner. That was exactly why I opposed Dr. Esfahani, but look at us now... and it's my fault."

"Lotte, you're perfectly aware that I was never comfortable about keeping that thing, but you know what? I've come to believe I was wrong. Without the Afrit's help, Charun might still be out there killing people, and sweetie, it helped us free you too. Okay, maybe these people didn't intend to hurt you, but they might easily have changed their minds if I didn't give them this new portal, which you know perfectly well we can't do. Trust me, I'm not happy about it either, but this is different from using the creature... how would you say it... *proactively*. We didn't start this. This isn't our agenda, it's his. What do you think would happen if we're right about what this thing is, and this guy got his hands on it? We didn't start this, Lotte, but we have to finish it. This isn't your fault at all. I know, deep down, you recognize this is the truth. I'm just trying to give you a little reminder."

Tears welled in her eyes. "Eric Schneider, I knew I kept you around for some reason." She quickly turned and began to rummage in her bag for some clothes. "Now go shower. You're right, our time is short. We have to go see this thing and figure out what to do."

He did as requested, forcing his aching muscles to lift him from the bed, and forcing his eyes away from his beautiful love as she threw off her towel and began to change.

Just past noon, they finished unloading the flight cases from the van into a corner of the barn that now served as a storage area and garage for Uncle Clint's truck.

"We'll go to the fishing lodge and see if he's there," Olive suggested. "If so, we can all go to lunch together. I'm Starvin' Marvin!"

It sounded good to Lotte and Eric. Breakfast had been quite a while ago.

The lodge was on Catfish Circle in Little River, a somewhat indistinct township tucked between Longs and North Myrtle Beach farther to the southeast. It was only about a fifteen minute drive, but once they got south of Longs on Highway 9, evidence of the floods rapidly became apparent. It looked like part of the road had been washed out at some point. The pavement was still strewn with mud and debris from the winding Waccamaw River, which had jumped its banks.

Olive and Lotte shared the passenger seat of the van. Lotte sat squashed next to the door, but didn't particularly seem to mind.

She must travel like this a lot when she's doing fieldwork.

He took pleasure in getting a small glimpse into a part of her life that was largely closed and mysterious to him, and noted with some amusement how his normally fussy and demanding girlfriend could so easily and without any commotion go with the flow when it suited her.

Olive surveyed the damage. "I never seen nuthin' like this! It was way worse when I was here last week. The river was still cresting, and this ain't even the part that flooded worst. Take this here left, then Catfish Circle is straight ahead. When Uncle Clint and I came down here last Thursday, we couldn't even drive all the way to the house. The road was a mess. We put the boat, the one you saw back at the house, into the water down yonder and cruised right up into the back yard. That's where I took the picture, after my uncle waded through the muck and opened them back doors."

The road was still a mess, but at this point seemed passable. Thick mud covered the weathered asphalt, which became a barely navigable dirt path when Catfish Circle proper began. To the right sat a large pond, which Eric guessed was the source of catfish.

Imagine that.

The fishing lodge lay ahead and to the left, down an incline that led toward some sort of tributary of the Waccamaw. There were no other houses in this area, and he saw little evidence of other traffic, but some vehicle, or vehicles, had been this way. Several tire tracks crossed each other, though nothing looked particularly fresh. When they reached the point where Catfish Circle looped to the right, an opening in the dense underbrush appeared to the left.

Olive pointed. "That's it. The lodge is down there, probably two hundred yards or so."

Eric drove a bit closer, and a narrow dirt road came into view. The rutted trail was barely wider than the cargo van itself, which, after its muddy journey, no longer gleamed quite as brightly.

"Boy," he said. "I don't know. I can't tell if we've got enough wheel clearance for this. I can see truck tracks, so your uncle has clearly done it. I'm just not sure the van will make it, and I can't under any circumstance afford to damage this vehicle. I think we have to walk."

Olive and Lotte begrudgingly agreed, and both grabbed their hats and water bottles from the dashboard and jumped out.

Eric parked by the side of the road and joined them. Soon, all three trundled along the winding, muddy path. The steady hum of insects provided the only sound in this remote place, still warm and muggy despite it being mid-October. The soft ground absorbed their footsteps and permitted only the slightest *squish* to be audible. They passed a lazy pond to the right, birds visible as they darted between the trees, their branches overhanging the surface like waterfalls of green.

Eventually, the dense underbrush started to thin, and the roof of a small house peeked above the trees ahead. The trio entered a cleared area, and passed a beat-up old red Chevrolet pickup truck parked near the end of the winding road. Two intimidating rifles were visible, secured in a rack inside the back window.

The lodge itself was an elaborate cabin of weathered wood, stained a dark brown. It had two stories, sort of. The top floor sat at ground level where they stood, but a lower level straddled a fairly steep incline that led down to the river. The portal was apparently set up in this semi-basement area. The double doors visible in Olive's photo were toward the back of the structure, where they faced the water.

Olive walked up to the front door and knocked. "Uncle Clint! Y'all here? It's Olive, and I brought some friends."

Almost immediately, a dog began to bark behind the house, down the incline toward the water. "That's Rebel. They must be round back. Let's go down over here."

She led them to the left of the house, where a stairway of long wooden frames filled with gravel skirted the side of the building. They'd hardly started descending when a large gray dog with floppy ears, short hair, and a stubby little six-inch tail rounded the corner at the bottom of the hill and froze in eager anticipation.

"Here Rebel. Here boy!"

The dog bounded up the stairs toward her. They met with a surprisingly gentle impact, given the dog's size and momentum, and she stroked his head and told him what a "good boy" he was, though she gave a yelp of her own when her hands came away caked with mud.

"Gawd, you're a dirty mess! What the hell you gotten yourself into there, and what happened to your front paws? They're all ripped up and bloody. Your daddy's gonna be right furious with you. Let's go find daddy. Come on boy!"

Rebel gave Lotte and Eric a quick sniff, but then ran ahead as Olive started back down the stairs. Eric noted that the dog's paws were quite mangled, as if he'd been scratching incessantly at something, but then, dogs will be dogs, and what did he know about this beast? Maybe he did that all the time.

When they reached the bottom, they saw a scraggly yard, now bestrewn with mud and debris from the flood. It sloped gently down to the river. A couch, two chairs, and a decimated pressboard coffee table, which now looked more like soaked kitty litter than furniture, sat on the mucky grass. Eric recognized most of the items from Olive's picture. Clint had clearly dragged them outside to dry after being immersed in the overflowing waters.

If Lotte noticed these things, she gave no indication. Once around the corner, she made a beeline for the double glass doors that still stood open, presumably to air out the lower level. She walked to the threshold and eagerly looked inside, but then stopped cold.

"It's gone! It's not here! Where did it go, and what the hell happened to the floor?"

Olive and Eric walked to her side and looked over her shoulder. Eric didn't know what to make of what he saw.

Olive gasped. "Oh, my gawd! What the H-E Double L happened to the fuckin' floor? Pardon my French."

At the back of the room, near the stairs that led to the upper level, a circular crater had been left in the floor. It seemed about three or four inches deep at the sides, and sunk down about a foot in the middle. The entire indentation was about four to five feet in diameter, exactly the size of the circular part of the portal, which Olive had described to Lotte because it had been underwater in her photograph. It was as if the whole thing had burrowed directly down into the ground, churning the earth within its perimeter and shredding the cheap linoleum flooring, parts of which still littered the sides and the bottom of the circular depression.

"This cannot be good," Lotte commented with dread. "Olive, where's your uncle? We need to find out what's going on here."

"Uncle Clint!" Olive called into the room. "Are you upstairs? Uncle Clint, it's Olive! Where are you?" Rebel started to bark again from where he stood, close to the river near a copse of trees. "I don't think he's in there. It's a small place, and the walls are paper thin. I remember hearing my daddy snoring in the next room when I was a little girl. 'Bout drove me bonkers. My uncle would have heard me for sure if he was in there."

"Where else could he be?" Eric asked. "His truck is here. He has to be around somewhere."

She slapped her forehead. "Well dang! He's probably in the boathouse, over yonder. That's why Rebel is over there barking his fool head off. Come on, it's just past those trees there."

Lotte and Eric followed as she led the way toward the water. A small wooden dock came into sight. It listed precariously to one side as it stretched out into the river. Rebel seemed overjoyed they were headed in his direction. The big, but by all indications friendly, dog leapt and circled, then led the way toward the structure that incrementally came into view from behind the trees. A large, corrugated metal shed with a sliding door, big enough to house two good-sized motorboats, sat near the end of the wooden dock. A padlock held the door shut, but the lock wasn't closed. Rather, someone had simply hooked it into the slots that secured the opening.

"He can't be in there," Lotte observed. "He didn't lock himself inside. We need to be careful. There may be something that he wanted to keep contained."

Cautiously, Eric went up to the door and rapped his fist on the rusty metal. "Mr. Carter, are you in there?"

They all listened and heard a noise. It sounded like rough, hoarse breathing, then a cough, then more hoarse breathing, then another cough, and then—

"Help!" The voice was choked, and constrained, but unmistakable.

Olive surged forward. "I think that's him! Uncle Clint, are you okay? Is that you?"

They heard more coughing. "Olive Oil, is that you? My gawd, Honey, if that's you, get in here and help me! Please!"

She madly started fighting to remove the padlock from its slots. "That's him! Nobody calls me Olive Oil but Uncle Clint. He sounds terrible."

Eric gently removed her shaking hands from where she struggled. "Okay, calm down. We need to keep our heads and stay alert. Don't rush anything. There could be serious trouble here. You two stand back. I'll get the lock out and open the door. Get ready to run if necessary. Why the hell didn't we bring the baseball bats?"

"My uncle's guns are in his truck. Maybe we should get them."

"I assume those are locked in the rack, and the keys are probably on him. I think we just need to be ready. Are you ready?"

Both women nodded and retreated a short distance back. Rebel sat by their side, silent and expectant, like Eric had been at the airport when Lotte arrived from Berlin two years ago—back when life had been overflowing with *Möglichkeit.* Now, it seemed as if dangers lurked around every corner.

He slipped the unfastened lock from the slots and cracked the door. Rebel instantly made for the opening and began to paw pathetically at the threshold. Eric looked down and saw scratch marks on the corrugated metal, exactly where the dog feebly churned his blood-stained forequarters.

He's been desperately trying to get in.

Encouraged, he grabbed Rebel's collar so the dog wouldn't rush inside, and pulled the door open a bit more. He peered into the darkness. The shed stunk from stale pee. In the light from the cracked door, he could see a boat to the left and that the right berth sat empty.

That's probably the space for the boat we saw on the trailer at the farm.

Suddenly, something moved—something on the ground behind the boat, at the left and the back of the shed. It was a person, a big person. It looked like a man, and it looked like he fought against ropes that bound his ankles together and his arms behind his back—exactly like they'd tied up Wayne last night—restrained, unconscious, and unknowingly, waiting to die.

Eric shuddered. He threw the sliding corrugated metal door wide open and released Rebel's collar. The dog shot into the reeking, dingy shed, and he reluctantly followed.

"Come on!"

Olive and Lotte didn't hesitate, and soon all three were crouched around the man who struggled on the floor.

Olive tried holding back the dog, who practically smothered the prone man in his excitement. "Uncle Clint! What happened? Are you okay? Well, obviously you're not okay, but I didn't mean it like that. I mean are you okay, like are you seriously hurt... or, like, did somebody hurt you... or like—"

"Olive," Lotte sternly but sympathetically cut in. "Let's get him untied and give him some water. He's clearly been here for a while. One step at a time."

She got the point and focused on untying her uncle's feet while Eric worked on his hands.

Soon, the poor man was free of his bonds. He righted himself with difficulty and sat with his back to the wall as he massaged his rope burned wrists.

"Water, please," he croaked. "Water."

Olive handed him her water bottle, and he downed it instantaneously. With minor hesitation, Lotte handed him hers, which he likewise consumed. "Oh, my Gawd!" he said as he gulped for breath. "Thank you so much. I've been here for almost two damn days. Jesus, I'm so sorry. I pissed my goddamned pants. I know I smell awful. I'm so embarrassed. After all I did for that motherfucker, he ties me up and leaves me here like this! I'd have died had y'all not come along. Olive Oil, Honey, you saved my miserable life."

"Uncle Clint, you ain't miserable. I love you! I can't believe someone did this to you. What happened?"

Lotte knelt directly in front of the shaking man. "Yes, Mr. Carter, we need to know exactly what happened and where the portal... umm... the *object*, or *sculpture*, or whatever you call it—the thing in the room that was flooded.... Where is it?"

"I'm right appreciative of the water you gave me, but can I ask who you are, missy, and what all this is to you?"

Olive jumped in. "These are my friends, Uncle Clint... Lotte and Eric. Lotte is an archaeologist, like me. Well, actually, not like me at all. She's really smart and knows all about technology and computers and such, and digital modeling and data archiving. She's what I wish I was. This is her boyfriend, Eric. They're just super wonderful, and know all about... well, things that you just wouldn't believe. They think that dang ol' sculpture Daddy brought back from Iraq is important somehow. And Uncle Clint, I've seen things with my own eyes, incredible and unbelievable things, so I think they're right. Please tell 'em what happened. It's super important. I just know it is."

Clint seemed slightly stupefied by the onslaught of information and Olive's obvious elation.

"Please start from the beginning," Lotte quietly prompted him. "Any detail might be critical."

"Well, my Olive Oil speaks highly of you two, so I'm pleased to make your acquaintance. I've seen some gawdamned unbelievable shit these past couple of days myself. Pardon my language."

Lotte made a dismissive gesture.

Wait until Olive's uncle hears her swear in German. He'll stop worrying about his foul language then.

"Anyway, on Monday afternoon, I come out here after lunch to start fixin' things up after that damned flood. Waters had finally gone down, and I was able to get the truck down the driveway. I started loadin' out the furniture, and noticed that ridiculous sculpture my dumbass brother brought back from I-Rak had sunk into the gawddamned ground. Now how the hell am I supposed to fix that?"

"Was the sculpture still there?" Lotte urgently asked. "If so, where is it now?"

"I'm a-getting' to that. Yeah, it was there, sunk into the damned mud. Ripped right through the flooring too. I figured I'd get the furniture out, then deal with that stupid thing. It comes apart, you know. I was the one put the fool contraption together."

"How did you know the way to assemble it?"

He laughed. "Well, missy, damned if it didn't come with instructions. There's marks on the ends of each piece, like little scratches. All you gotta do is find the two marks that match and slide the pieces together. Sets up in no time. When I got it, it was all taken apart in a couple of boxes Lucas mailed to me when he got back Stateside."

"I assume Lucas is your brother? Do you know where and how he got the sculpture?"

"Yeah, he's my dumbass kid brother. Sorry, Olive Oil, no offense to you."

Olive simply shook her head. She seemed to have heard things like that from her uncle many times.

"Anyway, Lucas got the thing in I-Rak, and there's supposedly an interesting story behind it, though I personally think it's all bullshit. You kids remember the I-Rak invasion in 2003? Well, about four months after our troops kicked the living shit out of their country, they trapped two of Saddam Hussein's sons in some kind of safehouse in Mosul, which I guess is north of Baghdad. They tried to get them out, but that place was fortified, like, and those bastards decided to fight. So, we blew the motherfucking shit out of the house in a missile strike and killed everyone inside."

"Yeah," Eric interjected. "Uday and Qusay Hussein. They were both killed."

Everyone stared at him, surprised.

"Hey, I'm a history major. What can I say?"

"Right," Clint went on. "So, the Army plans to bulldoze this house. They don't want it to become some kind of shrine to the damn Hussein family. Before they can flatten the place, though, the fucking CIA go in there souvenir hunting. It was a big outrage, but what the hell were the I-Rakis really gonna do about it? Supposedly, that sculpture was one of the things they pulled out of the rubble. Apparently, it had been disassembled in a couple of metal boxes, so it survived the bombing and the collapse of the house."

"That was 2003," Lotte said with astonishment, "twelve years ago. Your brother can't have had it that long, and how did he get it from the CIA?"

"He didn't... well... not exactly. These CIA guys, they took the thing back to their safe building in Mosul. They had no idea what the fuck to do with it, so for a while, it just sat around. Eventually, when things started to settle down, what's the first thing come into these people's minds? Drinking... but try to get a damned drink in Mosul! So, they set up their own gawddamned tiki bar in the safe building, and someone has the bright idea to put this sculpture together and use it as a decoration."

Lotte put her palm to her forehead. "I don't believe it."

"I told you. The whole story reeks of bullshit to me. In any case, that thing sat there until Blackwater took over protection services for VIPs and State Department people from the CIA. They moved into the building, and now it was Blackwater's tiki bar. Apparently, nobody thought this thing was especially valuable. Honestly, I think they're right. It's as ugly as all get out, and it's just made of damned plastic. Hard as shit, but it can't be worth a good gawddamned."

"You'd be surprised," Eric wryly commented, "but didn't Blackwater get kicked out of Iraq at some point?"

"They sure did! Bunch of stupid fuckups. That's why I hate this private military crap. Serve your damned country and behave like representatives of the greatest nation on Earth. This for-profit war shit is disgusting, and I've told Lucas that. He just laughs, says I'm old fashioned. Anyway, yeah, Blackwater got their asses tossed in 2007 for all manner of nefarious crapola. That's when Black Arrow, among others, got the I-Rak contract. They took over VIP protection services in Mosul with offices in the same building."

"Daddy went over in... when... 2009?" Olive asked.

"Yeah, around then. He was there about two years, but round about the end of 2011, the American troops started to pull the hell out, and most of the contractors went with them. Lucas and a few other Black Arrow employees were tasked with shutting the place down. They shredded documents, destroyed computers, gawd knows what else. Then, he remembers the gawddamned tiki bar and this stupid statue. Apparently, my dumbass brother took a shine to the fool thing and decided to pack it up and take it with him. It fits in a couple of duffle bags. In fact, that's where it is now."

"It is?" Lotte shrieked. "Where?"

Clint gestured in the direction of the fishing lodge. "Up the house. I had to pack it up. I was under orders."

"From whom?"

"Oh, missy, this is where it really starts to get interesting."

CHAPTER 11

Eric began to get nervous.

Someone tied Clint up, and that someone, or someones, might be coming back.

"Mr. Carter," he said, "do you think you can move? Much as I want to hear the rest of your story, I'm feeling like we need to get going."

"I hear you, son. My legs are just starting to loosen up, and I'm not feeling as dizzy-like. Gimme just another few minutes and I think I can walk. Anyway, it won't take me long to tell you what happened."

Eric reluctantly assented. "All right, but I'm gonna keep watch on this door. I just want to make sure no one is coming."

"Makes sense. I'll see if I can get these loosened up quick. The ropes cut off the circulation in my feet, and they're stinging like hell right about now." He massaged his legs and slowly moved his boots back and forth. The labor of that activity was clearly apparent. "Anyway, as I was saying, I'd just about finished bringing out the furniture when Rebel starts a-barkin'. I look over at what's bothering him, and gawddamn, what do you think I saw?"

Oh, I don't know, a giant bird-like man with wings and a massive hammer? A demonic-looking creature made entirely of shining black ash? I truly can't imagine.

"Out of the trees comes this tall guy, naked as a damn jaybird, like Arnold Schwarzernurger, or whatever his damn name is, in that *Terminator* film. He's just walkin' all casual-like across the yard, right toward us. Rebel is freakin' out, making all kinds of noise. Then, this dude gives the dog one sharp look, and Rebel just whimpers and runs off behind the lodge. Never seen anything like it. Nothing scares that dog. After that, the guy comes right up to me. I'm six foot, but this feller had to be eight, maybe 10 inches taller. He's got a big ol' beard, sort of like ZZ Top, except trimmed all neat and square-like at the bottom, and all thick black hair... just like on his head. And his body... holy shit! I ain't never seen nothing like it. It was like he was chiseled out of granite—perfect muscles, nice, deep tan... not a blemish on him."

"What did you do?" Olive asked, mesmerized.

Clint gave an almost fearful laugh. "Well, I asked him who the hell he was, and this guy, he just looks me straight in the eye and says something in a language I've never heard before... but gawddamn if I can't understand him. It's like he's speaking in my head. He says his name, actually starts rattling off a whole bunch of names... 'I am Ninu, also known as Ningsu,' or maybe it was 'Nanu-Nanu.' I don't know what the hell all he said. I can't remember. Goes on to claim he's the fucking 'god of thunder and storms,' and is the greatest warrior ever born. I mean, seriously? What a load of horseshit. I, of course, didn't say that, because the feller is almost seven foot and built like a brick shithouse. Still, that's a pretty outrageous claim."

"*Scheiße,*" Lotte intoned. "Hold on." She reached for her phone and typed madly. "Here! I found this on Saturday afternoon when I was resting in Olive's hotel room. I wanted to see if I could figure out what had been stolen from the Louvre, and I think I got it." She held up her phone to show a picture of a worn, slightly conical stone. Images of lions were carved on the surface. "They said it was a votive mace head, and I believe it's this one—the Mace Head of Mesilim."

"Okay," Eric said. "What does that have to do with any of this?"

"Listen! This is what I just remembered. The Sumerian inscription on the mace head says, 'Mesilim, king of Kish, builder of the temple of Ningirsu, brought this mace head for Ningursu, Lugalshaengur being prince of Lagash.' Turns out, Ningursu is another name for Ninurta, an ancient Mesopotamian god of agriculture, among other things, and later a god of war for the Assyrians. Mr. Carter, are either of those names familiar to you?"

"Yeah, that may well have been what the feller said his name was... or names. I think he rattled off one or two more as well."

"What else did he say?"

"Well, he told me to kneel before him and bring him food, except he called it 'sustenance.' Real fancy with the words, he was. I was about to tell him to go stick it where the sun don't shine, that I don't kneel for nobody but the Good Lord, but this feller puts his hand on my shoulder and starts pushing me down. This dude isn't strong, he's a gawddamned *powerhouse*! I realized he could snap my neck like a twig, so I knelt... not a particularly peachy spot to be in with his John Thomas swingin' around in my face, if I do say so myself, but he didn't pay it no mind. When he was satisfied... umm... sorry, poor choice of words.... When he was done with me kneeling, I get up and tell him I ain't got no food."

"I'm sure that went over well," Eric dryly observed. "What did he do?"

"Surprisingly, he wasn't upset at all. He just said, 'Come.' I followed him inside the house. He pointed at that stupid sculpture thing sitting in the muddy crater, and says, 'Destroy that gateway to ensure none can follow.' I'm like, 'Gateway? Gateway to where? The puddle of mud at the bottom of the hole?' This guy might be strong, but he's clearly missin' more than a few marbles. But hey, what the hell do I care? I had to take the damned thing apart anyway. So, I disassemble it, and ol' Arnold there, he just watches. All that 'Mr. Strongman' routine, and he don't lift a pretty finger to help. Treats me like a gawddamned slave. I went upstairs, got a couple of Lucas's old Army duffels, packed the thing up, and threw it in one of the bedrooms. That seemed to satisfy him."

"To ensure none can follow...." Lotte repeated the words as if trying to absorb their meaning. "So, Mr. Carter, how did you wind up here in the boathouse?"

"Well, that was later, and please, call me Clint. I don't have no fancy airs or nuthin'."

"All right, Clint, but only if you call me *Lotte* instead of 'missy.' Deal?"

He smiled. "Deal! I like your name anyway, it reminds me of Led Zeppelin, *Whole Lotta Love*!"

She grimaced, but didn't reply, to Eric's unqualified amazement.

"Anyway, when I was done 'destroying the gateway,' ol' Arnold was asking for food again... said he was starving, hadn't eaten in three thousand years, or some fool number like that. Gawddamned idiot. So, I says, 'Okay, feller, I'll take you to get some food, but you gotta put some damn clothes on. You can't be walking around with your dork hangin' out.'"

Olive laughed. "You really said that?"

"I did, and I meant it! Dude didn't seem to care one way or the other, so I went up and got some of Lucas's old gym shorts, a t-shirt, and some flip-flops. They was too small, so they looked stupid, but my shorts are too big and woulda' just fallen off. He didn't really seem to care, and at least now, we could drive somewhere. I figured if I didn't get him food, he might get angry and violent, and I knew I was no match for this fucker. When he got dressed, we loaded into the truck. I briefly thought of taking out one of my guns, but they's locked up, and he was sittin' right next to me and, well... I just didn't think it was a good idea to get him all mad. Something was just not right about this here feller. So, I just up and took him down to the Chick-fil-A in North Myrtle Beach."

"Wait a minute!" Lotte cried. "You took the Mesopotamian God of Thunder and Storms to Chick-fil-A? Are you serious?"

"Well, he seemed to like it. Plus, they had a drive through, so we didn't have to get out of the car. Dude's dork was still hanging out of his shorts. No shame at all, this guy. I tell you, I never seen nobody eat that much chicken. Not looking forward to my next credit card bill, that's for damned sure."

Lotte briefly buried her head in her hands before she gathered the composure to continue. "All right, Clint, what happened then? When did you get tied up?"

"I was just gettin' to that. When we got back here, he looked me up and down, real strange-like, and asks me if I have any 'cord.' I assumed he meant 'rope,' so I took him down here, unlocked the shed, and showed him what I got hanging on the wall. He looks it over, unrolls a fair bit, and just literally rips it off the coil. Told you this fucker was strong. Then, of all the gawddamned things, he grabs me, tosses me on the ground, and starts binding up my legs."

"Why?" Olive yelped. "What did you do to deserve that?"

"Absolutely nothing, but that's exactly what I was asking him. 'Why the hell are you doing this?' When he gets to tying up my hands, he leans over and tells me he's waiting for 'Sharon' to show up. Says Sharon's gonna be awful hungry when he arrives. I don't have the heart to tell him Sharon is a damned girl's name. Dumbass. I figure he'll want me to take her to the ever-lovin' Chick-fil-A too. What does he think I am, made of money?"

"What? Just a moment!" Again, Lotte furiously typed and scrolled on her phone. "*Verdammt!* I'm not nearly good enough with Mesopotamian mythology. Greek, Roman, Etruscan, some Egyptian... I can handle that, but Mesopotamian? I'm totally out of my element. *Alter!* There's just too much to know. All this technology, it takes so much time and focus, but that's the bloody future, so what can I do? Something has to go. I can't do everything, I just can't. Ah, here it is!"

She frantically read for a moment, and then dropped the phone to her side. "It's not *Sharon*. It's Sharur... the 'Smasher of Thousands,' Ninurta's weapon. Sumerian myths describe it as an enchanted talking mace that has the power to fly, as well as communicate with its wielder. In some stories, it acts as an emissary between Ninurta and his father, the god Enlil, one of the principal three deities of ancient Mesopotamian religion. This is the weapon from the Louvre."

"What makes you think that?" Eric asked with astonishment. "Okay, it can fly, but there's no way a little mace head could cause that much damage to the glass roof of that Louvre courtyard. You saw it yourself on the news. That was a gaping hole. It can't be possible."

She turned to face him, a mixture of terror and fascination in her eyes. "There's more. According to legend, Sharur can also take the form of a winged lion. A creature of that size could *easily* have made the hole in the Louvre's roof, not to mention utterly destroying the case where the item had been displayed. There was no robbery at the Louvre last Friday... there was an escape! Ninurta has somehow returned to our world through the portal in that fishing lodge, and he's summoned his weapon, Sharur. It's coming... here... as we speak... and it's not going to want bloody Chick-fil-A! *You're* what this creature is going to eat, Clint, and probably us too! We have to get out of this place right now, before it's too late."

The fear and conviction in her voice was all the incentive they needed to get moving. Clint did his best to rise on still shaky legs. Eric and Olive helped, but the man was quite large, with a belly that only a lifetime of drinking Budweiser tallboys while trawling for catfish could produce. Finally, they got him to his feet and agonizingly shambled toward the truck. Rebel happily skirted their heels, blissfully oblivious to the danger they were in.

"Wait a minute!" Lotte shouted when they reached the lodge. "We have to get the portal. We've got to take it with us."

Clint gestured inside. "It's upstairs. We can all go up this way and get out the front door. I need to use the bathroom anyway."

They passed through the glass double doors and went into the muddy lower-level room. Clint seemed to have gained some strength as his legs slowly remembered how to move, but he still clung to Olive's arm for support. The crater of mud and debris where the portal had once stood gaped up at them as they ascended the stairs. A door stood open at the top, which led into the rest of the small house.

Clint pointed to the right. "The bags with the sculpture, or gateway, or portal, or whatever the hell it is, are in the bedroom round there. I'm gonna use the bathroom. I'll be out in a minute."

While Olive helped her uncle navigate the narrow hallway, Lotte and Eric veered into the bedroom, which was toward the back of the house over the semi-basement room below. Two duffel bags sat at the foot of a sturdy old wooden bunk bed. Unable to contain her curiosity, Lotte loosened the ties on one sack and extracted a piece of the now disassembled structure. It was about a foot long and had a narrow curvature to it. One end was slightly fluted while the other thinned out, obviously to facilitate assembly. As Clint had described, there were small marks at each end, little impressions that seemed to have been made by a stylus, as if worked into clay.

"That's Cuneiform," she remarked, "the earliest form of writing. This looks like an especially primitive variant. This object is ancient, possibly five to six thousand years old. I have no idea what the material is. It looks like clay, but the texture and color are wrong. As you can see, it's almost like wood... or driftwood... but that's not it either. It's as smooth as plastic, and obviously extraordinarily hard, and look... it's hollow, like some sort of liquid was meant to run through it."

Eric was about to take the piece from her hand when something outside cried, or roared—or both simultaneously. The terrifying sound seemed to come from above. After a moment, the call repeated, this time with greater intensity. To their horror, from somewhere toward the front of the house, concealed in the trees and underbrush, a deep voice bellowed in triumphant response.

"What the H-E Double L is that?" Olive gasped as she bounded into the bedroom. "I never heard anything like it in my life!"

"That," Lotte replied with a defeated tone, "means we're too late. Sharur is here, and we're in big trouble!"

Eric ran to the rear of the lodge and the window that overlooked the back yard and the river beyond. "There!"

Sharur was definitely as advertised, a great maned lion with the wings of an eagle. The beast's front paws ended in the massive talons of a bird of prey. This creature was every bit as formidable and frightening as the Afrit or Charun, and Eric felt his stomach churn with dread at the prospect of meeting a gruesome death in the maw of such a monster.

"It landed over near the boathouse, just behind the trees. This may be our only chance. We have to get to the truck and try to get out of here."

Lotte furiously stuffed the piece of the portal she had been examining back into the duffel bag. Once finished, each of them grabbed one of the sacks and ran out into the hallway, where they met Olive and her uncle.

"Olive told me what's happening," Clint said with a worried tone. "Front door's this way. Olive Oil, take the keys and get the truck started. I can't run. I'll come as fast as I can."

She hastened to the door, Rebel at her heels and Lotte just behind.

Eric hung back. He'd help Clint move as fast as possible.

Olive exited the little house and began to race toward the truck where it sat near the tree line, maybe 30 yards away. Seeming to sense the excitement of the moment, Rebel also dashed out of the door, barking elatedly.

"*Shush*, Rebel!" Olive yelled. "Quiet boy!"

Sadly, the damage had been done. From near the river behind them, the terrifying beast emitted another caw-like roar.

"We've got to move!" Eric commanded, as he pulled Clint reluctantly forward. On stiff and shaky legs, the large man struggled as best he could, but they'd barely crossed half the distance to the truck when Eric heard a loud *thump,* and another ear-splitting, terror inducing shriek from the monster.

He looked behind to see Sharur, crouched on the roof of the lodge, looming above the still open front door. The creature's wings were tucked tight to its massive torso. The beast had them in its sights.

Panic-stricken, Eric tried to double their pace. He pushed against Clint's weight to propel him forward, but it was hopeless. After a few steps, the big man stumbled and fell to his knees.

"You go on. I can't do it."

"No! I'm not leaving you. Never again."

Tears welled in his eyes as he thought of Mason being dragged out of the jagged scar in the roof of the old white van.

I won't lose another person that way! I'll fight to the end to keep that from ever happening to anyone else!

The ground shook behind them as Sharur landed hard on the earth. Eric looked back and saw the beast was easily within striking distance. He tried to think, but his mind was petrified with fear. Flight was no longer an option. The monstrous lion had them cornered.

That leaves only fight*!* With grim resolve, he raised his fists and prepared to meet Sharur's inevitable charge. *I hope the end is swift.*

Again, the creature crouched, its charge imminent. The beast's lips curled back from razor-sharp teeth. Its talons rose from the ground and spread like sharpened knives that glistened in the sunlight, with the sure promise of bloody and painful destruction.

Then, to his side, Rebel streaked past him... directly at Sharur. The dog hurled himself at full speed and launched his body toward the monster's neck. This time, the collision was anything but gentle. Sharur reared back, stunned, and shook his head wildly from side to side, but Rebel held fast with clinched jaws.

Eric came to his senses. "Come on! This is our only chance!"

From somewhere deep inside him, Clint seemed to find the strength to stand. Together, they falteringly covered the remaining distance to the truck, where Lotte and Olive gaped in abject horror.

"Uncle Clint! We thought you was dead for sure. Come on, we gotta get outta' here!"

"Y'all get in the truck," Clint gasped as he reached the driver's side door. "I'm getting my gun. I'm gonna fetch Rebel and show that fuckin' thing what's what." He reached in his shirt pocket and produced a small key, which he desperately fit into the lock on the gun rack.

Lotte ran to him and put her hand on his shoulder. "Mr. Carter! Clint. You can't kill these things. They're immortal... or at least it takes incredible power to overcome them. Rebel's given us a chance. We have to take it!"

Clint didn't stop removing his gun from the rack. "Can you hurt 'em? Slow 'em down?"

"Yes, we've hurt them with guns and other weapons. You might be able to scare Sharur off, but I can't say for sure. I've never met this creature before, so I have no idea what it's capable of."

"That's good enough fer me," he said with determination as he released the safety on his weapon. "Y'all hop in the truck and get ready to move out. Here, son, can you shoot a gun?" Clint offered up the second rifle in the rack to Eric.

"I've never shot a gun like that." In truth, the only gun he'd ever fired was the pistol he used against Charun on the hill in New Hampshire. The semiautomatic rifle Clint held looked a lot more daunting.

"I can work it," Olive interjected. "Daddy taught me how to shoot one of these. Give it to me, Uncle Clint."

Eric just shrugged. On this issue, he had no ego to bruise.

Clint passed her the rifle. "That's my girl, Olive Oil. Your daddy would be so proud, if he could ever get his head out of his hindquarters and see how wonderful you are. Stay here and cover me if I have to retreat, or if that other bastard shows up. I heard him out there yellin' too." With that, he shuffled back toward where Rebel and Sharur still battled.

"Where you going?" he asked, noticing Eric walking by his side. "I told you to get in the truck."

"I told you I wouldn't leave you. You might need my help. You're still not walking well. I'll run if I have to."

There wasn't time to argue. Rebel had found a nearly perfect spot, clamped to the ruff of Sharur's neck where the monster couldn't easily reach the dog with its talons. Blood poured from the wound and streamed down the beautiful, sandy-golden fur of the terrible creature, as it thrashed in a frenzy. In the end, the otherworldly beast proved too strong for the courageous dog. One mighty swing of Sharur's neck sent Rebel skidding painfully across the ground.

Clearly dazed, the dog righted himself and, seeming to sense the imminent danger, tried to skulk off into the trees.

Sharur moved too quickly. The monster lunged forth and grabbed Rebel around his back legs in its mighty jaws and lifted him high in the air. The dog yelped pathetically as the beast, with a quick thrash of its head, slammed his limp, gray body into the muddy earth. For a brief moment, Sharur hovered over Rebel, growling with seeming disdain at the tiny creature that had managed to inflict so much damage on a being so mighty. Then, satisfied its opponent was subdued, the terrible lion-eagle reached in for the kill.

Clint's gunfire rang out like cannon blasts into the hot and hazy air. "Get away from my damned dawg, you motherfucker!" Shot after shot pierced Sharur's side. Blood and sinew exploded from the ghastly wounds, and the beast howled in agony. "Don't like that, do you? Have a little taste of what a gawddamned AR-15 can do!"

Sharur staggered back and quivered as bullets riddled its exquisite golden hide. The creature's flank became a panorama of gore. It spread its wings and attempted to fly to safety, but Clint merely directed his fusillade into the joint where wing met body. Feathers flew wildly in all directions and more blood spewed from the creature's side as its left wing collapsed into the mucky ground, almost severed from the beast's back.

Eric wondered how many bullets this rifle had. Clint had to be approaching thirty or forty shots. To his amazement, it really looked like the man might slay the monster.

Maybe we actually can kill these things!

Without warning, Sharur suddenly, and instantaneously, vanished. Left twirling in the air was a small stone about seven or eight inches tall, and perhaps six inches wide. At first, it flew upward as if propelled by an explosion, but then, gravity drew it to the ground in a small arc, and it landed with a *plop* into the muddy soil.

"What the...." Clint voiced his confusion.

Eric had no words as he ran to the strange little stone, the top of which now poked miserably out of the turf.

"Surprise, surprise. Lotte was right. Look at this. It's the fucking Mace Head of Mesilim, straight from the Louvre for our viewing pleasure. First stop on its world tour, I'm sure."

"What are we gonna do?" Clint asked as he staggered to Eric's side. "Take it?"

"Oh, hell no! We're not touching that damned thing. Who knows when it might turn back into the 'winged Simba,' or start flying around and talking to us, if the legends are to be believed... which might be even worse. This may be our last chance to get out of here alive. I'll go grab Rebel. You start making your way back to the truck. Nice shooting, by the way."

The man smiled, flashed a worried look in the direction of his seemingly lifeless dog, and then did as instructed.

Eric took one more glance at the mace head. A menacing winged lion with empty black holes for eyes glared up at him from the dirt. He shuddered and went to collect Rebel.

The dog was severely injured. An angry and oozing bite mark outlined his hindquarters, but Eric pressed his ear to Rebels chest, and could hear labored breathing.

"Thanks, boy, I think you saved our lives," he whispered in the dog's ear as he gently picked up the poor creature and hastened back to the truck.

"Is he alive?" Olive desperately asked as he ran up to truck with the wounded dog. "Uncle Clint's gonna be devastated if he's not."

"He's alive, but we need to get him to the vet, ASAP... which is fine because we need to get the hell out of here anyway. Damn, there's a lot of crap in the back of this truck. Unhitch the tailgate. I'll ride with Rebel, but see if you can fit the bags with the portal materials in the cab. I don't want them bouncing out if we have to move fast. We'll move them to the van when we get there."

"You were so brave. You nearly lost your life helping my uncle. I don't know how to thank you."

He laughed. "Thank Rebel. He saved us both. You can thank us all by getting a move on so we can get going."

She got the message. She passed the bags to Lotte and Clint, who already sat in the cab, and then hopped in. Thankfully, driving wasn't as difficult for Olive's uncle as walking. The high-suspension truck slowly but effectively navigated the rough road, a feat the other vehicle couldn't have accomplished. Soon, Catfish Circle loomed ahead, and Clint pulled up behind the white cargo van. Still armed with her AR-15, Olive jumped out of the cab and unhitched the tailgate.

"I'll put Rebel on one of the blankets in the van," Eric said. "Can you sit back there with him?" Olive nodded, and he gingerly carried the injured dog to the open side cargo door.

Lotte had already loaded the bags with the portal materials into the van and had positioned herself in the passenger's seat. "Eric, you scared me! I thought you were both going to die. You could have run, but you didn't. I saw you. You were going to *fight* that thing."

He placed Rebel on a blanket and draped another over his limp body. "I didn't feel like running would have helped. Maybe I was wrong. Maybe Sharur would have been satisfied with Clint, but... *shit*. I couldn't do it. I couldn't leave him there. I don't know... my mind was a blank. It was probably stupid."

"Oh, my love, not stupid at all! It's so... *you*! Don't you see that this is why I love you so much? Back then, when we were kids, you never hesitated. You told me I couldn't keep you away even if I tried. You'll never know how much that meant to me, how much it still means. I push people away. I intimidate them by being so blunt. I waste all my time trying to out-achieve all the other overachievers, and you still love me... for who I am... who I've always been. You're still here, doing what you've always done. I don't know what fate brought us together, but I know I'm the better for it. You're incredible."

He didn't have time to process all of that. He knew the truth was different, that he'd had many hesitations, many misgivings, and he didn't feel brave for having stayed with Clint. In some ways, he felt it only reflected his cowardice, his fear of having to live on, knowing that another person had been swept out of his grasp to die in agony. There was only so much of that he could take, and he felt he might already be past his limit.

He also knew that as much as he'd cast his lot with the girl who now looked lovingly back at him, draped across the seat of another white van, he'd come to recognize that his decision had been made without a full reckoning of the consequences. The ramifications of that choice had defined his life—all that was good, and all that plagued his peace of mind—not to mention his very existence.

I'm glad she appreciates it. It cost me nearly everything. "Thanks. I love you too, more than you could ever know. Now let's get out of here."

Olive ran up behind him. "Uncle Clint is ready to go. He's gonna follow us. Let me get in here with Rebel."

Eric closed the side door and circled around the back of the van. He waved at Clint as he passed, and the big man saluted with his index finger in reply. The relief of having survived the almost impossible ordeal showed clearly on his face. Eric jumped in and started the engine, and the two vehicles began to slowly roll along Catfish Circle, back toward the main road.

They had almost reached the asphalt part of the street when Lotte screamed beside him.

"Someone's there! Someone walked out of the underbrush on my side, just as we went by. Look behind you."

He looked in his side mirror and saw a huge man who couldn't be anyone other than Ninurta. He wore gym shorts and a t-shirt that were too tight for him, but more tellingly, he'd stepped into the road directly in front of Clint's truck and stopped it dead. He pressed against the front of the hood as the vehicle's rear tires spun uselessly, throwing muddy rubble and rocks into the air behind. Clint hadn't been going that fast, as he had to follow the van on the bumpy and debris-littered dirt road, but it obviously took incredible strength to stop a truck, not to mention with one hand.

In Ninurta's other hand, Eric saw with horror that he held the mace head Sharur had become. With a slight hop, he slammed the stone down through the hood of the red Chevy, straight into the engine. Metal screamed against metal as a thick cloud of black smoke streamed into the air.

"What the hell happened?" Olive yelled from the cargo space where she cradled Rebel. "What was that noise?"

Eric had no reply. He couldn't speak as he watched the huge man lift his fist with the mace head from the utterly destroyed engine block of the truck. Through the smoke, he saw Clint reach frantically for his rifle, and he suddenly remembered Olive had a gun as well.

"Olive! Open the back door and shoot Ninurta! He just smashed the truck. Your uncle's in deep trouble!"

Without hesitation, she jumped up and ran to the back of the empty cargo space. Lotte and Eric breathlessly watched as she unfastened the catch and swung open one of the two doors.

With alarm and dismay, they all saw Ninurta hurl the mace head at the windshield of the truck. Glass exploded in a shower of sharp, gleaming fragments. The weapon battered savagely into Clint's chest. His head whipped forcefully back, then bounced unnaturally forward. His limp body slumped across the steering wheel of the truck, and the vehicles horn sounded a lonely and monotone wail into the silence of the afternoon.

"No!" Olive screamed as she brought her gun to bear on Ninurta.

He turned at the noise behind him, but then, the cab of the truck burst apart. The doors and windows were blown outward in different directions, and most of the roof launched high into the air. Sharur, again in lion-eagle form, rose from the wreckage. The terrible monster raised its one healthy wing into the sky and emitted a screech-like roar. Then the beast looked down and plunged its jaws into Clint's body.

Sharur's sharp teeth and talons tore at vulnerable flesh. Eric turned away as the upper portion of Clint's torso ripped away from his legs. He hit the gas as Olive fell to the floor of the van, sobbing miserably.

Lotte tore off her seatbelt and ran to her. "Olive, hold on! You'll fall out the back door! *Scheiße*! Eric, he's coming. Ninurta's following us!"

Eric again looked frantically into the mirror. Sure enough, the Mesopotamian God was running toward them. Flip-flops long lost, his bare feet lightly skirted across the muddy road. The van could only move so fast due to the condition of the road, so the brute was rapidly gaining ground.

He looked over his shoulder and yelled. "Olive, shoot him! Please, I know it's hard, but you have to get yourself together, or we're all dead. Your uncle wouldn't want that for you. He loved you. Come on, Olive, you can do it!"

He turned back to focus on the road and caught a glimpse of Ninurta in the side mirror. He'd gotten even closer, but abruptly, a shot rang out from behind, then another! He risked a quick glance over his shoulder and saw Lotte with her arms around Olive's waist, legs braced in an indentation on the floor of the van. Olive pointed her rifle out the open door, trying to aim as the vehicle bounced awkwardly across the dirt road. It didn't seem she'd hit Ninurta yet, as he still ran menacingly toward them.

Eric did the calculation. *Will we make the asphalt before he reaches us? If so, can we then speed up enough to get away? I don't think so.* "Olive! Lotte! Brace yourselves and get ready!"

He hit the brakes. The van came to a rapid but not excessively sudden stop. He didn't want to pitch his companions out the back. Lotte released her grip around Olive's waist as she tipped backwards and fell to the floor. Olive steadied herself against the one closed door at her side and managed to remain upright.

"It's now or never, Olive. Get him. You can do it."

She shakily raised the rifle and fired. The shot missed, and Ninurta drew even nearer. She took more careful aim and fired again. The large man's left shoulder exploded in blood, and he spun around in pain and surprise. Pulling his hand from the wound, Ninurta examined the blood on his palm and fingers, then turned toward the van with an infuriated expression and let out an angry bellow.

Olive let loose a flurry of shots at nearly point-blank range. Several penetrated Ninurta's chest and created gaping, bloody holes, but the final burst hit him square in the head. The angry god fell over backwards in a cloud of blood and brain matter. His body twitched and spasmed where it lay on the ground.

Eric cheered. "Olive, you did it! He's either dead or disabled. Let's not stick around to figure out which. Close that door! We're gonna go as fast as we can to get out of here."

He threw the van into drive as the two women shut the door then collapsed side-by-side. Once they hit the asphalt, he looked once more into the side mirror. He couldn't see Ninurta anywhere. He'd vanished, practically in the blink of an eye. Clearly, he wasn't dead, but at the moment, he seemed unwilling to pursue the chase.

For now, that was enough. Eric hit the gas and sped through the remainder of the side roads that led back onto Highway 9. In the empty cargo area, Lotte held Olive as she wailed and heaved in sorrow.

You're gonna see things that will change your perspective on life forever, and Olive, I won't lie to you. People are gonna die, and you'll be party to their death.

His words to her hung over him like a dark and ominous cloud, as if the God of Thunder and Storms himself had transmitted them through Eric to this young woman as a warning—a harbinger of what was to come.

Just as he had all those years ago, she'd heard the admonition, and like him, she'd probably felt the inner rumblings of trepidation. In contrast, she experienced the thrill of uncommon adventure, just as he had, and the burning desire to help her new friends—to be wanted, to be *needed,* to rise above what she was and become something... *better.*

Like Eric, she'd made her choice, and in so doing, became yet another to cross the threshold of a portal to a new state of being.

CHAPTER 12

Olive's heartbroken cries of anguish were not out of place in the lobby of the animal hospital. Eric felt sure they'd seen all this before, though in truth, they hadn't. He sat with his arm around her as Lotte stoically talked with the receptionist after the still unconscious Rebel had been rushed into surgery.

"What's the dog's name?" the kindly woman behind the desk asked.

She struggled to answer. She seemed far away, not in focus, not in this space or time. *"Er ist Mutig,"* she finally muttered. "He is *Mutig*. Mutig...." Her words trailed away as her eyes drifted.

"Okay, darlin', it's all right. You say it's that woman's dog, but you're going to pay? That's awful sweet. If you can just sign there, there, and initial in these three spots, you can go have a seat."

She listlessly scratched her signature on the authorization and indemnification forms, then shuffled mechanically back toward them.

"Why didn't you tell them his real name?" Olive croaked, eyes bloodshot from near hysterical crying that had only just begun to subside, unsustainable even in her agony.

Lotte sat beside her and gently touched her arm, seeming to regain some of her concentration. *"Shhhhh.* He can't be who he was before. I don't know if this is where your uncle brought him for veterinary treatment. That's why I removed his collar in the van. You can't be who you are, either."

"Who should I be?"

"If they ask your name, just make something up. It won't matter. It's my name on the bills."

"I can't think of nothin' right now. You make something up for me."

She thought for a moment. "All right, if anyone asks, your name is Amanda Palmer. She's a musician I admire, but I doubt anyone here will know who she is. Your dog's name is Mutig."

"What kind of name is that? It sounds foreign."

"It is. It's German. It means 'brave.'"

Olive raised her head slightly. "I like that. Mutig. Brave. That's what he was. Thank you."

She gave a tired smile. "Hopefully, he still is. Let's see what the doctor has to say."

They had nothing to do but wait, so wait they did. Eric wasn't sure how much time had passed when he woke up and heard Lotte talking with someone. To his surprise, Olive was fast asleep, nestled under his arm.

"So, what does this mean?" Lotte asked of a woman with graying blonde hair who wore a white coat over scrubs—presumably, Rebel's, or rather *Mutig's*, doctor. "Will he live?"

"If there are no internal injuries, then I think so. The bite marks *look* awful, but they didn't penetrate that deeply. I don't think whatever got hold of him had that good a grip. What did you say did this again?"

Lotte fudged. "Well... umm... we don't really know. We were all out for a walk and Rebe... er... Mutig ran off. We heard this horrible yelp and hurried as fast as we could toward him. Whatever did this, we must have scared it off."

The doctor gazed at her skeptically. "I've never seen bite marks like this. At first, I thought it was a gator, but the pattern is wrong. More like a panther, but these wounds are bigger, and there aren't many panthers in this state anyway. Not a bear. I'd say a lion, but that's ridiculous. Whatever it was, you were damned lucky it didn't drag your dog off with it."

"Her dog, actually," Lotte said, nodding toward the still sleeping Olive. "But yes, we were lucky. What do we do now?"

"We're going to have to keep him here. He'll recover from the anesthesia and then hopefully wake up in the next four to six hours. We'll see what he's like then, but it's hard to know the extent of the damage. It may take a day or more to see if he comes around. We'll call you and keep you up to date. Monica said you were from out of town. Do we have your number?"

"Yes, I left it with the receptionist. We'll find a place to stay around here. We were just passing through. You can reach me any time."

"All right. Would your friend like to see her dog before you go?"

Lotte glanced at Eric, and he nodded.

"I think she would," he replied. "She's pretty torn up, and we were all exhausted. Let me wake her, and she'll be ready in a minute."

The doctor walked to the reception desk to give them a moment, and he carefully shifted his arm to wake Olive.

"Hey, would you like to see your dog?"

She shivered slightly as she returned to harsh reality. "Is he gonna live?"

"We don't know for sure, but there's at least a chance. They need to keep him to see how he does, and whether there are internal injuries. Why don't you go back with the doctor and tell Mutig to get better for us?"

Slowly and stiffly, she got up and started toward the desk.

From behind, Lotte took her hand and whispered in her ear. "We must not be connected with your uncle. Remember who you are,"

"I do. I'm Amanda Palmer. What kind of music does she play, anyway?"

"Umm, it's complicated. Does Brechtian Punk Cabaret mean anything to you?"

Olive gave her a blank stare.

"Never mind. Just go see your dog."

As Olive staggered away, Eric glanced at his watch. "Oh, crap! It's almost freaking four o'clock. Blake Harris is supposed to call. What the hell are we gonna tell him?"

For a moment, Lotte seemed stunned. Too much was happening too quickly, and like him, she appeared to be having difficulty keeping up. With uncanny speed, however, she seemed to assess the situation.

"We'll let him lead. He's going to want us to bring the portal to him. Let's see what he has in mind. He doesn't realize how far away we are, and we're not driving all the way back up to Raleigh right now. So, we'll just have to improvise. You go out to the van in case he calls. I'll tell the receptionist where we went so Olive isn't confused, and I'll meet you there in a minute. Go, go!"

He went, and a good thing too. His phone rang practically the second he got out the door. He put the device on speaker as he briskly walked toward the van. "John, so nice to hear from you."

"Fuck you. Stop playing games. You got what I want?"

"We have it. What do you want us to do?"

"That's more like it. You know where the Triangle Town Mall is?"

"Can't say as I do. Remember, we're from out of town."

"Well look it up on fucking Google. You'll need to be there in an hour-and-a-half. When you get there, go to the food court. I'll call you and give you your next instructions."

When Lotte exited the veterinarian's office, he motioned to his phone, and she sprinted toward him.

"Umm, that's not really gonna work, John. We're not anywhere near Raleigh anymore."

"You said tonight, asshole! It's tonight, or I start to take other... *actions*. You got me?"

"I got you, I got you," he stammered as Lotte breathlessly joined him. "Hold on, let me see what we can figure out."

He put the call on hold and frantically explained the situation to her. "He wanted to meet at a mall near Raleigh in, like, an hour. I told him 'No way,' but he wants it tonight. He's making threats, and I'm afraid of what he might do if we don't give him something. I have no idea how far his reach might be. Your father, my family... Olive's? I just don't know."

She nodded. "Right. You're right. We just don't know. We can't stall any longer. He wants to meet in a public place. Let me think... hmmm. That Waffle House we were in this morning, didn't they advertise they were open twenty-four hours?"

"Yeah, I think they all are."

She pulled her phone from her pocket. "Okay, stall him for a minute. I'll find an alternative location."

Relieved to have her sure assistance, he turned back to his phone. "Give us a second. We're looking for another spot. It will have to be later, but it will be tonight. Promise."

"I swear to God," the man irately shot back, "if you're lying to me, there will be all manner of shit coming down on you and the ones you love."

"I hear you. Just give us a second. Hold on."

Lotte urgently held the phone up and he read the address. "Okay, we have something. There's a Waffle House on 3090 West Fifth Street in Lumberton. Can you meet us there around—"

She grabbed his arm and whispered in his ear. "Tell him to come later. It needs to be very dark... for the Afrit!"

"Say, like eleven p.m. Will that work? We'll have it for you. I swear."

The man he presumed to be Blake Harris was silent, but Eric could hear the faint sound of typing on a computer keyboard in his phone's receiver.

He's looking it up. He's considering it.

Finally, he spoke. "Okay, but here's what you're gonna do. You get yourself a nice table right near the window. Only you, nobody else! What's the deal with this thing? Is it portable? Does it fit in a car?"

"Yeah. We disassembled it, but it's easy to put back together. There's marks on it that show you what pieces go where. Right now, it's in two army duffel bags, but it's not heavy, and it's easy to move."

"Great. Have the duffel bags with you at the table. Eleven o'clock, sharp! Don't kid yourself that I won't be looking for an ambush after that shit you pulled. This time, I'm taking precautions. I'll be ready. So, you just sit there and wait at that Waffle House, and do exactly as I instruct. We clear?"

"Crystal clear. I'll be there. I'll be alone, and I'll have the thing with me." He nervously wondered what Blake might have up his sleeve, but he knew they had something up their sleeves as well.

The phone went dead.

He turned to Lotte. "Okay, we're in play. What do we do now?"

"We go back to Clint's house," she somberly replied, "and we summon the Afrit... and we hope the poor creature has had time to digest its last meal."

Misery battled in Eric's mind with exhaustion and nervous anticipation of what had yet to be done this night.

Olive broke down again when they arrived back at the farmhouse on Happy Drive.

Not so happy now. I wonder if we should have even come back here. If someone finds the remnants of Clint's truck, not to mention what might be left of his body after Sharur finished with it, then the next stop will surely be this house. We need to summon the Afrit, though, and we all need some time to rest and regroup. I guess there's not much choice. There didn't seem to be any traffic on that part of Catfish Circle. Hopefully, it'll be at least a few days before they find the truck.

"Come on, just a little bit farther," Lotte said encouragingly.

She supported Olive, who stumbled toward the door, but about halfway there, her legs gave out and she collapsed in a tearful heap on the ground.

"Eric, help me get her up!"

He ran to Olive's side, and together he and Lotte gently set her back on her feet. The weary and dispirited trio maneuvered into the unlocked house. Once inside, Lotte led the inconsolable Olive to her room down the hall.

Eric stood alone in the living room. He felt dizzy. Lack of sleep was catching up with him, and he'd need to rest before they went out again. He started up the stairs toward his and Lotte's room, when he suddenly froze.

Shit! I haven't called Margot yet.

The thought made him even dizzier. He crumpled onto the bottom step and closed his eyes until the spinning sensation diminished. Then, upon regaining his focus, he reached for his phone and pulled up Margot's number.

Her friendly voice rang out on the tinny little phone speaker. "Hiya! You guys back in town?"

"Not even close," he creakily replied. "There have been... well... complications, as usual. I have no idea when we'll get back."

"God, you sound like shit. Are you okay?"

He fumbled for words. He'd been right that having Lotte back diminished his need to open his heart to Margot. Still, he found it difficult to conceal the truth from her. It gave him an odious feeling, almost as if he were lying to himself.

"I'm just super tired," he finally sputtered. "We're all about to take a nap. I'll be better after that, but listen, I'm calling you for a reason. I need a favor."

"Anything."

"You're gonna get a phone call from someone. His name is Siddique Alieu. I gave him your number and told him you'd help him. He needs a place to stay—nothing special, just a room somewhere. He's got money, so he can pay. I also want to see if you can place him on one of the teams. Didn't Ernie just lose somebody? Have him start at the bottom, just lugging stuff around, cleaning up, getting coffee—like I did when I started. Whatever is fine."

"Who is this guy, another one of your long-lost high school buddies? Or is he from college? Can't wait for this story."

Despite himself, he chuckled. "No, nothing like that. He's just a guy we met here. He helped us out, and now we're helping him out. I know it's against your nature, but please don't ask him too many questions. He's had kind of a hard time. He's gonna be coming in on the bus, hopefully to Worcester, but it might be Boston. He'll need a lift to Southby, and one of the guys will need to pick him up for work because he can't drive. I know it's a lot to put on you, but it's important to me. Really important."

The phone was silent for a moment as she took all that in. "All right, it's not a problem. Ernie does need someone. We'll probably look for a place closer to Worcester rather than Southby. That's where most of Ernie's guys live, so it will make transportation a lot easier. We'll work it out, but I want something from you."

"Anything," he offered, knowing full well he didn't mean it... at least not in certain areas.

"I want to know what you're gonna say to your dad, and if he's selling, I want to know how you plan to approach it. I don't care what you do—that's up to you—but I want to know. I just don't want to be in the dark. It's making me nervous."

Right. I forgot all about that. How life so often laughs at your priorities. On the plus side, though, this isn't something I have any problem sharing with her. In fact....

"Tell you what... I'll go you one better. When I'm back, let's you and I talk about it. I haven't given it any thought. I've been too busy, and you know how scrambled-up I can get over decisions like this. I'd like nothing better than to talk it over with you. Of course, that just means you get to help me... yet again."

She laughed. "Apparently, helping you is my life. Maybe we *should* get married. Shit, maybe we *are* married, and we just didn't realize it. It's like some weird parallel universe."

Isn't it, though?

"Anyway, that would be awesome. I actually have some ideas, and I'd love to talk with you about them. If you're serious, that would be really great."

"I'm totally serious. As usual, I can't thank you enough. You're the best."

"I know. Now go get some sleep. You're getting hoarse, and that can't be good. Say 'hi' to Lotte for me."

He promised he would, signed off, and stumbled upstairs feeling substantially better for having something off his mind that he didn't even know had been on his mind in the first place. He collapsed on the old-timey bed that rocked precariously on its ancient bedspring.

Just as he was on the verge of sleep, Lotte came in and quietly closed the door. She met his gaze with a troubled look. "She's obviously terribly upset. Understandable. I don't get the sense her father is particularly supportive. I think she got on better with her uncle. Poor man. I kick myself. We should have gotten out of there more quickly."

"It's not your fault. I tried to get us moving too. Clint just needed more time after being tied up. I don't think he really understood the danger. I guess, in the end, none of us did."

She scowled, then nodded. "I suppose. It's just awful. Olive keeps apologizing to me, saying how sorry she is, over and over. I tell her it's okay, but she says it's not, that she's so terribly sorry. What in the world is *that* all about?"

He gulped. "Umm, who knows? She's exhausted and upset, probably doesn't even know what she's saying. Don't worry about it. Anyway, we have to figure out what we're gonna do. We don't want to get sloppy. There's too much at stake. I'd forgotten to call Margot."

"About what?"

"About Siddique."

"Oh, right." She frowned at the memory of her captor.

"See? We're so wound up about this, and so exhausted, that we're beginning to forget things... make mistakes. Margot even reminded me about something else. Fortunately, that can wait, or I guess it will just have to. Whatever. I'm damned lucky she's there to cover when stuff like this happens."

"You certainly are lucky. I glanced at my emails while we were in the veterinarian's office. *Alter!* I don't even know where to begin. Things are just piling up. I barely keep my head above water in the best of times. Now it's almost hopeless. I can't even bear to listen to my voice mails. I'm beginning to wonder if maybe all this *isn't* worth it. Is it too late to just surrender and go teach high school German?"

He laughed. "High school German students are the worst, bunch of lazy good-for-nothings. But seriously, this too shall pass. Once we get through what we have to do tonight, there will be time to get everything together. I know you've hit a kind of rough patch, and I'm... well... I'm not trying to push you, but I know you. I know how much everything you do means to you. It's no surprise you feel overwhelmed. You're only trying to integrate every field of study known to freaking mankind. It's a lotta work, Lotte. Yeah, you can walk away any time, and I'll love you just the same, but you chose all this for a reason. After what happened, I think you should take some time before you make any big decisions. Tomorrow, we'll work on your emails together, just do them one at a time. That's what tortoises are good at. We just plod through. I'll help you. I've got Margot, and you've got me."

She walked to the window by the old timey dresser and stared out into the back yard, and he followed her gaze. A small pond sat at the end of the scraggly grass, near the tree line of the woods beyond. When she spoke, her voice was monotone and barely above a whisper.

"I live five years in the future, sometimes ten. Most everything I do, or ever have done, is meant to facilitate something down the road. I tutored you in German because I wanted to see if I could teach, whether I liked it, whether that's what I might have wanted to be in five to ten years. It's as if there's this endless string of *blocks* that are five to ten years out, and I hop from *block* to *block*. It's all well and good, but where does it end? When I get my PhD? Not likely. I suppose when I'm old, after I've had my 'distinguished career' and can sit back on my laurels and accolades. But what if I don't get old? What will I have missed in all that time I spent working for a future that never happened? None of this ever dawned on me... until now."

He didn't have an answer. Maybe he never would, but deep down, he felt—*he knew*—that somewhere in her usually impeccable logic, a flaw existed. He also knew better than to say that out loud, especially right now.

He changed the subject. "What time do we need to wake up the Afrit?"

She turned to him and raised her eyes toward the ceiling as she calculated. "We have to be there at eleven. It'll take us an hour or so to get there. We want to be early, scope things out, so I'd say eight, at the latest, and seven-thirty would be better. Why?"

"Because we all need sleep, and if we sleep now, we'd get about two and a half hours. You want to start living more 'in the moment,' let's start with *this* moment. What do you say?"

She smiled. "I'd say that was spoken like the lazy, good-for-nothing German student you truly are."

He cheerily parried. "Hey, last time I checked, you were registering a .9873 happiness correlation with me on the patented WHG Love-O-Meter, or am I off by a decimal place or two?"

She giggled. "Stupid machine. Can't even find a simple underground temple with a portal. Who'd trust those readings? In any case, you're right. We need sleep, and right now, nothing would make me happier."

It felt as though he fell asleep before his head hit the pillow, but not before he felt the press of her warmth and the safety of her gravitational pull. Despite all counteracting forces, that tug somehow continuously grew stronger. He felt the faintest kiss of her breath on the back of his neck, and somewhere, deep in the most primal part of his mind, he sensed she felt a similar attraction, and that truly, they were one.

The summoning went far more quicky than Eric and Olive's attempt the night before. Either Lotte had the magic touch, or the Afrit was feeling better.

Hmmmm... feeling better. Does the Afrit even have *feelings?*

As usual, Lotte had been right. The thing really was the world's most interesting science project. What humankind could learn from such a creature about its nature, or the very structure of the cosmos. He couldn't imagine where to begin. These were questions his mind couldn't even conceive. In some sense, the existence of the Afrit changed everything, completely altered the paradigm of man's place in the universe.

Talk about boldly stepping forward where none have gone before.

Sadly, Lotte was probably accurate in her assessment that humanity would botch this amazing opportunity, given even half a chance. The lure of power seemed too strong to resist, and the creature's value as a weapon had always overshadowed the benefit of the knowledge it could bring. Eric wondered what insane motives drove Blake Harris to desire the portal that seemed to have brought forth Ninurta. If all went well, he'd soon have an answer. That, or the answer wouldn't matter anymore, as either he and Lotte, or Blake Harris, would be dead.

The empty barn had been the perfect place to set up the fire portal. They had plenty of room, a high ceiling, and a large door for the Afrit's egress. The beast swayed before them, definitely larger and bulkier now for having consumed poor Wayne, but still not the size it once had been.

Eric almost surprised himself that he felt sympathy for the man who would likely have killed him, but for Olive's intervention. Wayne's manner of death unnerved him, but this was the terrible price of dealing with a being that was beyond any human morality. It had no civilization to tame its inner drives for food, or for power.

Well, maybe that's not entirely true. For all its horror, the Afrit plays by the rules, and it wasn't the monster that called out to be unleashed to hunt someone else's blood, or carry out another one of these hideous pacts. I rang that bell. I started that cycle, just like we do now, and countless people in the past have done – all for reasons of their own, or like us, because they simply couldn't see any other way.

Lotte spoke to the beast with her commanding tone. "We again call upon your service, great Afrit. Someone threatens us. We've tried to reason with him, but he won't be swayed. He must be eliminated, and we promise him as spoils in exchange for your assistance. Will you help us?"

The creature's voice sounded in their heads as its harsh and rasping words filled the air of the dimly lit barn. *'Show us the one you seek. Give us his image, and you will have our answer.'*

"His face is not known to us, but we'll see him soon. Would a picture suffice... an impression of the man we're after, not the actual person?"

'Impossible. In ancient times, the Sadat Alnaar showed us drawings, likenesses of those sought. We cannot find the quarry you seek from such an image. It must come from the eyes of one who has seen.'

She bowed slightly. "Understood. As I say, we'll see him later. Will you accompany us until that time?"

The Afrit swayed from left to right in its familiar way, wings slightly pulsing and dark eyes twinkling in the reflected light from the candles in their bowls. *'We are still weak, still diminished. We demand your assistance in transporting our spoils back to the portal. If you accept, then let the rings bind our pact.'*

It seemed a reasonable concession, and given they had little choice, she readily agreed. They left the Afrit to its devices and went inside to make final preparations.

Lotte went into planning mode. "Let's make sure our phones are charged. We'll need the rope, and definitely bring those bats, along with the knives we have. Quite a little collection we're building, eh?"

Eric nodded. "Yeah, never thought I'd be happy to see an AR-15 in action, either. Speaking of which, are we bringing Olive?"

They'd left their poor friend asleep while they conducted the summoning, feeling rest and time would be the only balm for her heartache.

Lotte scowled. "I'm not sure. If she's going to mope and apologize all night, then no. *Alter!* That sounds terrible. I feel awful for her. Really, I do. It's just... well... we only have *one* chance at this. We don't need something else to worry about. If she can pull herself together and help, then absolutely. I'm just not sure what to do."

"Yeah, me neither, but we can't just leave and not let her know we're going. Tell you what, let me go talk to her. You're totally right. If she can't help, then she can't go, but if we need that gun...."

He didn't really need to finish the sentence. Instead, he marched dutifully to Olive's room. The sleep had helped, but he still felt weary to his bones, not to mention the bruises from his fights the night before. Even Lotte's coffee hadn't revived him this time, though in fairness, the resources in Clint's house were fairly meagre—some cheapo ground supermarket brand, and skim milk.

Blah!

He rapped gently on the door. "Olive, you up? We need to talk about what we're gonna do. We have to leave soon. Are you able to get up? Are you okay?"

Silence ensued for a few moments, then she spoke in a weary voice. "Y'all can come in. Click the light on. It's by the door."

He did as instructed and entered. Once he flicked the switch, he saw a small room with shelves along one wall, clogged with a potpourri of camping and fishing equipment. Olive lay on a small, single bed, jammed between a beat-up dresser piled high with boxes, and a tall, metal gun locker. She still wore all her clothes, other than her shoes, which Lotte had likely removed. She held up her arm to shield her eyes from the sudden burst of light.

He sat on the bed next to her and tried to smile encouragingly. "Hey, how are you? Did you sleep?"

"More like 'passed out.' I don't think I've ever been this tired, or upset, or scared. You tried to tell me, didn't you? You tried to make me understand what I was gettin' into. You've seen this before. Maybe I should have stayed in Boston, but... but I thought you needed me. I thought you wanted me here."

"I did. I wanted you with me, and I needed you every step of the way. Your help was critical. You saved my life. You saved us all from Ninurta. What you did was amazing."

She threw her head back on the pillow in disgust. "Not amazing enough to save my uncle. What am I gonna do? How do I explain this to my daddy, or my momma, or anybody?"

He sighed and took a deep breath. "You don't. You can't. For one thing, people wouldn't believe you anyway. Think about it. Would you believe it if a friend of yours told you this story? At a minimum, you'd want proof, and we're not in a position to be proving anything to anyone. We can't. The knowledge we have is too dangerous. That's what it means to be in on this. It's lonely and isolating. Let alone having to live with what you've seen and the loss of your uncle, there's nobody you can talk to about it, except me and Lotte. That's what it means to be part of our team. It's a small team, and our victories, such as they are, come at a terrible price."

She silently stared at the ceiling.

As much as anyone could, he understood. He'd been where she was now, particularly when he thought he'd lost Lotte. In many ways, Olive was worse off, or would be when he and Lotte went home and left her alone.

She finally stirred. "You said we needed to talk about what we're gonna do. Do we have to summon that ol' Afrit thing?"

"Already done. We meet Blake Harris tonight at eleven o'clock at a Waffle House just across the border. When I see him, I'll give him the portal, but I'll be able to communicate his image to the Afrit. The monster will track him down, capture him, and we'll take him back here. The portal is set up in the barn. That's where Blake Harris will be... absorbed... and that'll be that."

"So, when do we leave?"

"Well, Lotte and I, and the Afrit, I guess, are leaving basically now. Are you up to it?"

"Oh, H-E Double L yeah, I am! Blake Harris is responsible for my uncle's death. If we didn't have to mess around with his BS, pardon my fuckin' French, then we'd have gotten down here days ago! My uncle would still be alive. He's gonna pay for that, and I'm gonna help you. Oh, yes, I am."

Her resolve encouraged him. "That's the Olive I know. That's the Olive I need with me, and want, and have enjoyed having with me."

She propped herself on her elbows and gazed into his eyes. "You really mean that?"

He turned from her and stared at the floor. "I do... but let me ask you a question. Who was the love of George Washington's life?"

"That's a funny question," she said, somewhat taken aback. "I assume his wife, Martha Washington."

"Well, that's a good assumption, but it's most probably wrong. Good old George knew a woman before Martha. Her name was Sally Fairfax, and it's pretty clear he had strong feelings for her. He wrote a really sentimental letter to her late in his life. There's no question, he loved Martha too, but she was extremely wealthy, and marrying her was more a 'means to an end.' It's likely Sally was the true love of his life."

"That's interesting, I guess."

"Isn't it? The little things you learn when you study history, but it gets even more interesting. When Washington left the military around 1760 and married Martha, Sally and her husband were the Washington's nearest neighbors. They were all friends."

"Really? Did Martha and Sally's husband know anything about their past?"

He turned back to face her. "Nobody knows. As I understand it, they probably had some suspicions, but apparently nobody talked about it. And the more nobody talked about it, the more it became a thing of the past. They all just... well... moved on."

Her eyes narrowed a bit. "I think I know why you told me this."

"You do, though to be clear, Lotte is without question the love of my life. My point is, I like you, and I want you around, in whatever way is possible given the specifics of where we all live, but there's nothing to say to Lotte about... you know, what happened. No apologies, no explanations... nothing. And the more we don't talk about it, the more I think it will simply become a thing of the past, and we'll all just move on."

She sat up, brought her knees to her chest, and hugged her legs. It reminded him of Lotte in the hospital after her father's fall.

So many years ago.

"I think I better change before we go," she finally said. "Can you please excuse me?"

"Of course."

He got up and headed for the door. He hoped he hadn't been too blunt with her, but he needed to make his point. Anything less seemed unfair to Lotte.

He was about to exit when she called from behind. "That was pretty slick there, Mr. Schneider. I get what you're saying, but that was in me, and it needed to get out. Even if she doesn't know why, I know I apologized. I had to, and I meant it. Lotte's a good person, and so are you. I'm glad I'm on your crappy team that loses even when it wins. Kind of the story of my life. Maybe right now, I'm exactly where I ought to be."

He smiled and closed the door.

Maybe. Maybe I am too. I hope we all live long enough to find out.

CHAPTER 13

"Y'all want more coffee?"

The waitress oozed that characteristic Southern charm that Eric had come to recognize and, to some degree, appreciate. The service in Boston was much more perfunctory, far less overtly friendly, though in his experience never "rude," as some described it. His visit to the Carolinas had given him a taste of something different, both the people and the cheese grits, which he'd ordered with his coffee and promptly devoured. He'd envied Olive's when she'd ordered them at breakfast this morning.

Was that really just this morning? Time flies when you're having fun, I guess.

Not exactly having fun, given what they'd endured the past twenty-four hours, not to mention the last five days.

Right now, however, he owed his friendly waitress a response. "Yes, thank you. You can top me up."

She did, and then meandered back behind the counter where her sole other customer sat on one of the stools, eating a plate of pancakes.

At nearly 11:00 p.m., Eric glanced out the window hoping to see a car pull up, but nothing yet.

They'd played it cautiously and parked the van in the lot of a motel next to the restaurant. He'd then snuck across a large field to get to the Waffle House, hoping darkness and a small thicket of trees near the side of the building would hide his approach.

Meanwhile, Lotte and Olive waited in the van with the dour Afrit. The beast didn't appreciate being cooped up in the cargo space, but Lotte wanted the creature nearby in case things started happening quickly and they needed its immediate assistance.

Eric felt certain that by witnessing what he perceived to be an unearthly being *mope*, he'd now seen it all.

At least, I hope I have.

A car pulled into the Waffle House lot, and a man and a woman got out and walked arm-in-arm toward the door. They smiled and chatted as they came inside. The waitress showed them to a booth at the back of the restaurant, and neither cast a glance in his direction.

Not him. I wonder if I have time to pee. All this coffee, along with what Lotte made before, is going right through me.

He was just about to get up when another car pulled into the lot, an older silver Honda Accord that had seen better days, with several dents and scratches, as well as a missing hubcap. A woman got out, tossed a cigarette to the pavement with agitation, and scanned the front of the building until her eyes found him. They stared at each other through the glass, and she hurriedly scurried to the front door.

What the hell is going on? Is this one of Blake Harris's employees? Is that what he meant by taking precautions?

The woman didn't wait for the waitress when she came inside. She made a beeline straight toward him. She appeared to be about thirty, and wore a uniform, like perhaps she worked in a grocery, or another restaurant. Her eyes were puffy and red, like she'd been crying, and her stiff gait made her look like a marionette, being controlled by unseen strings.

She stood by his table and spoke in a ragged voice. "Are you Eric?"

"I am," he answered, suddenly uneasy with the situation. "Who are you?"

Her eyes darted restlessly toward the window, as if looking for something, or someone. "That don't matter. I'm here for what you promised that man. You got it, right?"

He nodded his head toward the booth seat across from him, where the duffel bags sat. The portal was there, at least most of it. Lotte had refused to risk giving the whole thing to Blake Harris, just in case the unthinkable happened and he got away with it. She held onto one piece, stowed away in the van—enough, hopefully, to prevent its future use.

The woman looked at the bags. "God, are they heavy? How am I supposed to carry all that?"

His mind started to race. *If she takes the bags, I won't see Blake Harris, and I can't send the Afrit after him! Wait, I can send it after her. She must be taking the portal to him. Everything is still okay.*

He carefully examined her features, trying to memorize her image to impart to the monster after she left.

"Umm, they're not that heavy, but I can help you get them in your car."

She again glanced furtively toward the window. "No, you can't! You can't leave the seat you're in right now. If... if you do...."

She began to cry.

"What? What is it? What's the matter?"

With effort, the woman regained control. "He's... he's got my little girl. I picked her up at daycare after work. I stopped at the 7-11, just for cigarettes on the way home... real quick was all. When I got back, Katie was gone. There was a note on the seat sayin' to meet this guy behind a strip mall a few blocks away. When I got there, he had a mask on. He told me to come to this Waffle House at eleven o'clock, get this thing from you, and drive to a location where he'd meet me. He said if I told you where I was going, he'd kill her. He told me he's watching us right now, with some kind of camera he set up, and said if you got out of that seat, he'd kill her. He said you can't move for an hour after I leave, and if you do, he'll kill her. You understand me? He'll kill my little girl if y'all don't do what he says!"

A wave of nausea washed over him, and it wasn't the cheese grits. He hadn't anticipated anything like this, nor had Lotte. Panic started to set in.

"Okay, listen, I hear you. I understand. I'm gonna do exactly what you just told me. I'll sit right in this seat for an hour after you go. I won't do anything to jeopardize your daughter's life. The bags are right there. Take them and do what he told you to do. It's gonna be fine, I promise you. It'll be okay."

Again, the woman looked out the window, and then down at the bags on the seat before her. "I'm gonna take one, and I'll come back for the other. Please don't do anything, mister. Please just sit there." She hefted one of the bags and walked toward the door.

The one good thing about this, is that I won't mind a bit when we feed this asshole to the Afrit. Of course, this assumes we can get the Afrit to Blake Harris in the first place. I can't impart her image to the monster. The damned thing can't just walk into a freaking Waffle House. It'll have to follow the car. Can it follow a car? It can't follow a person from a picture, so maybe not. Shit, shit, shit, shit! Think! Ah, I'll call Lotte. She'll know what to do.

The woman returned and slid the second duffel bag off the seat.

"Please don't follow me, mister. He says he'll be watching. I know he's watching us right now... from somewhere. It's my little girl. My little Katie. She's all I've got. Promise me. Promise me I won't lose her."

"I promise you," he replied, his voice hollow. "I won't move from here, but do just one thing for me. Drive slowly... carefully. Obey the speed limits, even go slower if possible. Use your turn signals. Trust me, this will all be okay. You'll get your daughter back. I swear."

She nodded and hoisted the strap of the bag over her shoulder. "I hope I don't ever see you again, but if I get my Katie back, please know how thankful I am." She turned and left.

He frantically pulled out his phone, placed it on the table, and called Lotte. If he truly was being watched, he didn't want Blake Harris to see him holding the phone to his ear, so he put it on speaker, watching as Katie's mother put the bag in the back seat and got behind the wheel.

Lotte answered. "Hey! What's going on? Did he come? Did he take the portal?"

"Lotte, listen, it wasn't him! He sent some poor woman to get it. He kidnapped her freaking daughter! He won't give her back until he gets the portal. She said he's got a camera set up, that he's watching me. I can't move from here, and you can't tail her in the van because he might see you. The Afrit is gonna have to follow her car."

He saw the lights of the Honda go on as the engine started. There wasn't much time.

"All right," she replied after absorbing the shock. "Is the car coming our way?"

A new rush of panic swept over him. *Shit! How can the Afrit see the car if it goes the other way?*

"Just a second. She's pulling out now. She's in an older silver Honda Accord... it's missing a hubcap in the left front. *Fuck!* She's going left, back toward the interchange where we got off. We should have thought of that and put the van in that direction. What are we gonna do?"

"Olive, open the back doors!" she commanded. He assumed she directed her next comments to the Afrit. "If I describe a car to you, can you follow it? If I give you the color, the shape?"

He heard the Afrit's grating words in reply to the question, but couldn't understand what the beast said. *I must be too far away for the creature's telepathic connection to work.*

"What did it say?" he eagerly asked.

"It said, 'What is a car?'" she sourly replied. "For that matter, it asked what a damned *color* was as well. Who knew the thing could only see black and white, or if it can even see that."

"Shit! What are you gonna do?"

"Sir!" the waitress snapped as she approached, a serious look replacing her previously friendly demeanor. "Can you please keep your conversation quiet, and watch your language? There's other customers here. Please mind your manners!"

"I'm... I'm sorry... really sorry! This is just super important, but I'll try to be quiet. Promise."

She scowled, but seemed satisfied. In truth, it didn't seem anyone in the Waffle House was bothered but her.

"Okay, please see that you do. Can I get you anything else?"

"No," he squeaked. "I'm fine. Just fine. Thanks." He flashed her the best smile he could muster and prayed she'd just go away. Amazingly, she did, and he returned his attention to the phone.

"Lotte! Sorry, I had to deal with something! What's happening?"

Her reply was curt. "Just a minute!"

He heard her talking, but she held the phone away from her so he couldn't hear her words clearly. It sounded like she was pleading with the Afrit. Suddenly, his phone rang with another call.

It was Olive.

What the hell does she want?

He panicked as he tried to remember how to put a call on hold.

Stupid cell phones! Why isn't there just a hold button?

At that moment, he saw the hold button prominently displayed on the screen.

Sheesh.

Since Lotte wasn't talking to him, he put her on hold and took Olive's call. "What? What's going on?"

"Eric, I'm sorry, it's just, well... it's Lotte!"

"What? What the hell is happening?" He realized he'd spoken far more vigorously than he'd intended. "Sorry, I'm just freaking out here. What's going on?"

"Well, she wants that thing to carry her, so she can follow the car. She wants you to conference all three of us together. Can you do that? I have no idea how."

He practically screamed, stopping himself just in time to avoid another verbal chastising from his formerly hospitable waitress. "Carry her? Is she crazy? Never mind, don't answer that. Let me see if I can figure out how to get us all together."

He hit the only possible button on the screen, the famous, "...," as he beseeched every benevolent god, spirit, or phone design engineer within range, that the answer to his quandary lay on some easily found submenu. Amazingly, "add call" was the only option that came up. He pushed the button, and Lotte's voice came back into the speaker.

"I'm light enough," she pleaded. "Just take me! There's no time to argue. The consequences are on my head, just—*aaaaaaahhhhhhhhhhh*!"

"Oh, my gawd, Eric! The Afrit just grabbed her and shot right up in the air!"

"Lotte! Lotte! Lotte, can you hear me?"

He definitely heard her. She was screaming, first yelling in terror, and then he heard her all too familiar verbal scalpels, slashing the Afrit as if it were a giant obsidian birthday cake—*one piece for everyone at the table, just... no candles, please.*

"You infernal idiot," she spat. "You practically broke my spine! Can't you be more careful, or has the concept of *mortal* not sunk in on you? A little bloody *warning* would have been nice as well! Thoughtless fool. Really, like a child." Her tone suddenly softened as she sang into the phone. "*Oh, my*. Eric, can you hear me? I'm flying!"

He almost cried. "I can hear you! I can hear you! Are you okay? You had me worried there."

"Us!" Olive chimed in. "You had us both worried. What do you see? Can you find the car?"

"I'm just getting oriented," she breathlessly replied. "Can you loosen your grip just a little, you're about to crush my chest! Oh, 'we don't want to drop our *Sadat Alnaar*,' do we? You may as well drop me if all you're going to do is squeeze all my breath out. There, that's better. Now, go in that direction, and stay low so we don't go too high for the cell towers. What? Oh, never mind. If you don't understand what cars are, I'll never be able to explain cell towers. *Idiot*."

Hearing his love being so *Lotteesque* definitely cheered him. "Now that you can breathe, can you see the car? It's probably near the interchange now, likely getting on 95 going north, or north-ish—the direction we were going when we got off."

"Fly that way," she instructed the Afrit. "Get a bit closer to the road so I can see the cars. I don't see anyone on the ramps. She's either on the highway or she went another direction. There are cars on the street that runs parallel, maybe it's one of them." Again, she directed the Afrit. "Fly over that strip of buildings. I'll be able to see both the highway and the other road. That's it."

Eric held his breath as she searched for the car. If they lost Katie's mother, he wasn't sure how they would track down Blake Harris. Their only hope was that he didn't have the entire portal, but it would be bad news if things came to that. Blake would be pissed, and who knew what he would do when he found out.

"Wait!" Lotte suddenly shouted. "Go right, that way. Down a bit. Eric, I've got her! Silver car, missing a hubcap in front on the driver's side.

She's not on the highway at all. She went the other way, onto the parallel street. She's just passing a store called 'AutoZone.' The road is starting to loop off to the right, away from the highway."

"Awesome! Keep on her. Olive, can you call up the AutoZone on your phone? See what road that is and start making your way in that direction, but go slowly! If Blake Harris is tailing the girl's mom, we don't want to be noticed. Let Lotte follow her from above. She'll direct you."

"Okay," Olive affirmed. "Am I supposed to just leave you?"

"There's nothing else you can do. If Blake really has a camera on me, and he sees me move, he'll know something is up. Plus, he'll see the van and link that to us. Just leave me. You're gonna have to get close enough that you can jump in if, and when, necessary. You can do it. Just go slowly and stay well behind for now."

"All right, I found the AutoZone. It's right on West 5th Street, the road we're on. I'll head to their parking lot, and Lotte can tell me what to do next."

Lotte chimed in. "She's staying on the same road. I think your plan is good. By the time you get there, I'll be able to give you more directions. I can't see behind me, I don't know if anyone is following, and I don't want to lose her. We'll just have to take our chances."

Eric agreed, and shortly the white van passed by the Waffle House. His heart jumped, but he tried to subdue his reaction to avoid tipping off Blake Harris, who might be watching. All was silent for a bit, save the sound of rushing air and Lotte's breath in the phone's speaker, until she spoke again.

"Wait. She's slowing down. She's turning left. I can't see the street sign, but the road is between an auto dealership and some kind of motorcycle shop. I can't believe it. It's almost German! *Hog Werks Custom Cycles*! Take the left immediately before that shop, but not now. It's only a short way. Just stay at that AutoZone place for now and let me see where she's going. This road doesn't appear to be too long."

"All right," Olive verified. "I'm at the AutoZone now."

After a brief silence, Lotte gave another update. "Now she's turning right. She's headed toward some huge water tower. Hold on... I think she's stopping. Yes, she is. She's pulling over. There's a bend in the road right behind the big tower. She's stopped by some trees there."

"Do you see any other cars?" Eric queried with apprehension. "Is she getting out?"

"She's shut off her lights. I can't really see. It's quite dark here, no streetlights, and the light from the water tower complex is blocked by the trees." Again, she spoke to the Afrit. "Circle low, above the road... there. Try to go as slowly as possible. I need to see if anyone else is around. That's it. Good. Hmmm... I don't see anyone else. The woman is just sitting in her car with the engine off. Perhaps she's waiting. We're going to circle back above and see if any cars come. *Verdammt!* I wish I wore my sweatshirt. It gets cold around here at night, especially up this high."

"What should I do?" Olive asked. "I see right where y'all are. She took a left on Branch Street, then right onto Lowery. I see the bend in the road, right behind the water tower. I can be there in about two-and-a-half minutes."

"I think you can try to get a bit closer," Lotte replied, "but not all the way. If he's watching the main road, any car that turns down Branch Street will alert him. Just go another minute or so up the street, find another quiet parking lot, and wait for my signal. We're going to circle here until I see something, then I'll let you know."

Eric heard the sound of the van's engine as Olive complied with Lotte's instructions. In a short time, she announced she'd found another spot in the lot of an auto repair shop only a minute away.

They all silently waited as Lotte and the Afrit circled above for any sign of Blake Harris.

After what seemed like hours, Lotte said, "There's another entrance to this area farther down 5th Street. I'll try to keep my eye on both in case he comes from that direction. I can't stay up here too much longer. My hands are so cold I can barely hold the phone, and I think the Afrit is getting tired. What? All right, my apologies, I meant no offense. Apparently, it just needed to get a better grip on me. Afrit's allegedly don't get *tired*. We'll see about *that.*"

Minutes ticked excruciatingly by with no activity. It was now past 11:30 p.m. and Lotte had been in the air for over twenty minutes.

"I can't take much more of this," she said. "We may have to set down somewhere, but then I won't be able to see both directions. *Scheiße!* Where is this bastard? Hold on."

"What do you see?" Eric expectantly asked.

"There's a gas station across the road from the entrance to Branch Street. I've seen a few cars pull in, either to get gas or to go into the convenience store. They've all left, but a car near the street that's been there all along just put its lights on. It's a black SUV. It's had a perfect view of that road this entire time. It's pulling out now, and it's taking the left, toward me. This may be him!"

"Can the Afrit put you down? If so, he can take Blake Harris out before he gets to the water tower."

"That won't work. That little girl is likely still in his car. She could be injured, or certainly scared to death—another young girl, scarred for life with memories of monsters."

Eric heard the Afrit's angry retort. Even unable to understand the beast's words, its meaning was entirely clear.

Lotte backpedaled. "Yes, I know, it wasn't your fault! I'm sorry, and truly, in the end, it's been for the best. It's just... well, if involving another can be avoided, then that's my preference, especially with one so young."

That seemed to mollify the creature.

"What are you gonna do?" Eric again inquired.

"Let's give it a moment to see if this is him. If it is, Olive, start easing in our direction, and turn off your lights when you go right on... what did you say... Lowery? Hopefully, he won't see you as you approach. We'll land nearby, and once the exchange is made and the girl and her mother are safely off, then I'll send the Afrit to capture our Mr. Harris."

That actually sounded like a good plan. Eric anxiously waited for word from Lotte, which came quickly.

"The SUV made the turn. He's on Lowery now. He's rounding the bend. He's pulling in behind the other car. It's him! Take us down, take us down! Over there, by those trees across the street where he can't see us. Perfect! Eric, I have to be quiet, so I'll update you when I can."

"Right," he numbly agreed as his heart raced. He prayed Lotte was correct, that it would be a simple exchange, then the Afrit could complete its—or rather *their*— ghastly business. He railed at his inability to help if something went wrong, but now it was up to her, and he could do nothing more.

Her voice was barely a whisper as she spoke. "Eric, I'm on the ground behind some bushes. I can see them, although our Mr. Harris still has his ski mask on. No matter. The Afrit will dispense with him once the little girl is free. He has her with him. I think she's handcuffed. Wait a minute. I can't believe this. He's put a bloody gun to her head! He's ordering her mother to load the bags into his car. She's practically hysterical, and the little girl is crying. This is horrible!"

Despite his own escalating blood pressure, he tried to soothe her. "I know. Is Katie's mom getting the bags?"

"*Ja.* She just put the first one in the back, and she's just now getting the second one. How do you know her name is Katie?"

"Her mother told me when she got the duffel bags. Sorry I didn't mention it before."

"It doesn't matter, but it's nice to know. *Katie*. Okay, her mother's got the other bag. She's walking to the back. All right, it's in. She just shut the hatch. She's asking for her little girl now. He's... wait a minute... *scheiße*... no! He's not turning her over! He says she's his insurance policy! He's taking her, and when he feels he's safe, he'll call her and let her know where Katie is. No, Eric, this cannot be! This cannot happen!"

"Lotte!" he screamed. "Don't do anything foolish! Wait for Olive. We'll follow him!"

"Sir!" the waitress called from behind the counter. "I'm gonna have to kindly ask y'all to leave. I tried to ask you nicely! If you don't go now, I'm gonna have to call the police!"

At this point, it seemed to matter little whether Blake Harris saw him leave or not. "Fine! I'm sorry. I'm going. Here." He tossed a twenty-dollar bill on the table. "Keep the change. I apologize for the inconvenience, really."

The waitress eyed him as he rushed out the door. Once outside, he turned his attention back to his phone. What he heard confused him.

"Eric!" Olive pleaded. "Eric, are you there? Eric!" In addition to Olive's frantic appeals, he could hear Lotte's distant voice.

"Olive, I'm here. Be quiet. I need to hear what Lotte's saying."

Once she was silent, Lotte's voice came into focus.

"I don't care!" she defiantly yelled. "You're not taking that little girl! You have what you want, now just *go*!"

In the background, he could barely make out Blake Harris's angry reply. "And for the last fucking time, it's your presence that convinces me I need her! How the hell did you get here? Nobody followed that woman. There's no way you can be here now, but here you are, just like the last goddamned time! That means there may be others, and that's why she's coming with me!"

"You want a hostage to secure your safety? Take me! I'll go in her place. You had me before, now you'll have me again. Just leave these poor people out of it, especially the little girl. I know monsters, but their behavior pales in comparison with yours. Don't do this. *Please*."

He scoffed. "Right, and have your friends track you down again? Fat fucking chance."

"My friends didn't track me down, you idiot. They were tipped off, by one of *your* men! They only found me because *you* were betrayed, by someone who *realized* what you were doing was wrong."

A clever lie. Will it be enough?

"That's impossible," Blake retorted. "How could they have known who I was calling?"

"A quick glance over your shoulder at the number you dialed. Siddique told me how he did it. He said he couldn't accept what he'd gotten involved in. He wanted to make it right, and he did. We let him go for his efforts, with *your* money! You were betrayed, and it serves you right."

"That little motherfucker! Okay, so that's how they found you, but that was then. Now you've had time to get ready. You're probably wearing a wire, or some kind of tracking device. If I take you, they'll just trace you."

"Are you quite insane? I realize you live in the dark world of private militaries and espionage, but do you think a person like me would think of doing something like that?"

"Okay, prove it."

"Prove it? Prove it how?" There was a brief silence. "You can't be serious. Fine! What the hell do I care!"

The phone made some sharp noises as it banged around, and then seemed to come to rest on the ground.

"Lotte?" Eric asked, fearful of what may have happened, or may be happening.

"Eric?" Olive's voice interrupted his intense concentration. "I'm here. I can see them. They haven't noticed me. My lights are off. Eric, you're not gonna believe what Lotte is doing."

"What? What is she doing?"

"Well, it looks like she's a-gettin' undressed. Yep, there goes the shirt. Pants were already gone. Socks. Nope, not enough. He's wavin' her on with his gun. There goes her bra... and... goodbye undies. She's buck naked. Eric, she's gorgeous! I had no idea. She don't exactly dress to impress, if you know what I mean. Smart and beautiful. What a combination."

Yeah. Smart, beautiful, and utterly reckless!

Lotte's voice could barely be heard in the phone she'd placed on the ground beside her. "Are you happy now? Please, let her go. I pose no threat to you. Do what you want with me, but do this one good thing. Let her go."

"All right," Blake finally said, his reluctance obviously diminished by the pleasant sight before him. "Get over here. Here's the key. Get the cuffs off her. My gun is still on her. You do anything, she gets it. Don't move, little girl... not until *I* say so!"

Eric heard Katie's mother crying.

"Don't worry," Lotte consoled her. "I won't do anything to jeopardize your daughter. It'll be fine. There, she's uncuffed. What now?"

"Toss me the keys then sit in the back. Wrap those cuffs around the door handle and lock 'em around your wrists. When I see they're secure, I'll let her go."

"Can I get my clothes?"

"Hell no, girl. If the goddamned tracking device is in your pocket, then I'm fucked. 'Course, if things work out, maybe I'm fucked anyway... if you know what I mean!" He chortled to himself. "Oh, don't give me that look. I'm just playin' around. I have a jacket in the car. I'll give it to you. Just gimme' those keys and do what I tell you. That's it. Okay, little one, run to Momma. You two go on and get, and not a word of this to anybody, you hear me!"

"Eric," Olive interjected. "He let her go. He's letting Katie and her mother go."

He pictured her in his mind. *Lotte Schwarz, Smart, beautiful, and utterly... tenacious. May it ever be so.*

Suddenly, a thought dawned on him. "Olive, he'll probably leave the way you came. Can you drive the van out of sight, into some underbrush by the side of the road or something? We don't want him seeing you."

"Umm, it's dark, but I'll try. Hold on."

He waited as patiently as possible as she moved the van. "Looks like Katie and her mom are just going straight, they're on their way. Blake is getting back in... oh, *shit*!"

He heard a loud scraping sound. "Olive, what was that?"

"Oh, gawd, Eric. That was the sound of me scraping your van up against a big ol' tree that I didn't see. I'm so sorry. Ricky is gonna kill you!"

Yes, Ricky is gonna kill me, and if that's the worst thing that happens to me at the end of all this, so fucking be it.

"It's okay, Olive. Don't worry about it. As long as you're safe and out of sight. Just back it out when you can. Far worse has happened, so let's not worry about that right now."

"Thanks, Eric. You were right to be concerned. He's turnin' around, and he'll be heading my way. I don't think he can see me. Hold on, he's just about to pass... *holy shit!*"

"What? What the hell now?"

"Oh no! They're coming this way! Shit, Eric!"

He heard a loud crash accompanied by the sound of glass shattering. The phone emitted a series of jostling noises, punctuated by distant screaming. "Olive! Olive, what happened? Are you there? Olive!"

"I'm here," she finally said, seemingly breathless. "It was the Afrit! It hit Blake Harris's car so hard that he lost control, and damned if he didn't swerve right into the trees where the van was! I barely got out in time. The Afrit has him on the ground now. He's screaming his fool head off, not that I blame him."

"Where's Lotte? Is she okay?"

"Hold on, let me go see."

The sounds of Blake Harris screaming got louder as Olive approached the wrecked black SUV.

"Lotte, honey, are you okay? Here, somebody wants to talk to you."

Lotte sounded dazed, but she was clearly all right. "Hello? Eric, is that you?"

"Yeah, it's me," he answered with fabricated indifference. "I was just hanging out here at the Waffle House and wanted to see if you'd like to join me for some cheese grits."

"I can't right now. I'm handcuffed, and I'm naked. Unless the Waffle House is rather more risqué than I'd imagined, I don't think they'll let me in."

"Well, if that's the case, maybe we could think of something better to do."

She laughed. "I can think of a few things. Right now, we need to get me un-handcuffed and get Blake Harris tied up and in the van."

"Speaking of the van," he broached the subject with trepidation. "Did the SUV hit it dead on?"

"Not quite. The SUV hit a big tree mostly, and the van partly. I think there will be a big dent, but it's not so bad. Well, I guess that depends on your definition of 'bad.' The SUV is totaled. The Afrit came right in the passenger side window. It was amazing! Blake never saw it coming. Thankfully, I was in the back seat and only got tossed around a bit. Oh, here's Olive with the key for the cuffs. Thank you."

He heard Olive's voice in the background. "No problem. Let me go get the rope to tie up that nasty man, and your clothes, unless you're happier like you are?"

"Clothes would be nice, though I know at least one person who'll be sorry he missed the show."

I didn't miss a damned thing. I heard it all on Lotte Radio, and my imagination filled in the rest.

CHAPTER 14

"What the hell is that thing?"

Blake Harris nervously glanced back and forth between the fire portal and where Lotte, Olive, and Eric sat as they prepared candles on the floor of the old barn.

He was a rather average-looking man in his mid-sixties, with salty hair and a goatee, portly, but not obese. He had more the look of a salesman than a soldier, and he'd spent the better part of the past two hours trying to smooth-talk his way out of the jam in which he now found himself.

"Don't worry, Mr. Harris," Lotte casually explained. "Soon, you'll know everything there is to be known about this object. It's a portal, to another place—another plane, or dimension, or universe. It's where the creature who captured you came from. You'll see how it works shortly. It's quite similar to the portal you were trying to get your hands on, and almost did."

He again launched into his familiar litany. "How do you know my name? I had no goddamned clue what that fucking sculpture was. Portal to another plane? I call bullshit! Even if that's true, I had no idea what it was. I swear! It was all just a big mistake!"

"Then can you please explain to us why you wanted it so badly? What was it that drove you to kidnap me, and that innocent little girl? What was so important to you?"

"For the tenth time, why should I tell you? What good will it do me? You aren't gonna let me go. In fact, I think you're gonna let that... that... fucking *thing* kill me! So, why should I say anything?"

She considered for a moment, then answered, a chill in her voice. "For your wife... the smiling lady on the 'for sale' sign in front of the house where you held me. It won't be hard for us to track her down. She'll share your fate unless you answer our questions. Do you have children, Mr. Harris?"

"Goddamn you. You leave my family out of this!"

"Like you did? Doesn't feel so good to be on the other end of threats like that, does it?"

He hung his head. "No, it doesn't. What I did was wrong. I understand that now, but listen... I know you won't believe me, but just listen. I didn't mean it. All I wanted was that thing, and I thought this was the easiest way to get it. I was wrong. I wish I never even heard about the damned sculpture, artifact, *portal*, what-the-fuck ever."

He finally seemed to be breaking down under her incessant interrogation. Eric could tell that she almost had him.

"How *did* you hear about it? Tell us what you know. For all the wrong you've done, this may be the way to make at least something right."

He finally capitulated. "Okay, you win. What the hell have I got to lose at this point, anyway? Early November last year, I got a call from the State Department. They had a visitor from the new Iraqi government. Malaki had finally gotten kicked out in September. I figured this guy would be from the new Adabi regime, hopefully about a contract providing security. Business had been shit since we all got kicked out of Iraq in 2011, and fucking Obama is useless."

"Yes, isn't peace terrible? But please, do go on."

He scowled, but then continued. "Anyway, this guy was from the Adabi government, but not security. He was from the State Board of Antiquities and Heritage, or some such. He was inquiring about some stolen artifact. Goddamned thing was taken back in the early 1950s. They showed me a picture of it right after it was unearthed in 1949, after which it seemed to go completely off the radar. Supposedly, though, some Iraqis had seen it in the safe house in Mosul where Black Arrow, among others, had their offices. Apparently, it had belonged to Saddam Hussein himself. Actually, that's not true. It belonged to his first wife, or her family. I don't know, I couldn't keep it all straight. Anyway, after the U.S. Forces and Black Arrow pulled out of Iraq in 2011, the thing apparently disappeared again."

"Why wait so long to raise the issue with the State Department? For that matter, why hadn't they pressed for its return before then? It had been in the building since 2003."

"How the fuck do I know, and how the hell do you know that? How do *you* know so much?"

"In this case, because Olive's uncle told us. Her father is your employee, and he's the one we believe removed it from the building in Mosul and shipped it to the United States. He had no idea what it was.

Like you, he thought it was a sculpture, though he also knew it was linked to the Husseins, because it was reportedly taken from the house in which his sons were killed."

"Hmmm... maybe I should have questioned Lucas's brother. I was in the house. I've even been in this barn before."

"Really? For what reason?"

"Well, I'll explain. The Iraqi guy from the Board of Antiquities had a strong suspicion a Black Arrow employee had taken the sculpture. That meant it could only be one of four of my guys, one of whom was Lucas Carter, Olive's dad. I got the clear impression from this Iraqi guy that the thing was valuable, like there might be a 'no questions asked' reward, or hell, maybe it could even have value on the black market. Like I say, business has not been exactly flourishing. Yeah, we probably over-expanded when shit was good, when we were all like pigs feeding at a trough when that war started. But now, I have major debts. Black Arrow is gettin' close to bankruptcy. I stood to lose everything I'd built, and I'm too old to start over. The ISIS situation helped, but this sculpture thing looked like my chance to cash in."

She shook her head in astonishment. "So, you did all this for money? Is that what you're saying?"

"That's exactly what I'm sayin', little lady. First thing I did was break into the houses of all four of my employees who shut the Mosul building down."

"It was you!" Olive cried. "You broke into my daddy's place in December, and that's why his buddy was robbed too... the quiet one. That was you too, lookin' for the sculpture."

"That's right, sweetheart. That was me, and knowing how close Lucas was with his brother, I even made a stop down here. Didn't even have to break in, as your stupid uncle leaves the house unlocked. If I'd only known about that fishing cabin, I'd have had it then. Instead, I put all four of my guys under surveillance. I watched their emails, monitored their calls. It all went through our server, so I had complete access. It took a few months, but then... *bingo!* A little email with a picture, and there the goddamned thing was, plain as day."

"So, you knew Lucas had it!" Lotte angrily interjected. "Why kidnap Olive? Why go through all this?"

"Because it was the perfect crime. Get a couple of goons to kidnap Lucas Carter's ditzy daughter—"

"I am actually standing right here," Olive angrily protested.

"Sorry, darlin'. You know how your daddy is. I just picked it up from him. He don't mean nothing by it. He loves you. Anyway, I don't expect precious little Olive here to be a particularly tough nut to crack. I get the sculpture, she goes free, nobody knows who took it, and I don't have to split the reward. I'd have never hurt her, and when those dunces grabbed the wrong damned girl, I never intended to hurt you either! I just wanted the damned sculpture. I didn't expect the kind of resistance y'all put up, or that goddamned... *thing*. Whatever *it* is! That's how they found you, isn't it? It wasn't Siddique at all. It was that monster who broke through the window. I wondered how y'all did that. I guess, now I know."

"And now we know. Thank you, Mr. Harris. Eric, are we ready?"

"I think so," he replied, as he moved to place the candles in their bowls.

"Olive, light a candle, open the barn doors, and go outside. See the Afrit in when it arrives."

"What the hell is happening," Blake Harris asked, struggling at the ropes that bound him. "What are you doing?"

"We're fulfilling our end of the bargain, Mr. Harris," Lotte replied. "The Afrit is quite demanding that its contracts be completed. Sadly, this particular agreement involves you. Whether purposefully or not, you left us no choice. If it makes you feel any better, we have no intention of going after your wife or children. Losing you in this mysterious way, I'm sure, will be punishment enough, though I wonder if they ever truly knew you at all. I bid you *auf Wiedersehen*, Mr. Harris."

With that, she helped Eric light the few remaining unlit candles, then sauntered out the open barn door. The Afrit and Olive entered as she exited.

"Are you people insane?" Blake Harris desperately cried. "This thing is goddamned Satan! You're in league with the fucking devil, all of you! You've lost your damned minds! Olive, I'm your daddy's friend. Please, help me!"

Olive gave him a blank stare, then turned and exited the barn, gently brushing her hand against the Afrit as she passed by.

Harris turned frantically to Eric, who stood aside as the Afrit made its way with ever-surprising grace toward the black marble board and the un-mirror. The *Alkuartiz Alnaar* was heating rapidly. Soon, the portal would open, and the Afrit would feed on the spoils of its labors.

"Please, Eric. Please! I'll do anything. What do you want? You can have everything I have. Just, please, God, spare my life. I'm begging you!"

"Save your breath, Mr. Harris. I've heard all this before. As abominable as you think this is, you brought it on yourself. This creature isn't evil, and it wouldn't have acted had it not been for *your* actions. Try to use your last moments to think of good things."

"Good things? What the fuck is that supposed to mean? What exactly can be good about this?"

"Well, think of it this way: you'll never have to live through the misery of seeing your beloved Washington Redskins being forced to change their name."

"That will happen over my dead body!"

"Truer words were never spoken."

He quietly and joylessly left the barn. Blake Harris's cries pierced the night as Eric closed and latched the doors. Only when he reached the house did the shrieks of terror cease. A loud *snap* put an end to the matter.

Actually, that's not true. This will live on in my mind, like it will in Lotte's and Olive's. This isn't what any of us wanted, and it will haunt all of us for the rest of our lives.

Perhaps most horrible to him was the fact that he'd seen all this before, and that this time was, in so many ways, less horrible than the last. He realized the brutal truth that one can get used to anything. The world he'd stumbled into ten years ago continued to make and remake him... shaping and reshaping... sharpening, and then blunting.

He wondered what would be left when the process had run its course.

Perhaps... nothing.

The unmistakable smells of coffee and bacon woke him. Sunlight streamed past the thin, old-timey curtains in the old-timey guest room, but light hadn't been enough to stir Eric from his profound slumber. It took bacon, and the hope of Lotte's coffee, to pry him from sleep. He reached for his phone to check the time.

12:33 p.m.? Holy shit, it's past noon already.

He jumped up, located some things that passed for clothes, and hustled downstairs. He shouldn't have been that surprised; he was making up for days of lost sleep. Even now, he could go back to bed and likely sleep for eleven more hours, but at the moment, the need for food held greater prominence in his mind. What he smelled cooking made him ravenous.

Lotte beamed as he stumbled into the kitchen. *"Moin, meine Liebe!"*

Olive smiled from where she stood over the stove, flipping pancakes and minding the sizzling bacon. She wore Lotte's Sisters of Mercy t-shirt that she had packed back in Somerville.

"We figured this would get you up!"

"Have you two been out?" he asked. "How long have you been up?"

"A couple of hours," Lotte explained as she poured a cup of coffee. "I got a text from the veterinarian this morning, and Rebel is awake and seems to be stable. They still want to keep him another day for observation, but Olive is going to see him after breakfast. Well, lunch really, but who's counting?"

"Lotte was so excited that she woke me up, and we decided to go get some food at the store, and real coffee. She said you'd like that."

"Speaking of which... here." Lotte handed him a perfectly prepared mug of his favorite beverage.

Either he was in withdrawal from not having her coffee for days, or she'd outdone herself. It smelled and tasted amazing, and he felt its warmth course through his body like some magical healing elixir.

Together, they sat at the table near the kitchen, dishing out pancakes and drenching them with maple syrup, sharing the crispy bacon, and avoiding any discussion of what had happened last night and the day before. He understood they all needed "normal" right now, perhaps him most of all—a respite from the onslaught of actions and reactions, punches and counterpunches, that had led to the deaths of three people. It was, in some ways, too much to bear. So, they ate pancakes, enjoyed the warm breeze from the open window, and tried their best, for a time, to forget.

"Olive," Lotte asked. "What will you do with Clint's dog, assuming he's all right?"

"I don't know. They won't allow him in the dorm at school. I suppose I could ask some of my friends that live off campus to take him until I figure something out, but I don't think they'd be able to take care of a dog. I guess I could take him to my mom's house in Marietta—tell her I saved him from one of those crappy shelters that kill unwanted dogs. She knows that makes me crazy, but she also knows Uncle Clint has a Weimaraner named Rebel. She'd wonder how and why I wound up with the dog, especially when she finds out what happened to my uncle. That'll raise a lot of questions, and I don't think that's what we want."

"You could keep calling him Mutig," Eric suggested.

"Yeah, I do like that name, but eventually my daddy will come home from overseas. He knows what Rebel looks like, and he'll know for sure that's him, regardless of what name I use. He also knows that my uncle would never willingly part with that dog, so he'd definitely suspect that I was here after Uncle Clint got... well... *eaten*, and all."

Lotte nodded. "Yes, you're quite right. I'm also afraid that once Clint's body is found and they begin to investigate, questions will come up about how and when Rebel came into your possession. They may even decide to trace your phone and see that you came back to Longs after the conference. That would be a major problem. It's something we'll have to think about. It'll be all right. Don't worry. In the meantime, let's just stick with calling him Mutig. It's bad enough that you suddenly acquired a dog that looks like your uncle's, but the fewer associations we have with a Weimaraner named 'Rebel,' the better for all of us."

When finished, they cleared the table and washed the dishes, then Eric accompanied Olive out to the van, dreading what he would see. As anticipated, a large, deep scratch extended from the front right bumper across the side door. However, that was nothing compared to the massive indentation above the front wheel on the driver's side. They were lucky they could still drive the van.

Gandalf the White Van no longer. Olive was right: Ricky is gonna kill me.

"Oh, Eric, I'm so sorry. This is awful."

"Don't worry about it. In the hierarchy of 'awful,' this is pretty minor. Plus, this wasn't your fault. It just... happened. We'll deal with it. Say 'hi' to Mutig for us. With luck, we can bring him home tomorrow."

She hopped in the van and drove off.

He went back inside, hoping to take a shower, but he wanted to check with Lotte first to make sure she didn't want the bathroom. He found her sitting on the back steps, sipping a mug of tea.

"Unless you need the bathroom, I'm gonna go clean up. When I'm done, maybe we can start looking at your emails? You okay?"

She stared out into the back yard, but her gaze seemed more distant. Occasionally, she glanced at the side of the barn. "I don't know. I feel tired—not sleepy tired, but tired to my bones. I'm still having dreams of being in that closet. It's part of the reason I got up, really. I just suddenly feel so... *vulnerable*! I hated that man for what he did to me—to all of us—but I take no joy in his death. It's like some horrible chore that simply had to be done, like cleaning the toilet or going through all my damned emails. Just like that, his life is over, and I realize how easily that could have been me. It's quite unnerving."

He had to admit, it *was* quite unnerving, but her reaction to the situation seemed so radically different than his, probably due to having been kidnapped, and likely further influenced by her completely different take on the world. He felt, in some sense, guilty, while she acted as if exposed and out of control.

Control! That's what she lost in that closet. That's what they really took away from her, her power to act... practically her defining characteristic.

Even when the Afrit had ripped at her mind, she'd still possessed volition, ceaselessly thinking of ways to manage the dreams and get out from the monster's clutches. He began to understand how deep this went for her, and how close to the core Blake Harris had cut.

"I'm here," he whispered. "I'll help you."

It sounded stupid, and out of context, but at some level, she seemed to understand.

"I know," she distantly replied. "I feel you always. Go take your shower. I'll get myself together. I appreciate your help. I think I need it right now."

He went upstairs and grabbed the towel he'd used the day before, and a fresh pair of underwear, then went to the bathroom and jumped in the shower. The water felt cool and refreshing in the humid, mid-seventies South Carolina weather. For a time, he just stood and let it wash over him.

Let it take what it wants of me, right down the drain. Whatever comes loose, the water can have. I don't need it.

He heard the door of the bathroom open, and to his great surprise, a completely unclothed Lotte joined him under the cool jets. She gazed up at him briefly, then fell into his arms and started to sob. Her tears mingled with the spray from the shower.

She sobbed for herself, and unknowingly, he let her sob for him as well, for the boy—gone now, though he still lurked somewhere deep in the shadows of his psyche—who had held this girl in his arms at the top of the stairs of his house ten years ago, as her feet barely brushed the floor. The boy had told her she couldn't make him go, despite the dangers, and surely, he'd meant that, without really knowing what it meant.

Now, he held her close and stroked her straight, raven hair. He didn't speak. He just held her and let the glorious water do its wondrous work, let it take whatever came loose with it... straight down the drain.

The water can have it. We don't need it. We'll have all we need in whatever it leaves behind.

"Okay, let's do this," he said with an enthusiasm he didn't really feel. "No more putting it off."

Lotte moaned. "*Alter!* If we must. You sit there while I get my phone. It's been charging." She bounded to the kitchen, hair still damp and dancing with each little hop.

He could tell by her gait that she felt better—surely not fully healed, but better. *He* certainly felt better, though he dreaded the prospect of sorting through her email as much as she did.

Jeez, what about my email? Whatever. I'll deal with that later.

She returned, flopped next to him on the living room couch, and opened her phone.

"*Alter!* People are going *nuts*! This is awful. Professor Sprich even emailed me, *personally*! He never does that. What am I going to do?"

"Well, let's start with that one. Just apologize and tell him everything is okay. Did he want something specific?"

"He needed results from the data analysis I was supposed to have been running. Obviously, I haven't touched it."

He grimaced. This was bad. "You'll have to tell him something came up, something personal, and that you're really sorry. You'll be back as soon as you can, and this will be your top priority. What else can you say?"

She rolled her eyes, but seemed to accept that. She started thumbing out a reply on her phone when he heard the van pull into the driveway.

"Sounds like Olive's back."

"All right, that's done. I'll do basically the same for these others, all people I'd promised this or that, though none are as important as Professor Sprich."

He smiled. "Great. See, you can do it. What the hell is that one?" He scowled at a long header in German.

"Oh, that's just the *Wöchentliche Archäologie-Überprüfung.* The Weekly Archaeology Review from the University in Köln. It's great because it has so much information on computational and quantitative archaeology, but it's a shitload to get through every week."

"Can't you just jet that one, or file it for later? There will be another one coming out soon anyway, right?"

She jerked her head and stared directly at him. "*Scheiße!*"

He was totally confused "What? What's the big deal? Hey, read it now if it's that important, I just figured—"

"No, no, it's not that. It's what you said, or rather, what you said reminded me of what Clint said."

"What did my uncle say?" Olive asked as she walked into the living room.

"I'd totally forgotten. He told us that Ninurta had instructed him to disassemble the gateway, so that 'none could follow.' That means to keep others from *coming out*!"

"What *others*?" Eric nervously probed. "You mean there could be more creatures that can pass through that portal?"

"I don't know for certain, but the implication of what Ninurta said is pretty clear. Where is the portal now?"

"It's in the barn, still in the duffle bags. We left it there last night."

"I think it's high time we have a look at this thing. Come on, let's go."

"What about your emails?"

"Oh, fuck the stupid emails! This is far more important... and interesting."

That's my Lotte.

They joined hands and jumped up from the couch, and followed Olive toward the barn.

"How is Rebel?" Lotte asked as they approached.

"Mutig!" Olive corrected. "His name is Mutig, remember?"

She smiled as she backtracked. "*Ja, ja...* Mutig! *Entschuldigung!* You're quite right. In any case, how is he?"

"He was still really woozy and weak, but he did wag his tail when he saw me. 'Course, that dang old dog will wag his tail just about at anything, so who knows what that meant? Anyway, they said they'd keep him another day, see how he does. They'll call again tonight if they can."

At least it wasn't bad news. Not sure I could have handled it had it been.

The doors to the barn were as he'd left them the night before. None of the three of them had worked up the courage to open them. Now, at least, they had each other for support. Eric unlatched the hinge and threw the doors open. Light streamed into the dingy barn, and the fire portal gleamed near the far wall. The bowls were empty, save some minimal remnants of melted wax. Otherwise, no trace remained of the Afrit, or Blake Harris, as if neither had ever been there, or ever existed at all.

The trio stood silently at the threshold, almost afraid to enter, or perhaps pausing in reverent tranquility, unwilling to disturb the sleep of the dead.

Lotte finally broke the stifling hush that had descended upon them. "Let's take the bags and bring them into the back yard. It's too dark in here to see anything, and it's beautiful outside. I don't want to be near *that* bloody thing right now, anyway."

Her words captured exactly what Eric, and surely Olive, were loath to say. They both happily obliged. Each grabbed a duffel bag and exited, while Lotte refastened the hinge that held the doors shut and returned the fire portal to its morbid slumber.

They carefully removed the pieces from the bags and placed them on the grass, not far from the back steps where Lotte had been drinking her tea. The discarded mug still sat where she'd abandoned it to join Eric in the shower, unable to further resist her sorrow. Now, her agile mind thoroughly engaged in solving the puzzle laid out before them.

"It's unbelievable," she said, as she examined the marks where they'd been inscribed at the end of one of the pieces. "I have no idea how they did this. The lines are nearly perfect, as if a stencil were used in clay, but this material is hard as a rock—I daresay even harder. It's like the magnetic stones of Charun's portal. This substance is simply not of our world. I'd love to get it under a microscope."

Once they'd spread the pieces out on the grass, they started to match them, which went remarkably easily. There were essentially two sections of the portal, the circular part that sat on the ground, and the semicircular portion that stood in the air. These two segments were linked by pieces on either side that had curved pipes leading out of the front, and legs with the feet of what appeared to be goats, which jutted out the back, presumably for support. The pipes fed into pieces at the circular bottom, which Lotte had already observed were hollow.

In fact, the pieces that connected at the top of either side to form the arch were also hollow. Each side of the arch ended in the middle with the same symbol, and only one piece bore that symbol on each of its ends. This piece contained a hole in its center where clearly the odd, stepped object that looked like a witch's hat inserted. As it turned out, that piece was also hollow, and its back opened into something resembling a funnel.

"If you poured liquid in," Lotte deduced, "it would run through the little hat, down each side of the hoop or arch, out of the pipes in the bottom, and through the circular area on the ground. There are small holes in the central piece on the left, right, back, and front of the circular bottom. That means the liquid would trail out of those holes into the area the circle encloses."

"No, it wouldn't," Eric countered. "There's no way the seals we made are tight enough. The pieces fit together, but not perfectly. Water would be dripping out everywhere. You'd have to caulk it up, or something, and I don't see any evidence of anything like that ever being used."

She pondered that. "You might be right, but what's the harm in trying? It's not like water will hurt the portal. I think we've established that. Olive, is there a source of water nearby?"

"I think the hose pipe is over on that side of the house."

"The *what*?"

"The hose pipe. Don't y'all know what a hose pipe is, or don't you have those in New England?"

Eric laughed. "We do. We just call them 'hoses.' I'm not sure what Lotte was picturing in her mind, but that's why she's confused."

Olive rolled her eyes. "*What-eh-ver.* Y'all want me to fetch the *hose*, or don't you?"

"Please do," Lotte said, repressing a giggle. She silently mouthed "*hose pipe*" to him as Olive rounded the corner of the house.

He tried not to laugh as well.

Fail.

Olive called out from around the side of the house. "I hate to interrupt your fun, but can one of y'all come help me? This dang thing is heavy and it's all twisted up."

With a slight pang of guilt, Eric ran to assist her with the hose. It was a big one, and almost hopelessly tangled. It took some work, but finally they got it uncoiled and walked the nozzle out to where the portal stood.

Olive went back to turn on the water. "Tell me when it's enough!" she shouted.

"That's good!" he called when the water poured out steadily, but not strongly. "This should work. You want to do the honors?"

He held the nozzle out to Lotte, who took it and brought it to the funnel in the back of the little stepped hat.

Olive joined them as water began to course through the hollows of the structure.

At first, nothing happened. As Eric had predicted, water seeped out where various seams were not perfectly tight, but then....

Lotte jumped. "What the hell was that? Did you see that?"

He wasn't sure what he had or hadn't seen. He was sure, however, that water had stopped seeping out of a particularly bad spot in the right arch, and he *thought* he'd seen the two pieces around that seam... move.

Suddenly, the entire portal erupted in a series of writhing motions, like the tentacles of a squid, squirming to life after being frozen. Each movement sealed another leak in the structure. In fact, the seams appeared to be disappearing altogether, as if the portal were made entirely of one living, undulating mass.

"*Scheiße!* It's responding to the water. The water is turning it on, bringing it to life."

"Should we be doing this?" Eric asked with trepidation. "We could be opening the portal. Who knows what might come out!"

She frowned. "You're right, but if we don't find out, we'll never know. Ninurta feared whatever else might come out of that portal. If we think he's a danger, which I believe we all do, and hope to get him to go back, then whatever else is in there may help us. The enemy of our enemy may be our friend."

"Yeah, and the enemy of our enemy may eat us first, then go eat our enemy! This could be a major mistake."

"I know. I know it's a risk. Let's just give it a bit and see what happens. We have to *know*, Eric, and this is the only way."

He bit his tongue. *Okay, sweetheart. It's your funeral if you're wrong. Actually, it's all of our funerals.*

"Olive," he said, "get ready to run if something happens. Don't wait for anything—me, Lotte, whatever. Get to the van and get out of here. You still have the keys on you?"

"Yep," she replied with a mixture of terror and determination. "Should I run 'n get the AR-15?"

"Yes, absolutely! Go get the AR-15! Why didn't we think of that before? Grab a bat or two while you're at it." He smiled at Lotte, who wryly smiled back. "Why have a nice collection of weapons if you're not gonna use 'em, right?"

As Lotte had predicted, with all the leaky seams sealed, water now flowed easily through the structure and streamed out of the small holes in the four pieces at each axis of the circle. At first, the water simply disappeared into the grass, but soon, small pools began to form.

"I don't get how this is gonna work," Eric said, bewildered. "Water is obviously supposed to flow into the middle area, but it will just seep under the bottom. There's nothing to hold it in. Maybe we're missing something?"

"I don't think so," Lotte responded. "Look. It's amazing."

He glanced down and saw that the bottom of the circular sides of the portal had extended outward and merged with the earth, like the walls of a shallow swimming pool. This seemed to trap the water, which built until it covered the grass with a smooth, sparkling sheen. The earth itself within the area of the circle seemed to ripple and churn, morphing into a slightly concave area that held, rather than absorbed, the water.

When the circular space was almost full, Lotte took the hose away from the funnel in the back of the stepped hat.

Just as Olive returned with her gun and the two bats, the water began to change color. The greenish hue of the grass faded, as did the murkiness of the muddy liquid, and a surface of pure blue glowed on the ground before them. Impossibly, a light emerged from the depths. In reality, the pool was only a few inches deep, but it appeared to extend into infinity.

"Oh, my gawd!" Olive said, slack jawed. "What have we done? Is the portal open?"

"I'm not sure," Lotte answered, equally in awe. "It hasn't dug into the ground like it did at the fishing lodge. It doesn't appear to have created that large crater, either, just a small concave area. So, I'm not sure if it's open or not. Perhaps it's only partially open, like the fire portal when it hasn't fully heated up. You can call, and the Afrit can answer, assuming it wants to, but the creature can't come through until the temperature is high enough. Maybe this is like that."

Eric tried to clarify. "You mean that, in the state this portal is in now, if we reach out with our minds like we do with the Afrit, something might hear us?"

"It's possible. Obviously, I don't know for sure, but based on what we know, I think there's a chance."

He considered for a moment. "Okay, let's give it a shot, but let's take precautions in case something comes shooting out of there to grab us. Olive, take out your gun and keep your eye on this water. If you see anything, and I mean *anything*... scream your head off, and shoot it if you have a clear shot. Lotte, you get on that side, and I'll go on this side. We'll both think into the pool and see if we can get anybody's, or anything's, attention. Is that a plan?"

"I see no harm," Lotte affirmed.

Sure, always the optimist. I can imagine about thirteen ways this could go seriously wrong.

She took her position, while Olive stood on the opposite side of the little pool from the hooped arch, eyes intent on the luminous water before her.

As he did when he'd called the Afrit, Eric reached out with his mind, casting his thoughts into the pool. Under normal circumstances, he'd have felt like an idiot, but this was hardly a normal circumstance, and past experience had proven the veracity of this otherwise questionable activity.

Similar to his recent encounter with the realm of the Eternal Flame, he felt zilch—all a big nothing-burger unless or until something responded. He broke his concentration to glance at Lotte, who like him projected her thoughts into the pool, eyes shut with intense concentration. He flashed a quick smile at Olive, who looked at him nervously, before returning to his task.

He quested with his mind, reaching out, casting into the void. He imagined his thoughts as waves, spreading ever outward into the abyss below him.

Wait a minute, waves travel on top of the ocean. We need something different, something that penetrates... like radar, or the WHG. I've got it... sonar!

He put the waves out of his mind and imagined his cry cutting through the water, permeating every space in its depths, leaving no area uncovered, radiating ever outward.

Is anyone there? Can you hear me? Don't be afraid. All we want to do is talk with you. Tell me if you can hear me. Is anyone there?

'Misery!'

The feeling washed over him like a tidal wave, but one that moved agonizingly slowly. The thought seemed to take forever to express itself. He reeled when it was gone, but then another slow-motion assault wracked his senses.

'Failure!'

He felt the emotion as if it were his own. All the failures in his life bubbled to the surface, like air from a diver's breathing apparatus. Each tiny pocket of oxygen seemed like a slash across his ego, an eternal strike against his confidence that he would never live down.

"Eric!" Olive called. "Are you all right?"

Her words broke the contact, and the withering self-recrimination that had caused him to partially collapse into the little pool of water quickly disappeared.

"What is it, my love?" Lotte said with alarm as she knelt by his side. "What happened? Here, let me help you." She supported his shoulder as he dizzily lifted himself from the water.

"I think I made contact. Whatever it is, it's not terribly happy, and its thoughts are almost overpowering. This thing packs a major punch, but I'm not sure it even noticed me. I want to try again."

"Are you sure? It could be dangerous."

"No kidding, but you wanted to know, and this seems to be the best way. In any case, I don't think it can really hurt me. It was just a really overpowering sensation. I wasn't ready for it. Now I am. Let me try again."

"All right, but I'm staying here with you, and if I see a problem, I'm going to pull you out. You hear me?"

He nodded and gave a hint of a smile. He felt safer having her by his side anyway.

Again, he closed his eyes and cast his thoughts into the glowing waters, concentrating on the idea of sonar that spread out and cut through the depths, leaving no area untouched by his message.

Very soon, the lethargic suffering reappeared. With anguish and agony, it lamented some dreadful occurrence for which this being took full responsibility. Eric tightened his focus and tried to shield his mind from the full onslaught of the emotional barrage. It seemed to work. He'd been *too* open, had cast *too* wide. That had located what he was looking for, but it had left him vulnerable. Now that he knew where it was, he could focus, and protect his mind from the creature's inner torture.

Cautiously, he projected out in a narrow, simple beam of thought. *Who are you?*

The waves of misery receded slightly, and he felt the presence of another mind. Its thoughts came so slowly—so long between ideas, between words, between images and emotions. Though alien, it felt somehow familiar. A word came to him. He didn't know why, but once in his mind, he couldn't get it out. It just... fit.

"Langsam," he whispered, as much to himself as to Lotte, whose tight grasp he felt on his arm.

"What, Eric? I didn't hear. What did you say?"

"I said... Langsam."

"What does that mean, Eric? What have you found?"

"You're not gonna believe this, but I think I'm in mental contact with a turtle."

CHAPTER 15

"Eric, that's ludicrous."

Apparently, Lotte didn't believe him. In truth, he had a hard time believing it himself, but the *sense* of it was simply impossible to deny. "I don't know what to tell you. It's this image in my mind, and I can't get it out. I... I think it's hiding... in its shell."

The look of skepticism didn't leave her face, but her natural pragmatism and curiosity quickly took over. "All right, you're getting sensations from... well... whatever this is. Can you communicate with it? Can you find out what has it so upset?"

"I don't know, but I can give it a shot. I just need to keep my focus very narrow, very small."

She pressed close as he again projected his thoughts into the glowing pool before them. He felt Olive brush his right arm as she knelt beside him. In most ways, their touch was indistinguishable—their bodies had such a similar feel.

Like sisters. My sisters of mercy, ready to plead for clemency on my behalf should anything in this pool try to harm me, or fight for it with whatever weapons they possess, just as I would for them. Like a brother. What a strange little family we make.

Once again, his mind filled with the tortured self-recriminations of the turtle-being. This time, he dared to project a tiny thought toward the miserable creature, just a whisper.

"Can you hear me?"

Silence.

All trace of the turtle's thoughts instantly vanished, and Eric felt as if he were suddenly alone in a great ocean, treading water, and incredibly far from shore. Lotte's touch grounded him, but he missed her counsel. There was nothing for it, her mind too far away. He had to keep trying. Again, he cast out into the nothingness.

"I mean you no harm. Can you hear me?"

'I... hear.'

The response, though tentative and laborious, encouraged him. Heartened, he tried again, but kept things simple for fear of overloading the mysterious being.

"Who are you?"

'I... am. I... serve. He... is... gone.'

"He who? Ninurta?"

At this, Eric felt a renewed rush of distress from the turtle, but also felt the being's mind open slightly, become less guarded and fearful of contact.

'Yes... Ninurta... Ningursu. You... wish... to... speak... with... him... but... he... is... gone.'

"I know he's gone. We met him in our world. I'm not here to speak with him. I'm here to speak with you."

He now felt a certain amount of surprise intermingled with the unhappiness and wariness that emanated from the creature.

'Me? I... am... nothing. A... failed... guard. Master... will... be... angry... if... ever... he... awakes.'

"Master? Who's your master?

The being arduously answered. *'Lord... of... the... Abzu. For... him... I... guard... Ninurta. For... centuries. Briefly... some... came... to... speak... with... him. But... no... more. Now... he... is... gone. Did... you... open... the... gate?'*

"No, we didn't. It must have been a sort of *accident* that it opened at all. Now, Ninurta is loose in our world, and we're afraid of what that might mean. We want to return him to you, put things back as they were. Can you help us?"

Briefly, he felt a surge of optimism from the miserable creature, but quickly, the dismal thoughts returned.

'Cannot... help. Gate... too... small... for... me. Only... master... can... help... but... I... fear... to... disturb... him.'

This thing must be massive if it can't fit out of the portal. It would probably be the biggest turtle ever seen! "Listen to me, you *must* disturb him. It wasn't your fault he got out. We'll explain that to your master, Lord of the Abzu, or whatever it was you called him. He wanted Ninurta guarded for a reason. I've seen firsthand what he's capable of, and I'm not sure if you know who, or what, Sharur is, but Ninurta has been reunited with his happy little weapon-monster, and I think they're dangerous... *very* dangerous. I know it's scary, but this is the only way. You have to wake your master and tell him. *Please*!"

He could feel the turtle retreat into its shell. Nonetheless, thoughts still emanated from the being, mostly terrible ambivalence. It obviously knew Ninurta could be formidable, and Eric had felt a tremendous shudder from the beast when he'd mentioned Sharur. Unfortunately, this, "Lord of the Abzu" seemed to produce an equal, if not even greater fear. It wasn't at all clear what the turtle would do.

The tortured being finally spoke.

'Mad!'

He feared he'd made the turtle angry, but quickly realized that wasn't its meaning.

'So... much... time. He... railed... at... his... captivity. He... called... out... to... his... father... but... the... Rope... of... An... and... Ki... no... longer... listens. With... only... me... to... speak... with... Ninurta... lost... his... mind.'

I hate to admit it, but I can sort of understand where Ninurta's coming from. If this turtle had been my only company for centuries, I'd probably be a little bonkers too.

He hoped that thought didn't seep out of his mind, but thankfully the turtle seemed completely preoccupied by its quandary and didn't appear to notice.

"I thought you said there were others who came to talk with Ninurta. Didn't that help?"

'Countless... time... passed... before... anyone... came. By... then... Ninurta... was... mad. Mad... as... the... one... who... spoke... with... him... the... most.'

"I see. Why does his madness concern you this much? Why are you so focused on it?"

'Anger!' the turtle shot back. *'Revenge! Madness! Dangerous... before. Now? Deadly. Must... be... stopped. I... go!'*

All trace of the being's presence vanished so quickly from his mind, it felt as if the oxygen had been suddenly sucked from Eric's body. He again partially collapsed into the pool, gasping for breath, and flailing for an invisible and unreachable shoreline to quell the overwhelming sense of drowning.

He felt Lotte's hands tighten around his left arm, and from the other side Olive also steadied him. "Eric, what happened? My love, are you all right?"

With their assistance, he lay back into the grass, gulping for air and fighting the dizzying effects of the rapid separation of minds.

He choked out a self-satisfied laugh. "Definitely a turtle. It's incredible. It says it was guarding Ninurta for his master, the 'Lord of the Abzu' for centuries. Recently, some others had come to talk with Ninurta, maybe the people who stole the portal back in the 1950s, but they never let him out. They probably didn't know how. Anyway, the turtle said

Ninurta has gone insane. He was dangerous before, but now he's pissed off and looking for revenge."

"What will we do?" Lotte exclaimed. "We have to stop this before he can cause any more damage. This is as bad as Charun, maybe worse. Can the turtle help us?"

"Well, yes and no. It's too big to fit out of the portal gate."

They all glanced at the pool, sizing up exactly how large the turtle would have to be for that to be true.

"That's a mighty big turtle," Olive observed. "Maybe it's just as well it stays put."

"Yeah, maybe, but it finally decided to go call its master, this 'Lord of the Abzu' guy. Apparently, he's been *sleeping* this entire time, if you can believe *that*. The turtle was afraid he'd be angry that it let Ninurta escape, and he may well be. I told it we'd say there had been an accident and that Ninurta had gotten free, which I actually think is true. I guess that offer, combined with its feeling that Ninurta *was* really dangerous, helped the turtle decide to go wake him."

Lotte pieced things together. "So, the turtle is going to wake up this Lord of the Abzu, and we're going to talk with him?"

"That seems to be the plan, best as I can tell."

"Abzu... I know this word. It's definitely Mesopotamian, something about water, but this isn't my specialty. *Verdammt!* I don't have my phone. Can you hang on? I'll run get it. I think we need to know what we're up against here."

She bounded back into the house, past the discarded and now forgotten mug on the back steps.

"Y'all okay?" Olive tentatively asked. "You look kind of worn out."

He finally found the strength to sit up. "Yeah, that concentration took a lot out of me. I felt like I swam out ten miles, and then got catapulted back. I've never been so deep into one of these 'other' places before. Calling the Afrit was totally different. This is just so much more... *powerful*."

"Should we even be doing this? I feel like we're in way over our heads. 'Course, I mostly feel like that, but this time, I know it means more than just gettin' a sucky grade on a paper."

"It's dangerous, but Lotte has good instincts about stuff like this. I think she may well be right that the enemy of Ninurta could be our friend, and after talking with that turtle, I'm convinced Ninurta is dangerous. Jeez, never in my life did I think I'd utter the words, 'after talking with that turtle.'"

She gave a nervous laugh as Lotte reappeared at the back door and dashed across the yard.

"All right," Lotte breathlessly said. "Keep an eye on the pool and tell me if you sense anything. Let me have a look." She rapidly typed and scrolled on her phone. "Here it is, Abzu... or Apsu. It's the name for fresh water from underground aquifers, which was given religious significance in Sumerian and Akkadian mythology. There's a link here to Mesopotamian gods. I'll see if one is connected with this water. I sort of remember Apsu being a god in his, or her, own right, in some kind of opposition to Tiamat, I believe, but that may be a later myth. It's all so damned confusing."

Eric completely agreed. Ancient history and myth had never been his specialty, or particularly his interest. *In fairness, though, I'd have probably studied it harder if I'd known I was going to meet some of the beings from the stories in person.*

"Here," Lotte went on. "You have An, or Anu, supreme god of the heavens and a prime mover in creation."

"The turtle mentioned An. Crap, what did he say? Something about the 'Rope of An and Ki.' I think he said that was Ninurta's father, although maybe I misunderstood that. It was hard to keep everything straight. Didn't you say something about Enlil being Ninurta's father, back when we were talking about Sharur? Is Enlil the Rope of An and Ki as well?"

"Great question. Why the hell didn't I do this research before?" Under her breath, he barely heard her mutter, "What's *wrong* with me?"

"It's okay. Just keep plugging. You're doing great. Olive, you see anything in the pool, any changes?"

"All clear far as I can tell," she called over her shoulder. "But y'all try to hurry, please? This is creepin' me right out."

Lotte rapidly digested the information from the web page on her phone.

"*Alter!* Here it is. *An* is the word for *heaven,* and *Ki* is the word for *earth.* This is linked to the second major god in the Mesopotamian pantheon, who is indeed Enlil. Anu is his father, and as we know, Ninurta is his son. Enlil is credited for separating An and Ki, heaven and earth, so he literally became the 'mooring rope' between them. It looks like he became a supreme god as well, eventually supplanting Anu, who it doesn't appear was worshiped directly that much after a certain point. It also looks like Enlil has a bit of a temper. According to one myth, he planned to wipe out humanity in a great flood because we were being too *loud,* and he couldn't bloody well sleep."

Olive scoffed. "Boy, these Mesopotamian gods sure like their sleep. What stopped him from killing us all?"

Her eyes widened. "Wait a minute! I remember a bit of that story from reading The Epic of Gilgamesh in my first-year classics class at Oxford. Hold on...." Again, she wildly flipped and scrolled on her phone. "Here it is! Right, I remember now. Most interesting. The man's name was Utnapishtim, and he's tasked with building a boat before the flood comes. He's supposed to save his wife and family, craftsmen from the village, animals, grain, and so-on. Sound familiar? It's just like Noah's Ark, probably the story off of which that was based. In the end, he winds up saving humanity and is made immortal. Right... I remember this now. He was tipped off by another god... what was his name? Ah, here it is. This one is called Ea, also known as—"

'ENKI!'

The word pummeled their minds as if hit by a blast of water from a fire hose. The trio fell to their knees and reeled from the battering, as they tried to keep the lovely brunch they'd recently enjoyed from rocketing out of their stomachs.

'I AM ENKI, AND YOU HAVE DISTURBED MY SLUMBER!'

Despite the almost incalculable power of the projected thought, Eric didn't detect anger. It was merely an announcement... a proclamation that a god had entered their midst, and to make no mistake about that fact.

"Please!" Lotte cried. "Your thoughts... they crush our minds! We didn't wish to disturb you, great one, but Ninurta has escaped your guard and is free in our world. We thought you should know. We want to help return him. Please, don't end our lives. We wish to serve you!"

With effort, Eric turned his head. The pool glowed more strongly now, but the surface of the water remained still as glass. Olive had collapsed onto her back and moaned miserably from the mental onslaught. He crawled toward her, praying there wouldn't be another assault. Surprisingly, there was not.

'Yes.'

The thought emanated from the pool, strongly still, but not overpowering as before.

'My creation told me. The priests are long dead. How did you open the gateway?'

"We didn't," Lotte protested. "It was an accident. The *gateway*, as you call it, was caught in a flood. I think it may have been totally submerged in water. That's the key, isn't it? The whole thing has to be under the water for it to be fully open, but it can be partially opened as we've done now, so your priests could talk to you."

'Long has it been since I saw the E-Abzu, my temple. Long has it been since I granted my gifts to its priests. All ended in eternal failure, eternal sleep my only recourse. Now, you noisy beings again seek my gifts, again wish to serve. Is even eternity not eternal?'

"Your priests weren't fools. They knew, one day, the world would need you again. I know nothing of this eternal failure of which you speak, but I've seen this before. Others have thought they were done with the likes of you, fearful of your power, and of their own superstitions. But they didn't destroy! Much as they feared, they couldn't bring themselves to do it. They knew that one day, perhaps, aid from another world would be needed again—that nothing is eternal, except change, and changing circumstances. Your priests were wise, great one. They preserved the chance for you to be called again, in our time of need. That time is now!"

Where the hell does she come up with this shit? And who talks to gods that way? I mean... really?

Even more astounding than Lotte's incredible display was Enki's response. He laughed, and waves of good humor came pouring forth from the pool, overwhelming the unnerved trio once again, but this time with warmth and benevolence.

'You creatures never cease to amaze me! So small, your lives, so short, but brightly you burn. You are wrong. Change is not eternal, not in the Abzu. Without your call long ago, all would be as it ever was, and as it ever would have been. But call you did, and we answered. Now, we are intertwined. You know what you must do, my brazen beauty. Having touched your mind and felt the force of your spirit, I cannot wait to set my gaze upon your lovely flesh.'

"Are you sure you don't want me to help?" Lotte asked with sincerity, but also a rather squeamish look on her face. "That looks terribly mucky. You two shouldn't have to do it all on your own."

"It's fine," Eric replied from where he stood, knee-deep in the murky pond behind Clint's house as he reassembled Enki's gateway.

Disassembling, or rather "de-animating," the thing had proven a bit of a puzzle until Lotte had the idea to simply remove the little stepped hat, which turned out not to have coalesced into unity with the rest of the pieces. At this, the entire contraption lost its cohesion, and broke again into individual parts. The water in the shallow pool vanished into the ground below.

"I think what you're doing is more valuable anyway. The greater our knowledge, the better off we'll be in dealing with our new friend... or friends. Who knows who else might pop out of this portal unexpectedly?"

"Yeah," Olive added enthusiastically. "Please keep reading. I could listen to you talk about history stuff all day. Why couldn't you have been one of my professors? They're all so boring. Plus, I don't mind. I've swum in ponds muckier than this since I was a little girl."

Lotte capitulated without significant protest. "All right, where was I? Right, so Enki is Enlil's brother, and is the Mesopotamian God of Water, among other things. *Alter!* It seems he's quite the ladies' man as well. The waters are associated with fertility, and it looks like he fully took *that* to heart."

Olive beamed. "He sure took a shine to you. Brazen beauty! He got you pegged pretty quickly, that's for sure."

"All right, all right," Eric interrupted, somewhat perturbed.

He'd also sensed Enki's interest in Lotte. It was hard to miss. With their mental contact, you could practically experience firsthand his, well... *excitement*. Competing with Mason had been one thing, but holding his own in Lotte's eyes against a *god* was a different matter. The prospect made him nervous and grumpy.

"Is there any other *useful* information in there, or is it just all about his prodigious sex life?"

Lotte scowled slightly, but went back to her phone. "It says his city was Eridu, which is actually thought to be the first city ever, potentially where civilization itself originated. In fact, in addition to being a water deity, Enki is thought of as the bringer of civilization—almost a god of 'progress,' or 'improvement,' as it were. Look, here's a picture of him."

She held the phone out so they could see. It was a photo of an ancient clay cylinder seal that depicted Enki flanked by two other gods and a great bird.

"He's got his little hat on," Olive sang with delight. "Just like the one on the top of the portal."

Lotte smiled. "Yes, I knew I'd seen that shape before when you showed me your picture. I'm certain this image has crossed my path more than once, but as I say, Mesopotamian myth and history aren't really my area... interesting as it is."

Eric squinted at the picture. "Speaking of shape, look how those two double lines with what look like fish inside them curve out on each side. It makes an arch, just like the curved part of the portal with the hat at the top."

She jerked the phone away and looked with astonishment at the picture, then started to shake with excitement.

"Eric, you're right! You're exactly right! Those are the Tigris and Euphrates rivers, each flowing from one of Enki's shoulders. That's why there's fish in them. It's showing the abundance of life that Enki's waters bring. I think the portal is emulating this image. The hat is on top, and the Tigris and Euphrates are flowing away on each side, carrying the water down. This is why it's an arch. This is why they're *all* arches! It says it right here: 'all rules laid down at Eridu were faithfully observed.' Eric, this isn't just *a* portal, it's *the* portal! It's the one all the others copied. This is the *first* one, the one *from the beginning*, at the very heart of civilization itself!"

Olive and Eric stopped what they were doing and stood, almost reverently, in the muddy pond, pieces of the disassembled gateway in their hands. The magnitude of what Lotte said hung in the air like a clap of silent thunder, shaking the earth with the stillness of revelation.

Olive finally broke the deafening silence. "Can I ask a question? What's up with them goat hooves on the anchor pieces?"

Lotte had to shake her head to regain some semblance of focus.

"I... I don't know. Let me look."

She read for a bit, still reeling from the realization of what they had in their possession, as if it weren't already priceless enough.

"Apparently, the goat-fish, what we know as Capricorn, is a representation of Enki, the 'Antelope of the Sea.' In ancient Babylonian myth, Capricorn correlates to the time the Sun embarks the tenth part of its orbit, and relates to the time of new knowledge. So, Ea, or Enki, is perceived as coming up from the oceanic abyss to teach humanity the wisdom of the gods. Our zodiac sign of Capricorn is an echo of these myths, still present in our southern skies in late summer and early fall."

"Southern skies," Olive repeated. "I like that."

She and Eric silently finished assembling the portal in the murky water of the pond. Together, they secured the final, central piece of the arch, which loomed about three feet above the surface, and he attached the little stepped hat.

"Are we sure this will be deep enough?" he asked. "Doesn't it have to be totally underwater?"

"I don't think so," Lotte answered. "I think it'll be enough that the circular part is submerged. It's likely the portal *was* completely covered during the flood, at least briefly. That's probably how the water got in, and that's what activated it and caused it to burrow down into the ground like it did. I think if we add water at the top, it'll do the same thing now."

"Hmmm, okay, but how are we gonna get the water into the funnel? Just use our hands and scoop it in, or grab a glass from the kitchen?"

She bit her lip as she considered that question. "It feels like the stream of water has to be more consistent than that. I'm not sure just dribs and drabs will get the material to activate, even submerged in the water."

"There's no way the hose will reach this far. Do we have anything to transport that much water?"

"I think there's some old cans in the barn," Olive responded. "I can bring them out here in the wheelbarrow, then use 'em one after another to put water down the hat and into whatever those rivers are supposed to be. You think that'll be enough?"

Eric laughed. "I hope so. I'll help you get all that together. Lotte, you stay here and watch that portal. Scream if it starts to swim away... or something."

She smirked. "I doubt that'll happen, but you'll be the first I tell if it does."

Her phone rang. "Oh, it's the veterinarian. Hold on. Yes, hello?" She listened intently. "Oh, great, thanks for calling." She put her hand over the receiver and spoke to Olive and Eric. "They have an update, just a second." She returned to her phone. "Yes, go ahead. Okay. All right. I see. Umm... yes. Just a moment."

She seemed subdued as she again turned toward Olive. "They think Mutig is ready to go home."

"That's great!" Seeming to sense Lotte's hesitation, she faltered. "Or is it?"

"They've done what they can, Olive. He probably has internal injuries and bleeding, but it's impossible to tell where, and he's not strong enough for surgery. He's heavily medicated, so he's not suffering. They say if we want to have some time with him, we can come get him, but if he doesn't slip away tonight, tomorrow, he'll likely have to be—"

Olive's sob stopped her.

Eric went to her side, but she pulled away.

"I'll get the cans and load them in the wheelbarrow," she choked, as tears streamed from her eyes. "We don't want to keep Mr. Fancy Pants waitin' or he'll swim off and go back to sleep, or some fool thing. Let's just finish this, so I can go see my goddamned dog and say goodbye... and so we can just keep on losing, even when we win."

CHAPTER 16

Olive and Eric retreated rapidly out of the pond as the murky waters began to bubble and churn.

The stream of water from two of the large fuel cans had been enough to bring the structure to life. The portal again launched into flurry of motion, and the motion carried it downward as it seemed to burrow into the pond's bed, just as it had in the basement room of the fishing lodge. Soon, only the stepped hat and a tiny bit of the arch remained above the surface.

From beneath, the water began to glow.

"Here we go," Lotte hesitantly observed. "For better or worse."

Like the little pool that had formed on the grass, the pond appeared frozen, like glass. Nothing stirred. Even the pervasive and ever-present sound of insects and frogs had silenced, the noise more noticeable for its absence. All was preternaturally still, as if time itself had stopped. The trio could barely breathe as they waited on the muddy shore for what came next.

They felt it before they saw it. The presence returned, emanating with unfathomable power from the depths, pulling at their minds like a great magnet.

Then... the tiniest of ripples, barely two feet apart. With uncanny grace they broke in perfect circles across the surface of the pond before they met and twisted into a myriad of cascading shapes.

From the epicenter of each circle, great horns slowly emerged.

"Oh, my gawd," Olive whispered. Her eyes were still red from a steady flow of tears, which, to her credit, she had brushed aside for what needed to be done. "Not what I was expecting."

It wasn't what Eric had expected either. With the mental contact came images, just as it had been with the turtle, and the image he'd had of Enki was that of a man. What emerged from the glassy pond was nothing of the sort.

Instead, he was a huge goat with great, sweeping horns like those of an ibex. His eyes were jet black. They seemed to pierce Eric's soul with their icy gaze as the massive creature glided silently toward the shore. As more of the beast's body became visible, enormous front hooves emerged, which recalled those on the portal now sunk deep into the murky bottom of the pond. From behind, the serpentine tail of a fish occasionally broke the surface as it gently propelled the great god through the water.

"How the H-E Double L is he gonna get around on land?" Olive asked with dismay. "He'll just be floppin' around everywhere."

"Look!" Lotte called out with amazement. "He's transforming."

As Enki emerged onto the muddy shore, the great hooves started to morph into arms and hands. The head of the goat rippled and undulated, almost like the material of the portal when it became animated, and soon the visage of a bearded man emerged. Likewise, the tremendous fish tail coiled inward to fill out the being's torso, legs, and feet. By the time he stood before them, the Capricorn had vanished, though a trace remained in the slightly scaled appearance of the god's naked, muscular flesh.

"Well," Olive dryly observed. "I guess we get the same treat Uncle Clint did. Mighty, er... *impressive*, if I do say so myself."

Enki wasn't as muscular as Ninurta. He lacked the other entity's barrel chest, and his arms and legs were lankier, more "elegant." Still, the being before them seemed to radiate greater power. He emanated a strength that lay not in physical, but rather psychological capacity, and perhaps, for lack of a better word... *magical*. It felt as if the entire and incomprehensible energy of the Abzu, the realm of the deep waters, lay at his command.

He stared at the three awestruck mortals before him, smiled, and without moving his lips, they heard his majestic voice in their minds.

'My children! I have missed you so. Long has it been. So immeasurably long. You failed me, as I failed you, but my heart leaps to see your ever hopeful faces once again – especially you, my raven-haired lovely.'

This last, he directed at Lotte as he grandly walked toward her.

'I happily accept your offer of service. You are now the priestess of my temple. All will bow first before you, and then you to me, as is prescribed.'

Lotte uncharacteristically fumbled for words. "Great one, I... I don't know what to say. I... I wish to serve, no doubt, but we were mostly hoping to help you recapture Ninurta before he can do more harm in our world. Truly, I... umm... appreciate this incredible honor, but the idea of people bowing before me is... well... really quite horrifying."

"Lotte," Eric quietly said out of the side of his mouth. "Ixnay on the contradicting a god thing."

"Quiet, my love."

Enki glanced quizzically back and forth between them. *'My love? Do you claim this one as yours, and does he claim you? Yes. Yes, I sense it. The bond flows strongly between you, like rapids on a mighty river – turbulent, but with great power.'*

Eric laughed to himself. *That seems about right. And now is the time on* Sprockets *when the great god gets rid of Eric and takes the brazen beauty for himself. Goodbye, cruel world.*

'A pity,' Enki dismissively said. *'Before me, you can have no other. You are unfit as my priestess, but there are always others.'*

His eyes fell on Olive, who busily wrung out the bottom of her soaked and muddy Sisters of Mercy t-shirt.

"Whuut? Why's everybody starin' at me? Am I makin' too much noise? Maybe I could just run get some dry clothes... possibly get y'all somethin' to wear there too? You do wear clothes, right?"

Enki looked her up and down, then started to laugh mischievously. *'Another raven-haired beauty! Yes, dear child, the priests took the clothes from my statue in the E-Abzu and adorned me when I deigned to visit them. It gave them much pleasure. Time has passed, but little has changed. Go, girl, fetch the appropriate apparel. It is a ceremony I remember well.'*

Olive turned and ran back to the house, seemingly happy to get away from the lascivious leers of the unclothed deity.

Eric was incredulous. *That was it? Lotte says* he's with me, *and Enki just moves on? Wow, gods are even more mysterious than I could have imagined.*

The strange entity rapidly changed his focus. *'Now, my minion told me what happened. He says the gateway was opened in a flood, and that Ninurta slipped away and has summoned Sharur. Is this true?'*

"It is, great one," Lotte responded. "The gateway, or *portal,* as we call it, was apparently found about sixty-five years ago after being lost, or perhaps more appropriately, hidden, for many centuries. It was then stolen, and from what we can gather from your turtle, those who took it were using it to communicate with Ninurta."

"Speaking of the turtle," Eric interjected. "I hope you went easy on the poor thing. Ninurta escaping wasn't its fault."

He regretted speaking so imprudently as Enki imperiously sized him up. *'My turtle has great strengths and great shortcomings. It can dig, straight and true, right through the clay of the Abzu, right into your world. It is strong, and it will never quit, but it is fearful, uncertain. It is terrified to act, and terrified to not act. Without direction, the creature dithers in eternal paralysis.'*

Eric rolled his eyes. *Ugh, sounds just like me. Turtles of a feather clearly flock together.*

'My creation should have woken me long ago. I know not what Ninurta told those who spoke with him. In his madness and anger, I fear what mischief he may have caused, but it was I who left the turtle as his guard. It was I who, in my grief, turned away from... everything. I wanted no more than to sleep and drown out the noise of you boisterous creatures, for whom everything is always so inordinately important, except that which is truly important! But enough of this. Continue your tale and tell me what happened.'

Lotte took a deep breath. "All right, where was I? Okay, Eric told me that, at some point, your turtle said the person who spoke with Ninurta the most had stopped speaking with him altogether. I think the portal had changed hands again, perhaps more than once, and that eventually it came to be set up in a building in a country we call Iraq. Your city, Eridu, is in the far south of this country. No one knew what the portal was, and while it was in this building, I don't think anyone exposed it to water. Then, the father of the girl who just ran to get your clothes brought it here, across a great ocean to this place. He set it up, and the house it was in experienced the flood. That opened the gateway and Ninurta got out. I don't think the turtle, or even Ninurta, was expecting it to open."

Enki gazed periodically into the sky as if searching for something while he considered her words. *'A storm will come,'* he finally proclaimed. *'Not yet, but soon. Ninurta must first regain his strength, as does Sharur. I told my brother not to give him such power, but without it he would not have defeated the Anzu, and the Tablet would have fallen into the hands of our father.'*

Lotte and Eric exchanged confused glances. Neither knew what he was talking about.

"What will happen in this storm?" she finally inquired.

'It is... complicated. My brother, Enlil, is Ninurta's father.'

"Yes, the Mooring Rope of An and Ki. Eric told me your turtle said Ninurta called out to him for help, but that he no longer listens."

'Yes. Long had he been troubled by our contact with your world... what it had done to you... what it had done to us. He was the first to see, and it angered him greatly. Once, he almost destroyed you all, but I could not let that happen. Enlil heard my words, as well as those of my wise advisor, who begged that you be spared. In the end, Enlil proved more patient than I. He remained active in your realm long after I retreated. Now, however, I cannot sense my brother's presence at all. I believe he has cut himself off in the space he created and is lost, even to me. But there is still one way to reach him. Sharur was Enlil's gift to Ninurta, and through Sharur, Enlil could communicate his will to his son. That connection still exists, and in the energy of a great storm, Sharur can penetrate Enlil's barriers.'

"Why? To kill him? Enlil didn't imprison him, you did. Why would he send Sharur after his father?"

'It is not his father Ninurta seeks. It is what Enlil possesses: the Tablet. The Tablet of Destinies. The item that led originally to Ninurta's imprisonment, and which now he covets above all else. For centuries, its power has clawed at his mind. With it, he can rule your world, and a cruel and terrible rule it would be, for, as I feared, the power Enlil gave him made him callous... indifferent... uncaring to the needs of the mortals who served him. Gone is the benevolent lord of grain and agriculture, which once he was. Ninurta became a god of war, and into endless wars he led his people. Sharur was the slayer of thousands, and they reveled in the blood they spilled.'

"Wait a minute. I thought you said he saved the Tablet from falling into the hands of your father, and something else... Anzu?"

'It is complicated. As you seem to know, Enlil is known as the Mooring Rope of An and Ki, heaven and earth as your kind render it. For us, Ki is the realm in which you people reside, the world you see around you, while An is a domain of air and wind. It fascinated my father, who claimed it as his own and gave it his name.'

"Like Anzu. Is that creature also related to Anu, your father?"

'Yes, but you jump ahead. At the time we arrived, this dimension of winds had suffused deeply into yours, likely a result of its insubstantial nature. Some of its beings had penetrated your world and, with time, they would have brought your realm under their control, leaving little to no place for you... or us. We created the Tablet of Destines to push the An away, sequester it to insulate this plane from eventual destruction. When this was done, Enlil crafted an intermediary space and took up residence there. This place became the single thread and conduit through which movement back and forth was possible – the Mooring Rope of An and Ki.'

"That's incredible, but it obviously wasn't the end of things, was it?"

A look of great sadness crossed the Lord of the Abzu's face, and they both felt waves of displeasure that emanated from the bitterest of memories.

'No, that was merely the beginning. Our father, Anu, was... well... difficult. Like the changing winds of the realm he adopted, or one might say, conquered, his moods would swing – kind at times, cruel at others. Our father adored Enlil for helping to enable the separation that allowed his domination and almost complete control of his newfound heavens, this realm of air and wind unfamiliar to beings of the deep waters. In reward, he granted Enlil the Tablet of Destinies, which conferred upon him supreme force and authority. The item has the ability to control time itself, in certain limited ways.'

Olive interrupted as she returned from the house. "Speaking of time, don't you think it's time you put on some pants? *Please*?"

Enki casually looked down at the bundle of clothes she held. *'Dress me. I welcome your dutiful service.'*

Both she and Lotte rolled their eyes while Eric wondered if Enki was the instigator of shameless patriarchal entitlement, or if he'd inherited that lovely trait from humans.

Olive sighed. "All right. Stick out your leg and I'll put the trousers on. Just be damned careful when you zip up your fly. I didn't bring no underwear."

"While our friend is *serving* you," Lotte disdainfully said. "Can you please finish telling us about what happened with Ninurta?"

The great god continued, seemingly unperturbed by Lotte's tone.

'Sadly, Anu could never remain satisfied. He plotted with his insubstantial minions to finish the domination of this world, and worlds beyond, all by his will and under his command. Where Enlil and I would stand in this new order would always be a subject of unease. We feared the ever-present threat of falling out of favor with our father, but realized he had unwittingly granted us the power to stop him. We both agreed that Enlil should seal the gateway inside the Rope of An and Ki to blunt us from his capricious ways and stormy temper. This he did. Anu was locked away in his adopted realm, and with the power of the Tablet behind him, my brother assumed the role of Supreme Deity. Much time passed this way, but Anu would not be so easily cast aside. There was a creature, a great bird called the Anzu, one of my father's earliest creations in your realm. Enlil had enlisted the beast as a guardian of the doorway to his sanctuary space, and for nearly two millennia, it acted with the utmost loyalty. At a time of great upheaval, however, the great bird stole the Tablet of Destinies and carried it into your world.'

"What good would that do?" Olive asked, as she handed Enki a well-worn t-shirt that probably once belonged to her father. "Anu wouldn't be able to get to it there, right?"

'You are correct. He could not, but it is not clear that my father knew of the theft. He must have had allies in your realm, likely creatures of air who were now permanently trapped here unless Enlil reopened his doorway. This, he could not do, lest Anu be freed. Never did we determine to whom the Anzu brought the Tablet. To our fortune, they did not possess the capacity to reverse our workings, which required our combined powers to accomplish, and even that barely sufficed. Instead, they used the artifact to cut off the flow of fresh waters from the great rivers.'

"The Tigris and Euphrates," Lotte interjected. "The lifeblood of Sumer and the entire Fertile Crescent."

'Yes. The people faced drought and extinction. Our kind too were threatened. Like the dimension of winds, the Abzu also bleeds into your world, though much less so. It connects through these fresh waters, and so our powers in your realm

were greatly diminished. Those of us here were trapped, unable to return due to the energy required, and greatly weakened. With time, we would have expired. Only Ninurta was strong enough to stop the Anzu and retrieve the Tablet, aided, of course, by the power of Sharur, whose energy does not depend upon the deep waters. Those who orchestrated the theft skulked away, leaving the great bird to its fate. It was a fearsome battle, one that Ninurta almost lost. In the end, the God of Thunder and Storms borrowed his weapon's energy to summon the power of the South Wind to rip off the Anzu's wings. The dangerous gambit worked. Once he had dispatched the beast, Ninurta brought the artifact to Eridu, and presented the precious item to me.'

"And for this, you imprisoned him?" asked Lotte.

'Of course not! I accepted the Tablet from Ninurta with eternal thanks. I promised to return it to his father, and assured him that all the gods would honor his name. As he handed it to me, however, he hesitated slightly before he let it go. I observed the look of hunger on his face as I drew the artifact to me. At that moment, I knew his heart, and that he would conspire to take the Tablet to use for his own ends. I could not immediately return the artifact to Enlil's protection, as it would require time to replenish energy before the doorway to the Rope could be reopened, nor could I return it to the deep waters for safekeeping. Needing a distraction to buy time, I summoned my ambassador, Isimud, to pay Ninurta an official visit. By fortune, my servant had not yet undergone his ceremony to surrender his mortal existence and join us in the Abzu.'

"Join *us* in the Abzu?" Lotte huffed. "How many are down there with you in the deep waters?"

'Once, there were many, including those from your world who sacrificed all to serve us here – only the purest of heart, who put no others before us. The promise of eternal life in the Abzu was a great honor for them, but as with all things, there were unexpected outcomes. With time, the mortality of your kind reasserted itself. Their souls became dissatisfied with the unending stillness of our realm, but once transformed, they could never return. Slowly, one by one, they all vanished... dissolved into the ever-seething currents. Even my beloved, Damgalnunna, perished this way. It was her choice, just as it was with the others. Their energy still feeds the deep waters.'

"Is it similar for those of your kind who were in our world, the ones whose power was weakened when Anu used the Tablet of Destinies?"

Enki gazed sorrowfully back over the little pond.

'Our children... our true children... the product of Anu's, Enlil's, and my seed with mortal women... they chose a life in your world. They were worshiped in their temples as living gods, and as living gods, they each died a mortal death, never thinking such a thing could actually happen. Indeed, none of us are immortal here in this realm – powerful, yes, but not immortal. Only Ninurta

was spared, because of his captivity in the Abzu, and with his lineage as a son of Enlil, he has not the option to simply... fade away as did the others.'

"Okay," she heaved, taking all this in. "So, what in blazes happened when you sent Isimud to see Ninurta?"

'Exactly what I expected. Ninurta was arrogant, dismissive. He dishonored the ambassador of a god. Initially, I did not react. Instead, I availed myself of the time afforded and laid a trap for Enlil's power-mad son. When I was ready, I summoned Ninurta to stand before me. I told him the honor of the gods awaited him for his great deed. He came for this, and surely for the chance to steal the Tablet from me before I returned it to Enlil, but come he did, and my trick worked. As I distracted Ninurta with praising words, I called forth the giant turtle I had surreptitiously created with what little power I had at my disposal. The creature grabbed my traitorous nephew from beneath in its jaws, and by its own volition dragged him into a great pit, and from there back into the Abzu.'

"What about Sharur?" Eric excitedly asked. "Wasn't Ninurta's weapon strong enough to save him?"

'Sharur was not with Ninurta. The mace was gorging itself on the body of the dead Anzu, replenishing its power that my nephew borrowed during the battle. Ninurta knew the risk, but the time remaining before I returned the Tablet to Enlil was limited, and he felt he had the upper hand. He called in desperation, but Sharur was too far away to reach him, and too weak to assist. All the way back to the Abzu, my turtle dug, and soon the connection between the weapon and its wielder was lost. Sharur became inert. So began Ninurta's imprisonment. Soon thereafter, the end came for Eridu, destroyed in another of your petty and all-consuming wars. Not the first time, but for me... the last. I chose to sleep, and leave you hopeless but ever hopeful beings to your own devices. Likewise, I left the turtle and Ninurta each to their own fate. It was wrong, I see this now, but just another wrong in a chain of misfortune, a chain I hoped to break by simply... going away.'

The sadness exhibited by this being so obviously capable of such great mirth was heartbreaking. Eric felt a sense of terrible loss from the intense emotional emanations, as if some great thing had fallen woefully short of completion—some noble effort had gone horribly awry.

Lotte pressed on despite the gloom that hung in the air. "So, what do we do now with Ninurta? Just wait for this storm to come?"

'It makes no sense to go to him now. With Sharur, Ninurta is powerful. I cannot best him physically in this realm, but I can slow him, and if we catch him by surprise, I have a plan to recapture him. So, yes, we wait for the storm, and for Sharur to leave Ninurta's side. Then, we strike.'

"Does that mean we can go get Mutig now?" Olive tentatively asked. "I just don't want to... miss him."

Lotte took her arm. "Yes, Olive, let's you and I go. Eric, stay with our *guest.* Make sure he's *comfortable.* We'll stop and get some food for dinner, and we'll be back as soon as we can."

In other words, watch this sucker and make sure he doesn't do anything dangerous. "Gotcha. See you soon, sweetheart."

He flashed a stupid smile in Enki's direction.

To his great amazement, Enki smiled back.

Eric briefly considered asking Lotte if he could go with Olive and let her stay behind to babysit the Lord of the Abzu instead.

What have I got to say to him?

Then he remembered the prospect of a now only semi-clothed deity potentially hitting on his girlfriend. Maybe that thought had crossed her mind as well. She'd certainly beaten a hasty retreat with Olive.

Probably for the best. I'll make it work.

For his part, Enki barely seemed to notice that Lotte and Olive had left. He sat by the pond and gazed into the murky water as he adjusted the pants that Olive had brought him. Like the shirt, they must have been her father's. They were tight in the waist, and too short in length for the lean and tall being. The faded t-shirt from a local bait and tackle shop completed the picture. He looked ridiculous, but Eric didn't think the great god really cared.

The silence became uncomfortable as he sat by Enki. Mercifully, the being had picked a sunny spot, and Eric's own damp clothes had begun to dry out.

"Umm," he ventured, "you said something about your turtle being able to dig right into your realm, the Abzu. Is that true?"

Enki's eyes grew bright with curiosity. *'Why would I lie? Of course, it is true. The turtle is, after all, my creation.'*

"I didn't mean to imply you were lying. It's just surprising to me. Lotte and I have encountered creatures from other realms, but they always come through portals, or 'gateways,' as you call them. I'm surprised to hear creatures can move back and forth in other ways, on their own."

'My father, Enlil, and I, as well as our creations, can enter or exit the Abzu without the use of a gateway. It is vastly harder, but possible. Consider... how could it be that your kind ever made contact with me, or my father or brother? The gateway was beyond their conception, and at that stage, beyond even ours.'

Eric vaguely remembered that the Afrit had hinted at something along those lines a long time ago. Humans had gazed into the fire, and the Afrit had gazed back.

Or was it Lotte who'd speculated something like that may have happened, or Dr. Esfahani? I can't remember. Remembering stuff is Lotte's department. Anyway, this is interesting. At least it gives us something to talk about.

"So, how did all this start? Lotte told us that Eridu was possibly the original city, where human civilization made its first appearance. Were you a part of that?"

The slightest smile creased the great god's lips.

'A part? One could say that, yes. A tribe of your kind settled near a marsh. There, an underground spring of fresh water flowed up into the salt water of the sea around it. In this spot, they farmed and fished, and in that special place, they worshiped. Indeed, it was a special place. Even they could feel it. There, the fresh water battled the salt, like the Abzu battled the Nammu, like order battles chaos, or chaos rips itself from order, depending on one's perspective. In any case, it was a location well known to us, a place that called to us from another realm, but a realm that connected to ours, both physically and in these uniquely special ways. For us too, it was sacred, a metaphor for the struggle that our own region experienced at its birth. From opposite sides, your kind and ours revered this site. It was inevitable that, eventually, we would see one another.'

Just like gazing into the fire. "So, you saw each other. What happened?"

He chuckled. *'Into this unique location, your kind poured their prayers. They begged the life-giving waters to help them. They had transitioned to a largely sedentary existence, risen above those who still followed game from place to place, but problems still plagued these people. Crops failed, pests destroyed their surplus, outsiders raided and stole their animals, and as their population grew, they found the old ways insufficient to make decisions for a larger group. They prayed for salvation, begged for help from gods that did not listen, because they did not exist.'*

"But... you did exist, and you heard. You listened."

'We existed, yes, but not in the way your kind thought we did. And we heard, and for us, it was something... different. *For an inestimable eternity, there had been the same, the unchanging Abzu. Then, suddenly, something new. So, yes, we listened, and we learned, and in time we became the gods you wanted, the gods you so desired. Anu and Enlil had their own priorities and desires in your realm, but it was I who took an interest in your kind, saw what you truly needed. I gave you new ways of organizing, new ways of thinking about lives that were no longer spent chasing game from place to place. I brought to your kind the* Me, *the gifts of civilization, and around my temple your existences, and mine, would henceforth revolve.'*

He hadn't understood it well, but Eric had seen *2001: A Space Odyssey* several times. One couldn't help but comprehend the beginning, the great black alien monolith that inspired the early hominid to use the bone as a weapon. Just a little nudge, and the next thing you know, humankind is waltzing in outer space.

The creatures in the film hadn't prayed for assistance, or, maybe they had. They'd been driven from their watering hole. Maybe they were desperate. Maybe they looked to the skies and, fearing almost certain death, asked the very stars themselves to save them. How could they have known what it meant, what it would lead to? That killing to slake their thirst on that day would seal a path from which their entire species could never turn—the path toward civilization.

Civilization, and its consequent and seemingly inescapable discontents.

"Your gifts... they came to us at great cost."

'You surprise me. Generations revered the Me, *basked in the glory of their benefits, but you are correct. There were unintended complications, for your kind and for ours. Your raven-haired female spoke of the constancy of change. It is not so in the Abzu. Little could we have imagined how rapidly you creatures adapt, and then outgrow. How quickly you came to chafe at the structure I offered, a life of reciprocity with my temple at its center. Power-mad little beings you can be, so few willing to play their role to create and maintain the stability that would have enabled your kind to live in prosperity and harmony for eternity. Too many revolted, unwilling to follow the laws and inhibit your natural urges and aggressions, even when that means being cast out, to live again as savages.'*

He nodded and laughed. "Yep, that's us in a nutshell. There's a man whose books I've read. He says almost exactly what you just did, that humans want the gifts of civilization, but so many of the benefits run counter to our basic nature. It can make us anxious, depressed, and I guess at the extreme, some people just completely lose their minds. He says there's nothing you can do but sort of 'make the best of it,' but this means that it's really hard for large groups of people to come together on anything, or stay together, because in the end, everyone wants or needs something different."

'This man is wise. Bring him before me. I would speak with him.'

"I wish I could. There's a lot of things I'd like to talk with him about too, but sadly, he's long dead. Only his books survive. I don't have any with me, but I could try to find one online and read it to you."

The great god silently turned his head back toward the water and projected a sorrow that pierced Eric's heart with its magnitude of despair.

'We tried. We entered your world and attempted to impress upon your kind the need for unity. To lead, we mated with your females to establish a ruling order that you could understand... that you could see, and touch... and who could keep up with your expanding and ever wandering populations. In the end, they became more like you, petty and covetous of their insignificant little domains, and as willing to fight with one another as you did among yourselves. But now, the conflicts became greater. They brought the power of the Me *to the act of killing. Oh, the carnage, and the noise! Ever clamoring, seething with passions that soon poisoned even the great and unchanging Abzu itself. Enlil saw it before I did. He felt the pull to return to what once had been and leave you miserable creatures to your fates. But I loved you! Love. A feeling solely of your world, but as your kind took from me, so I took from them. I am forever changed. There is no way back for me, just as there is none for you. It was all such a terrible mistake.'*

Eric reeled from this outpouring, clearly centuries in the making, almost like an unbottling of long-repressed memories.

Freud would love this guy, though I wonder how the diehard atheist would feel about having a living god on his couch.

He finally managed to clear his head of the deity's anger and misery.

"I hear what you're saying, but I don't know how else to put this... at this point, it is what it is. There's another man who says that a lot, and what he means is that, 'yeah, we made mistakes and didn't do as well as we could have, but it happened, and at this moment, the only thing we can do is move forward from where we are, learn from the past, and try to do better.' Humankind went through countless changes for countless reasons over millions of years before you ever entered the picture. We're the legacy of *all* of that. Nobody's crying over spilled Abzu water. We're just trying to live our lives the best we can. If what you say is true, Ninurta threatens that, for everyone. Help us get rid of him, and let us worry about our civilizations and their discontents. If it wasn't you kicking things off, it would have been something else. At this point, that just... is what it is."

Enki took all that in. *'Is the man who says these words also dead?'*

"Well, he's pretty *deadpan*, but no, he's alive. He coaches a football team that I like. That's a game, played with a ball."

'That you touch with your foot, I presume?'

Eric smiled. "Exactly. Want to see some video of football? You might enjoy it."

'What is... video?' the great god asked, curiosity again in his eyes.

"Oh, you're going to *love* this. Video is... well... it's like a waltz in space. It's one of the good things about civilization. You'll be proud."

Lotte called out as she walked up behind them. "Eric, we're back. Can you please go help Olive carry.... What in the world are you doing?"

He smiled over his shoulder. "Hi! So, we started out watching football, but Enki got curious about... well, basically everything, so now we're just surfing around. He says most of what we know about Mesopotamian history reeks of the entrails of rotted fish. His words, not mine."

Enki beamed out his sense of delight in warm waves. *'This small tablet is a wonder! There is much good in your world. Perhaps I was hasty to have abandoned you, or perhaps, my work was completed.'*

"What is he talking about?" Lotte asked with confusion. "He's not thinking of leaving, is he?"

"No, no, nothing like that. I'll fill you in later. You said Olive needed something?"

Her shoulders slumped. "Yes, I think she'd appreciate it if you could help her carry Mutig inside."

Riiiiight. "Ugh, how is he? I mean, I know it's not good, but does it seem like he's suffering?"

"He's just extremely weak, both from the fight and all the medicine. Even so, I think he'll be happier being around people tonight rather than alone at the veterinarian's office. We bought some barbeque. Olive thought we'd like that, though I don't think she'll be much in the mood. I'll heat it up while you help her."

She turned to where Enki still held Eric's phone in rapt concentration. "Great one, are you hungry? We have food, if you'd care to join us."

Enki handed the phone back to Eric and stood. *'I have no need for human sustenance. I get my power from the Abzu through the fresh waters of your realm, but I will accompany you.'*

"Please, this way."

Eric circled around the house and approached the dented white van. The now badly scratched side door stood open. Olive sat on the floor in the cargo space, gently stroking Mutig's head and shoulders.

"Can I help you?" he quietly asked. "Get him inside, that is. Help bring him in?"

She turned to face him. Her reservoir of tears had clearly not yet been exhausted, but he could see the look of grim acceptance on her face. "The vet gave us a blanket, so he didn't have to sit on these dirty ones. They said we could keep it. For how much Lotte paid, I guess that was about the least they could do. I'll pay y'all back, I swear I will."

"Olive, please, don't worry about that. Let's just get Mutig settled."

Together, they lifted the listless animal and Eric cradled him in his arms. The dog gave a slight wag of his tail, perhaps sensing his home. Together, they shuffled inside, and Olive set up the blanket on the couch in the living room where Lotte and Eric had sat earlier when they looked at her emails.

She wiped her nose, then staggered across the room and turned on the TV, leaving the volume muted.

"He'll be okay here. Y'all go on and eat, you're probably Starvin' Marvin. I'm just gonna sit here awhile with Mutig. I ain't hungry anyhow. I'll be in—oh, hi there, Mr. Enki... person... god... whatever-thing you are. I hope you don't eat ribs like Ninurta ate chicken. We didn't buy *that* much, but we got enough if you want some, and you can have my portion if you want. I was just tellin' Eric I ain't that hungry. Plus, I suppose we could always go get more. So, actually, y'all eat what you want, never mind what I said. Really, I don't know what I'm sayin'. I think I'll just shut up now."

Enki seemed to sense Olive's distress and distraction. *'I will not consume your sustenance, but your offering is noted. Why do you cry, child?'*

She started to reply, but tears again welled up and quickly choked her words.

"It's her dog," Eric explained. "He actually faced off against Sharur in its lion-eagle form—saved my life, probably all our lives."

Olive cried out in sorrow.

"Shit, I'm sorry. Scratch that. Not *all* our lives. Olive's uncle was killed. That was later. Ninurta stopped his truck, and... well... Anyway, Mutig's injuries—Mutig is the dog's name—are really serious... fatal."

Enki looked from Eric to Olive and then to where the miserable animal lay cowering on the couch. *'You mourn the loss of this creature? This beast who fought Sharur?'*

Olive's renewed onslaught of tears appeared to be answer enough for the Lord of the Abzu.

'Come, child. Bring your animal to the water. All will be well.'

She immediately stopped crying and looked with shock at Eric.

Don't look at me. I have no idea what he means, but if he means what I think he means, we should have summoned him before Lotte spent $3,426.28 on vet bills!

Without hesitation, he scooped up the unresisting dog and fell in line behind Olive and Enki.

"Where are you all going?" Lotte asked with surprise as they traipsed through the kitchen on the way to the back door. "Eric, why are you carrying Mutig?"

"I'm not totally certain, but I think you'll want to come with us. My guess is you're going to want to see this."

Her curiosity piqued, she needed no further enticement.

Enki led the group back to the muddy shore and strode into the waters with casual impunity. The glow from the portal was even more noticeable now that the sun was setting. In full darkness, it would shine brightly.

Lucky there's no neighbors close by, but I wonder if there's an airport around here? I'd hate for this thing to be seen and have someone sent out to investigate.

'Hand the beast to me!' Enki commanded from where he stood in the shallows of the pond.

Eric complied, not worrying about getting his pants wet yet again.

The great god took the dog in his arms and slowly lowered him into the water as Eric rejoined Lotte and Olive on the shore. The light from the portal began to glow with even greater intensity, pulsating like waves emanating from far below the surface of the pond.

"He's calling energy from the Abzu," Lotte observed with fascination. "He's going to heal him. *Scheiße!* This is incredible. Think of what he could do for humanity."

Ooooooh, let's not go there. "Not to be a buzz-kill, but don't you think that sounds a little bit like something Dr. Esfahani might have said?"

She briefly shot him a savage glance, but then cast her eyes downward, as if she again looked into infinity like she had that day outside the high school. "You're right, damn you! I knew I kept you around for some reason. Will you always be there to pull me back from the edge?"

"I hope so. It's a dirty job, but somebody has to do it."

She tried desperately to repress a smile. To Eric's complete satisfaction, she utterly failed. "Little shit. Oh, there he goes. *Alter!* I hope this works."

So do I.

They watched as Enki submerged Mutig in the now luminous pond. Energy pulsed from the portal as the God of Civilization raised and lowered the injured dog in and out of the water. Suddenly, Mutig *barked.*

Tears once again streamed down Olive's face, but she was smiling, overjoyed. "Oh, my gawd! He's moving! He's gettin' better! Look, the scars are going away."

Indeed, the vicious wounds on Mutig's haunches began to fade, replaced by healthy skin, and the dog's signature short gray fur. Soon, Enki released him into the water, and the animal swam joyfully toward the shore.

Olive was there to greet him, and while the impact was gentle, it was extremely wet and muddy. She squealed with joy when the rejuvenated dog vigorously shook the water from his healed and now healthy body.

Suddenly, she froze. "Wait a dang minute!"

"What's the matter?" Eric asked, as he crouched beside her on the muddy and now well-trodden bank of the pond. "Mutig is fine. It's all good."

"Mr. Enki," she firmly asked as she rose from the ground. "Can you do one more thing?"

From the luminous waters that gleamed in the rapidly darkening sky, Enki gazed curiously at her. '*Ask, child. I know not if I can do a thing until I ascertain what is desired.*'

She took a breath and seemed to summon all her courage. "Well, you just healed my dog, and I couldn't be happier about it, but, if it's in your power, and you'd be willing, could you just... *change* him a little? Make him look just a little different? Bigger, smaller, different color, different look in his face? I don't care. It's just... well, it's hard to explain. If he looks like he does, then he can live, and I'm happy as all get out for that, but he can't be *my* dog no more. Too many people know what he looks like, even if I do change his name. So, if it ain't too much trouble, or asking too much from you, it sure would make me happy. Would you do this for me, Mr. Enki? I'd be forever in your debt."

Lotte did a facepalm while Eric gulped. *Does Olive know what she might have just agreed to?*

For a long moment, Enki was completely still, then convulsions of amusement engulfed them as the Lord of the Abzu laughed with joy.

'A small thing such as this would bring you such pleasure? You beings are beyond belief. I revel in your unpredictability. Given that you, and the beast upon whom you place such value, are mostly water, your forms are mine to command, provided enough energy. Return the creature to me and I will do your bidding with pleasure. Your eternal debt will be my reward, and I will ruminate upon how I can avail myself of your... assets.'

The deed was done. No backing out now, especially as Olive had already scooped Mutig up in her arms and gleefully carried the almost hyperactively excited animal back into the water.

The changes, though not astronomical, were more than enough. Rebel was now well and truly gone. In his place was Mutig, who stood larger, beefier, with a shorter tail, stockier and more muscular legs, smaller ears on a wider head, and a larger snout and jaw. The personality remained, but should the need arise, this dog was built to fight... to kill, if necessary.

Somehow, Eric sensed that Enki's interventions were completely by design. He waded into the water and removed the little stepped hat from the portal, stifling its iridescent shimmer. Led by the rejuvenated dog, the wet, muddy, and hungry party went back inside.

Olive demanded everyone change their clothes so she could toss them in the wash, and even provided Enki with fresh trousers and a new t-shirt. "This time I brought you some underwear too, but I ain't helping you put them on. You can figure that one out for yourself."

In the end, Eric showed the Lord of the Abzu how it was done. The great god smiled contentedly at the small wonder of the added comfort.

Lotte and Eric set the table while Olive loaded the washing machine. When they heard her approaching from the laundry room down the hall, they began to fill their plates with ribs and sides of collard greens, black-eyed peas, and cornbread. It smelled wonderful, and Eric wondered how Enki could stand it not to at least *try* some of their food.

To his surprise, Olive's troubled voice called from the living room. "Uh... y'all? I think you better come in here."

Reluctantly, Lotte and Eric dragged themselves to their feet and away from the food they so craved. Olive stood like a statue in front of the flickering television she'd left on.

"I was gonna turn it off, but then, I saw...."

Police cars. Ambulances. A ticker at the bottom of the screen said at least five were dead, mutilated and dismembered in a horrible crime thought potentially to be an act of terror. In the background, they saw pictures of a North Myrtle Beach building.

Chick-fil-A

The screen flashed a grainy black and white security camera image of a bearded man, wearing nothing but short pants that were far too short, and a ripped, bloody t-shirt.

With mechanical movements, Olive retrieved the TV's remote from the coffee table and raised the volume.

"...image was taken just before the power went out in the entire neighborhood from what witnesses described as a bolt of lightning that came from out of nowhere. If you have seen, or know the whereabouts of this man, contact local authorities immediately. Do not approach him. He is thought to be armed and extremely dangerous. Police are still investigating the possible motive for this brutal crime that has rocked the North Myrtle Beach community. Stay tuned to WMBF News for updates on this breaking story...."

"Possible motive," Lotte angrily spat. "He wanted more fucking *chicken*, and probably additional lives to feed that damned weapon! We *have* to find him, before he kills more innocent people."

'Patience, my raven-haired child,' Enki said as he entered the living room. *'Agonizing as it may be, we must wait until Ninurta is distracted and Sharur is occupied in retrieving the Tablet. Their strength in this realm is great, so we must be cautious. The storm brews. It will not be long now. Soon, you will have your wish and Ninurta will stand before us, and before long we shall know whose power will ultimately prevail.'*

CHAPTER 17

He'd sensed it for some time, but only now had the slight jiggling become enough to rouse Eric from deep slumber. He opened his eyes and saw Lotte next to him, head propped on two pillows, one bare leg casually splayed on top of the covers, phone held intently in her hands.

She smiled. "*Moin.* I'm sorry, did I wake you?"

He yawned, not yet fully free from sleep. "You did, but it's okay. What are you doing?"

"Research," she replied, again focusing on her phone. "What else? I'm utterly astonished how little I know of Mesopotamian history. It's quite a scandal, really. So, I'm taking a crash course online. Want to see the best thing I've found yet?"

She flipped through her phone a few times and then held the screen so that he could see it.

"You've got to be kidding me. *Ninurta and the Turtle?* It's a damn Mesopotamian myth? What does it say?"

"I know, it's absolutely crazy. It says almost exactly what Enki told us. Of all the damned stories to wind up being fairly accurate, this is probably the last one I'd have bet on. It's part of what's called the 'Anzu myth.' There are a couple of variations, each involving the Anzu bird stealing the Tablet of Destinies, but the one with the turtle parallels Enki's description almost perfectly."

"What is this 'Tablet of Destinies' anyway? Did you find any more information on that?"

"That's actually where I started. Basically, it's a sacred clay tablet, essentially a legal document, that supposedly grants Enlil his authority as master of the universe. Enki mentioned it had the power to alter time, and that's actually described in the Anzu myth, where the Anzu bird, probably with the aid of the people who were behind the theft, uses the Tablet to reverse time. During their battle, this causes Ninurta's arrows to fall apart in midair and revert to their original components. The shafts turn back into cane, the feathers into live birds, and the arrowheads back to uncut stone. Even Ninurta's bow returns to the forest and the wool bowstring turns into a bloody live sheep!"

"You can't make this stuff up."

"Seriously. It makes you wonder if all these crazy ancient stories have some grain of truth to them. Who knows. What I'd like to understand is why the Tablet of Destinies confers such great power to Enlil. I mean, I can see how it would be useful, but this can hardly be an item that would allow you to control the entire universe, otherwise whoever the Anzu turned the Tablet over to would have easily been able to defeat Ninurta. I think there's more to it."

"Yeah, just like there's more to what was going on with that portal. I'd like to know who was talking with Ninurta all this time, and how it wound up in the house where Uday and Qusay Hussein were killed."

She put down her phone. "Right... I'd forgotten all about that. Things have just been so completely crazy. Wait a minute. What time is it?"

"I don't know. *You've* got the phone."

"Of course, silly me. It's just past eight. That means... what... four hours, five hours? Stupid daylight savings time, I can never tell. So idiotic. Whatever. It's basically around lunchtime in England. Hold on."

She picked her phone back up and began to furiously scroll through it. "I hope I still have his number, and that it's still good. Wow, it's been ages since we talked. Here. Just a second, I'm going to call a friend of mine."

She selected the number, and soon the familiar double beep of an English phone rang out on the speaker.

A man's voice answered, his accent a pleasant mix of English-from-England and something else, similar to Lotte's, yet different. "Hello? Lotte, is that you?"

"Yes, Arif, it's me. It's so good to hear your voice! It's been... wow... years. How are you?"

"I'm well!" he cheerfully replied. "I'm here at University College in London, working on my PhD, just like you. Are you still at Harvard? Are you still with Eric?"

Eric was surprised to hear his name, as apparently was Lotte. "I... I am. In fact, he's right here with me, but how did you know? I haven't seen you in well over two years."

"Sabrina. How else would I know anything since you never call any of your old school friends." He laughed, and she gave a feeble pretense of humor despite the uncomfortable look on her face.

Well, at least it wasn't just me she basically ghosted.

Arif went on. "Sabrina told me she stayed with you when she was in Boston for a lecture. It was right after you two had moved in together. She was so excited to meet him, she called everyone. Of course, there was money involved too. I lost fifty quid! I'm sorry, Eric, I bet against you actually existing."

He laughed. "That's okay. I have doubts about it sometimes myself."

Lotte scowled a bit, but then turned her attention back to her phone. "Listen, Arif, I need to ask you a bit of a favor."

"Of course, you do. Why else would you call me? I'm just kidding... sort of. What can I do for you? You know I'm always happy to help the person who got me through non-parametric statistics."

Non-parahoosy what? Jeez, and I thought geometry was bad.

Her demeanor softened a bit with Arif's expression of gratitude. "Well, that was my pleasure. I hope all your distributions since that class have been normal."

They both seemed to find this tremendously amusing and laughed heartily. Eric didn't get it.

"In any case, we've... well... stumbled onto something. It's a long story how it got here, but it's an item that we think might have at one time belonged to Saddam Hussein."

Arif's laughter immediately ceased, and after a moment's hesitation, he said, "Go on."

"You told me once that some of your family had been... well... involved with Saddam Hussein's security forces, or some such. I wonder... if I sent you a picture of this item, if one of them might know about it? It's an artifact that was discovered, and then stolen in the 1950s. What do you think?"

"Lotte, you put me in... a difficult position. Things are just insane right now, with Islamic State, and the recent regime change in my country. We're all trying to lay low, stay out of trouble, just go about our business. This part of my family's life is in the past. We left Iraq and came to the U.K. to get away from all of that."

Lotte winced. "I know, Arif. I know this is asking a lot, but it's *terribly* important. Let me send you the picture. You think about it, and do whatever you feel is right. I'm sorry to have asked you, but you're my only connection into this world."

After a few perfunctory pleasantries, Arif signed off and she texted him Olive's picture of the portal.

"Should have done that before. I just can't seem to get my concentration back, or it sort of comes and goes. I don't know. I never felt like this before, except maybe once, after my mother... well... died."

"Lotte, you went through a scary experience. It may be perfectly normal to feel this way. When we've dealt with Ninurta, assuming we live to tell the tale, maybe you should talk to somebody."

"Talk to who, Eric, and about what, exactly? How I was *kidnapped* and kept in a dark fucking *closet*? 'Well, that's a crime, Ms. Schwarz. Did you report it to the police?' No, doctor, I damn well didn't because then they'd be onto the gateway into the freaking *Abzu* where Ninurta, Enki, and his bloody *turtle* are cheerfully swimming around! 'Perhaps it's time for a bit of a rest, Ms. Schwarz, at a nice, serene little place in the woods, eh?' Oh, I look forward to that conversation! I so *fucking* look forward to *that*!"

The scalpels weren't meant for him, but that didn't lessen their bite. It felt as if they stripped the very flesh from his body, and exposed every nerve to an onslaught of never-ending agony.

It will be months before I can walk around in public again, except Halloween. Actually, that's coming up in a couple of weeks. I've got my costume totally covered.

It was, of course, a stupid suggestion. He saw that now. He also saw how much raw emotion still lurked under the relatively serene surface projected by the beautiful girl who lay in the bed next to him.

"I'm sorry. You're right, of course. You're always right. Dumb suggestion. I... umm... I guess that means you're stuck talking to me, or Olive, if you want. I know you're hurting, though, and you know it too. Don't ignore your feelings on this. They aren't like a friend you don't call for a few years. They won't let you off the hook so easily."

She stared at him as tears welled in her eyes. "Eric, I'm so sorry. I shouldn't have spoken to you like that. It's just... theses dreams. I'm still having them. I wake up afraid. I'm jumpy all the time. I hear a noise and it scares me. I don't want to go into dark rooms. I'm always anxious. I'm always... angry. I'm so *angry*, so... hurt. Why does it hurt so much?"

He had his guess, but he wasn't an expert, and he didn't want to get it wrong and further anger her.

He pulled her into his arms. "It's gonna take time. Be patient with yourself. Let the clock work its magic. And you can speak to me any way you like, any way you need to. That's why I'm here—for you, anything you need. You're the one thing in my life that I have a deep conviction about. There's nothing I wouldn't do for you. To me, you're totally worth it."

She clung tight in his embrace, the measured expansion and contraction of her breath the only movement. For a time, this was all there was, and all there needed to be.

"Do you want pancakes again?" she finally asked. "I'd like pancakes, and bacon. I wonder if Olive is up. Let's all go make them together and see Mutig, and Enki. Who bloody knows what *he's* been up to. And I love you, Eric Schneider, who's always there to pull me back from the edge."

Without another word, she jumped out of bed and began to rifle through her bag for clothes.

I love you too, Lotte Schwarz, my black hole sun. Even though it hurts sometimes to do so.

As it turned out, the Lord of the Abzu had spent the night near the pond, gazing silently into its dark, still water. Lotte asked if anything was wrong.

'Merely resting, building my strength for what inevitably will come. I suggest you do the same.'

That was all the encouragement the trio needed. Soon breakfast was underway, Mutig excitedly underfoot with all the activity and the smells of food being prepared.

Olive finally shooed him outside, and smiled. "I guess I got my wish. That'll teach me. Anyway, better get used to it. He's a handful."

"What about school?" Eric asked. "Have you figured out what you're gonna do?"

"I think I can talk my friends who live off campus into letting Mutig stay with them. Maybe me too, if they have room. If not, then I'll just have to find time to go over and take care of him, make it work for the rest of this semester. I'll find something more permanent after that, maybe with my momma. Now that he don't look like Rebel no more, it makes things a lot easier."

Of course, this assumes Enki doesn't cash in on your debt of eternal gratitude and take you back to the damned Abzu.

He saw no sense in voicing that concern. It would happen, or it wouldn't, and they'd deal with it accordingly.

Lotte's phone rang as they were doing the last of the dishes. "It's a number I don't recognize. Overseas. I think I better take it." She laid it on the table.

Olive and Eric took seats to either side.

Lotte clicked the speaker button and said, "Hello?"

A man's voice with a distinct Arabic accent replied. "Yes, hello. Is this Lotte?"

"Yes, I'm Lotte. Who is this?"

"Well, I'd rather not say, but I'm a friend of your friend, who shared a picture with me. Is your phone safe?"

"Yes, I believe so. I have no reason to think it's not. I sincerely appreciate your calling."

"I'm here with someone. He knows of this item, the one in the picture. His English is not good, so I will translate. He wonders how you came upon the artifact?"

"It's a long story. Put simply, it was purportedly taken some time ago from the house in which Saddam Hussein's sons were killed in the city of Mosul. It was stored in that city for nearly a decade, and then brought back to the United States when the U.S. forces left Iraq. It's been here since then, and starting last year there seems to have been renewed interest in it on the part of the Iraqi government."

His mouth away from the phone, the man spoke rapidly in Arabic. When he was done, the three could vaguely hear another voice in the background, seemingly that of an older man. This person spoke for some time before the original voice returned to the phone.

"Quite incredible. This item you have was found on an archaeological dig in Eridu in 1949, the last one at that location. It was secreted away by 'Abd al-Ilah of Hejaz, regent for King Faisal the Second, but apparently anti-monarchist, pan-Arab nationalists stole it in about 1951. It wound up in the hands of Kharaillah Talfah."

"I... I don't know who that is."

"He is, or rather, was, Saddam Hussein's father-in-law. He's dead now, but he was Sajida Talfah's father, Saddam's first wife. Kharaillah Talfah was an outspoken critic of the monarchy, and was instrumental in the early years of the Ba'ath party in Iraq."

"All right, that explains the connection to Saddam Hussein, but what's the item's significance? Why would pan-Arab nationalists be interested in stealing an archaeological artifact?"

"Well, this is what is so incredible. The man you hear me speaking with was in Saddam's Republican Guard for many years. He rose in rank, and was eventually assigned to guard the palace. There, he heard... rumors."

Again, he spoke in Arabic to the man in the background, and they went back and forth for some time.

"Sorry, I had to clarify some things. The rumor he heard was that this item gave Saddam some sort of knowledge. It was a closely guarded secret. Few knew about it, and frankly most thought it was a hoax.

Supposedly, the information Saddam got from the artifact helped him rise in the ranks of the Ba'ath Party, eventually becoming its leader."

The three stared at one another, and Eric shuddered, recalling the turtle's words. *By then, Ninurta was mad – mad as the one who spoke with him the most.*

"*Alter!* What happened? How did it wind up in Mosul?"

"To understand, you have to go back to 1990, the First Gulf War. The gentleman I am with was a guard in the palace during that time. He said that when Saddam's armies were crushed in battle, he was furious. Apparently, he blamed the artifact for misguiding him into a war he couldn't win. He wanted it destroyed, but it wasn't really his to destroy. It belonged to Sajida Talfah, and she snuck it into the hands of Nawaf al-Zaidan."

"Again, I'm sorry. I don't know who that is."

"No, you wouldn't. Back in the 1990s, he was simply an ambitious man hoping to rise in favor with the Ba'ath Party. He looked upon doing the wife of Saddam Hussein a favor as an opportunity to ingratiate himself with the rulers of the country, and it worked. With his connections to Sajida, he became a wealthy man, and he used his money to build a fortified house in Mosul for his protection, and the protection of his precious charge. This was the house where Uday and Qusay were killed in 2003, likely trying to retrieve the artifact for their mother before they fled the country."

"Unbelievable. It all makes sense now. Except why the sudden interest on the part of the Iraqi government?"

Again, the trio heard a muffled conversation in Arabic on the phone. Finally, the younger man returned to them.

"That is a hard question to answer. It likely has to do with the replacement of the pro-Shia Malaki regime by the more Sunni-friendly Adabi government, but that could mean any number of things. It's possible that a pro-Sunni government has encouraged those who know of the item to come forward and speak of it, simply as a matter of national pride. Another potential explanation is that, somehow, the influence of the Hussein or Talfah families, or the interests they represented, are reasserting themselves. In that case, you have to assume that these rumors about the artifact are true, that it does confer some sort of power, or knowledge. This seems almost laughable to me, but take my word, the man I'm with is not laughing. Not at all. He is deadly serious about this, otherwise he'd have never agreed to take a risk in speaking with you."

"Please, give him our thanks. We now understand better what we might be up against."

"The thanks he wishes is to see this artifact destroyed. If the rumors about it are true, then going back to the Iran-Iraq conflict, it has caused three horrible wars that have been devastating to our people. The ripples from those events are still in evidence today. He says the item is evil, malignant, its knowledge not of this world. If what he says is actually true, then I would have to agree with him. I assume this thing is in your possession? What do plan on doing with it?"

"Well... umm... it's made of a highly unusual material, extremely hard and exceptionally difficult to destroy. However, it comes apart, and the pieces can be separated... hidden... and we're not on anyone's radar, so it's unlikely the artifact could be tracked to us. Tell your companion that we agree, the item *is* dangerous, and we plan to keep it from those who would use it for harm. In fact, we don't intend it be used at all. On this, he has our word."

She looked feebly from Eric to Olive, well aware of her blatant lie.

Again, there was a conversation on the other end of the phone. When it ended, a voice spoke to them... an older voice, heavily accented, but completely succinct and utterly clear.

"I will watch you."

Eric's spine tingled. He felt as if eyes icily observed him from behind.

The younger man returned to the phone. "Don't call this number. This mobile will be destroyed. Don't try to contact us again. You put your friend in danger, as well as us and yourselves. Honor your commitment. See that this item never falls into the wrong hands."

The phone went dead.

Absolutely. We'll get to that right after we finish using the portal to save the world as we know it. Then we'll pack it safely away. Really. Promise.

"It's gotta be 'round here somewhere," Olive said with determination as she searched through the drawers of her father's dresser. "I just can't believe Uncle Clint would have that combination memorized. He can't even remember his own phone number."

"How many bullets have you got left?" Eric asked. "Clint shot close to fifty rounds and didn't seem to be worried. You only fired your gun... what... a dozen times?"

"Something like that, but did you see those circular magazines my uncle had on his gun? Those hold more ammunition, maybe up to a hundred rounds. Mine is stock, only has about thirty, maybe less. If I can get in this gun safe, then I can get more ammo, or maybe there's more rifles, or pistols. Whatever. I'd take any darned thing I can get my hands on at this point."

He agreed, though experience had taught him that an otherworldly creature's second encounter with a modern firearm might not produce the same results as the first. They adapt quickly and cunningly, but she had little better to do, so he left her to hunt for some clue as to how to open the gun locker.

He went back downstairs and found Lotte sprawled on the couch, Mutig curled up beside her. The dog had finally exhausted itself outside and was enjoying a late-morning nap while she again struggled to plow through her emails. She seemed pretty focused on the task, so he quietly slipped into the kitchen and out the back door. Other than his fight with Wayne, he hadn't done anything physical in days and yearned to move his body. The beautiful weather also called to him.

He began to cycle through his familiar stretching routine. As always, he heard Jennifer's soothing and encouraging voice as he executed the various exercises. He closed his eyes and joyously felt his muscles loosen.

Waiting plays a peculiar trick on the mind. Time seems to drag, as if the weight of what you're anxiously anticipating contributes to the gravity and mass around you, slowing your clock. It's like staring into Lotte's eyes, radiant little black holes where everything just... stops.

Lotte wasn't the only one changed by her kidnapping. In this quiet moment, perhaps the first he'd had in a week, he admitted to himself how shaken he'd been. The question of what to do on a typical Tuesday night suddenly seemed very small. His focus now fixated on what Lotte meant to him—her drive, her determination, her *calling*. He needed that force in his life, a propulsion to which, in some sense, he had become addicted. He found losing that unthinkable, but even modifying it, or blunting ever so slightly her single-minded dedication, just felt somehow... *wrong*.

What does this mean? What do I do with this understanding? How do I react if, after this episode, Lotte is no longer the Lotte I've known? What's been gained, or lost? How can I help her get back to where I feel she ought to be?

He had no answers, only seemingly endless questions. It felt like the more they did in their lives, the more chaotic and difficult things became, as if they moved toward incomprehensible and endless complexity. It all seemed simpler, back then—whenever *then* was.

Maybe this was just time again, playing another trick on the mind. Were things really that much less complex when he and Lotte had battled the impish Afrit in her kitchen, or when they faced a myriad of other seemingly impossible challenges? With these conflicts being in the past and now resolved, their power over one's emotions diminished, because the outcome no longer stood in question. It was frozen in time.

For better or worse, someday, this will all be in the past too. The key is that, somehow, we have to muddle through all that uncertainty and try to make the outcome as positive as it can be, so it doesn't fuck up the future.

Though of little practical use, he felt as if he were onto something, and suddenly felt better.

Maybe the stretching is helping as well.

With enthusiasm, he launched into some pushups. That turned out to be a mistake. His back and arm still ached from the trauma of the fight. He lay face down in the grass, hoping he hadn't further exacerbated his injuries.

'Rise.'

He heard the word in his mind, and looked up to see Enki standing above him. The God of Civilization and Progress called on him to stand and again face the chaos of an insecure and unpredictable tomorrow.

'It begins. We must commence preparations.'

Eric rose.

More time must have passed than he'd thought. They found Lotte and Mutig sleeping in a jumbled heap on the couch, her discarded phone on the coffee table.

He gently touched her shoulder. "Sweetie, I hate to wake you up, but it's time."

She yawned and stretched. "Time? Time for what?" She looked around as if dazed while she pushed an extremely reluctant Mutig off of her chest. Then she saw Enki where he stood in the entryway, arms crossed. "Oh, right, the storm. But look at the weather. It's gorgeous. Where is this storm supposed to be?"

'It forms in the direction of the rising sun, near a great sea, which will feed its power. It is not far. It will still take time for the rains and lightning to come upon us, but we must be ready.'

"The ocean is quite nearby to the east," she said. "Are you ready? Have you summoned all your strength?"

'All the power of the Abzu is mine to command, but many centuries have I slept. The energy used to affect your world is diffuse and degraded. It may be enough, or it may not. We shall soon see.'

"There is... another, one who might possibly be able to help us, but... well... there are contingencies to working with this creature."

'Explain yourself.'

"Perhaps it's best we just show you. I think you'll find it fascinating, and familiar." She got up and led the curious god through the kitchen and out the back door.

Eric went to find Olive. He located her in her father's room, toiling over the combination on the gun locker. "Any luck?"

"No. I couldn't find anything, so now I'm just trying every darned thing I can think of. His birthday, my birthday, daddy's birthday. I know the days of Grandma and Grandpa, but not the years, so if it's one of them, we're fucked. Pardon my French."

Despite his anxiety, he chuckled. "Hey, you gave it your best shot. But listen, Enki says we need to get ready. The storm is starting."

She shot a skeptical look out the window of the little room into the sunny front yard.

"I know, the weather's beautiful, but I'm gonna bet our pal is right on this one. He and Lotte went out to the barn. She wants to show him the Afrit portal. She thinks it might be able to help us. You want to come?"

She stared with frustration at the gun locker. "Darn it! I don't think I can get this thing open. I'll just try to save my ammo best as I can."

She got to her feet and they both scurried to the barn. A happy Mutig joined them at the back door. When they arrived, Enki was closely examining the fire portal.

"So, here," Lotte explained. "Imagine your portal tipped so that the base is in the air and the arch is on the ground. You see the similarity?"

The great god didn't reply, but his look made it clear that he grasped what she was saying. *'Tell me of the being, the one who comes forth from this gateway.'*

"The Afrit is a creature of fire. It calls its realm the 'Eternal Flame,' and the beast is composed of some sort of dark ash, possibly the combusted remnants of other creatures."

He looked somewhat askance at her final words, but other thoughts appeared to take precedence in his mind. *'A realm of fire. This is... new to me. Never have I detected it in your world, and it does not border on the Abzu. It is beyond my kind's experience, unless Anu has seen it from where he now resides.'*

"What do you mean? Are you saying other realms aside from our world *do* border on the Abzu?"

'Of course,' he matter-of-factly replied. *'Two others. One we have discussed, the domain of winds. Only when we entered your world did we realize it for what it was, the place where the Abzu first dissolves into misty droplets, and then vanishes into an impenetrable haze. This is where Anu, my father, went – to explore, and to rule. Ultimately, it is where Enlil imprisoned him, but it is only accessible through your world.'*

"And the other?" Lotte asked.

'Here, the Abzu turns gradually to clay, the material used to create the gateway, and later, the Tablet of Destinies. Eventually, this clay solidifies, becomes like rock. What lies beyond is unknown to us, it is impermeable. Never have we found any evidence of this realm in your world.'

"Astonishing. Eric, where's the magnetometer?"

He jumped at hearing his name unexpectedly. "Umm, it's... it's... hey! It's in the flight case with the papers! There wasn't room for it in the other boxes. Aren't you glad I brought that one now?" He smiled, a bit smugly.

She rolled her eyes. "Yes, very clever, my love. Can you please get it out? I'd like to use it to test something."

With quiet satisfaction, he went over to where the cases were stored in the barn and started unlatching the box.

'But enough of this,' Enki interjected. *'You say the creature from this realm of fire may be able to help us. Summon it to stand before me. Let us enlist its assistance.'*

Lotte returned her attention to the great god. "It's not quite that simple. For its service, the Afrit demands a reward. *Spoils*, it calls them, like the spoils of war. Over the years, this being has been used by humans to... well... eliminate other humans. These people, the Afrit took as its spoils, feeding on their energy, growing and changing with each passing century. If we wish this creature's help, it'll demand such a tribute. I don't know if we're in a position to honor such a debt."

Enki's eyes widened in horror and disgust.

'This is what you have transformed my gateway into, a path for a being such as this to enter your world to kill others? For what? Vengeance? Political gain? Like the blood from your veins, you poured your hopes, your dreams, your aspirations into the Abzu to be free of all these petty squabbles. We tried so hard to help you nullify them, so your kind could live in peace and prosperity, so you could live the lives you prayed so fervently for us to deliver unto you. Did you lie to us? To yourselves? How can you strive for such lofty goals, and then sink back into the very muck from which you wish to be free? You are my children, but you are mad, all quite mad! Enlil was right: we should have been done with you long ago.'

Eric saw Lotte stiffen at the severe chastening. He'd located the magnetometer, but he froze, afraid to move and further upset the furious god.

To his complete surprise, Olive broke the thunderous silence. "Mr. Enki, I know it don't look too good, but what you said... it's not so simple. We aren't all of... like... one mind. Some people want one thing, other people want something totally different. Some are bad, some are good, and some are bad sometimes and good at other times. You can understand that. You even said your father could be... what did you say... unpredictable. All happy as get out one minute, then pissed-off the next. We're the same way, all of us, and there's a whole lot of us. So, we make a lot of noise, just like you say."

Enki's eyes narrowed as he listened.

Lotte tugged on her arm. "Olive, perhaps we should—"

She pulled free. "I ain't done. It's true, Mr. Enki. People have used this Afrit thing for bad purposes in the past, but Eric and I used it to free Lotte from people who had kidnapped her. Now Lotte's offering that maybe it can help us save our dang world! We still want all those peace and love and togetherness things you said. It's just taking us a long time to figure out how to get that to work for everybody. Don't take away our chance. Don't give up on us. Let us stick around, and maybe in another thousand or whatever years, someone will wake you up, and it will be just like you hoped for—possibly even better."

Enki looked at Lotte, who simply shrugged her shoulders. There really wasn't much to add to Olive's argument. Eric stood motionless and hoped beyond hope that it worked.

'Utnapishtim,' the great god finally projected into their minds. *'He argued in much the same way. He was high priest of my Temple in Eridu when Enlil threatened your destruction. His words aided in your salvation. Patience, he counseled. He said that time was needed for your kind to adapt to a new way of being. Like so many other things, time is a concept with which we have no familiarity. Only now do we experience the passing of hours, days, years... centuries... and only in relation to your realm.'*

"But I thought you said the Tablet of Destinies could control time?" Lotte tentatively interjected. "This is what gives Enlil his power, the power Ninurta now seeks."

'This is true, but our ability to control time in your realm is only possible because we exist outside of that time. From the Abzu, we can look upon it as you cannot from within, and in simple ways, we can control that time. Sometimes, however, the very simplest thing provides inestimable power.'

"In our ancient myth, it's you who counsels Utnapishtim to build a boat to save his family, his animals, and some important people in his village. Our kind celebrated you as a savior. We don't need the Afrit if you object. I, for one, share many of your reservations about summoning the beast, and have done so in the past only with a heavy heart. But we need *you*! Let's forget the Afrit and get on with our plan. Help us by being the savior of humankind once again. You said yourself that there's much good in this world."

He turned from them to once more behold the gleaming fire portal. Its *Alkuartiz Alnaar* captured the light from the open barn doorway.

'No. I taste Ninurta's power. The risk is too great. I fooled him before, but he will be wary now. Much as I remonstrate against such an abomination, we may well need this fire creature's assistance. The question is how to satisfy this beast's terrible pact.'

"If one is to be sacrificed for such a cause," Lotte said, "let it be me."

Eric grabbed the magnetometer from the flight case and stormed back. "No! Absolutely no fucking way! You can take *me*, but not *her*! The Afrit would like nothing better than to crush my spine over his knee anyway, so, if that's the deal, so be it. But nobody is taking Lotte! You hear me? Nobody!"

Everyone stood in stunned silence as his final word echoed in the cavernous barn.

He handed the device he held to a wide-eyed and tight-lipped Lotte. "Here's your magnetometer."

Enki shook his head in apparent disbelief. *'Peculiar and temperamental creatures, such great potential, so frequently unfulfilled, but you three give me hope. You would have risen far in Eridu, each in your own way.'*

Again, the Lord of the Abzu turned toward the fire portal.

'Summon the creature of fire. I will strike a bargain with the beast. Ninurta is, after all, my burden... the legacy of my kind.'

That was enough for them. Eric and Olive hastened back to the cases to fetch more candles.

Lotte ran out the door with the magnetometer. "I'll be right back. I just want to test something." They were just beginning to unbox the candles when she breathlessly returned. "It's dead. Olive, are there any AA batteries in the house? It takes three."

"I... uh... I can go look."

"Please do. I'll help Eric until you're back."

Olive left on her task, and Eric turned to Lotte, who had a slight twinkle in her eye. "What have you got in mind? You think something might be magnetic, obviously."

She smiled. "Yes, it's all starting to make sense to me. Think about it... a realm of *water*, bordered by a domain of wind, or as Enki says... *air*. Then, in another direction, the deep waters connect to a dimension that starts off as clay, then becomes hard *earth*. Of course, we already know about the Eternal Flame... *fire*! It's the four bloody elements. If Enki's gateway is magnetic, then I think what Charun called 'The Zone' is the realm, or *plane*, of earth."

"Wow, I guess it makes sense. What I don't understand is why Enki didn't detect any evidence of the realms of earth or fire when he and his kind entered our world?"

"Because they were discovered later, or else earlier contact occurred in areas the creatures of the Abzu didn't explore... far away from Mesopotamia. I believe we hadn't yet made contact with the beings that eventually became the Afrit and Charun. Enlil and Enki had long gone back to sleep, so they never saw them."

Olive called out from the open barn doors as she returned. "I found a pack of them in a drawer in the kitchen. I hope they still work."

Lotte ran to her and inserted the new batteries. "It's on!" She bounded back out toward the pond, Mutig barking happily at her heels.

Olive sighed as she grabbed a candle and knife and began the now familiar preparation. "Whew. She sure has a lot of energy when she gets going. What in the dang world has her so excited?"

"I'll tell you later. It's a lot to absorb. Truth is, I'm just thrilled to see her so happy. I'm a little worried about how she's handling what happened, the kidnapping and all. This is the Lotte I know."

"And love. I heard what you said to Enki. I guess just about the whole town did."

He laughed with embarrassment. "Sorry about that. It's just... well... I don't know. Something about the prospect of losing her has always made me very... *emotional*. It happened when we were kids, when she was having these terrible dreams. She said maybe it wasn't worth the risk of bringing the Afrit back into our world just to save her life, as if somehow, she wasn't worth the effort. That was just unthinkable to me. It still is. Sorry I yelled like that."

"You don't have to apologize to me, dum-dum. If you hadn't piped up, I was about to say the same fool thing. I'd sooner be taken by the Afrit myself than see her talents wasted that way. I'd say that girl has her back covered, huh?"

He stared at her, amazed. "She sure does, Olive."

She sure does.

CHAPTER 18

Once again, the Afrit loomed before them.

Its bat-like wings tensed and flexed, and the otherworldly beast's head slowly swayed as its solid, inky eyes cautiously surveyed the occupants of the cavernous barn.

Outside, the daylight faded as clouds began to obscure the delicious sunshine—fitting, somehow. Fire or no, this was a creature of darkness, of shadows, its business death. Only the dull glow of its all-consuming flame seemed fitting illumination for such a monster.

The creature spoke in its coarse and abrasive tongue, its words clear in their anxious minds. *'We hear your plea,* Sadat Alnaar. *We come to your service, to bargain. Strong have we become since you and your minion once again summoned us.'*

Minion? Umm... ouch. Largely true, but still... ouch. On the other hand, I do have my own union.

The Afrit's assessment of its own prowess also seemed accurate. Eric could clearly see the beast had grown after consuming Blake Harris—perhaps not quite up to its previous stature, but far closer.

That's good news if Chuckles can help us, and bad news if he ever gets loose like Ninurta is now. But if the God of Civilization and Progress wants this thing's help, I'm not about to stand in the way.

Lotte confidently spoke as she rose from her spot at the apex of the arched black marble board. "Thank you for answering my call, great one. We need your assistance, and we wish to bargain, but I need you to speak with this being. Like you, he's a creature from another realm. He's here to help us recapture one who is similar to him, but behaves dangerously. This other being poses a threat to us all, possibly even you. Will you let him speak? His name is Enki."

The Afrit cast its unfathomable gaze toward the Lord of the Abzu, who for his part casually stood, arms crossed, with a look of mild detachment on his face.

'Speak,' the Afrit impatiently spat. *'We will listen, but only because the* Sadat Alnaar *bids us to do so.'*

Enki flashed an amused smile. *'She really can be quite convincing, can't she?'*

He projected a mental laugh, and the Afrit seemed momentarily caught off guard that the great god's lips didn't move at all.

'Sadly," Enki continued, *'what the dark-haired one says is accurate. My nephew, Ninurta, whom I imprisoned for his impudence, has escaped. He seeks a mighty and baleful artifact, which if secured, could pose a great threat to this world. Indeed, it may be able to seal off contact with your realm as well, and mine. He must be stopped, but his power is great. Your assistance would be... useful.'*

The Afrit turned its head questioningly toward Lotte. *'What is offered for our services? Again, you wish us to face a being of another realm, one whose power exceeds that of you puny mortals. The last time, we nearly met our end in this gloomy place. For what, precisely, would we now take such a risk?'*

Having no answer, she looked helplessly and hopefully to Enki, who further elucidated.

'I hoped that perhaps the prospect of losing touch with this little... feeding ground of yours... might be sufficient motivation. Am I wrong in this aspiration?'

The Afrit stared icily in reply.

'Mmmm... a pity, but not unexpected. Perhaps it will all be for the best. Very well. Should you assist us, Afrit, you will have your pound of flesh. On this, you have my word. Complete your bargain with the one whose heart you know. She recognizes that, on this point, I speak truly and will honor the covenant. It is the founding principle of all I hold, and all that I have ever held, dear to me.'

With this, the great god leisurely walked out of the barn, leaving Lotte, and seemingly the Afrit, somewhat confused.

Eric suddenly had a terrible feeling. *Could he possibly mean he's willing to sacrifice Olive? She did say she would be eternally in his debt, and Enki said he would ponder how to... well... avail himself of her allegiance. Shit!*

"Umm, Lotte?" He tried to get her attention, but she waved her hand for silence.

"Is this sufficient?" she cautiously asked the Afrit. "It's not very... specific... but we've done that with you before. Enki obviously has something, or someone, in mind. Will you complete the arrangement on these terms?"

The creature spread its bony wings and began its familiar rocking motion. Its barbed tail lashed like a whip as it deliberated. Finally, the obsidian creature spoke.

'Do you trust this one, Sadat Alnaar? *Is what you ask of us this important to you?'*

"It is. I'd never have initiated the summoning if it weren't. I know how dangerous this is for you, for all of us. All our lives, our existences, will be put at risk, but that's nothing compared to the potential consequences if we fail. So, yes, it's important to me. I also trust that Enki believes your help might make the difference, and that he'll be true to his word. So yes, and yes again."

The Afrit ceased to sway, then gently extended its talon toward her. *'Then let the rings bind our pact.'*

While she completed her ceremony, Eric and Olive exited the barn to finish making preparations. The sky had darkened considerably, the sun now completely concealed behind a veil of thick and ominous black clouds. To the east, flashes of lightning split the darkness, followed by deep thunder.

He counted. "Twelve, fourteen seconds. That lightning has got to be striking near the coast. Get your gun, and we'll meet up at the van. I'll doublecheck, but I think all our other weapons are in a bag in the cargo space already."

Olive ran inside just as a light rain began to fall. The weather was degenerating quickly. He ran to Enki, who stood in the dirt driveway leading away from the barn, gazing eastward.

"Can you tell where Ninurta might be? That lightning is striking near the coast."

'I sense him. We must get closer for me to determine his precise location. Do we have a means of transportation?'

"We do. Come with me and I'll show you. You can sit in the front and tell me which way I need to go."

He was explaining how the van worked to the ever-curious deity when Olive returned, gun in hand, and Mutig close at her heels.

"Are you planning to bring the dog? Is that a good idea?"

"H-E Double L yeah, I'm bringing him. Think about what happened last time! We need every advantage we can get. Plus, look at him now. He still ain't no match for Sharur, but he can hold his own a lot longer than before. I don't think it would be smart to leave him behind."

A part of him wanted to argue. He feared for the dog's life if it acted solely on instinct, without an understanding of the tactical situation. However, Mutig wasn't his dog, and he also partly agreed with her. They might need him. One never knew.

"All right, load in the back. Enki needs to sit up front with me so we can locate Ninurta. Where are Lotte and Chuckles?"

She giggled. "Lotte came in when I was going out. She wanted to change, said her clothes all smelled like *dog* after they was sleeping on the couch. *Chuckles* is out back, waiting for her."

He wasn't sure whether to laugh or cry about the delay Lotte was causing, but he felt relief when he saw her round the corner of the house.

The Afrit followed dutifully behind her.

What the hell is with this thing? Does the Afrit somehow bond with its Sadat Alnaar? *This is just getting too weird.*

As she approached, he saw that she wore her freshly washed Sisters of Mercy t-shirt that Olive must have returned to her. It was the first time Eric had ever seen her wear that particular garment, which he now associated more closely with Olive. He shook his head and attempted to cast out these useless and somewhat uncomfortable thoughts.

"Are we ready?" Lotte asked.

"Yeah, ready as we'll ever be. Hop in the back and hang on. I think it's gonna be an interesting ride."

The rain had increased, and the winds had picked up speed. Dense and threatening clouds roiled above as they shot toward the eastern horizon.

Lotte directed her attention to the Afrit. "Can you fly in this? Can you follow us from above by tracking me?"

The creature looked into the air and spread its wings. '*We can, for a time. If this worsens, we shall see.*'

She reached out and briefly grasped the beast's immense arm, then quickly turned away, climbed into the van, and pulled the scratched side door closed.

When Eric started the engine, the Afrit launched into the air and disappeared almost instantly into the tempestuous sky.

The van rocked as he maneuvered cautiously from Happy Drive onto Freemont Road. By the time they hit Route 905, the trees swayed violently from a mighty wind, and debris flew through the air.

Olive shouted from the rear where she and Lotte hunkered on a dirty packing blanket with Mutig. "This is like a hurricane! I bet nobody had *this* on their doppler radar forecast for today."

Soon, they pulled back onto Highway 9 and headed southeast toward North Myrtle Beach. Rain whipped the windshield, and Eric had to slow to a virtual crawl to move forward. Many cars had simply pulled over, caught completely unaware by the sudden and violent downpour. He barely registered the entrance to Catfish Circle as they passed, but their destination was farther ahead, where immense bolts of lightning now cut across the blackness of the stormy sky.

'This way.' Enki pointed to his right as they came upon an interchange.

With great concentration, Eric guided the van onto Highway 17 and headed south. The streets here were more urban, and would normally have had more traffic, but with the weather, they sat largely abandoned. Sheets of rain had caused flash floods as water rushed toward suddenly overloaded drains. It also appeared the power had gone out, and darkness made the waterlogged roads even more treacherous.

"I thought streetlights would have some kind of battery backup," Eric complained. "This is ridiculous. I can barely see anything."

The great god spoke beside him. *'It is Ninurta. To instigate the storm, he summoned all the energy in this area that powers your technological devices.'*

"That's probably a good thing," Lotte interjected from behind. "If the power is out, and all the batteries are dead, there won't be any cell phones working. We'll have no footage showing up on the six o'clock news of Sumerian gods summoning storms or commanding lion-eagles. We must have been out of range. Good thing. Otherwise, our car wouldn't have started."

Eric did his best to navigate the treacherous route. He trembled as the van passed by the shattered and shuttered Chick-fil-A to their left.

We seem to be on the right track, but we'd better be getting close. I'm really not sure how much farther I'll be able to drive.

For a time, they crawled along Highway 17 in tense silence. Mercifully, the road was straight, and even the few cars they'd seen before had now dwindled to nothing.

Enki finally pointed to his left, over the steering wheel. *'We must go that way, toward the water.'*

They seemed to have passed the area of fast-food restaurants and strip malls. In the more residential area, Eric wasn't sure which road to take. Seemingly out of nowhere, a huge mall appeared on the right, and immediately after that, another interchange. He took the van left in front of yet another Walmart Supercenter onto Kings Road, which skirted east, and then south.

'There!' Enki suddenly shouted in their minds. *'He is there, atop that great ziggurat! See how the storm circles around that point? That is where we will find Ninurta.'*

Olive leaned over Eric's shoulder and looked out the rain-soaked window. She pointed at a rather dull and faceless high-rise whose appearance was redeemed slightly by an unusual red, slanted roof, almost like a series of little Italian villas glued to the top of the building.

"That's Margate Tower. Bunch of luxury condos for the fat cats. Gawd, Uncle Clint *hated* this place. How the heck do you figure Ninurta got up there, and why?"

'Doubtlessly,' Enki replied, *'Sharur transported him. As to why, perhaps better to control the storm. It poses a great hurdle for us. For my plan to work, Ninurta must be on the ground. We will have to engage him there, in the heights, and try to force him to the earth before he reunites with Sharur and has the Tablet in his possession.'*

"Mr. Enki, how are we supposed to get on the roof of that building? I don't think they're gonna let us just waltz in there and take the elevator. That ain't workin' anyway, if the power is out. It'll take us forever to climb all them stairs."

'Quiet, child, all will be well.' He turned to Eric. *'Take us to the base of that structure in this rolling apparatus. Quickly. Time grows short.'*

Doing as instructed, Eric banged a left onto Queensway Boulevard, a long, straight road that led directly toward Margate Tower. He noted that Olive's description of a hurricane was apt. As they approached the nearly thirty-story building, he could see that the skies around the high-rise were clearer. It still rained, but not quite as heavily. Nor was it as windy and dark. Spider-webs of lightning pierced the sky, followed by mighty roars of thunder that shook the ground, but here there was no delay. The noise came right on the heels of the intense and terrifying flashes.

He followed Queensway until it dead-ended into the beach near the side of the great building that rose above them. "This is the best I can do. There's nobody around here, and we can get to the building past those trees. What's the plan?"

'Come!' the Lord of the Abzu commanded as he rose from his seat. *'Wait! Free me from this point of egress. I do not understand how it works.'*

Olive hopped out and opened the door for the trapped deity.

Whew, Eric thought with relief. *Glad he didn't just rip the door off. That would have been hell explaining to Ricky.*

Together, the unlikely foursome walked toward the towering structure, leaving a forlorn Mutig in the van. Eric wasn't surprised when he saw the Afrit drop from the sky and land gently near them. The beast was soaking wet.

Hmmm... no flame for you this time. He remembered with some concern how that had been the difference maker for the creature in its encounter with Charun.

When they reached the wall of the building, Enki looked up. *'Afrit, can you carry one of the females to the top?'*

'We can,' the ashen monster shot back, *'but is it not madness to go without you?'*

'Indeed, it is, but I will accompany you. I will bring this one.' He nodded his head slightly in the direction of Eric. *'Prepare yourselves!'*

With that, Enki's flesh began to ripple and convulse. His legs stretched backward until the colossal serpentine tail again took shape, while his arms stretched forward and once again became sturdy hooves. The massive sweeping horns unfurled outward from the great god's now goat-like head. When the transformation was complete, he focused his imposing gaze directly at Eric.

'Climb upon my back. Together, we will swim within the liquid in this air, right to the top of the ziggurat. Hold onto my horns tightly. It will be a turbulent ride.'

What? Eric couldn't believe what he was being asked to do. One slip at the wrong moment, and he'd fall thirty stories to his certain death. He looked at Lotte, who seemed equally horrified.

"Great one," she cried. "Is there no other way? This is terribly dangerous!"

'If you know a way, then speak! We have not time for the climbing of stairs. As we stand here, Sharur could be on his way back to Ninurta, Tablet in its clutches. What alternative do you propose?'

She stiffened and fell silent. Slowly, she turned her head toward Eric. Her dark eyes shone with the lightning in the air, as if absorbing it, like a black hole that devoured everything that came within the pull of its event horizon. He knew he was in there... somewhere... that like the electricity, he had also been consumed, and that as her gaze now transfixed him, more of him was taken into what lay beyond those little portals into her soul.

He knew what he had to do.

He gently grasped her by the shoulders and brought his face close to hers, that place where gravity and mass gave way, and where he always felt that possibilities were endless. "It's fine. I'll be fine. I just have to hold on tight. Let the Afrit take Olive. She's got the gun. You stay down here with Mutig and watch for us. Enki says we need to get Ninurta to the ground, so... *I'll be back.*"

She hesitated, but then tearfully laughed at his lousy Arnold Schwarzenegger impersonation. "That's the worst German accent I've ever heard! Did I teach you nothing?"

"You taught me everything... everything and more. I'm just out of practice."

A quick kiss was all they had time for, but it had to suffice.

He handed Olive his baseball bat. "Can you strap the gun around your shoulder and carry this?"

She nodded in reply, took the bat, and walked over to the Afrit.

Eric flashed a quick smile at Lotte, then turned to Enki. "Okay, let's do it."

His only experience on a horse had been a stupid pony ride at some two-bit county fair when he was a little kid. Somewhere, his mom had a photo of him, staring uncomfortably into the camera as he tightly clutched the reins of the tawny creature. This felt nothing like that. This was a wild ride on a bucking bronco, or some strange mix of a salmon swimming upstream and a gazelle running for its life while being pursued by a cheetah.

The Capricorn's great horns were not sharp, and had many protrusions that aided his grip, but this didn't help when Enki launched forward. Eric's body repeatedly rose and then slammed against the back of the immense creature to whom he so desperately clung. The first jolt nearly knocked his breath out.

Well, so much for having children! He groaned as he battled to focus all his attention on his arms and hands, refusing to let go.

Somehow, his tenacity won the day. With a final, great surge, the Lord of the Abzu thrashed his serpentine tail as if cutting through the ocean itself, and cleared the red roofing they had seen from the ground. This turned out to be little more than a decorative façade, roughly twelve feet high, which enclosed the top of the building. With a mighty thump, the great god skidded to a stop on the roof beneath.

With incalculable relief, Eric pried loose his nearly fossilized fingers and slid to the slick asphalt. As he stretched his hands, he detected movement behind him.

"I can't believe you did that," Olive whispered. "I thought for sure you'd let go, gettin' slapped around like you was. Come on over this way. You too, Mr. Enki. I think we found him."

She stayed low, and Eric followed suit. As they rounded a corner, he saw a long metal ventilation duct that stretched across a good portion of the roof. The Afrit crouched behind it, like a gargoyle, and peered around a corner where the structure disappeared straight down into the bowels of the building. Enki proved surprisingly capable of locomotion in Capricorn form, though his fish tail likely benefitted from the soaking wet asphalt over which it slithered. Together, they peeked around the corner where the Afrit kept its vigil.

Above them, about 30 yards away on an elevated catwalk that spanned the back of the red façade, stood Ninurta. He gazed toward the eastern horizon, out over the beach and the ocean beyond. With each bolt of lightning, his head twitched and shifted, changing direction as he searched the skies.

Enki projected his thoughts to them in a tight and quiet beam. *'He awaits Sharur's return. We are not too late. I can slow him, but you three must get him to the ground. Throw him over the edge of this structure.'*

"Well, that'll pretty much kill him," Olive said with quiet alarm. "Won't it?"

'He will be stunned, perhaps, but it shall take far more to kill a being such as him. Get my disobedient nephew to the ground. From there, I shall deal with him properly.'

Eric assessed the situation. "Olive, there's a staircase up to the catwalk here, and another one over there, past Ninurta. Have the Afrit carry you to the one on the far side. You and I will approach him from opposite ends." He turned to the Afrit. "When we have Ninurta distracted, you fly right at him. Try to push him over the edge, or lift him up and over, if you can. He won't be expecting you, so hopefully you can get leverage."

Olive nodded her assent and calmly walked into the arms of the Afrit.

Wow, Eric thought with amazement. *You really can get used to just about anything. If Olive had seen that monster two weeks ago, she'd have been screaming and running for her life.*

The beast took her in its grasp and lifted silently into the air. It circled wide around the front of the building, opposite where Ninurta stood, to avoid being noticed, then crested the red roofing and settled to the asphalt below.

There was no ductwork to shield her on the other side, so Olive hugged close to the façade until she reached the staircase. When she'd gotten into position, Eric gave a final nod to Enki, then cautiously crept to the stairs near him and began to climb. Ninurta was still distracted by his search for Sharur, but Eric knew that when he rounded a slight corner, the terrible god would surely notice him. That was fine with him. It would give Olive a shot from behind, perhaps several.

Trusting that Enki would do as he said and somehow slow Ninurta, Eric cut right and then sharp left. A mere ten yards now separated him from Ninurta on the straightaway of this portion of the catwalk, but the God of Thunder and Storms still had his full attention on the skies. Heart pounding, Eric summoned all of his courage and stepped forward, baseball bat in hand.

That was all it took.

Ninurta detected the movement. The deity angrily swung his head toward Eric and screamed. Like the Afrit, his words were in an ancient and foreign tongue, but Eric could understand their meaning in his mind.

'How dare you! Discard your pathetic weapon and drop to your knees, insolent mortal. You have no hope of stopping me.'

Eric took another bold step forward. "Probably true, but you'll have to excuse me while I give it the old college try."

At that moment, a gunshot rang out, adding to the clamor of thunder from the skies. Ninurta shuddered with the bullet's impact and staggered slightly forward. He clutched his right shoulder and collapsed heavily on the catwalk, his back to the wall of the façade.

Eric saw Olive near a bend in the roof's outer wall that mirrored the one on his side. Her location gave her a slight angle that prevented him from being in the line of fire, as long as he held his position. He watched as she again took aim.

This isn't good. Ninurta needs to be standing for the Afrit to have any leverage to get it over the side.

She fired again, but with uncanny quickness, Ninurta jerked forward, and the bullet sprayed stucco and cement from the wall where his head had been just a fraction of a second before. On hands and knees, the terrible god locked her in his sight, then vigorously waved his arm.

Olive launched away as if caught in the backdraft of a horrendous explosion, or a supernaturally powerful gust of wind. The AR-15 flew from her hands and landed hard on the asphalt below. The force pummeled her into the railing of the catwalk, and her head whipped violently as her body rag-dolled along the metal poles of the barrier. Eric quickly lost sight of her as she was fiercely whirled away.

The power of the South Wind.

He realized he'd just seen the force that had torn the wings from the body of the mighty Anzu, though probably weakened from the energy Ninurta had expended calling the storm, and not further augmented by Sharur's vitality. Had he been at full strength, Olive would likely have been ripped to pieces.

Despite concern for his friend, fury took control. He charged and slammed his aluminum bat into the bleeding spot in the noxious deity's back, right where Olive's bullet had pierced his flesh. It felt like striking concrete. Ninurta howled with the pain of impact, but Eric knew his weapon couldn't beat this monstrous being into submission.

The surprised and greatly angered god stood and turned to face him. *'Pathetic mortal! Like an insect, I shall cast you away. You think you can combat the power of a god with a metal stick?'*

Ninurta again raised his arm, and Eric braced for impact. If the gust the god summoned was as powerful as the one that dispatched Olive, it might lift him right over the edge of the roof. He went low, grabbed the railing of the catwalk with his left hand, and prayed he could withstand the onslaught.

Strangely, it never came.

When he mustered the courage to look up, Ninurta was struggling to move his arm forward. It appeared that a thin layer of ice had formed on his rain-soaked body. It chipped and cracked as the god fought to free himself, but the frozen coating didn't give way.

Eric felt a rush of relief. *Enki came through.*

Gaining confidence, he rose and again swung his bat. Fragments of ice shattered and flew away as he unloaded with all his might on Ninurta's barrel chest.

The confused deity stumbled backward as he battled to free himself from his frozen cocoon.

Eric gave no quarter, no mercy. Fear for Olive's condition drove his frenzy, and his aluminum bat's signature ring resounded with each strike.

Suddenly, a black shape enveloped the target of his aggressions. He checked his final swing as the Afrit swept the now frantic deity toward the wall of the façade. They both crashed into the barrier, which shattered behind them and sent more stucco and concrete cascading to the floor of the catwalk.

The Afrit had surprise, and had gotten a good grip, but Ninurta was huge, and far heavier and bulkier than his winged opponent could lift. Even hindered as he was, the terrible god still possessed incredible strength.

The two supernatural creatures wrestled, each exerting a force that would crush the bones of any mortal being. To Eric's dismay, Ninurta emerged victorious. He flung the bat-winged beast over the wall, where it vanished into the menacing sky.

Once again, Eric faced the mad deity on his own, now with little hope of forcing him past the edge and to the ground below.

'Ninurta!'

The cry, or its mentally projected equivalent, came from the roof of Margate Tower below them. He looked down and saw Enki, still in Capricorn form, with a look of unmistakable determination on his goat-like visage.

'Cease your struggles! Leave this world in peace, or at least to its own fate. Our kind has meddled enough here, and little good has it done. Return with me to the Abzu, and we will rule there together.'

Ninurta heartily laughed.

'Uncle! I might have suspected, especially when the gateway was taken. Clever little creatures, these humans, despite the fragility of their short lives. To rouse you from slumber is quite a feat. I give them credit where I surely failed! But do you take me for a fool? Return with you to the Abzu? To do what, exactly? Sleep for an eternity, like you? You forget, Uncle, I am part human. The passions of their kind run strongly in my veins. Like all from this plane who went to the Abzu, in the end, it is not enough. The unity, the singularity, the passage of time that does not pass – endless, everlasting, continual! You feel it not, but we do. You know I speak the truth. Even Damgalnunna once said these words to you. They broke what heart you have come to possess, but you knew the veracity of what she said, knew that she chose the proper path, even as the last of her essence slipped through your scaled fingers.'

Enki bristled at Ninurta's outburst. He reared on his serpentine tail as his mighty goat hooves flailed angrily in the air.

'Speak not her name, you who have betrayed us! If hers was the proper path, then you defy every tenet we set forth! By all means, go... as she did! Not into the Abzu – I recognize that path is not open to one of your birthright – but into this world where you have options. If you cannot live in harmony with these creatures, then live no more. Even your father, angry as he was, in the end realized this was true. We have no place here as rulers. To these beings, we are as gods, but we are not gods! We are not the answer they seek, nor are they ours. Make peace with that concept, and give up this worthless venture. It suits you not.'

Seeming to sense the détente, Eric felt the Afrit land gently beside him. For all he had feared, and sometimes hated, the beast, it now bolstered his flagging confidence to have the creature beside him.

'Failure. The goat-man speaks true. This being is powerful, both physically and in the forces he controls.'

"We did our best. Don't give up yet. Let's see what happens."

Ninurta had digested Enki's words, to which he now scoffed in reply.

'Oh, Uncle! Do you seriously believe that I wish to rule on this insignificant little speck of cosmic dust? You have my word, I will leave these creatures in peace, whatever is left of them when Sharur has consumed his fill of their energy. Then, we will be gone, along with the Tablet of Destinies, with which we can rule the varied worlds we will encounter. Long have we all known there is much more to this realm than simply one happenstance nexus point. Were this not the

accidental location where our planes collide, this little globe would have circled in endless darkness, eventually to be consumed by its own exploding star. Nothing here would have mattered at all. Why cry for these mortal beings? Their sacrifice will propel me to the ends of this cosmos. They should rejoice in such a fate, that they aided a being the likes of me. Go back to your Abzu and sleep, Uncle. Eternity awaits me.'

As if to underscore his final words, a blinding flash of lighting erupted in the sky, followed immediately by a deafening and earth-shaking clap of thunder. Margate Tower swayed under Eric's feet, and he momentarily feared that the building might collapse.

'There! Sharur returns! The Tablet is almost in my grasp. You are too late to stop me, and too weak. All of you, leave now, and I may be merciful and spare your pathetic lives.'

Eric turned to the Afrit. "You're our only chance. Fly out to meet Sharur. He won't be expecting you. Get that Tablet out of its grasp. We can't let Ninurta get his hands on it. We'll keep him busy... *go*!"

For a brief instant, the obsidian creature considered, but then resolutely flew into the air.

Ninurta noticed the Afrit take to the sky, but had no time to react as Eric lunged at the terrible god and pinned the being's neck to the wall of the façade with his bat.

Enki seemed to redouble his efforts to keep the ice formed on their struggling opponent.

Even with this assistance, Eric was no match for the angry deity's strength. With effort and deliberation, Ninurta brought his hands to the bat that choked him, and slowly he began to push back. Eric fought with all his might, but it simply wasn't enough. In the end, even Enki's ice started to give way. Sensing his advantage, the terrible god kicked Eric's feet out from under him, and fiercely cast his body backward. He slammed onto the floor of the catwalk and skidded painfully to where the wall turned. His head cracked as it crashed into the stuccoed concrete, and he felt warm blood pool in his hair and drip down his neck from a nasty gash in his skull.

Through eyes that refused to focus, he watched the vengeful god walk toward him, murder in his fiery gaze. Somehow, the bat still rested at his side, as if it had refused to slip through the openings in the grated metal walkway to stay diligently and obediently with its owner. He groggily fumbled for the weapon and rose shakily to his feet, but it was hopeless. Dizziness overcame him as blood clouded his vision. He could manage only to prop himself on the wall to await the end.

Ninurta came within three steps, but suddenly, his legs launched into the air. He fell backwards and smashed heavily onto the catwalk.

Eric saw Enki's serpentine tail flash by as it completed the sweep that had tripped the terrible god. He wanted to strike again with his bat, but his limbs simply wouldn't respond. He struggled for balance on the wall, and caught sight of Sharur as he approached.

The lion-eagle was nearly upon them, over the beach now and closing quickly on the roof of the tower. Its talons clutched a great clay tablet about the size of the large atlases that Eric remembered from the Southby High library.

With effort, Ninurta righted himself, then sidled toward the back wall to avoid another strike from Enki's dangerous tail. Again, he glared menacingly in Eric's direction, but noticing his adversary's gaze, he also looked toward the water. The terrible god briefly rejoiced seeing Sharur so close, but his joy was short-lived.

At that instant, the Afrit rocketed out of a dark and cloudy patch of sky, and dove directly into Sharur from above. They could almost feel the mighty impact. Feathers flew from the weapon-creature's eagle wings as the almost incalculably powerful blow bent the beast's body into an unnatural, almost back-breaking, shape.

Both Sharur and Ninurta emitted screams of dismay and agony as the Tablet flew out of the monster's talons and dropped directly down toward the beach below.

Ninurta abandoned Eric, savagely leapt over the catwalk's railing, and descended on Enki with a mighty shriek. The Lord of the Abzu had seemingly not expected such a maneuver. His tail still pointed in the direction of the catwalk, presumably in hopes of again tripping his opponent. This gave Ninurta easy access to Enki's back, where the enraged deity found solid purchase. He grasped the Capricorn's goat fur in one hand, and one of the great, sweeping horns in the other.

The God of Civilization fiercely bucked and thrashed, trying desperately to dislodge the furious Ninurta. However, as the Afrit had observed, and Eric had learned firsthand, the God of Thunder and Storms was incredibly strong, and while Enki flailed, he couldn't maintain concentration on the ice barrier that gave them all a fighting chance.

Ninurta ignored the pain of the bullet wound, or perhaps used it to further propel his rage, and pushed upward against the great horn he held.

Eric watched in incapacitated horror as the sweeping appendage began to give way, making a ghastly tearing sound as bone and cartilage ripped and tore. Enki emitted howls of agony as, finally, the entire structure wedged away in a gloppy expulsion of blood and gore from the Capricorn's skull. The Lord of the Abzu instantly collapsed to the wet asphalt roof.

Ninurta spat into the steadily increasing rain, and tossed the once majestic horn to the ground. *'Your time is done, Uncle! You cannot stop me, try as you might. I go now to retrieve what is mine. Crawl back to your deep waters and lick your wounds, and kiss your children goodbye! Your failure will mark their end, and to me, it is high time. Ungrateful little wretches, they are! We offered all, but it was not enough. Now, they will reap what they have sown.'*

The Mesopotamian god of Thunder and Storms marched indignantly across the roof of Margate Tower. He found the door to the stairway, ripped it from its hinges, and threw it angrily aside, then glanced behind one final time. He shook his head sadly, then turned and disappeared inside.

CHAPTER 19

'Come, quickly.'

Eric heard the voice in his head, but couldn't determine from where it had come. He'd recovered somewhat, not as dizzy and unstable now, though blood still dripped from the gash on his head. He searched from left to right, trying to find who had spoken.

'Here. Come to me. Quickly!'

He looked down to where the Capricorn stirred. Thick, ichorous blood still seeped from the gaping and grisly wound on the creature's mighty head, but Enki wasn't dead. He didn't even appear to be immobilized.

Eric marshalled his strength and concentration, grabbed his now heavily dented aluminum bat, slipped through the inner railing of the elevated catwalk, and dropped to the ground. For his battered body, the move proved painful, but time was short, and the stairs were not close by.

"Holy crap! I thought you were dead, or at least knocked out!"

'Precisely. I am a trickster. Ninurta's anger and arrogance blind him. He forgets that I have no mortal component as he does. This body is for me but a shell. He hurt me, no question, but I let him see what he wanted to see. Now, he approaches the ground as we intended, believing that we are out of the way. Come! We must get to the Tablet before he arrives. Climb again upon my back.'

"I don't know if I can do this. You have only one horn to hold onto, and I'm still pretty weak."

'Going down will be far easier. I will be as gentle as possible. I still need you. Hang on with all your might.'

Eric heeded Enki's instructions. He grabbed a fistful of blood-stained goat hair and dragged himself up. Then, with his left arm, he clutched the Capricorn's remaining horn, maintaining the bat in his right hand.

Enki coiled his serpentine tail and launched into the air. Eric's stomach lurched as they vaulted over the wall of the façade, but he was heartened when he caught a brief glimpse of Olive as she dragged back toward the stairs she'd used to reach the catwalk.

Enki had been correct: going down was easier, almost like hang-gliding. Not that Eric had ever been hang-gliding, but he imagined it might be like this as they smoothly sailed and banked on pockets of air. Of course, the Lord of the Abzu used the water of the rain to perform this near miracle. He circled wide and descended cautiously so as not to put undue stress on Eric's arm or hand, which clung desperately to the sweeping horn. They neared the ground toward the side of the building that faced Queensway Boulevard, and the Capricorn flew almost directly in front of the windshield of the white van.

Lotte was bound to see that. Not that she'll be able to do much, but at least she knows I'm alive... for now.

As they approached the beach, Enki lowered and dragged his tail along the rain-soaked sand. It made for a bumpy ride, but it decreased their momentum. Soon, Eric felt the mighty creature's front hooves touch the earth. He trotted at first, then slowed, as the Capricorn came to a remarkably gentle stop.

Eric had barely dismounted when the huge goat-fish again began to undulate and change. Enki's man-form soon reemerged, stripped of Olive's father's ill-fitting clothes, and bearing the mark of the terrible wound he had suffered at Ninurta's hand. The entire side and back of the great god's head had been torn away, revealing broken bone and the bloody pulp of exposed and mangled brain tissue. To another being, this injury would be fatal, and Eric shuddered at the realization that soon, he would likely face their superhumanly powerful adversary once again.

Enki turned and strode purposefully toward the waters of the ocean as they furiously lashed the beach in the great gale. He had picked this spot to land for a reason. Here, the Tablet of Destines stuck out of the muck and sand like a half-buried obelisk. It seemed unbroken, not surprising given its construction from the same material as Enki's gateway—clay from the Abzu itself. The portal had been magnetic, as Lotte surmised—highly so. These objects were, in some ways, a product of two realms, both water and earth—truly a wonder, but Eric had no time just now to fully contemplate it.

The Lord of the Abzu lifted the Tablet out of the wet sand, and Eric could see the now familiar linear scratch marks, similar to those on the portal, though more plentiful and varied, and interspersed with other shapes, both large and small. For such a powerful item, it seemed rather mundane, and of crude construction, like the gateway, or like the many broken and crumbling tablets and seals he'd seen in the ancient history wings of various museums.

Enki projected to him with an unusually serious tone. *'You must guard me... buy me time. I have him, but it will take effort, and I must concentrate. I will lend you what assistance I can, but....'*

Eric knew what "but" meant.

I know you want to have a dog, *but....* I know you don't want to go to school today, *but....* I know how much you hate geometry, *but....* I know you want to talk with Lotte, need to hear her voice so badly that it feels like your heart is being ripped from your chest, *but....* I know you want to live to see tomorrow, *but....*

'He comes. Make ready.'

Eric made ready, which wasn't a particularly complex process. He turned around. He hefted his dented bat. He kissed his ass goodbye.

A large double glass door at the back of the towering building exploded outward in a shower of crystalline shards and twisted metal. Ninurta burst through and strode angrily along the manicured path, past the pool, and toward the wooden gangway that led to the beach—and to them.

To Eric's left, he caught sight of Lotte, maybe a hundred yards away. She had crept out into the trees near the building that overlooked the scrubby embankment, which the wooden gangway politely bridged for the pampered residents of Margate Tower. Mutig stood beside her, and she clutched the collar around the dog's throat.

Eric could hear Enki speaking behind him—really speaking—intoning words not meant for others to understand—long, droning syllables that only reluctantly gave way to those that followed.

Ninurta was halfway down the gangway when he saw them. The terrible god screamed and waved his arms.

Eric knew what that meant, and immediately slammed his body into the muddy beach below, letting himself be sucked in by its moisture. Wind-whipped sand blasted at the top of his head and scraped at the raw, exposed laceration on his scalp. Grains of rocky grit embedded deeply and painfully into the gash.

Literally pouring salt in the wound. What's next, a plague of locusts?

Thankfully, the forceful wind soon abated. Despite the sand-blasting, he remained in place, and still heard Enki incanting behind him. That was the good news.

The bad news was that Ninurta now stormed toward them. He seemed to have abandoned his little wind trick, realizing that the wretched and puny mortals were onto his game. Now it looked like he just intended to pulverize, which, in the end, was probably simpler and more effective, anyway.

Eric stood, repositioned his bat, and waited for the inevitable.

Ninurta closed to within about ten yards when, again, the ice encased him. The terrible god screamed as he struggled and furiously fought to free himself.

This is my chance!

Eric ran as fast as he could toward the hindered deity, using the distance to build momentum. This time, he didn't bother with the noxious god's barrel chest. He went straight for the head, right where Olive had shot him from the back of the van. A ragged scar still remained from that devastating, near point-blank strike.

This feels like tee-ball, only the ball is much bigger, and I'm gonna hit this one out of the park... if it's the last thing I ever do.

The God of Thunder and Storms attempted to raise his arms to shield his head from the force of the impact, but the ice slowed him just enough.

Eric made solid contact with his adversary's face, just a bit lower than he'd been aiming.

Oh, well.

The blow struck Ninurta directly in the bridge of his nose, right between the eyes, and for once, Eric experienced the satisfying curdling of flesh and bone under the impact of his trusty bat.

To his wonder, the terrible god toppled over backward. He screamed in agony, and blood sprayed from between fingers that belatedly and desperately grasped at his demolished nose.

Not wasting a moment, Eric whirled around and struck again, this time on the side of Ninurta's face. The head of his bat brutally cracked against the struggling deity's cheek. Blood and dislodged teeth spewed onto the sand as Ninurta's entire upper body whipped with the ferocious impact.

Once more, Eric brought his bat to bear. This time, he attempted an overhead strike aimed at the back of the reeling god's skull, but Ninurta powered into action.

With anger-fueled desperation, coupled with the inevitable dimming of the ice's capacity to hold him, Ninurta managed to arch his back at the last moment, causing Eric's strike to deflect across the being's hard-as-concrete shoulder blades. Then, with a blindingly quick sweep of his arm, Ninurta caught Eric off guard.

Eric splashed into the wet sand and madly grasped for his bat, which had landed just out of reach.

Again, the terrible god was too fast. On hands and knees, he reached out and grabbed the weapon before Eric could secure it, then slowly rose to his feet, took the object in both hands, and brought it down over his knee. Like the spines of the Afrit's victims, the aluminum bat split in twain with one final and mighty *klank*, before being silenced forever.

Ninurta spat thick blood into the wind-lashed rain that enveloped them, then turned his bleeding and ruined face to Eric. '*I give you credit, mortal. You fought bravely, and wisely. You could have served me well, but now, your short life must end.*'

The terrible god reached down, clutched Eric, and lifted him into the air. Eric struggled, but it was useless. This being had far too much strength. He would die on Ninurta's knee, suffering the same fate as his bat. He would even be denied the dubious pleasure of feeding the Afrit, and perhaps endlessly warming some small part of himself beside the Eternal Flame.

It happened quickly. In one second, he rose as the angry god lifted him. In the next... he fell, but it wasn't the fall he'd expected. Instead of feeling Ninurta's knee as it shattered his spine, he tumbled headfirst into the muddy sand. Again, he screamed in agony at the fresh aggravation to the gaping wound on his skull. It took him a moment to regain his bearings, scrape the mud from his eyes, and assure himself that, indeed, he still remained all in one piece.

It was a sound, however, that ultimately brought him back—the sound of a savage struggle, the sound of... *growling*. He looked up and saw that Mutig had embedded himself in the terrible god's shoulder, near the throat. Fresh blood streamed down the embattled deity's mighty chest as he twirled madly and flailed his arms at the audacious animal. He struck Mutig in the sides, and the dog emitted heavy snorts and deep, guttural noises with each blow, but he didn't let go.

We were right. Enki did more than just change Mutig's appearance. No normal animal could withstand blows like that.

Eventually, Ninurta seemed to determine that he couldn't dislodge the beast by pummeling him, so he changed tactics. Bleeding and staggering, he grabbed Mutig by the shoulders and laboriously tore the dog from his neck. The agony must have been unbearable. A huge gouge of flesh ripped away in the vice grips of the powerful canine's jaws. Part of Ninurta's collarbone appeared, exposed through the torn flesh and torrents of blood that gushed onto his hopelessly stained and shredded t-shirt.

Mutig fought to free himself from the furious god's grip, but the dog had lost his leverage. Seemingly oblivious to the excruciating pain in his shoulder, Ninurta grasped the struggling creature in his left hand, and punched him directly in the face. Mutig's head lashed backward, and he instantly went limp. Ninurta then raised the dog above his head, and vigorously hurled him directly at Eric.

The two collided, the impact anything but gentle, as Mutig's refashioned body felt like a stone. Eric's breath violently expelled as he smacked into the wet sand. He fought for air, nearly unconscious. He sensed Mutig's body beside him, surely dazed, if not dead, but the dog was beyond his assistance.

Reluctantly, he opened his eyes. Far above, illuminated by the frequent and massive discharges of lightning, he could see the Afrit and Sharur. There, they darted and lashed at each other in the air, as the ashen monster had once confronted Charun. This time, the Afrit appeared to be faster, more agile in flight, but the obsidian beast fought with caution, seemingly fearful of falling into Sharur's powerful clutches. For now, the struggle appeared to be a standoff.

Ninurta suddenly appeared, towering above him. The terrible god seemed to have moved beyond anger, beyond more words of praise to an opponent who had shown bravery. His intent was simple, and it would be delayed no longer. He reached first for Mutig, and Eric could see that that dog gave no resistance. Like him, the animal had been rendered incapable of further delaying the inevitable.

Eric clenched his eyes shut, unwilling to watch the valiant beast's miserable and brutal end.

The ground seemed to shake as Ninurta exacted his vengeance on the stunned creature.

Strangling him, probably, or lashing his body into the fucking mud.

He felt the sand give way to his side, and imagined Mutig's pulped body being repeatedly pummeled into the earth, creating a hole into which Eric now felt himself being drawn. He tried to move, but a wave of nausea washed over him, and he began to shake. Unable to hold back, he turned his head and vomited into the wet sand. The shaking worsened, and he feared he might be going into shock.

After a few moments, the nausea lessened, having cleared his stomach of all its contents. The shaking, however, grew ever stronger, as did his sense of slipping downward. His ears rang, but Ninurta's terrible and familiar cries cut through the haze that enveloped his senses. Coughing and sputtering, Eric reluctantly opened his tear-filled eyes.

He'd slipped into a pit, and from the bottom, a great, black, reptilian eye gazed impenetrably at him. Two huge holes punctuated the front of a blunt, snout-like nose above bony protuberances that formed the top of the giant's mouth.

It's a turtle. It's the *turtle!*

Enki must have again summoned his creation, and it had somehow tunneled all the way from the Abzu to once more ensnare the arrogant and overconfident deity. The massive creature had pinned Ninurta under one of its great claws, and now attempted to ensnare the frantic god in its questing jaws and drag him downward. With Herculean strength, Ninurta fought to fend off the beast's gigantic maw.

The turtle's head was the size of a sofa, and Eric now understood why the monster couldn't exit though Enki's gateway. It was even larger than he'd imagined.

Ninurta howled in anger and frustration, but one word, mixed among his desperate shouts, rose above all others.

'Sharur! Sharur!'

Panic shot through Eric.

I don't know if Sharur can save him, but at this point, I don't really care. If I can't get out of this pit, I'm gonna be killed in the battle, or accidentally dragged down to the Abzu. Either way, it's the end for me, and at this stage, that's a needless death. Problem is, I can barely move. Also, where the hell is Mutig?

He frantically scanned the pit.

There!

A flash of lightning revealed the dog's location, farther down in the depression that trapped them, close to the left side. He'd probably been in Ninurta's grasp when the turtle tunneled-up from underneath them. To get to the animal, Eric would have to descend back into the pit, but the slope steepened, and the sand was wet. He might lose his footing and slide directly into the struggling titans.

Too risky. It'd be better to get out of the pit and try to grab Mutig from above. That'll work, if the hole doesn't get any deeper, and if I can actually move in the first place.

Every instinct his body exerted told him to stay put, but he knew his life, and Mutig's, depended on his ability to act. He struggled to pull himself to his elbows, agonizingly rolled onto his stomach, and began to claw his way out of the fissure. Pains he hadn't even noticed before asserted themselves, and pervasive weakness, along with the return of the nausea, made every motion a chore. Somehow, he lifted his upper body up and over the sandy lip of the depression, then collapsed into a muddy pool, gasping for breath.

When he again raised his head, he beheld a disheartening development.

Sharur had seemingly evaded the Afrit. The terrifying lion-eagle had landed a bit closer to the water, and to Enki's left. It hesitantly pawed at the ground, while its maned head searched the skies.

Once bitten, twice shy, I guess. The Afrit clearly wounded it, and it doesn't want to be taken unaware again.

Sure enough, from out of nowhere, the ashen creature dove at the lion-eagle. It seemed a desperate move, perhaps a final bid to delay the beast before it found its way back into the hands of its master. It looked as if the Afrit had succeeded, as Sharur was flattened to the ground by the savage impact. The monster fiercely swung its lion head around, but the shimmering black being wildly fluttered its batlike wings, lifted its legs high of Sharur's bite, and drove its barbed tail deeply between the lion's shoulder blades.

Sharur shrieked in agony, but the supernatural being was not finished. Its eagle wings clamped mightily together above its back, trapping the Afrit between them. Like a bronco, the monster then bucked with its mighty, leonine hind legs.

The Afrit tumbled uncontrollably forward and landed hard in the wet sand.

The creature of flame struggled to right itself, but Sharur acted too quickly. Its mighty lion jaws clamped down on the back of the Afrit's thigh. It lifted the ashen being into the air, and with three mighty shakes of its head, tossed its prey viciously aside. The Afrit's leg severed almost at the hip.

Head, over heels, over wings, the Afrit tumbled. It finally came to rest in a jumbled and motionless heap near the water, directly behind Enki.

Sharur turned and lined up his erstwhile adversary for an easy killing blow. Ninurta desperately beckoned, but the weapon-creature was wise. He knew he had time, and if his dark, otherworldly opponent recovered, it could still cause mischief.

Sharur crouched, preparing to strike, when suddenly gunshots rang out and the beast's side exploded in a haze of blood and gore. Eric turned and saw Olive, closely followed by Lotte. She fired her AR-15 with deadly accuracy, Sharur having given her a nice big target by turning broadside. Again and again, she fired. Blood and feathers flew, and one wing again collapsed, its tendons severed from the forceful impact of the bullets.

Then, as before, Sharur capitulated under the terrible onslaught, and morphed from lion-eagle back into the form of a mace, now with a new wooden handle attached.

I'm not sure how Ninurta managed that, but right now, I don't really give a shit.

The weapon twirled in the air and landed with a soggy *plunk* in the muddy sand.

Olive stepped in the path between where Eric lay, half-in and half-out of the pit, and where the inert weapon had fallen. She smiled at Enki, who clutched the mighty Tablet to his chest. With difficulty, the great god attempted to smile in return, but he struggled to lift the right side of his mouth where most of the muscles had been torn away.

She beamed, and looked back toward Eric. The lightning over the ocean behind created almost a halo around her. Vengeance on the creature that killed her uncle was hers. She had proven herself to that terrible beast, to Ninurta, to Enki, and to her friends. She had proven herself to herself. This was the moment she'd waited a lifetime to accomplish.

Ninurta broke the spell. The furious and desperate god roared with anger. Lightning, thunder, and a stiff breeze answered his mighty cry. To Eric's horror, so did Sharur. The mace swept out of the mud and into the air, head pointed straight for the pit where Eric lay, and where the frantic god struggled with the gigantic turtle.

Directly in the weapon's path to this hole, stood Olive.

Eric feebly cried out as sand from the fierce wind again lashed his face "Olive! Look out! Look behind you!"

She couldn't hear, his weakened voice lost in the din of the great storm.

He desperately began to wave his arms and point behind her, but she didn't seem to notice or understand his danger signals as she basked in her victory.

The mace took off. Like a missile it sped toward her, the head of the weapon leaving a wake as it sliced through the heavy rain.

Olive still didn't hear, didn't understand... but Lotte did.

She and Eric had their own private language, one that wasn't predicated exclusively on words. She could read the signs. She knew when something was wrong.

The mace had come within a few feet of impact when she shouldered Olive aside. She surely intended to have ducked, for both of them to hit the ground together, and let the mace fly harmlessly overhead, but there were a million variables... an almost countless number of things that needed to go right, and an equally countless number of ways in which something could go horribly wrong. Lotte didn't have time to run the computation. This time, uncharacteristically, she acted on impulse to save Olive.

With a dull thud that rang like a shot in Eric's ears, the weapon split her skull.

A madness drove him, or a possession.

It wasn't Eric who slid down into the pit and furiously hurled dirt into the face of the God of Thunder and Storms. It wasn't Eric who kicked at the embattled deity's arm, who tried to aid the great turtle in its strenuous task. It wasn't Eric who heard the terrible god's ever more plaintive cries, nor was it Eric who knew, or at least assumed, they would go unanswered.

It wasn't Eric who watched as Ninurta abruptly went stiff, eyes wide and empty, or saw the gigantic reptile cease its struggle. Its gargantuan claw now seemed enough to hold the suddenly silent deity. It wasn't Eric who felt the turtle's black gaze upon him, recognition and gratitude in the mighty creature's expression.

It wasn't Eric who staggered in the wind-lashed rain of the storm to drag a still unconscious Mutig out of the pit. Someone, clearly not Eric, then handed the animal to a weak-kneed and nearly hysterical Olive.

It wasn't Eric who traversed the distance to where the strange little group had gathered. It was twenty, perhaps twenty-five yards, but for whoever made the trek, it seemed like miles.

They were four in all – three moved, one lay perfectly still. Enki and the Afrit sat elsewhere in the muddy sand, enduring the torrents of rain, and reeling from their efforts and injuries. Another small creature played almost carefree in a nearby puddle, close to the body that lay motionless on the ground.

But it wasn't Eric who saw any of that. Eric wasn't there at all. He was clearly possessed, because without an entity to animate him, he'd be incapable of movement. He knew he'd be curled tightly in a fetal ball, sobbing in boundless despair, and praying for the end to be swift. So, he let whatever daemon had apparently come along have its way with him, and the daemon brought him to Lotte.

She had rolled onto her back after the impact, and a bloody pool had formed around her shattered skull. Her lifeless eyes stared toward the sky, the black holes extinguished and empty, no longer inexorably capturing any object that attracted her ever voracious gaze. The Sisters of Mercy proclaimed themselves on her chest, but there would be no mercy, no opportunity for clemency. No quarter. No second chance.

Olive walked up from behind. She must have put Mutig down.

It wasn't Eric who hoped the dog was okay.

"I don't... I can't... oh, gawd, Eric... I'm so sorry. Mr. Enki, can you heal her, like you did with my dog? Make her good as new... better, even?"

The Lord of the Abzu sat with shoulders slumped in the soaking sand, the Tablet of Destines close beside him. '*I cannot, child,*' he answered with exhaustion. '*She is dead, beyond my power to heal. Even were she alive, it would be hard for me now. Vast quantities of power from the Abzu have been drained. What little remains I use to aid my turtle to stifle Ninurta. With Sharur destroyed, he is in shock, far easier to control. However, we must make haste and return him to the gateway before he recovers his bearings.'*

The daemon remembered.

When the mace had made its horrible impact, it had ricocheted toward Enki, propelled by Lotte's momentum, where it fell to the ground. The great god had seized it and, commanding the power of the Tablet of Destinies, began to reverse time on the dreadful weapon. Unlike a mundane item of the material world, Sharur had resisted. It had been a battle of wills, one that taxed both combatants to their limits. In the end, drawing on the powers of the deep waters, the Lord of the Abzu had prevailed.

It wasn't Eric who had given up on the battle before it was over, recognizing that if Enki lost, humanity's only hope was for the gigantic turtle to drag the noxious god down into the depths. The daemon inside him vented its fury on the one responsible for the death of his love, and only when Ninurta ceased his struggle did it realize that the God of Civilization and Progress had succeeded.

Now, it wasn't Eric's legs that a small lion cub rubbed against.

Or, maybe they are my legs.

He reached down and touched the tiny beast. It seemed friendly... fearless. Enlil had selected this creature to forge into a weapon, probably when the animal had grown up and proven its prowess in battle with others of its kind. Now, it was a baby again. The fledgling eagle had likely flown away.

An unadorned and uncarved stone sat partially buried in the wet sand near Enki – the remnants, or rather the precursor, of the Mace Head of Mesilim.

The Louvre's out of luck. They won't be getting their artifact back.

All the weapon's components had been returned to their previous states, their time reversed by the mighty Tablet of myth, and now almost impossibly... reality.

The Tablet....

Eric shook his head and the daemon fled. He was done with it, or perhaps it was done with him. With purpose, he walked to where the Lord of the Abzu gathered his depleted strength. The storm continued to rage around them, and before Enki could realize what was happening, Eric picked up the Tablet of Destinies.

'What are you doing? This is the artifact we sought, sacrificing much to regain. You are behaving as did my insubordinate nephew. Return it to me instantly!'

"I will, with pleasure, if you use it to bring Lotte back. I understand you can't heal her, but you can reverse time on her like you did with Sharur. Promise to do that, and it's yours."

Enki gave a great sigh. *'It is not so simple. First of all, the Tablet of Destinies does not reverse time. The past is immutable. Second, this artifact requires great energy to use. Mine is virtually depleted, and as I have explained, I call upon the last of the Abzu's reserves to check the mind of the still dangerous God of Thunder and Storms.'*

"How do you replenish the Abzu? You said the energy of people who willingly went into the deep waters fed its power. Is this the only way?"

'That is the quickest way. With time, the Abzu will restore itself, but to you, that would be as an eternity – far longer than a mortal human life.'

Eric's mind raced. *There has to be a way.*

"All right, so the quickest way is to find people willing to give themselves to your service. Is one person enough?"

He considered. *'For this purpose, perhaps.'*

"Okay. Do they have to travel through your gateway to enter the Abzu, or can you access a person's energy directly, like the Afrit absorbs its victim's energy?"

The great god cried out, appalled. *'I do not kill my children! What that creature does is an abomination!'*

"That's not my *point*! I'm asking how someone gets into the deep waters. Do you need the gateway, or can you summon their energy directly and deposit it in the Abzu later?"

Enki briefly held Eric's gaze, a stern look in his eye, but then, his demeanor softened, and he looked away. *'I have the capacity to do as you suggest. I can call the energy of any who are willing to come through the waters that flow in this world, or that lingers in the air. Long has it been since that was necessary, but it is possible.'*

"If that's true, then take me! Take me now. I'll go. Drop me in the Abzu later, whenever you feel like it, I don't care. Just bring her back. Promise me you'll bring her back."

'The bond between you is strong, but that is why you cannot go. Quickly did we learn that those who love in this world grow dissatisfied in ours. They poison the Abzu with their grief. So great is your passion that you, like your raven-haired beloved, would inevitably be insufferable. I cannot take you. I will not.'

"Then take me!" Olive forcefully interjected, as Eric, Enki, and the Afrit swung their heads toward her with great surprise. "Lotte died saving my miserable and stupid life anyway. If I wasn't such a dumbass, she wouldn't be layin' there right now. I have nobody before you, Mr. Enki, and you know I owe you one, for my dog and all, so take me. She's worth a whole heck of a lot more than I ever will be."

Eric protested. "Olive, no. This isn't your responsibility. It's not on you. I want Lotte back more than anything in the world. It's not worth living without her, but I can't let you make a sacrifice like that. I wouldn't be able to cope with that either."

'It is irrelevant! Even were I to garner an influx of energy, I cannot wield the Tablet and hold Ninurta simultaneously. The artifact requires too much concentration. It is out of the question!'

"Then let Eric do it," Olive screamed. "Lend him extra strength if you have to, but there has to be a damned way! Pardon my French."

"Is that even possible?" Eric inquired. "If you had the power available, could you allow me to use the Tablet?"

A look of frustration grew on Enki's face.

'It is possible, but I will not allow it! I know that for you, this means everything, but do you realize the power this item has? Have you not seen the way it corrupted my nephew? Yes, he craved authority in a way you do not, I grant you this, but at least a god's blood flows in Ninurta's veins. How am I to know what will happen when a mortal mind is exposed to such potential? Most likely, you will simply die, or go insane. It cannot happen. Hard as it is, face your loss and move on. I also grieve, but some things cannot be undone.'

'Wrong!'

The Afrit's word cut through the noise of the thundering sky. The beast had risen, and tightly flapped its bat-like wings to maintain balance on its one remaining leg.

'These mortals risk everything for no reward... sacrifice their lives for others whom they have never met. We marvel at them. Sometimes we wonder if they have lost their minds, and other times we ponder if, perhaps, there is something to be learned from the most courageous of them. The ones now before you have helped save this realm, and possibly ours. They are due their spoils. The risk, yet again, is mostly theirs. Let them take it. You have the power, so it can be done, or undone. You simply lack the will. Act with courage, and with the compassion you claim to possess. The Sadat Alnaar *is worth the effort.'*

Enki stood up and gazed at the unlikely trio. *'You are certain this is what you wish?'*

In answer, all three stared silently into the great god's eyes.

The Lord of the Abzu lowered his shoulders in acquiescence.

Eric turned to Olive.

She had stopped crying, and a look of defiance had spread on her face. "Don't even try and talk me out of this, Eric Schneider. You can't! I'm doing this for you, too. I kinda like you, in case you hadn't noticed, but I like Lotte too. I never had better friends than y'all. I only wish I could have known you longer."

He gazed deeply into her eyes as his thoughts whirled in desperation. She wasn't Lotte, and would never draw him as did the girl, now the woman, he'd known for ten years. Still, Olive touched his heart. As different as he and Lotte were, he and Olive were sympatico. He felt he understood her. He'd been in this place before.

He remembered his words to Lotte, all those years ago. *You can't make me go, and if you try, I'll be a total pest and you'll eventually give in.*

Arguing was hopeless. He knew this as surely as he knew the depths of his own mind, and with that, he reached his conclusion.

"You're as stubborn as I am, Olive. I know it's useless trying to talk you out of anything. You're also incredibly brave. Don't ever believe anyone who tells you otherwise. I'm glad, like you are, that we're friends. So is Lotte, if I may speak in her absence."

He hugged her tightly, then turned to approach Enki.

Olive called in a shaky voice. "Please take care of my dog. Mutig. Brave. Like me."

He looked over his shoulder, smiled again, and gave a slight tilt of his head.

With the Tablet cradled under his right arm, he walked up to the Lord of the Abzu and tightly grasped the god's upper arm with his left hand. He stared deeply into Enki's eyes, ignoring the gory ruin of the deity's head. They intensely locked gazes, focused fervently and purposefully on one another.

For a time, all was silent. Even the thunder abated.

'You are certain?' Enki finally asked with seeming surprise.

Eric slowly nodded his head.

The great god cast a forlorn look toward Olive, but Eric didn't flinch. The God of Civilization and Progress then closed his eyes and took a deep breath.

After a few moments, he again met Eric's gaze and whispered. *'It is done. Raise the Tablet.'*

He did as instructed, not looking back, and a power surged inside him as Enki granted him the ability to read the ancient script. The runes on the Tablet began to wiggle as they blurred and merged with one another. The face of the clay document soon became a torrent of images that rushed by at impossible speeds.

Deeper and deeper, his mind descended into the flow, until suddenly... he was gone... and he was everywhere.

CHAPTER 20

Not exactly what I anticipated, but then, what in my life has really gone as anticipated?

Given the whirlwind of motion the Tablet of Destinies had become, he'd expected to find himself ensconced in some sort of river, rushed along by the irresistible current of time, struggling to keep his head above water as history itself battered and buffeted him from any and all directions.

It wasn't like that. Not at all.

If it was a river, it was a frozen one, more like a great block of ice—dark and motionless. Images appeared and then rapidly vanished, as if having been briefly illuminated by a hopelessly inadequate flashlight—there, and suddenly gone.

Was that a dinosaur? Was that the Tower of Babylon? Was that William Sherman, gazing in horror at the carnage of Shiloh, intent that if he had his way, he'd find another path to win a seemingly unwinnable war? Was that a star, imploding on itself, giving birth to a terrible and mysterious black hole? Was that the birth of an entire galaxy, or it's death?

He couldn't tell. The sights flashed before his eyes too quickly, before he could absorb and comprehend them. He also knew they were not what he sought, and that his time was limited in this unfathomable dimension, this "where" that was nowhere, yet everywhere, this space that was nothing, yet encapsulated everything that had ever been, and eventually, everything that ever would be. The immensity of it terrified him.

Enki had been right. This place that wasn't a place strained the mortal mind—slashed at it. It said, "You belong here not. *Get out*!"

Eric was happy to oblige, but first he just had one thing to do. In the context of the immensity around him, it felt like a small thing, a thing so tiny it would hardly be noticed, would hardly register. For him, however, it was the most important thing in the world. His burning desire drove him forward into the abyss.

A flood of grief threatened to overwhelm him.

What have I done?

Desperation had driven him to make an almost unimaginable choice, trading one life for another. Did it matter that the one sacrificed was willing, ready to go, and fully prepared to take Lotte's place in a realm beyond flesh and blood existence—for all intents and purposes... dead? Had the exchange been worth *that*, just so he could sidestep the pain of losing her?

Of course, there was more to it. Lotte's life had an intrinsic value as well, separate from any connection with him, and he'd made his choice with both considerations in mind. Much as it wore on him, no good would come of fretting over it now. That would waste the opportunity so graciously and unselfishly gifted. His tears would have to wait. There would be time aplenty for those later. With a heavy heart, he forced the subject from his mind and concentrated on the task at hand.

He had two jobs. The first was to locate Lotte in all this... "this-ness." The second was to somehow figure out how to do the trick that makes a bowstring turn into a "bloody live sheep," or causes an ornamented mace head revert to uncarved stone, and disgorge its magically merged monstrosities as the cubs and fledglings from which they'd grown.

The Lord of the Abzu had claimed that the Tablet didn't reverse time, that time was immutable. As he looked around this frozen place, Eric could see this was probably true. So how was it done?

First things first. If I can't find Lotte, I can't save her.

He cast his thoughts outward, as he had into the Abzu. Like using sonar, he hoped to hear a little *ping* that would tell him where to go, or pick up some trace that he could follow.

Only silence greeted him.

Here, wherever "here" was, he heard no sounds, sensed no thought. He saw only the fleeting images from the corners of his eyes, and they disappeared before he could even focus on them.

This isn't the way. Maybe if I concentrate on Lotte... maybe that'll take me to her little thread in this gigantic tapestry.

He tried. He focused on her face, her sharp and shining eyes, her slightly slanted natural eyebrows, her luminescent skin. He imagined her laugh, and her characteristically sharp tongue. He reeled from memories of her incredible tenderness and her occasional but breathtaking passion, then felt the sting of her cold, casual inconsideration, and her self-centered yearnings. All this made up Lotte, all this and more, but no memory of the woman at the center of his life could help him locate her—not in this place that wasn't a place.

Wait a minute. I may not be able to find her, but I should be able to find myself. I mean, this is happening to me, right? Somewhere, back there, is my past. It has to be linked in some way to this moment. That's the thread I need to find, and if I find me, I find Lotte!

It turned out to be remarkably effortless, like looking over your shoulder, but also incredibly difficult to control. *Now*, the images surged at him, flooding him with memories too fast to process before another recollection supplanted it. Lotte was easy to find, she was *everywhere*, but he couldn't stop the deluge of his own experiences. It felt like being trapped on an old VHS movie stuck on rewind. He couldn't find the "play" button, or "stop."

In practically the blink of an eye, he found himself in high school, racing backward toward his meeting with the Afrit, the being that unknowingly brought him and Lotte together as they battled to rid her of the debilitating nightmares. Beyond that lay just the short time they knew each other before that. Then, their paths would diverge as he rocketed toward his past before her, and hers before him.

The incredible trip began to tax his limited energy. He wasn't sure he'd be able to repeat the journey forward.

I have to do something, but what? Until I figure out how to stop, I need to stay alongside her somehow... or do I?

He didn't know what else to do, so he risked it all, and reached out. He tried to abandon his own historical thread completely and desperately tried to implant his consciousness into Lotte's past, the flow of her experiences.

Somewhere, there has to be an opening, a way inside. If I can't do it, I'll lose her, and I'm not sure I have the energy to find her again.

His mind began to tear apart as an overload of information from the two historical streams ripped at his very sanity. He couldn't take much more of this. Enki's warning rang in his ears, but still he pushed and probed, battling for some point of entry into her track of time.

He almost gave up, almost pulled back into himself to flee the searing mental agony, but then he saw Lotte plunk herself down next to him and bring her face close to his, closer than they'd ever been. They were in the Southby High library. He sat on the orange seat cushion from one of the retro comfy reading chairs that Lotte had surreptitiously nicked.

Her black-stained lips, squiggly black un-eyebrows, scary black circles under her black-mascaraed eyes, and the scent of something vaguely sweet that came from her breath—the glorious gummy bears—once again became his entire world.

This time, however, he crossed the event horizon, and gravity and mass gave way.

He saw his own surprised reaction through her eyes, and heard his own hesitant voice through her ears.

"Umm, yeah, sure. Go ahead."

In reverse, Lotte told him what she wanted, "Eric, I need desperately to sleep."

He wished he could linger here to relive this wonderful moment, but again he felt himself swept away, trapped in Lotte's memories, which seemed to speed by faster and faster.

He barely noticed when he vanished from the picture altogether. Everything was a blur. He'd partially succeeded. He'd managed to hold onto the course of Lotte's past, but he still didn't understand how to stop the fast-motion rewind.

This is Lotte's whole life, rushing over us both like a waterfall. I need to find an anchor point, or even better, I need Lotte to find it for me – one exact moment in time, instead of all of them together, simultaneously. It has to be something important, something like that experience in the library. That *made her vulnerable, and it gave me an opening. It has to be something she'd remember, that she couldn't* ever *forget!*

Time came to a screeching halt.

Eric found himself in front of a doorway as he rummaged in his book bag for his keys.

Wait a minute. That's not my book bag. Those aren't my keys. This is Lotte's memory, and we're moving forward in time.

She placed the key in the lock of the big wooden door and pushed it open. He saw a plush carpeted hallway with other doorways off to the right, and a beautiful wooden staircase to the left. She slung her book bag over her shoulder and ascended the stairs. She moved slowly. She was tired. It had been a long day at school, but it was what lay ahead that truly made her weary.

She anticipated the silence of the now bleak and hushed house. She dreaded banging on her mother's door to see if she wanted something to eat, and her mother's inevitable failure to answer, or else a curt, "Go away," the only reply.

She sighed as she reached the top step and made the short trek to their front door. Again, she rifled through her keys, found the correct one, went inside, and removed her shoes in the little foyer. She was thirsty, and hoped there was still some Coca Cola left in the icebox. She grabbed her book bag by the strap and lugged it inside.

Glancing down the hallway on her way to the kitchen, she noticed her mother's door stood open.

That's odd. Maybe she's up. Maybe she's feeling better.

The optimistic possibility brightened her mood. The thought of another lonely afternoon of homework until her father returned from work had become almost too much to bear. Even when he arrived, they'd eat a silent dinner before he claimed he needed to work and sequestered himself away. She knew better, and that he simply hid from what was happening. In a sense, who could blame him? So, she didn't push, but it left her dreadfully alone.

Her mother wasn't in the kitchen, so Lotte dropped her bag on the counter, grabbed a Coca Cola out of the fridge, and went toward the living room.

Perhaps she's there, or out on the patio. It's nice today, and some fresh air would do her good.

She skipped down the hallway, her heart a bit lighter. "Mother! Are you feeling better? Do you want some Coca—"

Eric knew the experience of shock. It was still fresh with him from the beach. Now he felt it anew through the eyes of a thirteen-year-old girl, who saw her mother dangling from the chandelier of their dining room. Lotte stood unmoving, at first not believing what she saw. Then, the madness took her, or was it a possession? Eric felt the presence of the daemon once again.

It wasn't Lotte who righted the toppled chair, the one her mother had kicked away to separate herself irrevocably from the supporting gravity of the Earth. It wasn't Lotte who stepped onto the chair, and then to the top of their mighty, dark-stained, oak dining room table her mother had somehow managed to pull aside. It wasn't Lotte who reached over and grabbed the lifeless body, bare feet swinging slightly in sympathy to some imperceptible vibration from the depths of the building.

It was, however, Lotte who pulled her mother toward her and put her arms around her, who held her, as she'd wanted to hold her for nearly a year, since the sickness began. She rocked gently from side to side, knowing that this would be the last time she would ever feel her mother's skin, ever smell her smell, ever touch the body that brought her into the world—the body that now left her in this wretched, cold, and indifferent place to fend for herself.

She felt frightened and confused, abandoned and betrayed, and *angry*... so angry. Too angry for tears, she merely rocked back and forth—gentle rocking, like when she had been little. How she would miss that, but she knew that was now in the past. She took what solace she could in the firm resolution that nobody would ever hurt her this way again. She wouldn't allow it. She wouldn't let anyone close enough to touch her. It wasn't worth the pain.

Eric shuddered.

I have no place here. I wasn't meant to see this, but it was the only way I could figure out how to stop.

Now he began to understand.

Specific moments. You can't just ride the wave. I have to get out of here. Lotte has to take me to the next moment, right now!

Lotte followed him in silent exhaustion up the stairs.

We're in my house, back when we were in high school, back when her father was in the hospital, and we were trying to get rid of her nightmares.

Belly full, she hoped she'd sleep well, assuming, of course, that the monster left her in peace. Vexingly, that was out of her control... for now, but unbelievably, she actually had a plan. For the first time in two years, she felt as if there might be a way out of this torturous wilderness, and even more incredible, she felt she had allies, people who were on her side, who understood the dangers but nonetheless were willing to risk all... for her.

She suddenly felt panic. *That's impossible! How can they know what this might mean? They have no idea what we're up against. They haven't felt the power of this beast, like I have when it claws at my mind! The imp we faced was nothing in comparison, but look how the poor boy limps. The little monster practically clawed him to death.*

"Here, let me help you." She supported his arm as he painfully ascended the stairs.

When they reached the top, Eric saw himself speak, still wincing a bit from the pain.

"Thanks."

Through her eyes, he watched as she looked toward the floor, feeling a sudden and deep pang of remorse. "Eric, I should be thanking you. I can't believe I've dragged you into this. You could have been killed today, or seriously hurt. If you want out of this, I'll totally understand. This is my struggle, and it's unfair to put you at risk."

He saw himself gently take her arm and guide her down the hall. "I'll never abandon you, Lotte." His cheerfulness surprised him even now. "You can't make me... and if you tried, I'd be a total pest, so you'd eventually give in. I want to see this through. This is one of the coolest things that's ever happened to me... but the coolest thing to me is *you*! I'm better for knowing you. You make me better, and it'll take a lot more than this for me to let that go."

Scheiße! *This can't be happening. I can't allow myself to believe it. I can't! Out of all this misery, how can something like this happen? But I feel it's true. Do I trust this odd boy? Can I? I want to, so badly. I need to. I can't do this alone. I don't trust anyone, but maybe, this time, I need to break my own rule. I have no idea what might become of him when this is over, but for now, I need him more than anything, and... well... maybe not just for now. Who really knows? Who really knows what the future might bring?*

Within Lotte's body, Eric felt himself hang in his own embrace, limp, feet briefly brushing the floor as the two of them rocked in silent unison... gently rocked, from side to side, like when Lotte had been little. How she missed that. How she savored it now. How she relished being the object of someone's attention, the freedom to lose herself in the arms of a person who might just actually... care for her.

Astonishing.

Eric reeled with the heady rush of her emotions, far more intense than he could ever have imagined, both fueled and tempered by her experience with her mother. It created a push and pull within her, desirous of contact with others, but also fearful of it. He wondered if that was still at play, somewhere in the recesses of her mind.

Shit!

He suddenly realized with shock that he was being consumed. The energy he had in this realm was draining away while he feasted on the banquet of Lotte's burgeoning love.

This is just as bad as being trapped when she was thirteen. I have to focus on why I'm here. We have to move on, but it can't go on this way! We can't hop from one intense memory to another. Each one will draw me into her inner world like a magnet, and that'll use up all the resources I have to complete this mission.

He knew he could push her. He'd done it twice, sent little suggestions into the historical stream of her consciousness to fix on a single important moment in time. Now they needed to find *the* moment. He didn't want a thirteen-year-old Lotte, or the girl he fell in love with in high school. He wanted her as she was today, right before she'd been killed. That meant they had to travel to *that* memory, or one in far greater proximity.

The perfect moment dawned on him.

I've got it! Take us here!

He expended as much force as he could spare, and the two instantly whisked back into the maelstrom of images. As they rocketed forward, he observed the opposite effect he'd noticed when traveling backward. They began to move more slowly.

Why? What's happening here?

As the memories gradually became easier to follow, he sensed that things were also becoming more complex. Lotte's world expanded explosively when she went to college. New people and experiences broadened her scope, and exponentially multiplied the connections she had with an almost countless number of systems. It felt like a cone that grew ever bigger, and ever wider, as it stretched out into the future. The increased complexity seemingly made it ever harder to move quickly, though they still moved at a super-fast forward pace.

What did Enki say? It was something about being able to control time in simple ways, but that sometimes, the simplest thing provides great power. It doesn't make sense, though. Complexity obviously grows as time progresses. Things were simpler back then! Does that mean the greatest power is in the past?

He tried to reason it through. Lotte's life was like an ever-expanding funnel. Presumably, his own existence followed a similar pattern, a move from incredible simplicity to one of almost unimaginable complexity.

Wait a minute. I remember something about this. Lotte and I read about it when we were in high school, or we watched it together on NOVA, *or something. It's not just my life that moves from simple to complex, the entire universe is on the same trajectory! Things right before the big bang, or right afterward, were incredibly simple... immensely spread out, but extremely homogenous... like... only a few gasses or something. The most uncomplicated, lowest entropy state imaginable. How could this, presumably the simplest form possible in our universe, give the Tablet of Destinies such power?*

Like that, it came to him.

This is what Enlil was going to do when Enki stopped him centuries before. He was gonna turn the universe back into a monolithic field of hydrogen and helium. Enki was right. Time is immutable, but if you can see it from the outside, like I can now, and like these godlike beings have been able to do for millennia, you can borrow something from the past and bring it forward... insert it into the thread of time at the exact spot where the past meets the future, and that little piece of energy is what gets carried forward. It becomes that object's future. What you bring forward has to be something simple, otherwise, it would cause too many problems and take too much energy, but you can do it with uncomplicated things, and there's nothing less complicated in our universe than its original state.

This explained a lot, but not everything. He sorted through the possibilities.

There has to be a size component as well. You must be able to manipulate slightly more complex things if they're really small, really individual. That's how you turn a bowstring back into a live sheep, or cause Sharur to revert back into a lion cub, a fledgling eagle, and an uncarved stone. Ninurta wouldn't have to destroy the universe. He could easily cripple most modern technology. He'd bring us to our knees in no time, and if that wasn't enough, he could threaten to do what Enlil had planned. What would it matter to him? The Abzu, like the realms of fire and earth, and presumably air, aren't part of our universe. They're outside, which is why they can see the whole of our spacetime. He could retreat to his plane, or some other little dimensional fold, and just wait it out. Time would start again from scratch, and a new universe to dominate would be just around the corner.

"Great one!" Lotte cried. "Is there no other way? This is terribly dangerous!"

'If you know a way, then speak! We have not time for the climbing of stairs. As we stand here, Sharur could be on his way back to Ninurta, Tablet in his clutches. What alternative do you propose?'

Again, time had come to a mind-bendingly abrupt halt. Eric felt Lotte bristle at the Lord of the Abzu's words, but she knew he was right. Slowly, she turned her head and Eric saw himself come into view. He had been right, he had been in there... somewhere... but now, he needed to get out, get back into his own track, and from there, back outside of time itself.

"It's fine. I'll be fine. I just have to hold on tight. Let the Afrit take Olive. She's got the gun. You stay down here with Mutig and watch for us. Enki says we need to get Ninurta to the ground, so... *I'll be back.*"

Her thoughts flowed through his mind, and again, the depth of her feelings overwhelmed him.

You bloody well better be, Eric Schneider, my heart, my love – the one person in this cold and ridiculous world that I completely trust, who I know really sees me, and who has nothing but my interests at heart. How could I have been so fortunate to find you? How would I live if I lose you now? But this isn't the time for words like these. When is, really? We both have to be strong. You can't know how afraid I am.

"That's the worst German accent I've ever heard! Did I teach you nothing?"

He watched his mouth form a singularly unconvincing and feeble smile prior to his response. Then a quick kiss was all there was time for, but it had to suffice... and it did.

In that moment, he passed from Lotte back to himself, and from there, he passed back into... well... wherever "this" was. He had her now, frozen in front of him, merely a sliver of a sliver of a sliver of time in the thread of her life – in the vastness, so simple, so easy to call forth with his mind.

The last of his fading energy drained away with every second that wasn't a second. It would be nearly impossible to take more, even for a god. It had to be small things, uncomplicated things. The Tablet's terrible secret lay in simplicity, but in simplicity lay great power. He now understood.

He took a short step forward, and there he stood, Tablet of Destines clutched to his chest, eyes closed, body dripping with motionless raindrops, bloody hair pasted upright by an immobilized gust of wind. At his feet lay the lifeless Lotte. With care, he gently caressed that thin slice of her energy with his mind, and placed it with loving reverence toward the ever-unfolding haze of the future.

It cost him the last of his reserves. As the immense darkness closed around him once more, he tried with all his might to hold onto Lotte's face. He wanted to see her take a breath, wanted to see her open her shining black hole eyes, wanted to know that his efforts, and the monumental sacrifice, had not been in vain – but the darkness enveloped him, and his mind went still.

CHAPTER 21

An odd mixture of popcorn and petrochemicals assaulted Eric's senses as he pushed open the door and went inside, thankful to be free of the blustery wind.

This was a fantastic job for Schneider Industrial Flooring. A venerable cineplex on the outskirts of Worcester needed a facelift, and the uncarpeted concrete flooring was absolutely grody with the grit and grime of decades of use and abuse. Plus, they wanted to install a fancy new seating configuration, so the floors needed a lot of work. The job had to be done fast, in waves, with just one theater closing at a time. The whole project needed to be completed before Thanksgiving, which rapidly approached, now just ten days away.

They'll manage. Both Central Mass crews are on the job, and we haven't missed a deadline in years – not since Margot and I sorted out the inventories. It's hard to do your job when the materials aren't available.

He inhaled deeply. *Nothing will ever erase that smell of the synthetic butter-flavored glop they poured onto countless tubs of popcorn over the past... what... forty-five years? That's almost half-again my age. Amazing.*

He remembered the aroma from his youth, when his parents took him to the movies, not in this complex, but one quite like it that bore the same smell. The scent would probably linger in this spot long after the building had been demolished, when its cinder block life had come to a close. It was, he hoped with some amusement, indelible.

The fragrance brought recollections of the past to his mind. *Star Wars Episode II: Attack of the Clones* was a memorable excursion. He'd been about thirteen, and he remembered his dad playing TIE Fighter and X-Wing on the way home. He wove in and out of their lanes with reckless abandon. Eric had been near hysterical with jubilation, while his mom sat white-knuckled in the passenger seat of their Oldsmobile.

"Fred, stop it! We'll get pulled over!"

They hadn't been. The Southby roads were quiet back then, back when things were simpler.

Ernie wouldn't be out for a few minutes, so Eric sat in a low windowsill and pondered what had transpired earlier this morning. He'd finally had a chance to have that conversation with Margot, once things had settled down after the unforeseen event.

Well, unforeseen by most, anyway.

That had thrown everyone's life into turmoil for several weeks. Today had been the day to talk with his dad, who'd been surprised to see him at the office early on a Monday morning.

"To what do I owe *this* great pleasure?" his father asked, a touch of sarcasm in his voice. "Need to take another little unplanned vacation like last month, kiddo?"

Eric winced. He'd hoped his dad had forgotten about that, or at least put it behind him. There was nothing to do now but take his medicine and try to change the subject as quickly as possible.

"No, no, not at all. You know how sorry I am about how that went down, and how bad I feel that some things got screwed up."

His father gave a sigh. "Well, we were able to cover. Margot really did some scrambling for you."

Eric closed his eyes and nodded. Well did he know that Margot had saved his butt, which was a big part of the reason he was here now.

"Speaking of which," his dad continued, "did you ever get in contact with that Mexican restaurant in Burlington? What the hell was that place called, 'The Old Mole,' or something like that?"

Eric laughed. "I think it's supposed to be *Olé Molé*. Like 'holy moly!' Get it... *Olé Molé? Molé* Sauce. *Olé*!" He gave a little twist of his arms, like a matador waving his cape.

"Who comes up with this stuff? Do you actually think anybody is going to understand that joke? I don't even get it, and you just explained it to me."

"Hey, don't ask me. I just do floors... but to answer your question, yeah, I rescheduled my meeting with them when I got back, and the bid is in. They seemed happy. We should hear soon. It's gonna be a big place. It'll be a good job, if we get it."

"Great, but I assume that's not why you came all the way down here, to talk about *Holy Guacamole*, or whatever."

He giggled, recognizing his own sense of humor in his father's quip. "No, but it was worth the trip just to hear you say, 'Holy Guacamole.'

Anyway, I've been thinking that we never really talk much about the future of the business... like... how you see things unfolding, longer term. It's just been, sort of... I don't know... on my mind. So, I figured I'd ask you."

His father narrowed his eyes and clasped his hands across his chest. "What prompted this? Something going on with Lotte? You two moving to Europe?"

"No, nothing like that. She's just at the beginning of her program. We should be in Boston for a long time, longer than I think I'd realized a couple of years ago, or maybe *comprehended* would be a better word. Ten years, or whatever it winds up being, really isn't temporary. It isn't forever, but it's a long freaking time. I think I've been approaching things with the wrong mindset. I can't just sit in a holding pattern through this entire period. I have to *do* something. I *want* to do something. Lotte can't be my whole life, even if at some point, her job might take us both elsewhere. Even then, I'll still need my own thing."

"And you're wondering if the business might be your thing, at least for the time you *are* in Boston? Is that what you're asking?"

"It is, but it's more than that. I'm honestly curious what you want out of this... what *you* see as the future of the business. Do *you* want to keep doing this, or will a point come where you might want to sell? Maybe you want to get out and enjoy the rest of your life, be free of all the hassles of running this place."

His dad slowly got up and looked out the window to the street below. He stood where Eric had first seen Lotte when she surprised him two years ago.

"Margot! She put you up to this, didn't she? How did she figure out who they were?"

Oooh, busted! Maybe I shouldn't have mentioned selling. Oh, well, too late to go back on it now.

"Yeah, you know how hyper-curious she can be. She got suspicious back when they were here and went outside, saw the EastCoast van in the lot, put two and two together. Don't be mad at her, though. Neither of us have any illusions about whose decision this is. We just want to know what's going on, and whether we can help. I guess that's what I was trying to say to you. If you haven't made up your mind to sell, and you want to keep the business, but want to lean on other people more, I'm in. So is Margot. In fact, we'd kind of do it 'tag-team.' We talked it over. She's got a lot of great ideas. I could never do this alone, but together, I think we could do a lot."

His father turned to face him. "I'm not mad. Margot is good at her job because she's smart and curious, doesn't let things go. I like that. The truth is, EastCoast approached me. They heard we were making inroads in Boston and wondered if it made sense to partner up with a larger firm. It would be good for them too."

"So, what did you say? What are you gonna do?"

"I was intrigued, but now just didn't seem like the right time. This has been an interesting experience. Cracking into the Boston market is something I always wanted to do. Your grandfather was never interested. 'Stick to your knitting,' he always told me. Well, it's my business now, so I'll knit what I want to knit. This is what I always pictured in my mind, sort of what I'll look back on with pride that I brought to the operation. You being in Boston just seemed like the perfect opportunity to give it a shot. So, I'd have talked with you two if there had been anything to talk about. Since you brought it up, though, I'm curious about what you have in mind."

"Well, I was mostly probing about whether you were going to sell, but the truth is, I think I may be ready to commit more time. We'd talked about a second Boston team, but that seemed to fall off the radar last spring."

"I can't do it alone, kiddo. At the hours you work now, you're a big help, but the load is still on me. Skip and Ernie are great on the job, but I need someone who can run numbers, manage project schedules and materials, personnel allocations, meet with clients, and do sales calls. It also has to be somebody who knows the business. I didn't want to push you, but it's really *you* I want involved."

He hadn't expected that. He felt his throat tighten a bit with emotion.

"I know this isn't necessarily what you had in mind for your life, but the truth is, it wasn't what I'd always pictured either. Sometimes, things just work out how they work out, and you make the best of it. I'm happy with my life, but nothing would make me happier than having you more involved in the business. If you wanted to step up, it would be a *huge* help, and heck yeah, I think you and Margot make a great team. So, if this is really something you want, the three of us can talk it over. We'll conquer Boston together."

"Hey Eric!" Ernie called out as he walked out of the hallway that led to the cinemas. It startled Eric from his recollections. "You're early. You should have called me. I wouldn't have kept you waiting."

"No worries. I met with my dad this morning in Southby. It was nice to have a few minutes to recharge my batteries. How's it going?"

"It's going. Big job, but only two rooms left after the one we're on. I think we have the drill down now, so it's moving quicker. You here to see what we're doing? You can help us lay some base coat after lunch, if you want. You kicked ass doing that!"

Eric laughed. "Yeah, that was the first real flooring work you had me on. Beat the hell out of going on Dunkin' runs all day. I didn't know anybody could *drink* that much coffee! That's definitely where my habit started—thanks a lot, by the way."

They both smiled and laughed at the memories.

"But no, I'm not here to see the job. I know you guys are doing great, and my dad is probably running you ragged. I was actually wondering if I could borrow Siddique for a couple of hours."

"Uh-oh. Trouble?"

"No, no, not at all. Unless you have something to tell *me*?"

"Are you kidding? Siddique is doing great. I don't know where the hell you found him, but he was just what we needed. I mean, we had to start him at the bottom. He doesn't know fuck-all about flooring, but he's been working his ass off, does anything we ask, and not a peep out of him. Shit, man, he reminds me of you. Works like he's got something to prove, not to anybody else, but to himself."

Or like he has something to forget. "Well, that's great to hear. I'm glad it's working out. Siddique did Lotte and me a solid a few weeks ago when we were out of town. I've been so... well... busy, that I haven't had time to check in on him. I was hoping you could spare him for lunch. You guys will be breaking soon, right?"

"Yeah, we're wrapping it up now. No problem. Let me go get him. He'll be psyched. Man, it's good to see you. It's been a while. You look fantastic! I can't believe you're the quiet, out of shape kid that started with us... what... five, six years ago? Has it been that long? No offense, by the way."

"None taken."

He *had* been a quiet, out of shape kid. That was the tip of the proverbial iceberg. He was gratified people who knew him back then perceived a change. To him, it sometimes felt he was still stuck in many of the same ruts, frozen in time, like the images he saw in that "where" that was nowhere.

Ernie interrupted his thoughts. "Anyway, it's really good to see you. I'm glad you're doing so well. Give Lotte my best when you see her. Let me go get Siddique." He turned to leave but then stopped. "God, man, I totally forgot! This is the first time I've seen you since it happened. I'm so sorry about your grandmother. It was so sudden. You know I'd have been at the funeral, but we were just prepping for this job, trying to finish up in Leominster—"

"It's okay. I totally understand. My dad was happy you and Skip could hold things together for a couple of weeks. He was pretty torn up. We all knew where you were. You were with us in spirit. Plus, Marsha came, which was really nice."

"Yeah, well, Schneider has been good to our family. This is a great place to work, even better since you started. I was skeptical when I got the boss's kid on my team, but you won us all over with your hard work and the no-bullshit attitude. It's rare these days. My little brats are a couple of monsters."

Sure, they are. You want monsters, I'll *show you monsters!*

"Anyway, your dad should be proud of you. I know he is." He patted Eric's shoulder and left to find Siddique.

It would get easier, but it wasn't any easier yet. Eric just had to suffer the stab in his heart each time his grandmother was mentioned, and despite having his all too brief moment to mourn and cry, he still had to bite back the tears that welled in his eyes every time he thought of her, or what had happened.

He woke up in the van. He lay on one of the dirty packing blankets, Lotte by his side. Her face was the first thing he saw clearly, concern in her shining black hole eyes. In that moment, at least a portion of his universe righted itself in the pull of her gravitational field.

"He's coming around!" she cried.

Olive gave an enthusiastic hoot from the driver's seat. He cast a groggy glance in that direction. Mutig's face stared at him from the passenger's seat. The dog seemed cheerful despite a puffy, swollen eye where Ninurta had violently punched him.

He felt a weight on top of him that made it difficult to breathe. He pulled his chin to his chest and saw the lion cub curled in slumber on his stomach. He ignored the discomfort and enjoyed the warmth and succor of the tiny beast's proximity.

"Eric, can you hear me?" Lotte asked with anxious relief. "Are you all right?"

He nodded. He felt disoriented, and speech was still a bit beyond him. This wasn't what he'd expected. He'd anticipated that it would be him who bent over Lotte on the beach as she opened her eyes and returned to their realm from beyond, restored by the Tablet of Destinies from a sliver of her past.

Instead, it was he who returned from unconsciousness. He tried to focus his eyes, and glanced around the now wet and muddy cargo space of the van. He saw Enki, still completely nude. He sat majestically with his back to the side door, and next to him–

"Ninurta!" Eric cried with alarm, and immediately wished he hadn't. A wave of dizziness washed over him. "What the hell is going on?"

'Calm yourself,' the great god gently commanded. *'All is well. My nephew has become pliable. It appears losing Sharur was devastating, both to his power and to his psyche. The loss has sapped his will to fight. He is now under my control, and shall remain so.'*

In some sense, Eric sympathized. Without Lotte, he would have been in the same boat–no will to fight, no will to live on.

Thanatos fully in command.

Lotte whispered in his ear as she gently kissed his cheek. "We did it. We're taking him back to the gateway. We'll be there any minute. Enki said you battled Ninurta while he summoned the turtle, and that without your intervention, he would probably have gotten to the Tablet. I don't know what bloody well happened. Olive said I fell and hit my head. The last thing I remember was you flying off on the Capricorn. Then I woke up on the beach. It's really odd. I can't feel a bruise anywhere. In fact, I feel wonderful!"

'Think not of it, child. Focus on what must be done. Our task is yet to be completed.'

The Afrit met them at Uncle Clint's farm on Happy Drive. The creature still flapped its bony wings to stay balanced on its one remaining leg. Lotte and Olive led the way, Mutig joyfully, but still somewhat tentatively, at their heels, while Enki gently guided the now dazed and tractable God of Thunder and Storms out of the van and toward the house. Eric and the lame Afrit took up the rear. Rain still fell, but the storm was dying out, as exhausted and spent as the being who had summoned it into existence.

Lotte and Olive rounded the corner and began the trek toward the pond where the gateway to the Abzu awaited them.

'Where do you go, children?' Enki called out. *'We require your assistance.'*

Lotte replied with surprise. "We go to the pond, great one. You said we have to get Ninurta to the gateway as quickly as possible. I saw no reason for delay."

'Yes, the gateway. We must get my nephew to the gateway immediately, but that is not the gateway to which I refer.'

It took them all a minute to figure out what the great god meant.

Lotte finally said, "I see. Olive, can you open the doors to the barn and check if the lights are working? It appears we're going to have to prepare some candles."

Without a word, Olive did as she asked.

"Was this your intent all along, to give Ninurta to the Afrit?"

The Lord of the Abzu smiled enigmatically. *'It was one of several options, perhaps not the most likely, but dispatching Sharur settled the matter. Your raven-haired companion owed me, but I love my children. Had things unfolded differently, it could possibly have been me who satisfied the bargain with your creature of fire. Who knows? The future always holds many possibilities.'*

Once the portal of fire had been set in motion, Olive and Eric retreated inside, to clean and dress wounds that could wait no longer for attention. Lotte remained behind to witness the passing of the terrible god who would feed the Afrit, and conclude the dreadful bargain between the supernatural beings.

Eric went to his room, discarded his soaked and dirty clothes, and threw on a pair of sweats. He then staggered to the bathroom.

Olive soon joined him. She'd hurriedly changed into some flimsy sleeping shorts and a t-shirt.

He sat on the closed toilet seat and leaned over the old-timey sink. The cold porcelain pressed against his cheek as she ran water over his blood-stained hair.

"Ow, shit! That hurts like hell."

"I know, but we gotta get this cleaned out or you'll get an infection, and we don't want to be going to the hospital right now. Not around here. We gotta move."

"You're right. We've been lucky so far, and the storm will probably buy us another day or so. Nobody is gonna be looking for your uncle until things calm down, but we shouldn't risk it. We probably need to leave tomorrow."

"Suits me. There ain't nothing here for me anymore, anyways. I've got Mutig. That's all I need. What the H-E Double L are we gonna do with that lion cub, though?"

Good question.

He hadn't given that a bit of thought, but then, he'd basically been unconscious since they left the beach.

Olive shut off the water from the old-timey sink. "How's that, any better? It's a deep scrape, bleeds like crazy when it's on your head like that. I can put some band-aids on it, but it might need stitches. I'll try that, if you want, but it might be over my pay grade."

He felt the back of his skull. It still hurt and was painfully raw, but now his fingers didn't grind over sand when he touched the irritated abrasion. "It's much better, thanks. Let's use the band-aids and see if that does it. How are you? You got whipped into that railing pretty hard."

"It hurts when I breathe deep. I've got a bad bruise back there, maybe worse."

"Can I take a look? No funny stuff, promise."

She scoffed. "I think we're kinda beyond that, but yeah, I can't see back there, and I guess I oughta know how bad it is." She turned, lifted her shirt, and exposed her back to him.

He put aside any other thoughts and carefully probed for damage.

"Ow!"

"Yeah, you've got a pretty big welt there. I can't tell if it's just a bad bruise, or if something's broken. Let me just feel around it a bit more. I'll try to be careful."

He gently massaged his fingers around the angry red mark to see if he could detect anything.

"So? You gonna tell me?"

"Tell you what?" he distractedly countered.

"Tell me what happened... why I'm not swimming around in the freaking Abzu with a giant turtle right now."

"Do I have to?"

"Yes, Eric Schneider, you sure *do* have to! I was about ready to pee my pants out there, looking at you with that damn Tablet, going all stiff and quiet, and then just falling over five seconds later."

Five seconds. Wow, seemed like a lifetime to me. Two lifetimes.

"I kept sayin', 'I'm ready, I'm ready,' but Mr. Enki, he told me to hush. Not in a nasty way, mind you, but he said everything would be okay. Well, okay for me anyway. For you, he wasn't so sure, but he said I needed to keep quiet if Lotte woke up, that you didn't want her to know she'd been... well... like... *dead* and all."

"And you kept quiet, right?"

"'Course I did! I know I have loose lips that sink ships sometimes, but I ain't gonna mess this one up! This actually *is* life and death, which is why I'm so confused. I thought *my* death was part of the darned plan."

He lowered her shirt and sat back down on the toilet. He felt his face get warm, like the onset of fever, and he exhaled deeply. "I couldn't. That was a choice I could never have lived with. I had to do something... *else*."

The dam burst. He could hold back the waters no more.

She turned to face him as she began to understand the magnitude of her question. "Whuut? What did you do?"

He reached out and pulled her toward him, buried his face in her belly, and began to sob.

What have I done?

He shook with fury, and sadness, and remorse, and guilt, and thoughts of what had been lost so that others could gain. He choked words over his tears.

"She was... she was... starting to fade. She didn't want to end up in assisted living. She didn't want to lose her mind, the memories of the people she loved. She wanted it to be quick, painless, and... and... she said she wanted nothing more than for Lotte and me to live a long and happy life together. She loved Lotte! She loved her so much. I grabbed Enki's arm, and I stared in his eyes, and I did what I've done in the past with the Afrit. I gave Enki the image of my grandmother. He called... and she went... just like... *that*!"

He exhausted his reservoir of sorrow in heaving wails of grief. Slowly, he calmed in his friend's tender embrace.

Lotte rapped on the door. "Are you two in there? It's done. Ninurta's gone. The Afrit got its spoils, that's for bloody sure. Enki is going home, back to the Abzu. Do you two want to see him off? The rain finally stopped."

Olive opened the door. "Yeah, give us just a minute. Eric is such a baby, crying while I cleaned out that gash on his head. I'm just kiddin'. It was actually pretty bad. We'll be down in two seconds."

He saw Lotte give him a sideways glance as she looked past Olive to where he morosely sat on the toilet. If she suspected anything, she didn't voice the concern.

"Yes, fine, I'll see you down there. Thank you for taking care of him, Olive. Thank you for everything, really. Enki said it was you that incapacitated Sharur. Apparently, I was there to see it, but... I just can't recall. Very strange. Maybe it will come back to me... with time."

Lotte went back downstairs, and Olive closed the door.

"You can never tell her," Eric sputtered. "She can never know—not that she was dead, or how she got back, and certainly what my grandmother sacrificed so she could live. Lotte couldn't cope with that. It would destroy her."

Olive gazed at him where he sat, shivering with self-loathing on the toilet. "You have my word on that, but Eric... don't let it destroy *you* either. Y'all hear me? She did it for both of you. Don't forget that. Honor her final wish and live a long, and most importantly, *happy* life with her. Can you do that?"

"I'll work on it."

She was right, of course, but it would take time. Time, however, was exactly what his grandmother had gifted them, the most precious and misunderstood commodity in the universe. He resolved to make the most of it... somehow.

Olive let it go. "Good. So, you gonna answer my question now?"

"What? I thought I just did."

"Not about that, about the lion cub. What are we gonna do with that little critter?"

Seriously? We have to settle this now? Well, she did just let me spill my guts out to her, so maybe I should give it a moment's thought.

"How about this: we need to get out of here. Let's plan to hit it early tomorrow morning, like... *really* early—four a.m. early. We'll stop at a bank machine, and I'll get everything out that I can. I think that's around six hundred dollars. Did Rebel... err, Mutig, have a leash and another collar around here somewhere?"

"Probably. I can go look."

"Good. Get one of his dog dishes too, for water. We're gonna leash the cub to the door of the vet's office before they open. We'll leave them the money, and ask them to handle it. They'll have a far better sense of what to do than we have. How's that?"

She smiled. "Sounds like a plan! I'll get that stuff later. Let's go down there and say goodbye to Mr. Enki. I don't want to miss him."

He didn't either. He started toward the bathroom door when she suddenly hugged him.

"Thanks for saving my life, Eric Schneider, or sparing it, anyways. It ain't actually so bad being on this team that loses even when it wins. We lose some stuff, but we get other things in return. I like what I got, even though I'll miss my uncle a whole lot. I know you'll miss your grandmother."

It was good perspective. He wasn't the only one who'd lost something. He needed to be grateful for what he had, hard as that would be for a while.

The memory stung him when he suddenly heard his name.

"Eric, can you hear me? Eric? I don't mean to scare you."

He turned from the window where he'd been staring into the cold and largely empty parking lot of the cineplex.

"Siddique. Sorry, I was spacing out. How are you? It's good to see you."

"I'm... all right," he said with slight suspicion in his voice. "Working hard. Trying to stay warm. It gets so cold up here." He shot a quick glance over his shoulder, and then, seeming to sense they were alone, he whispered, "I haven't said nothing to nobody. I keep quiet, just like you told me. I haven't even called my cousin since I told him I left town. I'm working hard. Please believe me. I do what you say."

"I believe you. I'm not here to check up on you. You gave us your word, and that's good enough for me, but we do need to talk. You want to go to lunch? My treat, though you know the old saying... there's no such thing as a free lunch."

"Yeah, okay. Boss told me. I have my coat."

Together, they exited the cineplex into the chill of the New England November morning.

I'll have to explain the joys of long underwear to him.

Eric chuckled to himself as they walked toward the side of the building where his little red Mazda waited.

When they rounded the bend, Siddique screeched to a halt.

Lotte had gotten out of the car. She leaned against the hood, her dark eyes locked on them as her breath steamed in the chill. For a moment, nothing moved. The little wisps of exhaled carbon dioxide from their mouths provided the only evidence any of them were alive at all.

"It's okay," Eric finally said. "She won't bite you... much. She just wants to talk. Trust me, it'll be all right. Sometimes, the only way forward is *through.*"

She walked calmly toward them. "Hello, Siddique. I know this is probably a surprise, but give me a moment to explain. First of all, I want to apologize for how I spoke to you the last time we saw each other. I was... well... incredibly angry."

"You had pretty good reason to be angry," Siddique admitted, eyes to the ground. "What we did to you was wrong. I think about that every day. How I could do something like that... for money. I thought I was desperate, but I was just greedy. You don't owe me no apology."

"Well, I feel badly about it. I guess I just want you to know that. The truth is, Siddique, I feel quite badly about the whole thing. I've had nightmares for several weeks. I still get jumpy. I still don't like to walk into dark rooms. It's getting better, but I need... well... more. I need to talk to someone, but given the circumstances, I can't exactly go see a professional. So, I want to talk to you. I want you to help me make this better."

He looked at her with astonishment. "I... I don't know how to make this better for you. I don't know what to say, or what to do."

"Neither do I, but I feel like this is my path forward. If I can just come to some kind of... *understanding*... through you... with you... then maybe we can try to get beyond this together. You obviously have feelings about it as well. I just don't want to hold onto all this *anger* anymore. I don't want to keep flinching every time I hear your name. I want to talk about what happened, and you were there. You know. I want to know what you know. I want to see it through *your* eyes, because mine are... broken... and I can't think of any other way to fix them."

"I... umm... I can't say no. The truth is, I want this too. I got nobody to talk to neither, and I feel bad inside. So, okay, I'll talk to you. I can do this. I do the best I can."

"Great. That's all I can ask. Actually, that's not true. There's more. We need to talk about something else as well... talk about what you saw... the creature."

"I don't tell nobody about that. I don't even want to think about it!"

"But you do, don't you? You think about it all the time. Seeing that monster has changed your entire perspective about everything you thought you knew. You can't make sense of it, and you can't forget it. It'll haunt you for the rest of your days, just like it haunts us. There's only one thing for it."

"What?"

"It was an accident, seeing what you saw, but it can't be unseen. That's both a curse and a blessing. There aren't many of us who know, and we like to keep it that way. In this case, the choice was made for us. You've seen the tip of the iceberg. We're offering to let you see the whole thing, to truly understand, and to be able to actually get your mind around this. Then, if the need arises, as it appears it does from time to time, we'd like to call on you to help us, to be a part of our little team. We only have each other to lean on, but that's better than nothing—far better."

Siddique shot Eric an astounded gaze.

He smiled in return. "Don't look at me. She's the boss. I just work here, but in this, I fully support the offer. You live in a different world from us. You bring a whole different perspective, different skills. You've proven to be a man of your word, and when you make a mistake, you try to fix it. I'd go into battle with you, and as you well know, it can get bloody. It's a big decision, but like it or not, you've already taken the first step. You *know*, and that makes it hard to walk away. Believe me—" He chuckled. "—I get it. I've been there."

Siddique chuckled in response. "Well, you certainly tell the truth. There really is no such thing as a free lunch, is there?"

They all laughed a bit.

"What about my cousin, and my family? I just called him once when I first got here, told him I had a job, that I was starting fresh. Other than that, I did as you said—no contact—but I miss them, and I know they miss me."

Lotte cut in. "The man who orchestrated the kidnapping is dead. Do you remember Olive, the other girl who was with us in North Carolina? She's a part of this too. She's been keeping an eye on the Raleigh news. They found his car in Lumberton, but it appears the investigation has stalled. They think he may have committed suicide, likely because Black Arrow just announced that they're going into receivership. Nobody seems to be digging too deep. There wasn't even a report of a break in at the house on Chalk Road, which isn't surprising, given the questions that might arise about what was going on there. In any case, we're pretty confident that things have died down and that you aren't a suspect in anything that happened. You can contact your cousin, and your family."

An enticing smile spread on Siddique's lips, the first Eric had ever seen grace the unfortunate man's face.

Well, in the end, maybe not so unfortunate.

He couldn't help but feel a hint of pride at this small victory, one that assuaged ever so slightly the guilt and ambivalence to which he'd grown so detestably accustomed.

They loaded into the car and gratefully ran the heater on high.

I think I'll call Olive when we're at lunch, maybe try to do FaceTime. I miss her. It would be nice to hear her voice. She'd be happy to see Lotte, and know that we might have a new member on the team. The team that loses, even when it wins.

He had signed a long-term contract with a no-trade clause. He hoped his tenure with the club would be long and fruitful, even if their record never got above .500.

CHAPTER 22

Somerville Massachusetts, Thursday, November 19, 2015

Eric had intentionally left the back curtain in their living room open, so he saw the light go on, and felt a rush of excitement.

She's locking up her bike now.

Soon, he heard the familiar tread of Lotte's steps as she climbed the wooden stairs at the back of the house. He muted the Thursday Night Football game he'd been vaguely watching, Jaguars versus the Titans.

Not exactly a marquee matchup.

He laughed as he rose from the couch and headed for the kitchen.

Lotte smiled as she stepped inside. "Hi! How are you? *Oooooh* – "

He swept her into his arms and hugged and kissed her before she could reach down to remove her shoes. He felt the cold of her nose when it touched his cheek.

"Great! You could have called me. I'd have been happy to pick you up."

She still giggled a bit from the unanticipated display of affection. "Oh, it's fine. I had my bike. It's such a pain to put it in the car. Plus, I don't mind the cold. It's never bothered me. But what in the world has gotten into you?"

"Nothing." He smirked knowingly at his lie. "How was the talk?"

"It was a-*ma*-zing! They're doing such incredible work. The Amazon is totally out of my area, of course, but still, I could see so many ways they could use computational models and Werner technology to further their research. Do you want to go to Brazil?"

"Why not? You really want to get involved down there?"

"No, not really," she confessed as she finally removed her shoes and hung her coat on the rack near the door. "Plus, they have to get grants, work out logistics, the whole *blah, blah, blah,* and who bloody knows how it would fit with *my* program. It's just fun to think about. I get so excited when I see all these interesting projects happening. I might make some calls, see if anyone at Werner would be interested in talking with them. *Alter!* I'm doing it again, aren't I?"

"Doing what?"

"Going all crazy! Sticking my nose in places it doesn't belong, getting excited about projects that have nothing to do with *my* research. It's why I'm always overloaded. I go down all these rabbit holes, and the time just slips away."

"Well, you are a hare. No big surprise you go down rabbit holes."

"Oh, ha, ha, ha. It's not funny. It's exactly what I said I *didn't* want just four weeks ago, and here I am again, getting in past nine at night, and I still have lots to do."

"Well, go ahead. It isn't that late. If you're not tired, go get some work done."

She groaned, and a hint of conflict rang in her voice when she said, "No, I don't really want to. I just need to focus tomorrow. I'd rather just sit and have some tea. What are you doing? Watching TV?"

"Yeah, Thursday Night Football. It's not a particularly interesting game, though."

"Ugh, American Football. So boring! The games are four hours long and there's only like fifteen minutes of action. Is there hockey on?"

"Hockey? You want to watch hockey?"

"Well, it beats bloody football. Hockey is more like *Fußball*. The action is continuous. Plus, I like our team. They wear the black uniforms, right? With the big 'B' in front. For Bremen!"

He laughed heartily. "Yeah, that's exactly what it's for! The Bremen Bruins! Let me go check if they're playing. Maybe they'll be up against the München Maple Leafs."

"Great. Put on the kettle for me. I'll put my backpack away and check my email real fast."

She strode off into the hallway toward her office.

Yes, you do that... and... three... two... one....

"Eric! What in the world have you done?"

He ignored her, focusing on the kettle and prepping the mug for her tea.

It wasn't long before she wandered back into the kitchen, holding two books in her hands. "What's that in my office?"

He tried desperately to suppress a big smile. "What does it look like?"

"It looks like a little couch. What's it doing there? Where did it come from?"

"Well, it came from the furniture store. It's there for me. You spend so much time working, I thought it might be nice if I had a spot to hang out and read, like we used to work together, back in high school. I liked that. Sometimes, we even talked together about what we were doing. I liked that too. If you hate it, I'll get rid of it. Also, I'm sorry I had to move all your stuff."

"What stuff?"

"The stuff all over the floor—all those papers, and folders, and God knows what else. Stacks of them everywhere. I tried to keep the piles in order, assuming there was ever any order to them in the first place."

"Oh, those. That's just largely junk, stuff I pick up here and there at lectures and the like. There's maybe a page or two of something useful in some of them, but I never have time or the patience to go through it all. There's always new stuff to do that's so much more interesting."

He did a facepalm, but tried to mask his frustration. "Well, sweetie, for a bunch of junk, it's sure taking up a lot of space. Maybe we could go through it together some time, thin the herd a little bit. Would that be helpful?"

"Are you kidding? Of course! That would be great! I'd love my office to be less cluttered. I'll never do it on my own. It'll be dreadfully boring for you, but I'd love your help. But what are these?"

She held up the books.

"Well, those would be books."

"Oh, ha, ha, ha. Very funny. Little shit. I mean what are they *doing* there? *Babylonian and Mesopotamian History*, and *A Guide to Mesopotamian Gods and Myth*. Eric, these are wonderful. Thank you so much, but you know it'll be ages before I can get around to reading them, much as I need to."

"Who says they're for you? You found them on the couch, right?"

"I did, but... why would you want to read something like this? Not exactly your area of interest, is it?"

"No. Well, not until recently anyway, but that's not why I want to read them. I'm gonna do it because you can't—at least, not right now. As we learned recently, there's stuff in there we might need. This is just the beginning. I'm sure there's lots more history and myth we need to be familiar with. You tell me what you want me to bone up on, and I'll do that while you work. We'll be doing it together... sort of."

The kettle began to whistle as the water came to a boil. She stood, seemingly paralyzed, so he turned off the burner and poured water over the chamomile tea bag in the mug.

"That's incredibly thoughtful, Eric. Please leave the couch there. I don't hate it at all. Quite the opposite, really. Why didn't we think of this before?"

He handed her the steaming mug. "Here. Just put the books on the table and take this into the living room. Turn the TV to NESN, see if the Bremen Bruins are on. I have another surprise for you—two, actually. I got ice cream."

"Ice cream?"

"Yeah, your favorite."

"I don't have a favorite."

"It's chocolate with all kinds of cookie crumbles and peanut butter thingies in it."

"Oooh, my favorite! I'll meet you in the living room."

This is it!

He reached into the freezer and got out the ice cream. He dished out a tiny amount into two small bowls, squirted a bit of whipped cream on the top of Lotte's, added a couple of gummy bears for good measure, and then put in one additional treat, buried under the toppings. He grabbed a couple of tiny teaspoons from the set they'd inherited from Grandma, then gingerly carried the dishes into the living room, careful not to drop them for his slight shaking.

Apparently, the Bruins were playing the Minnesota Wild. Lotte seemed happy watching them.

She's probably just enjoying the black uniforms.

He handed over her dish. "Here you go."

"Wow. You went to a bit of trouble. Is there a special occasion I've forgotten about?"

He laughed. "No, nothing like that, at least nothing you've forgotten. Eat up, but go slowly. You don't want to get an ice cream headache."

She shook her head as she looked at the tiny bowls and teaspoons. "Seriously? It would be rather hard to eat quickly with these pathetically tiny spoons. Whatever is in your mind? You really are strange sometimes. Actually, you've been a little weird since we got back. Was it what happened, or your grandmother? *Alter!* I feel so awful. We should have gotten to see her. It's *my* fault, always so busy. See what I mean? All the important things pass you by while you're doing... what, exactly? It's just what Enki said about humans: never focused on what's truly significant. You'd think I'd learn my lesson, but it's like I can't help myself."

"It doesn't work that way. This is where I don't think you have things quite right. I know the idea of treating every day as if it's your last makes a great internet meme, but I don't think people are psychologically or practically able to live that way. Think about it. If you knew this was your last day on Earth, would you go to work, read a book, attend a lecture on archaeological excavations in the Amazon basin?"

"Probably not."

"Exactly. I wish you could have seen your face when you walked through that door. You were so excited... so happy. There's no place in the universe you'd have rather been tonight. That's who you are! You can fight against it if you want to, but the past is real. In fact, in some sense, it's the only thing that *really* exists, which is why losing your memory can be so terrifying. In the end, that's all we truly have. All this stuff about everything being just a series of interconnected *now's* is baloney. By the time you experience something, its already done, already part of the great cosmic permanent record. And to a huge extent, what we've done in the past sets up what we'll do in the future. The accumulation of those forces makes us what we are. They set the patterns that are so hard for us to break. So, absolutely, come up for air a little more often. Call you poor school friends once in a while. They'd love to hear from you."

"*Alter!* I need to call Arif. We really owe him one. Plus, I think he can help me... help us... down the road. I need to stay in touch with him."

"Then call him, but that doesn't mean you have to restructure all the priorities in your life. That's a huge undertaking, and it would take an awful lot of effort and focus to maintain. In the end, I think it would probably prove impossible, especially since what you truly enjoy so much, what you really *are,* dominates the majority of your time and energy. So, don't blame yourself for missing the boat occasionally. I'm just as guilty of it as you are, even when it came to my grandmother, and I don't have a *calling* like you do. I'm gonna try to do better too. We'll do it together. You're not alone in this. I'm with you, always."

Her eyes rolled with disgust. "You've got to be kidding me!"

"No, I'm not kidding at all. Why would you find that so unbelievable?"

"It's not that! What you said is beautiful, but there's something in my bloody ice cream!"

He smiled mischievously. "Well, whatever could it be?"

She eyed him suspiciously as she prodded the bowl with her tiny spoon. "It's metal. It's got bloody gummy bears stuck to it. Actually, stuck inside it. *Scheiße!* It's a ring!"

He said nothing as he handed her a napkin to wipe off the object.

"Oh, Eric, it's beautiful! What kind of stone is it? Where did it come from? And don't say the bloody *jewelry* store!"

"It's a fire opal. The stone is from Mexico. I'm not sure exactly where. It looks like the Afrit's portal, huh?"

"It does. I love it! But why would you get me something like this? It must have cost a fortune, and with all we spent last month, plus the van.... Has all that been settled? Was Ricky terribly angry?"

"He was pretty angry. We'll be using a different company when we move the flight cases out of my grandmother's basement next month. I think I have a buyer for Mrs. Binson's furniture in the basement. They're coming on Saturday to look it over. She said we could store our stuff there when it's gone."

Enki's gateway was already stashed in the closet in Lotte's office, packed once more in the green duffel bags from the fishing lodge.

"In any case, I figured in for a penny, in for a pound. Looks like I'll be going full-time with Schneider, so we'll pay it off eventually. But as far as why I got it for you, well...."

"Well what?"

She paid more attention to the ring than to him, turning it in her fingers with fascination and wonder. When he didn't reply, she looked up and they locked gazes.

"Oh, my. It's *that* kind of ring. Eric, I don't know what to say. I'm in shock. Why now? We've never even talked about it before."

"I know, and if now isn't the right time for you, or if this isn't what you want, I'd understand, but I guess it was like I was trying to say before. Living your life is like painting a picture. You want to look back and like what you see, because you can't change it once it's done. You have to take actions that are instantly locked in the past, but that guide the future in the way you want, and the time to do that can be... limited. You can't sit around and wait. I'm tired of making that mistake over and over. I could give you a lot of practical reasons about why we should get married—the tax incentives, that it's easier to go along and get along in society, that we already complete each other's sentences, almost have our own language, that both our families would love it, children."

"Wow. We've never even talked about children. I can't possibly imagine it right now."

"There's a lot of things we haven't talked about. I think your study would be a lot cleaner if we'd discussed all that junk in there six months ago. We can work all that out. Apparently, communication on this kind of stuff isn't either of our strong suits, but knowing the problem is the first step toward a solution. You hardly noticed, but we actually just had our first conversation about kids."

"We did? Yes, I suppose we did, didn't we. Sorry, didn't mean to interrupt."

"No problem. But when you ask me, 'why now,' my answer is because this is the picture I want to look back on for my life. This is far and away the most important thing in the world to me. There's nothing holding me back, and I want you to know today, right now, from this second forward, without any ambiguity, that I am yours, and that I want you to be mine—every freaky bit of you, just as you are, just as you want to be—and that I'll never leave you."

She started to cry.

He knew where to strike. He didn't do it out of malice, or to get what he wanted. He did it for the little girl whose mother abandoned her, and who hid thereafter in the armor of caution and suspicion, of doubt and denial. That armor had to be pierced for her to move on, to move forward. She had to get over her greatest fear, get past the rule that literally had to be *broken* in order for her to establish any emotional contact at all. It was time for that to stop. Everything has its time.

"I'm not very good at this, Eric," she tearfully explained as she blew her nose into the ice cream-stained napkin. "It's hard for me to say what I feel. I've kept things inside for so long... so hellishly long. I sense all that starting to unravel now. I'm not sure that's a bad thing, but it's scary. You can't even begin to know what you've meant in my life."

Yes, I can, but I can't explain how, so please continue.

"I just struggle for the words, or the courage to voice them, but maybe this time, I know what to say. You told me this is the most important thing in the world to you. In its own way, it is for me as well. I just have other things that call me equally, but differently. We've already been through all that, that and so much more, but thinking back over all we've experienced together, I've always trusted you, always felt you were there, that you really *saw* me for who I am. I'm far from perfect, but you seem to accept that. So, this time, I actually *do* have the words. For once in my life, I know what to say, and how to say it. I love you with all my heart. You *are* my heart!"

She smiled mischievously. "Let the rings bind our pact."

THE END

(...although Eric's and Lotte's adventures will continue. To help ensure that happens, please consider leaving a review on whichever

site you typically purchase books online. Your support is critical to the success of independent publishers like Evolved Publishing, and independent authors like William E. Noland. Reviews send a strong signal to potential readers and encourage online booksellers to promote the titles. If you'd like to see more books like this one, leaving an honest, heartfelt review is one of the best, and most sincerely appreciated, forms of support that any loyal reader can offer. Thank you so much.)

ACKNOWLEDGEMENTS

Once again, I'd like to express my sincere appreciation to the team at Evolved Publishing, especially my editor, Dave Lane (AKA Lane Diamond), from whom I continue to learn, and who continues to inspire my writing ambitions. I'm also thrilled that *From the Beginning* features another fantastic cover by artist Kris Norris. This one was quite a challenge, but I think it came out great, and perfectly captures one of my favorite moments in the story. Thank you, Kris!

To all my friends and family who have read earlier versions of this and other books in the series, your feedback and support continues to be indispensable, and you have my deepest thanks.

I also count myself fortunate that my wife, Madeleine, remains my biggest fan, and provides energy and support through every part of the writing process, and all aspects of my life. It's amazing to be on your team, and to have you on mine.

ABOUT THE AUTHOR

William Noland combines a lifelong love of speculative fiction with a passion for history, sociology, and psychology. Engaging and entertaining, Noland's stories carry his hallmark of strong character development that weaves through every book in this page-turner series. In addition to writing, William plays in multiple rock bands and loves international travel and reading. He lives in Massachusetts with his wife and two cats.

For more, please visit William E. Noland online at:
Website: www.WENoland.com
Goodreads: William E. Noland
Facebook: @WENoland.Author
LinkedIn: www.linkedin.com/in/william-noland-103804140/

WHAT'S NEXT?

William and his team at Evolved Publishing are fast at work on Books 4-6 of the "Uncommon Bonds" series. Stay tuned to the web page referenced below to keep up to date.

www.EvolvedPub.com/UB

MORE FROM WILLIAM E. NOLAND

PLAYING WITH FIRE
Uncommon Bonds - 1

FINALIST: Independent Author Network - Book of the Year 2022 - FICTION: PARANORMAL/SUPERNATURAL

WINNER: Pinnacle Book Achievement Award - Fall 2022 - FICTION: BEST SUPERNATURAL THRILLER

An ancient entity, trapped and suffering; a girl who inexplicably hears cries of anguish in her dreams.... What's their connection?

~~~

"I just kept turning the pages and could not put it down... The story was fast-paced and very interesting and kept me on the edge of my seat."
~ ***Readers' Favorite Book Reviews, Alma Boucher (5 STARS)***

~~~

"I seldom read a book and start laughing out loud, but with *Playing with Fire*... this happened more than once. ...Waiting for the next book is going to feel like an eternity. I can't wait to read more about these characters who later on felt like friends."
~ ***Readers' Favorite Book Reviews, Antoinette Wessels (5 STARS)***

~~~

Lotte has moved from Germany, and is new to Southby High School, where Eric is trapped with her as his German tutor. Despite being somewhat dazzled by her unusual beauty and keen intelligence, he quickly realizes there may be more to her crabby demeanor and the scary black circles under her eyes than anyone realizes.

The unlikely couple must discover the mysterious source of Lotte's debilitating nightmares... before madness overtakes her.
~~~

MORE FROM EVOLVED PUBLISHING

We offer great books across multiple genres, featuring high-quality editing (which we believe is second-to-none) and fantastic covers.

As a hybrid small press, your support as loyal readers is so important to us, and we have strived, with tireless dedication and sheer determination, to deliver on the promise of our motto:
QUALITY IS PRIORITY #1!

Please check out all of our great books,
which you can find at this link:
www.EvolvedPub.com/Catalog/

Thank you!

www.ingramcontent.com/pod-product-compliance
Lightning Source LLC
LaVergne TN
LVHW050955080826
845145LV00006B/1503

* 9 7 8 1 6 2 2 5 3 7 1 9 8 *